The Bridge

The Bridge

Solomon Jones

 St. Martin's Minotaur ♏ New York

THE BRIDGE. Copyright © 2003 by Solomon Jones. All rights reserved. Printed in the
United States of America. No part of this book may be used or reproduced in any
manner whatsoever without written permission except in the case of brief quotations
embodied in critical articles or reviews. For information, address St. Martin's Press,
175 Fifth Avenue, New York, N.Y. 10010.

ISBN 0-312-30615-6

To my daughters

Acknowledgments

First, I would like to thank my Lord and Savior Jesus Christ, who snatched me from the abyss, and gave me the greatest gift of all—new life. I would like to thank my life partner, my best friend, my inspiration, my lover, my wife, LaVeta Jones, who fills me up each time I look into her beautiful eyes. Thanks to my parents, Carolyn and Solomon Jones, my brother, Brian Jones, my daughters, Eve and Adrianne Jones, my aunt, Juanita Bryant, and my grandmother, Lula Richards. Each of you has placed hands against the clay that is my life. You've shaped me. And for that, I am eternally grateful. Thanks to my agent, Victoria Sanders, who sold this work in the aftermath of this country's most horrific tragedy. Thanks to my editor, Monique Patterson, who embraced the vision and helped to bring it to fruition. Thanks to the brave children who have endured stories such as this. And thanks to you, my readers. You are the mirror that reflects the essence of each story that I tell.

The Bridge

Chapter One

It started late Friday, with Kenya lingering in Miss Lily's arms and breathing in the mingled scents of baby powder and fried chicken on a hot summer evening. It was hard for Kenya to let go of Miss Lily, because the reality of Kenya's home was a far cry from loving hugs and sweet scents.

But Kenya Brown was strong enough to accept her reality and wise enough not to dream of something more. Dreaming only made the truth of the projects that much harder to take. So when she left Miss Lily's apartment and headed home for the evening, Kenya didn't look back. Regret was a luxury that neither she nor anyone else in the Bridge could afford.

As she walked down the fifth-floor hallway and entered the building's shadowy stairwell, she passed by a group of men who talked too loud and laughed too hard as they guzzled forties of Old English from brown paper bags. She ignored them and pressed on, trying not to think of what awaited her at her aunt's apartment.

Kenya was halfway up the first flight of stairs when she heard a sound like footsteps padding softly behind her. She stopped and turned around, but there was nothing. Kenya felt her stomach flutter and instinctively began to walk faster.

Seconds later, she heard the sound again. She looked toward the bottom of the poorly lit stairwell and listened intently. She didn't hear anything. But she saw something move.

Kenya picked up her pace, skipping every other stair as she trotted to the seventh floor. By the time she reached the hallway outside her aunt's apartment, she was nearly running.

But then Kenya remembered what she was running to. She stopped in the middle of the hallway and held her breath as the echo of her heartbeat reverberated in her ears.

She looked around, waiting for the source of the stairway footsteps to appear. When no one came up the stairs, her heartbeat slowed. But by now, Kenya was afraid.

She walked down the hallway toward her aunt's apartment, sliding her hand against the dingy white cinder-block wall and listening to the muted voices murmuring behind her aunt's door.

She stood outside for a moment, and the voices seemed to go silent, as if they were waiting for her to enter. Kenya opened the door, took a few tentative steps into her aunt's apartment, and immediately wished that she hadn't.

There was a cloud of gray-white smoke wafting a few feet above the floor. She narrowed her eyes and surveyed the room. Aunt Judy was in a tattered armchair in the corner, handing a capsule of crack cocaine to an emaciated man who hopped from one foot to the other with bug-eyed anxiety.

In the ten feet that separated Kenya from Judy, there were others wearing that same look—a look that Kenya had seen more times than she cared to remember.

Uncle Darnell and Renee were hunched over a small pile of white rocks, ensconced in their own swirling cloud of smoke. Two gaunt-faced men were seated next to them on milk crates, greedily sucking crack smoke from makeshift metal pipes. A rail-thin woman in a grimy miniskirt swayed absently before a gray-haired man who slurped corn liquor as he groped her.

The man looked familiar to Kenya. She always saw him there, and he always seemed to be watching her. Thankfully, he had someone else to watch that night.

She looked beyond the old man to the wall where desperate, hard-looking women sat in a line, silently appraising the men's pockets.

Aunt Judy's boyfriend Sonny was in the kitchen, his hooded eyes observing every movement. He rested his left hand on top of the counter, while his right hand, and the gun that it held, was hidden beneath it.

Kenya scanned the room, taking it all in as she squinted through the smoke. She saw the old man shuffle over to her aunt and hand her five dollars. Judy pointed toward the room where Kenya normally slept. The girl with the miniskirt rubbed her hand against the old man's crotch and led him into the room.

Kenya stared at the closed door and knew that there would be no sleeping there that night. Because after the first trick was turned, there would be another. And the parade of whores would not stop until dawn crept through the window and all the money in the projects had been swallowed up in crack pipes.

"Here," Judy said, speaking to Kenya for the first time.

She was holding out the five dollars the old man had just given her.

Kenya walked over to Judy's chair and took the money.

"Go down the Chinese store on Ninth Street and get you some shrimp fried rice or somethin'," Judy said.

Kenya's blank expression said nothing. She'd long ago learned not to seek sympathy from Aunt Judy.

"What the hell wrong wit' you, girl?" Judy said, her face creased in exasperation.

"I ate already," Kenya said quietly, glancing toward the bedroom.

"Well, eat again. Time you get back, they'll be outta there, and you can go 'head in and go to bed."

Without another word, Kenya turned from her aunt Judy and

moved toward the door. She turned the knob and looked back at Sonny, who ignored her. As she closed the door and walked out into the dank hallway, a cloud of smoke followed close behind.

She watched it float toward the ceiling and disappear, and wished in her heart that she could do the same.

Kenya walked nervously down the hallway, trying to block out thoughts of the footsteps she'd heard on the way up to her aunt's apartment. She contemplated taking the elevator, then thought better of it.

As she ran into the dark stairwell, she tried to think of someplace where she could sleep. She couldn't take another night of waiting for Aunt Judy's crack to sell out.

Just the thought of going back there was too much for her to bear. And so she ran, trying desperately to erase the images of smoke and rail-thin women, old men and scheming eyes, footsteps and burning crack.

She had almost outrun it all when she passed the third floor and found Bayot—a man who often frequented her aunt's apartment—standing on the landing.

She tried to run past him, but he folded his arms and spread his legs, blocking the stairway.

"You in the wrong place, ain't you?" she asked with all the sarcasm she'd learned from listening to grown folks. "All the crack upstairs."

He smiled at her, revealing teeth as gray as the smoke in Judy's apartment.

"Move, Bayot," she said, low and threatening.

He didn't move. Instead, he fixed his eyes on hers. They seemed to bore into her.

"Move!" she screamed, pushing past him and running down the steps.

She could feel his eyes at her back as she made her way to the first floor. The thought of him looking at her made her skin crawl. She shivered.

Kenya ran out into the night, panting as she walked quickly away from the building.

"Where you goin', Kenya?"

Tyreeka, a thirteen-year-old girl whom Kenya had befriended just months before, was behind her, walking in the same direction.

"I'm goin' with you," Kenya said, looking back nervously at the dark entrance to the building and wondering if Bayot was still there.

"You ain't goin' nowhere with me lookin' all paranoid like somebody after you or some shit."

"Ain't nobody after me," Kenya said, catching her breath and smiling at Tyreeka as she prepared to spin a lie.

"I'm glad I seen you, though. Aunt Judy told me to see if I could spend the night with y'all 'cause my cousins came up from down South today and they stayin' with us 'til they get a hotel room tomorrow."

"Why they ain't get no room tonight?" Tyreeka asked.

"I don't know." Kenya rolled her eyes with all the attitude she could muster.

"I'm 'bout to go out, Kenya," Tyreeka said, dismissing the lie and ignoring the attitude as she walked past her.

"Take me with you, Tyreeka," Kenya said with quiet desperation. "Please?"

The edge in Kenya's voice caused Tyreeka to stop and turn around.

Kenya forced her eyes to fill with tears. Then she looked up at the sky as if she was trying not to cry. She couldn't let Tyreeka put her off. Because in truth, Kenya had no place else to go.

Tyreeka could sense that this was more than just another one of Kenya's lies. But just as she was about to relent and take Kenya home with her, a bright green Mustang stopped at the curb.

"Come here, Shorty," said the teenage driver as he beckoned with a hand full of gold rings. "Lemme talk to you for a minute."

"Who, me?" Tyreeka said, hoping that the drug dealer she'd been watching had finally noticed her.

"Yeah, you," he said with a sly smile. "I don't bite, baby. I just wanna ask you somethin', that's all."

"Hold up," Tyreeka said, before leaning over and whispering in Kenya's ear.

"Go 'head up to my mom apartment, Kenya. I'll meet you up there in a few minutes."

"But, Tyreeka, I—"

"Go 'head, Kenya. Tell her you waitin' for me. I'll see you up there in a few minutes."

Kenya looked from Tyreeka to the boy and saw that she couldn't win.

"Okay," she said reluctantly.

Tyreeka walked over to the car, bent over, and leaned against the door with her cleavage resting on her forearms to give him a closer look.

Kenya walked slowly back toward the entrance of the projects, dragging her feet in the hope that Tyreeka would finish talking to the boy and join her before she went inside.

She turned around to look at them once more. The boy had gotten out of the car and was standing close enough to Tyreeka to kiss her. He said something, and Tyreeka threw her head back and laughed as she placed her hand gingerly on his chest. Kenya knew at that moment that waiting for Tyreeka was a waste of time.

But it would be okay, she thought as she walked back inside. Tyreeka's mother would let her in and allow her to stay the night. Kenya would be able to rest. Tomorrow, she thought, would take care of itself.

It always did.

The building seemed a little darker when Kenya walked into the foyer. The guard who should've been in the booth at the building entrance was gone, and the glow coming from the stairway was an odd yellow she hadn't noticed before. She thought that one of the lights must have blown out.

Kenya hesitated for a moment, listening as the sound of the all-night craps game echoed from the bottom of the ramp in the rear of the building. She glanced at the back entrance, where fenced-in Dumpsters hid used condoms and empty crack vials. Then she made her way toward the stairs.

As she was about to go up, five teenage girls in tight jeans and stiff hair weaves trotted out of the dark stairway.

"That nigga on the steps look crazy," one of them said, as they rushed out of the building.

"Girl, that's Bayot," her girlfriend said, as they walked away. "That nigga *is* crazy."

As soon as she heard that, Kenya knew the stairs were out. Even though she hated waiting for the elevator because it made her feel closed in, the thought of Bayot looming in the shadows frightened her even more.

Steeling herself, she approached the single working elevator and pushed the up button. The numbers above the elevator didn't light up to indicate its location. Like everything else there, the lights weren't working.

Kenya stood back in the shadows near the stairway, hiding in case someone she didn't want to see stepped off the elevator.

When the doors opened, Kenya looked to make sure no one was on board, then rushed out of the shadows and got on. She pushed 7, and when the doors closed, she leaned back against the wall with her eyes shut tightly, fighting against the trapped feeling she always felt in the elevator.

Her eyes still shut, Kenya counted the floors as the elevator ascended. When it reached the fifth floor, the sound of loud hip-hop poured in as the doors opened. Kenya stuck her head out of the elevator and saw a crowd outside 5B. Someone was having a party.

As Kenya scanned the hallway looking for people she knew, she felt someone slip into the elevator behind her. Startled, she turned and looked up into a familiar face. Kenya was relieved and smiled brightly as she reached out for a hug.

As the doors shut, Kenya closed her eyes and lost herself in comforting arms. She wished that she could always feel that way—protected and loved. But as Kenya began to melt into the embrace, the arms began to tighten around her. Kenya's smile disappeared.

Suddenly, there were hands at her throat. She was gasping as her windpipe squeezed shut. She tried to scream, but managed only tortured, animal-like sounds that died in the back of her throat.

Her struggle was silent, but violent nonetheless. She kicked her feet so hard that one of her sneakers fell off. She punched at her captor's back, but her arms were weakening as her muscles screamed out for oxygen. She reached for the hands at her throat and scratched at them desperately. But with each movement she made, their grip seemed to tighten.

Tears streamed down her face as the elevator lurched toward the top of the building. Kenya stopped fighting then. And at that moment, for the first time since she could remember, Kenya allowed herself to dream.

She closed her eyes and imagined that she was the smoke she'd seen at Judy's. She was floating toward the sky in great, looping wisps, coming apart and fading into air, into light, into nothing.

As her captor squeezed her breath from her body and Kenya Brown fell down into velvet blackness, she smelled the Bridge for the first time.

It was the smell of forties and blunts, swirling in a sweat-soaked summer. The smell of graffiti and urine sprayed haphazardly against concrete walls. The smell of fear trapped behind elevator doors.

For the first time, Kenya truly knew the smell of the Bridge.

It smelled like death.

Chapter Two

Lily squinted through a sleepy haze and tried to understand why Kenya was walking naked across the moonlit rooftop of the high-rise.

As Lily watched in disbelief, Kenya smiled at her, then leaned over the edge of the building and pointed toward the ground. Lily's gaze followed Kenya's pointing finger as she stared down into the courtyard outside the building.

Bewildered, Lily looked at Kenya, who smiled and met her gaze with large, almond-shaped eyes. Lily was disarmed by her loveliness. She smiled back.

Kenya pointed toward the ground again—this time with urgency. Lily looked down and saw moonlight reflecting against thousands of shining jewels. For a moment, they were beautiful. Then a cloud passed over the moon, and the brilliance dissipated. The jewels were nothing more than broken shards of glass.

Lily looked up at Kenya. And the little girl who'd seemed so lovely just moments before started crumbling to dust, right before Lily's eyes.

The gentle rooftop breeze kicked up into a swirling gale, scattering Kenya's naked, crumbling body across the rooftop. Lily ran to the edge of the roof in a panic, trying in vain to snatch pieces of

Kenya from the air. But as Lily leaned over the edge to save her daughter's best friend from the windstorm, someone pushed her.

Lily tumbled off the roof and spun toward the ground, falling, as the wind blew against her face. She tried to scream, but couldn't. She flailed her arms and fell faster.

Tears sprang from the corners of her eyes as she hurtled downward. And then someone called her.

"Mommy." The voice was soft, feminine, familiar.

"Mommy!" The voice was louder now, accompanied by hands pulling at Lily's clothes.

"Mommy!" Janay screamed.

And with that, Lily's eyes snapped open. She stared up into her daughter's face as she sat on the edge of the bed. Lily sat up and looked across the room at the oscillating fan that had whipped up the wind in her dream. Then she jumped from her bed and ran into the living room, looking desperately for a child she knew she wouldn't find.

"Where Kenya at?" she asked when she returned to the bedroom.

"She went home," said a bewildered Janay. "Remember? You said she couldn't spend the night 'cause Miss Judy wanted her home sometime."

"I remember," Lily said, sitting down on the edge of the bed and placing her face in her hands.

A tear rolled slowly down her cheek as she recalled the details of her dream. She whisked it away with a hard, bitter swipe of her palm.

"What's wrong, Mom?" Janay asked, her voice rising in panic.

"It's Kenya," Lily said as she reached out to cradle her daughter's face in her hands.

"Somethin' bad done happened to Kenya."

It was four in the morning when Judy realized that her niece had not come home. She knew—deep down in the secret place where women feel such things—that something was wrong.

She considered calling the police, but thought better of it. She was down to her last twenty-cap bundle of crack—hardly enough to sustain the pipers who were buying them two at a time as they waited for Sonny to return with more. On this, the summer's only first of the month to fall on a Friday, tens of thousands of dollars in welfare and Social Security checks were circulating through the projects. And Judy had to get her share.

No, she couldn't call the police. But as she looked around the room at sunken gray faces fixed in silent desperation, she knew that she had to do something. At this time of morning, with legions of addicts searching for their next hit, anything could happen to Kenya. And Judy knew it.

She looked up at the grease-stained clock above the stove. It read 4:05. As images of Kenya worked their way through her mind, she was immersed in something she hadn't felt in years. Fear.

Judy picked up the phone and dialed the only person who knew Kenya better than she did. She only hoped that Daneen was where she'd said she would be. Because more often than not, she wasn't.

"Hello?" a groggy voice came on the line after the fourth ring.

"Kenya with you?" Judy asked quickly.

"Who this?" Kenya's mother asked as she sat up in bed and tried to get her bearings.

"Daneen, it's Judy," she said evenly. "Kenya left outta here ten o'clock to go to the Chinese store. She ain't come back, and I was wonderin' if she was with you."

"What you mean is she with me?" Daneen said, suddenly wide-awake. "She supposed to be with you."

"Well, she ain't."

"How she gon' get up here with me, and I'm damn-near 'cross town, Judy?"

Daneen jumped out of the bed at her boyfriend Wayne's house, reached over him, and grabbed jeans and a T-shirt from the floor.

"Kenya don't even know where Wayne live at," she said as she pulled on her clothes.

"Look, Daneen. I was just—"

"You was just what, Judy? You was just so busy sellin' that shit you let my baby walk out and disappear? What's wrong with you? I swear to God, Judy..."

Daneen screamed and cursed and said all the things she'd wanted to say to Judy for years. Judy listened to the tirade, and when her niece's anger dissolved into sobs, she responded.

"I know you think you got yourself together now that you done stopped smokin' that so-called shit I'm sellin'. What is it, two months clean now?"

Judy didn't wait for Daneen to answer.

"Congratulations. Maybe you can run back to family court in a couple o' months and try to get your daughter back. Might even get your job back, too. Tell 'em you changed or some shit.

"But for right now, Kenya's out there. And it's a whole lotta folk who care even less about her than you do. So I suggest you get outta bed with Wayne, or whoever the nigga o' the week happen to be, and get down here and find your daughter."

There was silence on the other end of the line as Darnell and the other pipers in Judy's apartment stopped smoking long enough to stare wide-eyed at Judy. She hadn't meant for them to hear. But it was out now, which meant that word would spread before first light.

Judy knew that. But she didn't care. All that mattered was finding Kenya.

"I'm callin' a cab," Daneen said in a near whisper after she'd calmed down. "I'll be down there in a few minutes."

Judy slid the phone into its cradle, closed her eyes, and mouthed a silent prayer.

Daneen called a cab. And then she made the call that she knew her aunt wouldn't.

Somebody was going to find Kenya, Daneen thought as she hung up the phone. One way or another, they were going to find her baby.

It was four-twenty when Sonny parked his maroon Sedan de Ville on Watts Street, an alleywide passageway between Broad and Thirteenth. He got out and walked half a block, crossing to the hack stand in front of the deli on Broad Street.

He handed five dollars to a thin, unkempt man in an old white Mercury Marquis. Then he got into the car's passenger side and told the driver to go south on Broad.

The man glanced warily at the garment bag that was slung over Sonny's arm. He knew that it contained drugs, and that somewhere, tucked into the folds of Sonny's clothing, there was a gun. But it didn't take much to figure that out.

Anybody who knew anything about Girard Avenue knew all about Sonny. He was a fixture outside the awning-bedecked building in the middle of the block, where welfare recipients collected their biweekly checks.

He made loans to them at 50-percent interest, holding their welfare identification cards as collateral and escorting them to collect on check day. He bought their food stamps at seventy cents on the dollar and redeemed them at full value. He sold crack to them from Judy's cramped apartment and took what he wanted from those whose drug habits outpaced their ability to pay.

But if anyone ever crossed him in any one of his enterprises, Sonny did more than merely punish them. He made them disappear. Some showed up again, with scars that forever marked them as his victims. Others never came back at all.

The man driving the old white Mercury had the good sense to be afraid of Sonny. That's why he was glad for the short trip—one block south on Broad and a left at Poplar, then four more blocks to East Bridge Place—a one-block stretch of asphalt that ran along the front of the projects. Sonny would usually get out and walk to the building from there.

Sonny, as always, was relaxed during the ride. But when the car reached the corner, and the building came into full view, his calm demeanor was shaken. There was a police van parked out front.

"Stop the car," Sonny said quietly.

The driver pulled over and shut off the headlights.

Sonny placed his hand against the garment bag, checking its contents, as he watched two officers get out of the van and walk toward the projects.

He sat there for a few seconds after they went into the building, trying to tell himself that they weren't on their way to Judy's apartment.

But in his heart, he knew where they were going. He even knew why. So he did what his instincts screamed for him to do. He ducked out the passenger-side door, disappeared around the back of the car, scrambled onto Poplar Street, and walked back toward Broad.

The driver watched, glad to be rid of Sonny, who disappeared into the night.

Judy heard the sound of a baton against her door and knew that it was the police.

The pipers heard it, too. Darnell and his girlfriend Renee, along with the other two who remained in Judy's apartment, quickly scrambled to hide pipes and rocks in pant hems and sneaker tongues. Judy moved more casually, slipping the remains of her bundle and a thick wad of cash into her ripped chair cushion.

The baton rapped against the door again, harder this time.

Judy lit a cigarette and waited, contemplating whether to answer the knock as the scramble to hide the drugs continued.

"Somebody here call the police?" a male officer asked from behind the door.

Judy didn't answer, but raised her arm to signal Darnell and the others to stop moving. They did, and silence enveloped the room.

Judy waited half a beat to answer the door. To ignore it when the lights and movement had already made their presence known would seem suspicious. And suspicion was something that Judy could ill afford, especially with Sonny on his way back with their third package of the night.

Judy tousled her hair and kicked off her shoes. Then she wrapped her favorite robe around her clothes, walked to the door, and opened it a sliver.

She was nonchalant as she regarded the black cop and his white partner. For effect, she squinted and rubbed her eyes like she'd just been awakened from a deep sleep.

"I didn't call the police," she said after a long pause.

"You sure about that?" the black cop asked. "We got a call that somebody here wanted to file a missing person report."

"You must got the wrong apartment then." Judy dragged on her cigarette and exhaled slowly. "Ain't nobody here but me, and I ain't missin'."

The officer looked at his partner, then back at Judy. He seemed puzzled.

"Anyway," she said, taking another drag on the cigarette, "I ain't call no cops."

Before the officers could respond, she closed the door and locked it, then listened as their footsteps echoed down the hallway. When she was sure they were gone, she leaned back against the door in relief.

Darnell sat on the floor with a broken metal hanger, scraping residue from the hollow glass tube that served as his crack pipe.

"You coulda told 'em about Kenya," he said without looking up.

"And you coulda got the hell outta here," she said, crossing the room and retrieving her money and drugs from the ripped chair cushion. "I wish you woulda just kept goin' when you went out to get them matches."

"Yeah, I bet you do," he said as he deposited the residue he'd scraped from his pipe onto a bent matchbook cover. "Same way you wanted Kenya to keep goin' when you sent her to the store."

Judy retorted quickly. "You know what, Darnell? I think you need to shut the hell up."

Darnell glanced at his aunt as he struck two matches and held the flame at the end of his pipe. It hissed and sizzled as he sucked the glass tube. And when he exhaled, the smoke swirled in front of his face, giving his skin an otherworldly glow.

Judy watched as his almond-shaped, coal-black eyes danced with childlike mischief. She took in the straight hair that extended from his scalp in fine, black wisps. It was at moments like these that the resemblance between Judy's nephew and her great-niece was uncanny. Looking at Darnell was like looking at Kenya in a fun house mirror. He was her reflection, twisted into a gnarled, gray shell of itself.

"You look like you seen a ghost," Darnell said, reading Judy's expression.

"And you look like you chasin' one," she snapped back. "Ain't shit else in that pipe, Darnell. All the scrapin' in the world ain't gon' change that. Now if you spendin', you can stay. But if you ain't, you can get out. Matter fact, all o' y'all get the hell out right now."

The pipers got up without a word and slowly shuffled to the door. Judy opened it and pushed them into the hallway. Darnell, who was last in the procession, turned to her as he left.

"I know my sister," he said with a mirthless grin. "Same way she called the cops, Daneen gon' do whatever she gotta do to find Kenya."

"It's a li'l late for her to be tryin' to do whatever she gotta do for Kenya, ain't it, Darnell?"

At that, Darnell's eyes grew intense. He looked at Judy as if he was probing her for the truth.

"That's what I'm wonderin', Judy," he said, staring at her as he walked out the door. "I'm wonderin' if it's too late."

It was five-thirty, and dawn had begun to sift burnt orange sunlight across the cracked sidewalks outside the projects. A cab screamed to a halt, and Daneen burst from the backseat with a crazed look she hadn't worn in the two months since she'd begun her latest try at recovery.

She charged into the building, ran past the foyer's shrinking shadows, then bolted up the steps. But as she knifed through concrete passages that the light of dawn had yet to reach, she was reminded of all the ugliness that lived and breathed within the Bridge.

Huddled in dark corners of the stairwell were the faces she despised: men she'd tricked for half a cap, women she'd fought for less than that, boys who'd snatched her self-respect and locked it in crack-filled vials.

She saw them and hated them still. Hated the glint of recognition in their eyes, the way their smirks withered to pity as she approached, the way their glances turned downward to avoid the awful truth that had brought her back.

Kenya. The sound of her name was just beneath the silence. Daneen could feel it. And as she reached the seventh floor and ran down the hallway to Judy's apartment, she silently prayed that she would soon be able to wrap her baby in her arms again, the way she'd done in the days before things fell apart.

Daneen tried to hold on to the sound of Kenya's name as she stood outside Judy's apartment, trying to gather herself. But she couldn't feel it anymore. It was as if her name was merely an echo, a reflection of what she used to be.

Daneen tightened her gut in an effort to push out the premonition that lingered there, then forced herself to raise her hand to knock. But before she could do so, the door swung open.

Judy was wearing a robe and a blank expression as she stared at

Daneen. When she saw that Daneen was frozen between her desire to leave and her need to stay, Judy opened the door a little wider and stood to one side.

Daneen walked in hesitantly. When she looked around the room and saw that Judy was alone, her tension eased, but only slightly. She stood in the middle of the floor, not quite sure of what to do next.

"Ain't nobody call and say where she was?" she asked, her words dropping like hammers against the silence.

"No," Judy said. "And I ain't call nobody, either. Not even the cops."

"Why not?"

" 'Cause somebody already called the cops for me," Judy said, turning up the corners of her lips in mild disgust as she stared at her niece.

Daneen folded her arms and shifted her weight from one leg to the other. She was clearly uncomfortable. "Look, Judy, what was I supposed to do? Sit there and wait for you to do it?"

"Don't matter," Judy said. "I told 'em wasn't nobody missin', and they left."

"Well, call 'em back," Daneen said, her voice nearly a squeal.

Judy ambled to her chair and sat down, pulling her near-full bundle of crack from one of her robe pockets and making a great show of counting each of the plastic caps.

Daneen turned away and tried to ignore the sudden churning in her stomach. But there was no denying the rumble that soon grew to a growl. It echoed across the room as Judy placed one cap after another on the table beside her chair.

"I think we should try to find her first," Judy said, still counting the crack-filled vials.

Daneen couldn't hear Judy. Her nostrils were beginning to fill with the lingering scent of crack smoke. Her pores expelled tiny beads of sweat as her heart climbed out of her chest and beat wildly against her throat. The rumble in her stomach began to work downward until she felt that her bowels were going to burst.

And still, Judy counted. Daneen thought she could see a tiny smile playing on her aunt's lips.

"You know what I think, Daneen?" Judy asked as she counted. "I think Kenya gon' show up 'round nine o'clock talkin' 'bout 'What's for breakfast?' Same way you used to do when you was her age. Disappearin' and showin' up when you felt like it. Remember how you used to do that?"

Daneen's mouth was beginning to water. She could hear Judy now, but couldn't concentrate on what she was saying. The taste of crack was once again dancing on her palate. The smell of it was overwhelming her.

"What's wrong, Daneen?" Judy said, with a self-satisfied smirk.

"You always did like to fuck with me, didn't you, Judy?" Daneen said, turning to face her aunt. "Probably doin' Kenya like that, too, ain't you? Figurin' out how to push her buttons. That's probably why she got the hell up outta here."

"Kenya ain't weak as you," Judy said, taking out one of the caps and opening it. "She don't give me the satisfaction."

"I ain't gon' give it to you neither," Daneen said, moving toward the door.

"You sure about that?" Judy picked up the open cap and held it in the air. " 'Cause I sure could use some satisfaction right about now. You got some money, don't you, Daneen? First one's free."

Daneen swallowed hard, ignoring the taste in her mouth, the rumble in her stomach, the stench in her nostrils. She backed toward the door, staring at the crack, even as she reached behind her and pawed at the air until her fingers closed around the doorknob.

"I gotta find my baby," she said as she opened the door and stepped backward. "I just—I gotta find her."

And with that, Daneen was gone—without a word about the final call she'd made before coming to Judy's apartment.

Chapter Three

Not twenty miles from the chaos that was about to erupt in the projects, on the edge of a tree-lined section of Philadelphia called Chestnut Hill, Kevin Lynch could feel the quiet bearing down on him.

The solitude of middle-class living was the one thing Lynch hadn't mastered, even ten years removed from his last years in the projects. He still found himself wishing for profane tirades and breaking glass, childhood games and pulsing music. Sounds he had almost forgotten since leaving the richness of ghetto poverty.

Whenever the silence he hated was broken, he jumped to embrace the noise, secretly hoping to snatch a piece of the confusion that was so much a part of him.

That's what had happened when he had received the phone call shortly before five. He had snapped awake to the sound of the ringing phone and listened with growing panic to Daneen's sordid tale of crack dens and missing children.

It had taken him just minutes to get up and bathe and dress. When he came back to his bedroom and his sleeping wife, he moved quietly, strapping on his shoulder holster and his handheld radio before easing himself down onto the corner of their bed. He bent and twisted his broad shoulders to tie his sneakers, then stood to his full six feet as the moonlight streamed in from the bedroom window and reflected against his bald head. When he was about to leave, his wife, who'd been listening to him move about the room, decided to speak.

"Where're you going?" Jocelyn asked in a sleepy voice as she lay unmoving beneath a single sheet.

Lynch considered lying. He didn't want his wife to know where he was going. More important, he didn't want her to know that a woman he'd known since childhood had asked for his help. With the troubles they'd had in their marriage lately, he knew that Jocelyn would read more into it than was there.

Things had changed in the six months since she'd lost the baby.

Jocelyn had experienced complications five months into the pregnancy and was forced to go in for an emergency delivery that was supposed to be routine. The baby was a boy. They'd planned to name him Kevin. He didn't survive. Jocelyn nearly died, too.

Though she had come through the experience physically, she'd suffered a terrible emotional toll. And rather than cling to her husband, she withdrew from him. No sex, no communication, open bitterness.

It played on Lynch, made him tense, magnified everything he felt. His wife knew that, and it worried her. Because somewhere deep down, she believed that he would eventually look elsewhere—away from the staid environs of Chestnut Hill—to find what she refused to give at home.

She knew that a part of him longed for the raw energy of the projects. The Bridge, after all, was just like him. Concrete slabs, damaged and defiant, wrapped tightly around a steadfast will to survive. He still had old memories, old friends, and old connections in the projects. He claimed to want to forget them, but in reality, he cherished them. They gave him identity.

His wife, though she would never say it, believed those connections to the projects impeded his ability to smooth out his rough edges the way she wanted him to.

Even in the dark, Lynch could feel his wife's concern. He turned away from her as he answered her question.

"Something came up at work," he said vaguely. "I should be back sometime this morning. It shouldn't take long."

"Be careful," Jocelyn whispered in an anxiety-laden voice.

He mumbled a response, then strode down the hall and into his daughter's room. He stood silently beside her bed, watching her sleep, then brushed his massive hand against her face.

"I love you, Melanie," he said, sweeping her hair away from her forehead to get a better look at her.

He stood for a moment, marveling at the young lady his daughter had become. She didn't play the same childhood games as other girls her age. Rather, she immersed herself in black thought and high fashion—taking weekly shopping trips with her mother so the two of them could satisfy their cravings for revolution and Armani.

But beneath all that maturity, she was the same as Kenya—a little black girl who could very well be missing, too. A girl who, in the scheme of things, didn't matter much to anyone but her family.

That thought crowded Lynch's mind as he backed softly out of her room. He knew that it was only by the grace of God that he could still kiss his daughter good night. Not everyone was that fortunate.

It was six o'clock by the time he started down Germantown Avenue, breathing in the morning through the open window of his unmarked Chrysler Grand Fury.

The police car bounced along the cobblestones of the centuries-old street, the tires sliding on and off the trolley tracks that followed the winding road from affluence to poverty. Watching absently as the pristine sidewalks north of Mount Airy Avenue gave way to discarded beer bottles south of Chelten, he tried to think of where his best friend's daughter could be.

It had been years since the last time Lynch had seen Kenya. She was only two years old then, sitting quietly on her mother's lap as Lynch sat across from them in Daneen's apartment. Kenya had stared at him. And he stared back, his eyes filled with loathing for the project whore and her bastard child.

Lynch hated Daneen for what she'd done to his friend Tyrone. He despised the way she'd lied to him about the child. The way she'd conned him into the crack trade. The way she'd placed the sliding board in front of him and pushed, then stood back and watched as his addiction had spiraled down to a violent death.

He hated Daneen Brown for all that and more. He tried to hate the child, too. But he couldn't. Though nothing of Kenya physically resembled Tyrone, there was something in the way she'd looked at him. It was like Ty's spirit was alive in her, peering out from the sparkling, coal-black eyes. It was like he'd known her for years.

That day, when he'd finally seen for himself the woman and the child Tyrone had loved as his own, he knew that what he'd always suspected was true. Kenya Brown was not Tyrone's daughter—not physically.

But in spirit, she was bone of his bone and flesh of his flesh. She was all that was left of him. Lynch swore to himself after looking into her eyes that he would help Kenya Brown to make it out.

It was a promise he'd done little to keep. But that was about to change.

After leaving Judy's apartment, Daneen stood outside the building, waiting anxiously for Lynch to round the corner. Ten minutes turned into fifteen as she tried to ignore the stench of death emanating from the man-size weeds in the vacant lot on the corner.

By six-fifteen, she knew that she couldn't stand there any longer. She had to do something.

Daneen rushed back into the building. Up the steps, down a hall.

And then she was there, standing in front of Lily's door and pounding her fist against it. She pounded again, then waited, praying that Lily had allowed Kenya to stay the night with her. When Lily answered, Daneen didn't wait for a greeting.

"My daughter here?" she said, barging into the apartment and looking around the living room for signs of Kenya.

Lily felt sorry for her.

"No, Daneen, she ain't here," she said as she walked into the kitchen. "You want some coffee or somethin'?"

"Lily, I ain't got time for no small talk," Daneen said, standing near the front door and looking around nervously. "You seen Kenya or not?"

Lily came back to the couch with a cup of black coffee. "Sit down, Daneen."

"I don't wanna sit down," Daneen said, raising her voice. "I want my damn daughter. Now where she at?"

Lily sipped at the coffee and contemplated telling her about the dream she'd had concerning Kenya.

"I don't know where she at," she said, after deciding against it. "She played with Janay almost all day yesterday, then they came in here, and I gave 'em dinner. Kenya stayed 'til somethin' after nine, then I sent her home."

"She ain't come back here last night?"

"She ain't spent the night here in 'bout a week, 'cause Judy don't want her stayin' here no more. Least that's what Judy told me. If it was up to me, she could stay here all the time, 'cause it ain't like Kenya got a real home to go to."

At that, a simmering anger filled Daneen's eyes. Lily could see it. So could Janay. She had come out of the bedroom and was watching them from the hallway.

"I ain't mean that like it sounded, Daneen. It's just that—"

"Yeah, I know what it's *just*," Daneen said. "It's *just* that you one o' them bitches think they better than everybody else."

Lily stood up. "Look, you ain't gon' be standin' up here disre-spectin' me in my house."

"I'ma do more than that you don't tell me where my daughter at."

"Oh, so now all of a sudden Kenya your daughter," Lily said cynically. "Where was all that mother love when she needed you, Daneen? I probably done spent more time with Kenya in the last year than you ever did. Now you got the nerve to bring yo' ass down here like you gon' save the day? You shoulda been down here before somethin' happened to her."

Daneen's head reared back as if she had been slapped. "What you mean somethin' happened to her? How you know somethin' hap-pened to her?"

Lily answered in a near whisper. "I just know."

Daneen knew, too. That's why she didn't answer.

Janay watched it all from the hallway. But she couldn't let it go at that. So she walked into the living room, and through a haze of tears, asked the question that was burning on her lips.

"Why you let her stay there with Miss Judy and Mr. Sonny anyway?" she cried, her accusing eyes fixed on Daneen.

"Janay, go to bed," Lily said. But Janay would not be silenced.

"You know what they do in there, Miss Daneen." Janay's voice shook with emotion as it rose to a near shout.

"And you let Kenya stay there anyway. You ain't come get her. You ain't do nothin'. They was hurtin' her up there, Miss Daneen. They was hurtin' her and ain't nobody care."

Janay broke down, the sobs wracking her body as she collapsed against her mother. Daneen stood speechless, staring at the nine-year-old and wondering what she meant by *hurt*.

Lily glanced at Daneen, then took Janay's chin in her hand and raised her face until she was looking into her daughter's eyes. She wiped Janay's tears and ran her fingers through her hair. And then she asked.

"Who was hurtin' Kenya, baby?"

Janay looked from her mother to Daneen and back again. Then

she fixed her eyes on the floor and uttered the name no one wanted to hear.

"It was Mr. Sonny," she said. "He was doin' it to her. She told me it hurted."

It was six-thirty when Lynch parked the unmarked car on the sidewalk and ran into the building, bounding past the elevator and into the stairwell.

He moved with purpose, pulling himself up by the railing that ran alongside the stairs. He was passing the fifth floor when Daneen stumbled out of the hallway and into the stairwell, nearly bowling him over in the process.

Lynch reached out to grab her, and as his hand touched hers, they both paused, almost imperceptibly, before she tore away from him and bolted up the steps.

"What is it, Daneen?" he called after her, ignoring the electricity he'd felt in her touch. "Did they find Kenya?"

She rounded the landing to the seventh floor. With Lynch lagging behind, Daneen flew down the hall and burst into Judy's apartment.

Judy had barely looked up before Daneen was upon her.

She jumped headfirst into the chair where Judy sat, knocking it backward. Money and caps flew into the air as Judy's head bounced against the floor. Daneen was merciless, straddling Judy's chest and using her knees to pin her arms to the floor.

"Bitch! You knew what that nigga was doin' to my baby!"

She punctuated each word with punches and slaps. With her eyes stretched wide and a rope of saliva swinging from her open mouth, she looked like a madwoman. She drove Judy's head into the floor, punching her again and again as Judy struggled in vain to break free.

Lynch tried to stop her, but Daneen would not be denied. She continued to flail away as she repeated the words like a mantra.

"You knew!" she cried, pounding her fists into Judy's face. "You knew what that nigga was doin'!"

She continued until Lynch was able to force his hands under her armpits and clasp them behind her neck, pulling Daneen's arms into the air and dragging her away from Judy.

Daneen threw her head back and unleashed a tortured howl. Then she fell backward into Lynch's arms, weeping. He let her go quickly, as if he had touched something hot. She staggered to the far side of the room, sliding down the wall and sobbing loudly.

Lynch heard a movement behind him and turned to find neighbors standing in the doorway, staring openmouthed at Judy sprawled on the floor, her head surrounded by a fractured halo of money and crack.

He went to the door and closed it, then pulled his police radio from his belt and called for a paddy wagon before walking over to Judy.

"You're under arrest for possession of narcotics," he said, reaching down and placing handcuffs on her wrists. "Now, where's Kenya?"

"Like I told Daneen when she came in here a hour ago," Judy said through swelling lips. "She'll be back."

At that, Daneen jumped up and tried to charge, but Lynch held her.

"Back to what, Judy?" Daneen said. "Back to Sonny screwin' her every chance he get?"

Judy seemed genuinely confused. "What you talkin' about?"

"Sonny raped Kenya," Daneen said, enunciating each word for emphasis. "Molested her, whatever you wanna call it. And you knew about it, didn't you, Judy? You knew what he was doin'."

"Sonny ain't never touch Kenya," Judy said emphatically.

"Yes he did," Daneen said. "And you knew all about it. Just like you knew all about—"

"All about what, Daneen?" Judy asked quickly.

Daneen looked up at Lynch, who stared back and waited for her to answer Judy's question. Daneen fell silent as she looked at Judy, then dropped her eyes to the floor.

Just then, Lynch's radio squawked.

"Six-oh-two on location," the wagon officer said over the air.

"This is Dan 25," Lynch said into the radio. "Send me a car to secure this location. Hold them out on a crime scene detail."

"Okay, Dan 25."

Lynch placed his radio in his belt and spoke without looking up. "Daneen, I'm going to have an officer meet you here and take you around the neighborhood so you can look for Kenya."

"How I'ma find her ridin' around in a cop car? That ain't—"

"You asked me to help you, Daneen," he said in measured tones. "That's what I came here to do. Now, I already saw you running the hallways, so you obviously looked in the building. Now it's time to look outside."

She folded her arms like a petulant child, then opened her mouth to speak.

"We'll find her," Lynch said, looking Daneen in the eye. "One way or another, we'll get Kenya home."

As he reached down to help the handcuffed Judy up from the floor, Lynch wasn't sure if what he'd said to Daneen was true. In fact, what he'd seen in the last few minutes caused him to question more than Kenya's whereabouts. But he knew that the answer to it all lay in Sonny. And he knew that the sooner he was able to find him, the sooner he'd find the little girl.

A breeze rustled the vertical blinds that covered the picture window of the second-floor loft. It whispered through the room, kissing each of the trinkets that graced the tastefully appointed walls—from the Fulani tribal masks to the Andrew Turner oil paintings.

When the breeze finally brushed against a grim-faced Sonny Williams, he was standing in front of his walk-in closet, hastily changing his clothes.

Sonny had kept his apartment on Third Street—halfway between the historic Betsy Ross and Ben Franklin houses—for just such an occasion. He'd known for years that the day would come when he'd leave the Bridge for good. But he hadn't known that his plans would allow him to do it so soon.

But then, things had always gone better than expected for Sonny. In the Seventies, he'd sold the bulk of the heroin that fueled Girard Avenue's shadow world of prostitution, ruthlessly taking from a community that could ill afford to give. It was around that time that he took Judy. First as his lover, then as his tool.

By the late eighties, when the lucrative crack trade took hold in the projects, Sonny had convinced Judy to part with some of the welfare she'd collected through multiple identities and fake dependents. He took the money, then added some of his own to buy their first package of cocaine.

In a scant three years, Sonny and Judy became two of the most prosperous crack dealers in North Philadelphia. But to look at them, no one would ever know.

They eschewed the inordinate flash of the young dealers who passed away as predictably as time. Instead, Sonny and Judy carefully orchestrated their appearances to hide their success.

They dressed simply, never donning the jewelry and designer clothing their young competitors preferred. Sonny's Cadillac was eight years old, and Judy had never owned a car. They even let people believe that Sonny was merely the enforcer who allowed Judy to operate unharmed.

Neither the neighbors, nor the police, nor the pipers who bought their crack knew the extent of their enterprise. In truth, neither did Judy.

One year into their partnership, Sonny had begun skimming money from their packages. Soon, he'd taken enough to begin buying and selling quantities of powder cocaine to select clients in Center City. After the first kilo, it was easy. He merely reinvested the money and repeated the process again and again.

Sonny's nest egg was held in a bank account under an assumed name, and totaled over half a million dollars. Judy held the bulk of the profits from the day-to-day cap trade, which amounted to a little more than one hundred thousand in cash.

But five-to-one wasn't good enough for Sonny. He wanted it all. And in order to have access to the money he knew Judy had hidden away, he needed more control. Simply put, he needed to make Judy disappear.

He had decided that night, when he'd left shortly after Kenya did, to make Judy's disappearance happen quickly. So he stopped at a phone booth on his way back from Ninth and Indiana with their package, and he made an anonymous 9-1-1 call.

When he arrived at the building with the hack taxi driver and saw the police van outside, he believed the police were there to investigate his call about a man with a gun in apartment 7D. Of course, there was no gun. But there were drugs. And Sonny hoped that the drugs would get Judy arrested.

When he shuffled out of the hack taxi, ran back to his car, and drove to his Old City apartment, he waited an hour, then called one of Judy's neighbors. She told him that Judy had been led out in handcuffs.

Sonny called one of his Center City contacts and arranged for funds to be transferred to his bank account in exchange for the package he'd brought back to his apartment in the garment bag. He left the drugs in his normal pickup spot—a mailbox outside the building. Then he made plans to return to the Bridge.

He was going to pick up the money that Judy had hidden in a place that only the two of them knew about. That money, combined with the cash in his account that he planned to wire to his new location, would allow him to leave Philadelphia and never look back.

But as Sonny left his loft at seven o'clock on Saturday morning for the short drive back, he had no idea how very wrong his plan had gone.

Chapter Four

The heat in Central Detectives' locked interrogation room was stifling. Judy could feel her thighs sticking to her chair's vinyl cushion as an oscillating fan recirculated the hot air. It was difficult to breathe, much less answer questions.

But the heat wasn't the cause of the rivulets of sweat that trickled down Judy's back. Judy was sweating because she was starting to believe what the detectives had been saying to her for the past hour: Kenya was missing, and Sonny was somehow involved.

It didn't take much to convince her. She was tired after spending the night selling crack to the disheveled pipers who shuttled in and out of her apartment. To make matters worse, the effects of the beating she'd taken from Daneen were starting to wear on her. The copper-colored skin around her eyes swelled to a shiny blue, and there was a steady, throbbing pain at her left temple.

Though the crust of blood on her cracked lower lip made it difficult to speak, she opened her mouth and croaked a few words.

"Can I have some water?" she asked Lynch, who sat across the table from her in the cinder-block room.

"You can have some water as soon as you tell us where Kenya is."

"I told you I don't know," Judy said, slightly exasperated.

"What about Sonny?" the female detective on the other side of the table chimed in.

Judy glanced at the thick-framed black woman, whose piercing eyes seemed to look straight through her.

"What about him?" Judy said with an attitude.

"You know what?" the woman said, standing up and moving closer to Judy as she spoke. "You can talk that smart shit if you want. But we got you on possession, conspiracy, possession with intent to deliver, simple assault, aggravated assault—"

"I ain't assault nobody," Judy interrupted.

"You did whatever we say you did. Now where's Sonny?"

Judy looked at Detective Roxanne Wilson and knew that she would have to give an answer. The look in her eyes said she would stand for nothing less.

It was a look that had come from twenty years on a force where being a black woman pitted everyone and everything against her. It was the look of a woman who had survived shoot-outs and foot beats and unwanted advances, racism and sexism unchecked and un-punished.

And lingering just beneath the look, there was something else— a sadness that she'd earned from her struggle to raise two boys in a West Philadelphia neighborhood called the Bottom.

One of her sons had made it. He was a Temple University senior, studying to become a lawyer. The other was dead, struck down eight years before by a drug dealer's stray bullet.

Roxanne Wilson had buried her son and promised herself that she would never allow another child to die needlessly. That's why she had made it her business to be assigned to the Juvenile Aid Division.

Lynch had called her in shortly after he'd brought Judy to Central Detectives. He knew that Wilson was the one officer in the depart-ment who cared more about children than he did.

That's why he wasn't surprised by what she did next.

"You think I'm playin' with you?" Wilson said suddenly, nearly leaping across the table at Judy, who flinched just enough to let them know she was about to break.

"I want a lawyer," Judy blurted out nervously.

"And people in hell want ice water," Wilson said, scowling as she stood over her.

Lynch stepped between them. "Daneen's out there riding around with a cop looking for her daughter. But I don't think she's going to find her. And deep down, you don't either."

"I don't know what you talkin' about," Judy said, turning her head.

Lynch smiled. But there was no humor in his grin. "Just like you didn't know what Daneen was talking about when she said Sonny was having sex with Kenya?"

Judy looked down and didn't speak.

"Stop protecting him, Judy. You know, just like I do, what Sonny's capable of doing to little girls."

"That ain't fair," Judy said with tears welling up in her eyes. "It ain't about that."

"Oh, but it is about that," Lynch said, his stare boring into her. "It's all about that."

Wilson stepped back, looking at the two of them and trying to figure out what they meant.

"You remember, don't you, Judy?" Lynch asked. "I do. Sonny likes children. Always did. Even back when I was nine years old, I remember Sonny liking kids. He would come around to see you, Judy. He was all flash and smooth talk. You remember, right? Had a stroll you could see from a block away. Used to lean to the left and dip his shoulder, swing his arm and drag his foot just a little bit. And it all looked so cool. Had all the little boys trying to walk like Mr. Sonny. But we never could quite get it down.

"I remember the ice-cream man would come and Sonny always seemed to time it just right. We waited for him, too—spotted him walking down the street, swinging that arm and dipping that shoulder. We'd run up to him because we knew Sonny was always likely to pull out a whole bunch of money.

"I can still see it, clear as day. He used to take a rubber band off his roll, because a bill clip just wasn't big enough to hold it. He would fold all those bills back and peel dollars from underneath. Then he would give everybody one. A whole dollar. We'd run and go buy our little ice cream and still have fifty cents left over for the next day.

"I didn't know until later on that those dollars came from the money he made selling dope. Didn't know that the man we found in '72, slumped over in the stairway with a rubber tube around his arm and a needle in his vein, had died from the shit Sonny was selling.

"All I knew about was the ice-cream money. Remember the money, Judy? Remember the dollar bills he used to give all the kids whenever they wanted some ice cream?"

Judy was rocking back and forth in her chair now, wearing a blank stare and listing to the right, like a ship sinking low in an ocean full of dark memories.

"That was a long time ago," she said in a monotone. "Things different now."

Wilson looked at Lynch with a question in her eyes. And Lynch didn't hesitate to answer it.

"One day they found this little girl named Tish," he said, looking at Wilson but speaking to Judy. "She was in the trash bins behind the main building, underneath the garbage. She was naked. I remember that she was naked because that was the first time I had ever seen a naked girl.

"She didn't have a thing on her body, but her face was sticky, like she had been eating something sweet. Her hands were sticky, too. And they were closed real tight."

Lynch paused to allow the phrase to linger in the air.

"Maybe that's why they didn't see it at first," he said.

"See what?" Wilson asked.

Judy didn't give Lynch a chance to answer.

"The dollar," she said. "They found a dollar in the little girl's hand and tried to say it was Sonny. They tried to say he bought her some ice cream and lured her back there and raped her and killed her. But they never found nothin' to prove Sonny did that."

"And why couldn't they?" Lynch asked.

" 'Cause it wasn't Sonny," Judy said, a fire suddenly burning in her eyes. "I know it wasn't."

Lynch sat down in front of her and gazed at her with something approaching sympathy.

"How do you know it wasn't Sonny this time?" he asked softly.

A tear rolled down Judy's cheek, and she looked away.

"I don't," she said.

And with that, she began to tell them everything.

After leaving his Old City apartment and driving through a gentrified neighborhood called Northern Liberties on his way to North Philly, Sonny drove west on Girard Avenue from Third, watching as the morning rituals unfolded.

Men stood outside the Seventh Street bar where prescription drugs like Xanax were bought and sold. Dope fiends trudged toward the Eighth Street hospital, where methadone fed their heroin addictions. Desperate junkies stood on every corner, selling the bus tokens they'd received from a nearby outpatient program.

It was a drama played out by actors who didn't know or care that they were being watched. Sonny was their audience. And he was anxious to use Judy's money to leave the theater of the streets. Because anything would be better than another day in North Philly.

By the time he passed Ninth Street, he could see the projects, ahead and to his left. Almost immediately, he sensed that something was wrong. When he slowed the car and glanced down at the projects, he saw what had given him that feeling.

There were two police cars parked on the corner, and there was an officer standing on the corner, holding a notepad and questioning one of the neighborhood children. Another officer walked along the edge of the trash-strewn lot a few blocks down, near the corner where Daneen had waited for Lynch just hours before. He seemed to be conducting some kind of search. But Sonny couldn't be sure, so he kept driving.

His mind raced as he tried to figure out what the officers were doing. It took only a few seconds for him to decide that children and vacant lots had nothing to do with him. Still, he opted to be cautious, and rode to Eleventh Street, where he parked his car and began the walk back to Judy's building.

As he strolled the passageways that ran through the labyrinth of street-level houses surrounding the high-rise, he could feel eyes upon him. People were staring out from the closed windows of apartments where whispered rumors about the fate of Kenya Brown had already begun.

Sonny ignored the incessant buzz that seemed to ring louder with his every step. He walked in through a hole in the chain-link fence that surrounded the back entrance of Judy's building. Then he stepped between the Dumpsters that had replaced the trash bins where the dead little girl had been found years before.

The back entrance, like the front, was a large, open passageway without doors. He walked inside and stepped around a pole. Then he disappeared into the hallway near the front entrance to catch the elevator.

He pushed the button and waited for the car to descend to the ground floor, hoping that the officers wouldn't come inside the building.

When the elevator arrived, and the doors slid open, he stepped on and pressed the button marked 12. The rusting cables creaked as the elevator began its slow climb. Sonny looked straight ahead at the doors, then glanced offhandedly at a torn piece of cloth in the corner. It looked to be from a striped cotton shirt.

He turned away, thinking nothing of it. After all, there was always some random piece of clothing littering the projects. He'd seen everything from pants to skirts and panties, even used condoms and tampons. So a ripped piece of someone's shirt was nothing.

Or so he thought.

Sonny looked down at his watch, then cursed under his breath as the elevator slowed to a stop at the fifth floor. The doors lurched open and a little girl who looked vaguely familiar stared up at him, her eyes abruptly filling with something that looked like fear.

"You gettin' on?" he said, trying not to sound as aggravated as he felt.

"No," Janay said absently as she spotted the torn piece of Kenya's shirt in the corner.

Sonny jabbed impatiently at the twelfth-floor button.

When the doors closed, Janay ran down the hall to tell her mother what she'd seen.

Judy sipped the water Lynch had brought her a few minutes before, then glanced at him and Wilson and wondered how much longer they would keep her at Central Detectives.

She had spent the last half hour venting about Sonny. Judy knew the detectives needed to know more than she was telling them. But once she began to talk about the pain of loving Sonny, she didn't want to stop. Even as she withered beneath the words.

Lynch stood back and watched warily as her silken black hair fell down in strands around her bruised face. Before his eyes, it seemed, the rough sensuality of Judy's sturdy feminine frame began to fade. The light in her face went flat—stamped out by the words she spoke about Sonny.

She saw him watching her and tried to force herself to think of happier times. And then she tried to speak of them.

"I used to be somethin' else," she said with a wry smile that faded almost as quickly as it appeared. "Had men fightin' just to get next to me."

She paused, staring straight ahead as if she were caught in the memory.

"I used that pretty young skin and them long, thick legs to get their attention. Used that hard switch to make sure they seen how I looked in a skirt. Used my eyes to make 'em look twice in case they missed it the first time. If they was real cute, I'd lean down just so, 'til they got a real good look at everything. But they couldn't touch nothin' less they had some money. And if they had enough, they could touch it all they wanted."

Judy's face creased in a sly, flirtatious grin.

"You know how that song say 'you gotta use what you got to get what you want?' Well, trust me, I was usin' mine. But it ain't never work like that song. I would use it and use it and use it, and I still ain't get what I wanted."

"And what was it that you wanted?" Wilson asked, cocking her head to one side as she looked down at Judy.

"To get the hell out the Bridge," Judy said, then rolled her eyes because a sister should have known better than to ask such a thing.

Duly chastised, Wilson fell silent.

"Yeah," Judy said with a sigh. "I used it. I used it 'til I looked up one day and it was just all used up. Time I figured out I needed to do somethin' different, I wasn't twenty no more, wasn't even thirty. I was forty, with two kids, stretch marks, and varicose veins. Had to buy everything two sizes small just to make myself look halfway presentable."

Judy laughed. It was a guttural sound that rumbled deep in her throat. Lynch and Wilson looked at each other, then at her.

"By that time Manny, my kids' father, he was gone. Shot some nigga in the Liberty Bell Bar on Broad and Girard in '68. Got life in Graterford. 'Course life ain't last long for him, 'cause he got shanked in the shower a couple years later. I don't even know what for. All I know is he left us here all by ourselves, with no money and no idea what to do."

Judy's breath caught in her throat, and she lowered her gaze, slowly shaking her head as she gathered herself. Wilson stared at her and realized for the first time how small and frail Judy was.

When she felt Wilson's stare, Judy looked up at her. Their eyes met, and Judy's lips curled slightly at the edges. It was almost a smile, one that was tinged with unspeakable grief. Judy took a deep breath and continued.

"The Vietnam War was damn-near over by then," she said with a sigh. "But Man-Man—that's what I used to call my oldest—he dropped out o' Edison High and joined the Marines. Figured he was gon' come back with some G.I. Bill money and move us out the projects. I guess he thought he was gon' be different from the rest o' them boys who came outta that school and came back in boxes. But I knew better. So I just watched him go and held back the tears. I knew I'd have to cry 'em one day, so I figured I might as well just save 'em.

"Six months later some Marines came to my door. Told me Man-Man died fightin' on some hill he probably couldn't even pronounce. Funny thing is, I had them tears saved up, but when it was time to let 'em go, I couldn't. I guess I just went numb. I stopped thinkin' I could get out. And I stopped carin' about gettin' my kids out, too.

"My daughter Joan got real wild after that. Started runnin' with them boys from down Crispus Attucks Homes. Smokin' weed and bein' fast. I guess she was lookin' for another brother after she lost Man-Man. She ain't find no brother, though. All she got was pregnant. Poor child figured she wasn't gon' tell me. Figured she was gon' be slick. So she took a hanger and stuck it between her legs. I guess when the bleedin' started she just kept diggin', figurin' that's what was supposed to happen. I found her on the floor in the back room. Blood everywhere, hanger in her hand.

"Her baby was gone," Judy said, sniffing to contain a muffled sob. "And so was mine."

Her shoulders shook as she covered her face with one hand and cried silently. The detectives stood over her, watching and waiting for her to say something they could use. To this point, she hadn't, and they couldn't wait much longer.

Lynch reached out and squeezed her shoulder. "What does this have to do with Sonny?" he asked evenly.

Judy wiped her eyes, then picked up the glass of water from the table and sipped. She breathed deep, then she continued.

"He was like the one thing I never thought I would lose. After my kids and their father was gone, and the men stopped lookin' as hard as they used to, Sonny was there. Seem like he just popped up outta nowhere.

"He acted like he wanted to stick around for a minute and that was good enough for me. I guess by then I knew not to expect nothin' to last but a minute. I guess I knew I had to hold on to whatever I got and squeeze every last drop o' good out of it.

"I looked at Sonny the same way I looked at everything else. I was gon' use him up and get rid o' him before he got rid o' me. But it ain't work out like that. I fell in love with him."

Judy looked directly at Lynch. But this time she didn't see a detective. She saw the little boy she had watched grow up in the projects.

"Sonny was just like you said he was, Kevin. He loved children. Loved 'em so much that after my oldest sister died and Darnell and Daneen moved with me for good—it was like they lived there anyway, much time as they spent up there—Sonny ain't bat a eye. He just made room and made a way. Treated 'em just like they was his own kids.

"I watched him love both of 'em like they hadn't never been loved before. He gave Darnell and Daneen whatever they asked for—least 'til they started messin' with that shit. Then he backed away from 'em. And they knew he was right, so they never questioned him about it.

"He never backed away from Kenya, though. He always treated her like she was his granddaughter. Used to buy her gifts and give her money, hug her and kiss her and make her laugh.

"I watched it all, and at first I ain't think nothin' of it. But then one day I saw him tellin' Kenya a story. She was sittin' on his lap and lookin' up at him, and he had his hand on her thigh, squeezin' her legs, real slow. Looked like he was breathin' a little heavy. Had his mouth open and his eyes down to slits.

"That's when I knew. I ain't never see him have sex with her or nothin' like that, but I knew. I thought back to that little girl in the trash bins, and everything everybody used to say about Sonny. And I knew in my heart it was all true."

"So what did you do?" Lynch said.

Judy's face was a picture of guilt as she paused and looked down at her hands.

"I ain't do nothin'," she said quietly. "I acted like I ain't know, 'cause if Sonny left, what was I gon' do—keep sellin' crack by myself, so somebody could come in there and blow my damn head off? I needed that money, and I needed what he brought in from whatever other hustle he had goin' on.

"That money was gon' get me outta there," she said earnestly, as a tear formed at the corner of her eye. "That's what was finally gon' give me a life, Kevin. After everything I done been through in the Bridge, don't I deserve a life, too?"

Lynch and Wilson both looked at her, trying to understand. Neither of them knew if the sick feeling in their stomachs was contempt or sympathy. They only knew that they had to find Sonny. So Lynch called in a description, and had it broadcast throughout Central Division.

"Do you have any idea where Sonny is now?" Lynch asked hopefully.

"No," Judy said.

It was the first lie she told them.

"What the hell was you doin' out in the hallway when I told you not to leave this house?" Lily asked Janay as she picked up the telephone.

"I thought I could find her, Mom. I thought maybe I could—"

"Shut up," Lily said, cutting her off as she dialed 9-1-1. "I nod off for a minute and you got yo' ass out in the hall. You don't go nowhere without me 'til I say otherwise, Janay. You hear me?"

"Yes."

"Now you sure that was Sonny? Don't have me callin' these people if you ain't sure."

"Mom, it was him," Janay said. "He was goin' up on the elevator, and it was a piece o' Kenya shirt right next to him on the floor."

Lily motioned with her hand to quiet Janay as a dispatcher answered her call. "I'm at the East Bridge Apartments. My daughter just saw somebody y'all might be lookin' for."

The dispatcher asked a question.

Lily opened her mouth to answer. But then she saw Janay looking at her expectantly. She stopped to think about what she was doing, and the words she needed to say wouldn't leave her mouth. Lily froze for a moment, then hung up the phone.

"Mom, why you hang up? They could still catch him." Janay's eyes stretched wide as she fought to contain her frustration.

"I know they could catch him," Lily said evenly. "But I don't know if I want you to be the one who saw him, baby. I don't want nobody comin' 'round askin' you no questions later on."

"I ain't scared," Janay said, her voice rising.

"Yeah, but maybe you should be."

"Why?"

"You remember Charmaine?"

Janay fell silent at the mention of a neighbor who'd been the sole witness to a murder two years before.

It had happened around three in the morning on the first hot Friday in May, when a piper approached a drug dealer named June, who was sitting with Charmaine in the project stairwell.

Charmaine had always liked fast men and fast money. But she'd never been street-smart. She'd always believed herself to be invincible.

That night, she sat with June and watched as he collected thousands of dollars for the vials of crack he'd sold throughout the night.

By the time the last piper walked up the steps and asked if June wanted to buy a diamond-encrusted gold ring, Charmaine was caught up in the game.

June took the ring and began to examine it. Before long, it became clear that he didn't plan to buy it, or to give it back. Charmaine grew nervous as she watched it all play out. But she didn't move.

The piper asked June for the ring. June told him that the ring was a fake. The piper tried to argue, but June crushed his protest with his fists. The piper fell down beneath the weight of the blows, and June began kicking his head until it scraped against the rough cement floor. A gash opened above his eye, and tiny red droplets of blood spattered Charmaine's white shirt.

June drew back his leg and kicked again. The piper bounced against the wall and fell down a flight of stairs. Charmaine watched, horrified, as the man knelt down and begged for his life. She stifled a scream when June walked up to him, pulled out a gun, and shot him at point-blank range.

A few weeks later, June was arrested for the murder. When Charmaine was approached by detectives, she agreed to testify against him. The District Attorney's Office promised her protection. But when June made bail, Charmaine was still living with a cousin in the building.

June didn't waste any time. He and an accomplice broke into Charmaine's cousin's apartment. There were screams as June forced Charmaine and her cousin to kneel on the living-room floor. Then he ripped Charmaine's blouse from her body, tore it into strips, and used it to bind his victims' mouths. He shot each of them once in the back of the head.

A year later, June and his accomplices were sentenced to death. But that was little solace to Charmaine. She'd gotten the death penalty, too.

That stark reality swirled through Lily's mind as she looked at her only daughter and vowed that she would never lose her to the violence of the Bridge. Not for Sonny. Not for Kenya. Not for anyone.

"You all right, Mom?" Janay asked, stirring Lily from her reverie.

"Yeah, I'm all right," she said, then posed the question she knew the police would ask.

"What was Sonny wearin'?"

"He had on, like, this white, short-sleeved church-lookin' shirt. And he had on some jeans and some black sandals."

Lily sat for a moment, trying to weigh the risks of becoming involved. She knew that once her name became a part of it, the police would come back to her for more information. They would ask about things she might not want to tell. And find out things she might not want them to know.

But then, Lily thought of Kenya—the little girl who'd been as close as a daughter. Though Lily wasn't ready to put Janay's life on the line for her, Lily was more than willing to give her own. She loved Kenya that much.

"Come on, baby," she said, grabbing Janay by the hand and running out the door.

The two of them went down the hallway and up two flights to

the seventh floor. When they got there, Lily made Janay stand behind her as she opened the door and peeked down the hallway.

A police officer was standing outside Judy's door, jotting notes
on a pad. Lily knew that his presence meant that the rumors of
Judy's arrest were true. She stood there for a few seconds more,
watching and listening as someone said Sonny's name over the officer's police radio.

Lily stepped out from the doorway with her daughter in tow and
walked up to the officer.

"I just saw somebody y'all lookin' for," Lily said.

"The little girl?" he said, looking down at the pad as he wrote
the last few words of the description he'd just been given over the
air.

"No. Sonny Williams."

The officer stopped writing and looked up from the pad.
"Where'd you see him?"

"He was goin' up in the elevator a couple minutes ago," Lily said.
"He somewhere upstairs."

She gave him the clothing description that Janay had given her.
The officer wrote it down, then called it into radio, along with
Sonny's last-known location.

The radio crackled to life. "Six-A, have 611 and 613 go inside
that building and search the top floors," a sergeant said. "I'm en
route."

With the shift change about to take place, 6A was the only sergeant available in the district. He had a five-minute ride from City
Hall to the projects. Cars 611 and 613 were the only ones available.
But since they were already outside the building asking questions
about Kenya, getting upstairs quickly wouldn't be a problem.

When he got off the elevator at the twelfth floor, Sonny walked
down the darkened hallway, inhaling the dank air that escaped from

the open doors along the hall. Many of the apartments had been empty for over a year, and the Housing Authority had done little to secure them.

Doors swung from hinges that had rusted almost completely away. Chipped and peeling paint rolled from cinder-block walls like giant palm leaves. The apartments were like abandoned crypts—burial grounds that played host to the project's deepest secrets.

Names had been burned onto the ceilings with lighters and matches. Others were scrawled onto the walls with spray paint. Sonny moved past all of it, oblivious to the stories told by the dingy walls and crumbling floors.

He moved with purpose, walking out into the stairwell and up a short flight of steps to a chain-link fence held shut by a flimsy chain and lock. Pulling the fence back to create an opening, he squeezed through and trotted up the steps to the roof of the building.

He opened a scarred metal door, and swirling rooftop air rushed into the hallway. Muted voices floated skyward as people made their way outside. It was after seven-thirty, and the working folk in the projects were coming out from behind the locked doors, where they routinely spent their Friday nights. Which meant that Sonny didn't have much time.

He crossed the roof quickly, stepping over torn tar paper, then zigzagging between two vents until he reached a brick, chimneylike structure that protruded about three feet into the air. There was a rusting iron grate on the side of the brick chimney. Sonny reached into his waistband and removed a screwdriver, then stuck it between the brick and metal and began to pry.

There was a squeaking sound. A puff of red dust rose into the air and disappeared as the brick began to loosen. Sonny pried harder, pulling the grate out just enough to work his thick fingers into the space. He dropped the screwdriver and pulled. The grate gave way with a muffled pop, and Sonny dropped it before reaching into the chimney.

His face contorted into a determined grimace as his arm disappeared into the hole. He pressed himself against the bricks and reached down, his fingertips brushing against the top of a canvas bag. When he tried to grab the bag, it slipped and fell on a pile of leaves and trash that had been stuck inside the chimney for years.

Sonny pulled his arm out from the chimney and began to remove the bricks, overpowering the crumbling cement that had held them in place since the building was constructed. He reached into the space once more, and had just managed to grab hold of the bag when he heard the metal door to the roof creak open.

Sonny put his arms through the straps on the bag, hoisted it onto his back, and pulled his gun. Then he leaned against the chimney and peered around the bricks. Suddenly, the cool rooftop air seemed stifling.

"Six-eleven on location," the officer said as he walked out onto the roof with his gun drawn.

His partner, whose gun was also drawn, came up behind him. "Six-thirteen on location."

The two went in opposite directions—611 walking toward his left, 613 moving straight ahead. They had decided to start at the roof and work their way down, hoping to complete the search as quickly as possible. After all, it had been a long night.

After shuttling back and forth with disturbances and prisoner runs from twelve to seven, they'd spent the rest of the morning questioning neighbors about Kenya's disappearance.

The officer from car 613 was especially tired. He had seen too much since being assigned to the sector of the Sixth District surrounding the projects: murders over less money than he made in an hour; twelve-year-olds peddling vials of poison to their neighbors; mothers too young to finish middle school.

What he saw was enough to reinforce the beliefs he'd tried so hard to forget after growing up in the city's largely white Northeast: Niggers live like animals. And they should be treated like animals. All of them.

He knew that hating them was wrong. But it was hard for him not to do so. Especially when he saw children like Kenya disappear in the abyss, dying while their parents, aunts, and uncles smoked their lives away.

"Friggin' idiots," he mumbled to himself as he made his way toward the middle of the roof.

He walked past the first vent and stepped over the torn tar paper that Sonny had passed just a few minutes before. He passed the second vent, absently wondering if he would get overtime if the search stretched past eight. He walked toward the chimney, and paused as the stillness of the morning seemed to thicken.

He stood there for a moment, feeling like something was wrong. As he passed the chimney, he found what he had sensed. Or rather, it found him.

Sonny reached out from behind him, throwing both arms around the officer's neck and squeezing. The officer struggled mightily, and managed to plunge an elbow into Sonny's midsection.

Sonny let out his breath in a great whoosh, but refused to let go. The officer's finger tightened around the trigger of his gun. A shot rang out. Sonny pushed up from his legs and forced the officer's head into the brick wall. Then he ran.

The other officer spotted him as he ducked between the metal vents.

"Stop!" he said.

Sonny kept running, reaching back and shooting in the direction of the cop's voice.

The officer shot and missed, and Sonny dived toward the metal door at the end of the roof. The officer shot again as Sonny slithered along the ground and reached up toward the metal door. He pulled it open and crawled through, then struggled to his feet, ran down the steps, and popped through the twelfth-floor fence.

The cop started to give chase, then thought about his partner. He ran toward the brick chimney in the middle of the roof and found him—his head covered in blood and his breathing ragged.

"Six-eleven, officer down. Get me some help up here," he said into his radio.

"Six-eleven, what's your location?" the dispatcher said.

"We're on the roof of the goddamn building!" he said, growing angry as he watched the blood trickle down his partner's face. "Send me some help!"

"East Bridge Housing Project. Assist the officer, police by radio," the dispatcher said over all bands before calling Fire Rescue.

"Six-A, I'm on location," the sergeant said into his radio, running out of his car and heading into the building. "Six-eleven, where's that male we were searching for?"

"He just left the roof. Shots were fired and he escaped on foot through the door that leads to the twelfth floor."

As cops listening to the transmission scrambled to get out of morning roll call, and the sergeant went in through the front of the building, Sonny made his way down to the first floor.

Then, as sirens wailed in the distance, he disappeared out the back entrance of the building and ran toward the morning sun.

Chapter Five

The streets surrounding the Bridge were in chaos. Though the assist had lasted only a few minutes—long enough for the injured officer to be brought down to a waiting Fire Rescue vehicle—police still drove with swiveling heads and eyes stretched wide, desperately searching for Sonny.

Dozens of them rolled through the streets, riding slowly and then accelerating, cruising to the end of one block and turning recklessly onto another.

The people in the projects watched the drama from behind closed doors and windows, waiting with bated breath for the other shoe to drop.

They knew in the back of their minds that something was missing from the scene. They just didn't know what.

But Lynch knew. Even as he and Wilson left Central Detectives in an unmarked car with Judy's sordid tale swirling in their minds, he knew.

Still, he remained silent as they rode west on Vine Street—the northern border of Philadelphia's Chinatown. Wilson did the same because, like Lynch, she was wondering if the search for Kenya was in vain.

They had already spoken by radio with the officer who had spent the last two hours driving Daneen in circles, and arranged for him to bring Daneen to Eleventh Street. They would meet her there and take her back to Central Detectives to file a missing person's report. In the back of their minds, they were praying that Kenya would come home on her own. Because if she didn't, statistics said she wasn't likely to come home at all.

Lynch turned onto Eleventh Street and tried not to think about that. Instead, he thought of Judy's willingness to talk, and idly wondered if the Bridge would give up its secrets as easily. Of course, Lynch knew the answer. The streets would never surrender Sonny. Rather, the worn concrete would crack open and hide him in its bosom, like a mother protecting its child.

If the case dragged out, there would be noise about Kenya's disappearance. But it wouldn't be long before the people of the Bridge resumed living by the rules—rules that said if the wind blew, everyone bent, because it was the bending that allowed them to stand.

These were the same rules that caused the working people in the projects to labor to get out while pretending not to see the ones like Sonny. After all, they'd grown from the same concrete as he, in such close proximity that they could smell each other's breath in the morning.

No one could hide in such a place. Not even Sonny. But while Lynch knew that there was no love lost between Sonny and his neighbors, he also knew that very few of them would talk. Lynch had grown from the concrete, too, and he remembered the rules as well as they did.

He was cursing those rules when an alert tone from the radio broke the silence between him and Wilson. He reached down to adjust the volume just as the dispatcher uttered the name he had been waiting to hear.

"Flash information on Sonny Williams, black male, fifty-two years, wanted for an assault on a police officer within the last five minutes. Williams is six-foot-two, dark-complexioned, with brown eyes, black hair, and a mustache. He's wearing a white, short-sleeved shirt, blue jeans, and black sandals. He was last seen on the roof of the East Bridge Housing Project. He made his escape on foot. Direction unknown. Use caution. This male should be considered armed and dangerous. This is KGF-587. The correct time is 8:10 A.M."

Lynch flipped on the car's lights and punched the accelerator to the floor.

Wilson grabbed the radio and screamed into the handset. "Dan 25, we're en route, coming north on Eleventh from Spring Garden."

"Six-A," the sergeant said over the radio. "I'm on the roof at this location. I've got a neighbor saying she saw that male go out the back of the building heading toward Eleventh Street."

After that, dozens of voices exploded over the radio, and it was difficult to understand any of them.

"Dan 25, we're on location," Wilson said, adding her voice to the commotion as Lynch flew past Poplar Street and slowed to a stop at the rear of Judy's building.

They were cruising slowly, each of them looking out their respective windows, watching for movement. Lynch didn't see anything, but Wilson heard a rustling at the rear of an abandoned car they'd just passed.

She tapped her partner and pointed to the sound, then pulled her gun and leveled it out the window. She had never fired her weapon in the line of duty before, and the thought of it caused her palms to sweat. The gun felt slippery in her hands, so she squeezed the butt and hoped she wouldn't drop it.

Her breath began to come faster as Lynch stopped the car. Both of them got out, pointing their guns at a pile of trash in back of the abandoned car.

There was a sudden movement. Someone stood up and ran toward them. Wilson tightened her finger on the trigger. It was almost too late by the time Lynch realized what was happening.

"Stop!" he said sharply.

Daneen pulled up short as she saw the guns pointed in her direction. Wilson let out a heavy sigh as she lowered her gun to her side. All of them looked at each other and tried not to think of what could have been.

Daneen was the first to speak.

"Where y'all been?" she said, feigning calm as she reached for the door handle. "I been waitin' for twenty minutes. Anything coulda happened to Kenya while y'all got me out here wastin' time. I ain't—"

"Shut up, Daneen," Lynch said, reaching for his car door. "I probably care more about Kenya than you do, and I hardly know her."

Daneen got in the car and closed the door. "You don't know me either, Kevin," she said quietly. "Not anymore."

As they got into the car, Lynch and Daneen locked eyes as Wilson watched them both. When Lynch's glance turned into a stare, and Daneen turned away red-faced, he quickly dropped his eyes to the floor. For a moment, nothing moved except their thoughts.

Then something flew toward the curb, ahead and to their left.

They swung around to see what it was, and a green Mustang darted out in front of them, its tires screaming against the asphalt.

Lynch gripped the steering wheel tightly. Then he pounded the pedal into the floor.

And with that, the chase began.

Sonny looked in his rearview mirror at the blue Chrysler and instinctively reached for the bag of money he had taken from the roof. Nothing mattered more at that moment than the money. Nothing, that is, except escaping.

When he looked up from the bag and saw a police car screeching to a halt in front of him, Sonny swerved and skidded, slamming against a parked car. Then he spun the steering wheel furiously, the tires of the Mustang kicking up white smoke as he drove north on Eleventh Street.

He was going ninety miles per hour as he passed through a neighborhood called Yorktown, with its neat homes and striped awnings welcoming him into its midst. When he looked back again, the Chrysler was closing fast, flying through the residential streets with abandon.

Sonny didn't know his pursuer, but he was going to test him. Because catching Sonny would cost at least one life. And Sonny didn't care to whom that life belonged.

He spun the wheel suddenly, turning right on Oxford and plunging head-on into the street's one-way traffic. He dodged one car, then clipped another, causing it to spin out of control. The Chrysler didn't stop, but stayed close behind Sonny, plunging in and out of the traffic like a needle threading a seam.

At Tenth, Sonny turned left, barely avoiding an oncoming police car. When he looked back again, the Chrysler was upon him, banging against his bumper, pushing him toward the parked cars along the side of the street in an effort to make him stop.

Sonny didn't plan to stop. He found a space between the parked cars, jerked the steering wheel, and took to the sidewalk, skidding to avoid a child on a bike as he approached Montgomery Avenue. He made a hard left there, slammed the accelerator to the floor, and entered yet another of Philadelphia's one-way streets.

He looked in his rearview mirror again. The Chrysler was losing ground. He tore his gaze away from the mirror and peered through the windshield. There was a building to his right—Temple University's police station. He raced past it and onto the dormant campus.

As he approached Broad Street, a police car skidded to a halt one block ahead of him, blocking Montgomery Avenue. Sonny had a split second to react. He turned to avoid the car and zigzagged through the streets of Temple's campus. Then he raced through a student parking lot and crossed Diamond Street, blazing past the rear of a large church on the corner. There, he turned right, dodging Susquehanna Avenue's oncoming traffic before disappearing into a maze of tiny one-way streets.

When he looked into his rearview mirror again, the blue Chrysler was gone.

In a few minutes, Sonny would be, too.

"Six Command," the captain said over J band—police radio's main frequency. "Break off the pursuit. I repeat, break it off."

A dispatcher repeated the command, and the wailing sirens that had filled the air just moments before petered out and fell silent. In their absence, there was a strange calm, the kind of quiet that rushes into a space that has just played host to devastation.

The streets of North Philadelphia were accustomed to such silences. They followed every tragedy the neighborhood hosted—from the Columbia Avenue riots to the Ridge Avenue gang wars.

The chase that had just spilled from Central to North Central Division, with Twenty-sixth District officers joining in from their Girard Avenue headquarters, was devastating. The utter confusion and spotty communication between the officers had made a bad situation worse.

Two Sixth District officers called into radio to say that they were "involved," meaning that they had been in auto accidents. At least one child had been injured trying to avoid the speeding cars, and was on her way to Temple Hospital. Sonny had sideswiped two cars and caused two more accidents as drivers had tried to avoid him. A fire engine and a rescue vehicle were on the scene of one of the accidents, prying a man from his car.

Someone had to answer for all of that. And Lynch knew who that someone would be.

"Six Command to Dan 25, meet me at Broad and Cecil B. Moore," the captain said over the radio.

"Dan 25, okay," Wilson said into the handset before turning to Lynch. "You know he's gonna tear you a new one, right?"

"Somebody need to," Daneen said from the backseat.

Lynch clenched his teeth and ignored Daneen. Then he drove down Montgomery from Thirteenth—the spot where he'd lost Sonny—and hit Broad Street. Before he even got there, he could see the captain's face burning crimson against his starched white shirt.

Lynch parked his car, then got out and walked over to Captain Silas Johnson, the commanding officer of the Sixth District.

"You wanna tell me what the hell just happened here?" the captain said.

"We were just about to take our complainant back to Central, and—"

The captain walked over to Lynch's car and looked inside.

"You had a civilian in your vehicle during a pursuit?" he asked incredulously.

"That's the complainant, sir," Lynch said as he walked over to stand beside the captain. "Her name's Daneen Brown. She called me this morning to tell me her daughter was missing. I thought it would just be a matter of finding the child. But it turned out to be a little more than that."

"So you know this complainant."

"You could say that."

"I don't want to hear that 'you could say that' bullshit. Do you know her or not?"

"Yes, sir."

"Are you involved?" the captain asked, allowing the question to linger long enough to make Lynch feel uncomfortable.

"No, sir."

"And who's this?" the captain said, nodding toward Wilson.

"Detective Roxanne Wilson, sir," she said, getting out of the car.

"From Juvenile Aid. Lynch called me this morning to help him out on this."

"I see," the captain said, staring at Lynch, who returned the glare for a few seconds before looking away.

"Where's the child now?" the captain asked him.

"We don't know yet, sir. But we're holding her aunt back at Central. The suspect in the pursuit was the aunt's boyfriend, Sonny Williams. We have reason to believe that Williams knows where the girl is."

"And what reason might that be?"

"The aunt and a neighbor said he was molesting her."

The captain mulled the answer for a few seconds, then pulled Lynch aside, leading him away from his car. Daneen and Wilson looked on for a moment, then turned to watch a news van fly past them.

The captain shook his head and turned to Lynch.

"You know, you were going to get your lieutenant's bar next month," he said, turning around to watch as the news van disappeared on Oxford Street on its way to the accident scene.

"Were?" Lynch said, his face etched in confusion.

The captain paused.

"You're the best detective in Central," he said. "And I don't want to lose you. But what happens to you is out of my hands now, especially if the guy they're cutting out of that car on Oxford Street doesn't make it."

"I don't understand, sir."

"I guess you didn't hear with all the confusion of the chase," the captain said, searching Lynch's eyes for comprehension.

"Hear what?"

"It's Judge Baylor in the accident. He was on his way home when your suspect hit his car and it flipped. Rescue's been on the scene for about ten minutes now. They said it looks like his skull is fractured. He might not make it."

Lynch said nothing. But his mind raced as he digested what it would mean if Judge John Baylor were to die because of his decision to chase Sonny.

Baylor—who'd escaped his hardscrabble upbringing in the Crispus Attucks housing project with a thirst for education that had led him to law school—was a man whose influence went well beyond the bench.

In the midst of the drug wars that erupted in the late eighties, Baylor trod where even the police dared not to. When gunshots split the night air and dead bodies greeted morning, Baylor stood on corners and showed manhood to gun-toting adolescents by convincing them to lay down their arms.

When Charmaine and her cousin were shot to death by June on the eve of her testimony at his murder trial, it was Baylor who consoled her family and raised money to pay for proper burials.

Because of his rare combination of compassion and strength, entire blocks fell silent when his powder-blue Mercedes rounded the corner. When he emerged from the car, the distinctive white Afro that topped his diminutive frame conveyed wisdom even before he spoke. And when he fixed people in his gaze, the coal-black, silver-ringed eyes that peered out from mahogany skin were captivating.

John Baylor had gained with strength of character what legions of drug dealers had tried to gain with bullets. He'd gained respect. Not just in the black community, but everywhere.

For conservatives, his rise to the bench was proof that racism did not exist. For liberals, his commitment to equal justice provided hope for change from within the system. And for the poverty-stricken blacks who'd watched him escape the streets and then come back to tame them, he was simply a hero.

Baylor had been planning to run for district attorney as an independent candidate in the upcoming general election. He was just about ready to resign from the bench, announce his candidacy, and secure endorsements. And with the fund-raising ability of some of his key supporters, he was expected to win easily.

But none of that mattered now, because Baylor wasn't going to make it through the night. The judge's blood and the dashed hopes of an entire community would be on Lynch's hands.

As he got into his car and peeled away from the corner with Daneen and Wilson in tow, Lynch knew that the only way to make the impending furor die quickly was to find the man who was really responsible for what had happened to Baylor.

Lynch had to find Sonny Williams.

The news van arrived at the accident scene and parked in the midst of neighbors who'd been drawn out of their homes by the loud crash and screaming sirens.

When Jim Wright stepped out of the van with his receding gray hair and weathered, leathery skin, he knew that it was bad, because no one saw him—a newsman who'd spent the last fifteen years on the air. They only saw the accident and the firefighters working feverishly to free the bleeding victim from the wreck.

Wright loosened his tie as his cameraman arranged the apparatus they would need to report live from the accident scene. Then Wright removed a notepad from his shirt pocket and reviewed what he'd written on the way.

Because he'd spent the morning monitoring his police scanner and speaking with department sources, he knew the chase that had critically injured the judge was all about a suspect who'd assaulted a police officer.

He also knew that the suspect was wanted for questioning in connection with the disappearance of a little girl from the East Bridge Housing Project. Beyond that, he knew nothing. But that was easily remedied.

Wright walked slowly to the edge of the crowd, scanning faces that were fixed in the slack-jawed expression of shock that people wear when viewing death.

About twenty feet from Wright, a woman of about thirty was speaking to an officer from the department's Accident Investigation Division.

As the woman explained with animated hand gestures how the accident had happened, the officer took copious notes. Wright moved close enough to hear snatches of the conversation, and as she spoke, he took a few notes of his own.

"Blue unmarked police car . . . chasing this green Mustang . . . flying through here . . . wrong way . . . hit the car . . . kept going."

The officer asked the woman if the police car had stopped.

"No," she said.

The officer thanked her and said he'd be in touch.

As the AID officer walked away, Wright pulled out a cell phone, called a police department source, and asked him to run the tag of the wrecked car.

"Are you sure?" he said into the phone when he received the owner's name. "And neither the car nor the tag has been reported stolen, right? Okay, thanks."

Wright disconnected the call and moved through the crowd until he was standing next to the woman who'd witnessed the accident.

"Excuse me, miss," Wright said. "Would it be okay if I interviewed you on camera about what you saw here?"

She looked at Wright, and then at the camera. She shook her head no. And then, without a word, she resumed staring at the car.

Wright followed her gaze, and for the first time, looked hard at the twisted, powder-blue Mercedes Benz and the bloodied brown face of the man staring out from its shattered windshield. Like the young woman, Wright was at once repulsed and fascinated by the crumpled wreck. He stood for a moment in stunned silence, and decided, in a rare fit of humanity, not to press the woman for an interview.

As the firefighters worked to split open the roof of the car, Wright turned to his cameraman and nodded. The cameraman hoisted the camera onto his shoulder and Wright worked himself into a space that would allow the wreck to be seen on camera.

There was a countdown, then an intro, and then they were live.

"This is Jim Wright, reporting live from Eleventh and Oxford Streets, in the Yorktown section of North Philadelphia, where a police pursuit has ended in tragedy. A car apparently registered to highly respected Common Pleas Court Judge John Baylor—the man widely regarded as Philadelphia's next district attorney—has been involved in a serious accident. As you can see here around me, neighbors are stunned by what has happened here, and an entire city will most probably follow suit."

Wright stood aside as the cameraman zoomed in. "Behind me, firefighters are working to free a man who appears to be the judge."

Wright pressed against his earpiece as the anchor asked him a question.

"Well, Dick, details are sketchy, but the information we have is that the chase involved a suspect who was wanted for investigation in connection with a missing nine-year-old girl at the East Bridge Housing Project in North Philadelphia. When police approached him, he assaulted an officer and fled. There was a high-speed chase, resulting in several accidents, including this one, which has apparently seriously injured one of the most influential jurists this city has seen in a generation. The suspect is still at large, and police aren't releasing the identity of the missing child.

"We'll be following this story throughout the morning and providing updates as they become available. This is Jim Wright, Channel 10 News, reporting live from North Philadelphia."

The cameraman stopped shooting, and Wright snatched out his

earpiece. Then, as they headed back to the news van, Wright was on his cell phone, trying to find someone who could confirm the identity of the child whose disappearance had set the day's events in motion.

As he did so, Kenya Brown was suddenly more important than she'd ever been.

Lily sat still as the image of the crumpled car wreaked havoc in the quiet of her mind.

She'd been sitting in front of her television since telling the policeman that she'd seen Sonny, praying all the while that they would catch him without a struggle.

She never expected him to escape. Nor did she believe he'd leave so much damage in his wake. But she'd seen it all with her own eyes—from the crushed metal to the shattered glass to the bruised and bloodied face inside the car. She'd watched it all and shivered, because she knew it meant that Sonny was still out there.

Lily turned to Janay, who lay next to her on the couch, sleeping. As she reached out to touch her, Janay's brow wrinkled, and her mouth opened suddenly, as if to scream. It was like she understood, even in her sleep, that she, too, should be afraid.

Lily turned back to the television, and as the Saturday morning cartoons replaced the images she'd just watched, Lily remembered the way Kenya would laugh at these same cartoons, then make some womanly gesture minutes later. She remembered the way Kenya would play dolls with Janay, then manipulate her to get what she wanted.

Lily remembered that Kenya was struggling to be a little girl in a place where childhood was a liability, trying mightily to straddle the line between her age and her circumstances. Most often, Kenya succeeded. But in a place where the weak existed for the convenience of the strong, a single failure was more than Kenya could afford.

Lily knew that. Because Lily was one of the weak ones, too. At least that's what everyone thought. After all, a single mother trying to work her way out of the projects with two minimum-wage jobs was weak. A woman with her looks who refused to use them to do better was weak.

But the very things that made her weak in the eyes of some, made her strong in her own eyes. That's why Lily was not to be preyed upon. And neither was anyone whom she loved.

As she got up from the couch to get dressed and search for Kenya, there was a knock at her door.

"Lily," someone said softly. "Lemme talk to you for a minute."

She paused when she recognized the voice, then went to the door and cracked it.

"You seen Kenya?" Darnell asked through the cracked door.

"I figured you woulda seen her by now," she said with syrupy sarcasm. "Since you supposed to be her uncle and all."

"Can I come in for a minute?"

"I don't think so," Lily said, looking him up and down and taking in everything the crack had taken out of him.

"It ain't about me, Lily," he said, looking around before leaning in to whisper. "It's about Kenya."

She looked into his eyes and saw fatigue. There was none of the quick and flinching desperation that always accompanied his lies, none of the darting eyes and dry-mouthed gibberish that came with his addiction. There was only a sad, deflated picture of something she hadn't seen from him in years: the truth.

She closed the door and unhooked the chain lock, then opened it and let him in, leading him past the sleeping Janay and into the hallway between the bathroom and bedroom.

"How you been, Lily?" he asked quietly.

She didn't answer, but glanced at his sweat-stained clothes and the flaky residue that had dried to form scaly layers of gray skin on his face.

"Look, I know you care about Kenya," he said, fidgeting slightly as he spoke. "That's the only reason I came down here. I needed to talk to somebody who cared about her."

He paused and looked down at Lily. "And somebody I cared about."

She stared into his eyes, and for a moment, the man he used to be shone through. But instead of exciting her, the way it used to, the thought of being in his arms saddened her. His arms, like everything else, no longer belonged to the man who had held her through the worst time of her life.

In the fall of 1987, just weeks after Janay began first grade, her father died suddenly of a brain aneurysm. Two weeks later, Lily lost her job as a receptionist. Left with only a night job as a part-time barmaid, she was trapped once again in the mind-numbing poverty she'd been working so hard to escape.

That autumn, the loneliness of it all began to consume her. She was mourning. She was vulnerable. And so she did what she'd seen many others do. She lost herself in the pulverizing grind of the projects.

During the lazy afternoons when Janay was in school and the Bridge paused in preparation for its nightly ruckus, Lily would sometimes walk to the seventh floor to visit Judy. She knew that Judy's niece was in the same class as Janay, and that's what the two of them talked about at first.

By winter, Lily was revealing bits and pieces of the grief she felt over the losses she'd experienced, and Judy was listening. By spring, they had shared laughter and tears, gossip and secrets. Their friendship was genuine, and the trust was real.

When Kenya began to spend nights at Lily's apartment, Judy would send Darnell to pick up Kenya.

It was then that Lily saw something about him that she hadn't seen before. The way his broad shoulders gave way to the hard muscle of his arms and chest. The way his dark skin poured over his languid body like syrup. The way he looked at her when he arrived at her door, asking for his niece, but wanting Lily.

He was young enough to be Lily's son, but with the eyes of a man. He used them to see the soft caramel that was Lily, to take in the voluptuous curves that lingered beneath the cheap, silk dresses she'd wear on the mornings when he would come.

His hunger and her loneliness made their coupling inevitable. And when she took him, it was because they both wanted it to happen.

Lily didn't tell Judy at first, because she didn't think she would understand. But as she grew closer to Darnell, their relationship became more difficult to hide.

By the time Judy saw it in their eyes, it didn't matter that she knew. Everything about her relationship with Lily had already changed.

Judy chose the crack trade over friendship. And Lily, who had stopped coming to Judy's apartment because of the drugs, chose Darnell over gossip-filled afternoons.

Judy was resentful. She felt that Lily had only befriended her to get closer to Darnell. She thought that she was taking advantage of her nephew, that the age difference between them was too great.

Lily could do nothing to tell Judy otherwise. She knew that a black woman never lets go of the boys she raises. Perhaps that's why, a year into the affair, the mother in Lily wouldn't allow her to continue. When she suddenly broke it off, Darnell was never the same.

He poured his loneliness into other women. When that didn't suffice, he poured it into a crack pipe, slowly at first, then with increasing abandon. His magnificent body fell away to nearly nothing, and the spark in his eyes that had drawn Lily to him faded away slowly.

Before long, the deep, abiding loneliness that had always consumed him shone through. His mask of self-assuredness dropped into the pipe with everything else. He seemed to be a different person. And so did his aunt, Judy. She began to treat Darnell like all the others who filed in and out of her apartment, feeding him crack as if it were candy and despising him for what he had become.

Lily watched it all from a distance. By the time she decided to reach back for Darnell—to pull him from the loneliness that had drawn them toward one another—it was too late. He'd already surrendered to addiction. His youthful hunger had given way to deception and lies. His desire for companionship had been sated by the pipe.

All that Lily had left of him was his niece, Kenya. So she tightened her grip on that child, praying that she could keep her from being consumed by the flames around her.

Now, Lily realized that in spite of her best efforts, she couldn't save Kenya. She was gone. And the man standing in front of her was so depleted that she hardly knew him anymore.

It saddened her to see him that way. But as her mind came back to the moment, she knew that she couldn't show it. So she concealed it with the harshness she'd learned from all her years in the Bridge.

"I ain't got time to be talkin' about what used to be," she said sharply. "If you got somethin' to say about Kenya, I'm listenin'. But if you don't, get out."

For a second, Darnell's face looked as if it might crumple beneath Lily's stinging words. But he quickly recovered and looked around uncomfortably as he tried to find a way to ask the question that he must. When he realized there was no other way to say it, he was straightforward.

"Did you know about Sonny and Kenya?"

Lily searched his eyes and tried to understand what she was hearing. Because it couldn't be what she thought it was.

"I just found out," she said. "But you knew? You knew, and you didn't say anything?"

"No," he said. "I didn't know 'til this mornin', when I heard the cops was lookin' for Sonny. But Judy knew."

"Look, Darnell, don't be comin' in here on that shit talkin' all crazy."

"Look at me, Lily. Do I look like I'm high? I been walkin' around since seven o'clock this mornin' lookin' for my niece, tryin' to figure out what happened to her.

"Now, I know she told some people about Sonny. And I know she was gettin' ready to tell some more people—maybe even the cops. My niece was tired, Lily. She was tired o' watchin' me smoke, tired o' watchin' Judy sellin' crack, tired o' watchin' all that madness that went on in between. But mostly, she was tired o' Sonny doin' what he was doin'."

"So Sonny did somethin' to Kenya to keep her from tellin'?"

"Sonny ain't the one sent her out there ten o'clock at night to go to the store."

"What you sayin', Darnell? Just say it."

"I'm sayin' Judy couldn't have Sonny goin' to jail, 'cause Judy can't hustle by herself. So she sent Kenya out there and paid somebody to make sure she ain't come back.

"I'm sayin' the only thing that mattered to Judy was money, and if she had to get rid o' my niece to make sure her money kept flowin', then that's what she was gon' do.

"I'm sayin' Judy did somethin' to my niece," he said, cradling his head in his hands as the emotion of the moment overcame him.

He paused, and when he had gathered himself, he looked Lily in the eye.

"I just hope she ain't kill her."

Chapter Six

Judy looked at the dingy cinder-block walls of the locked room in Central Detectives and hoped that the minutes wouldn't pass too quickly.

She was afraid that time would allow things to spin out of control. Her fear wasn't about the possession charges that she knew would be filed against her. It wasn't even about Kenya anymore.

The thing that frightened Judy the most was the possibility of losing Sonny—a possibility that grew more real with every passing second. She knew that if she didn't get out and find him soon, she would never see him again.

Judy knew this because she loved Sonny in a way that allowed her to crawl into his skin and become what he was. She had studied him in the night, when their lovemaking was over and he lay spent. She had listened for him in the day, when the drop and slide of his feet announced his arrival. She had breathed in his essence when he awakened in the morning and tasted it when he lay down in the evening. She could sense his moods and experience his pain, rise with his smile and sink with his anger.

So when Lynch had asked her if she knew where Sonny was, Judy was certain that she did. She could feel it in that space where she had the ability to become as greedy and selfish as he was.

She knew that he had gone back to the projects to take the money they'd stashed there. And she knew that he would disappear once he had it. But she also knew that wherever he went, she would find him, because Judy could always close her eyes and feel where he would go next.

That thought reverberated in her mind as a police officer came to look in on her.

"Excuse me," she said, banging on the door when she saw his face in the square window. "I really need to go the bathroom."

The cop looked her up and down, his blue eyes lingering on the full breasts and hips insistently pressing against her thin cotton dress.

Judy let her eyelids droop slightly, then smirked seductively and placed her hands on her hips. "Please?"

The cop smiled before his face disappeared from the window. Judy heard keys, and then the sound of the door being unlocked. When it opened, he was still smiling.

"Come on," he said, taking her by the arm and leading her down the hall to the bathroom.

As they passed through the hall, Judy looked into an adjacent room and saw several detectives, seated at scarred steel desks with ancient word processors, looking up at her through a haze of cigarette smoke. Most of them were drinking coffee and sitting behind foot-high stacks of paperwork.

Judy counted six detectives and two uniformed officers in the room. The detectives appeared to be bored and entrenched in a daily routine. The two uniformed officers, on the other hand, were engaged in easy banter. They acted like they were only there to visit.

Beyond the officers, on the other side of the room, Judy saw a door leading out of the office space, which she knew led to another hall and at least one interrogation room. She looked behind her. There was a door at that end of the hall with a red exit sign above it. In front of her, there were two bathrooms and a door that appeared to lead to a broom closet.

"Right here," the officer said, opening the door to the bathroom.

Judy walked in. The cop walked in behind her and closed the door. She heard a latch click as he locked it.

"Y'all ain't got no female cops to take women to the bathroom?" she said, turning to face him. "I mean damn, you act like you—"

And then he was on her, pushing her against the stall and pulling up her dress, his hands grabbing her thighs and moving up hurriedly to the soft flesh above them.

One hand grabbed her everywhere, hungrily seeking out the warm places and finding them with his palms and fingertips. The other hand gripped her hair, holding her in place and forcing her against the stall as he ripped at her dress and squeezed her breasts.

She didn't resist. Instead, she reached down and touched him, caressed him, then squeezed gently. He stopped long enough to look in her eyes. Even with the fading bruises she'd suffered at Daneen's hands, Judy's eyes were still hypnotic.

She placed a finger against her lips and another against his pants. Then she loosed him, slid down the stall and touched him, then kissed him with every part of her mouth. He looked down at her, then threw his head back with pleasure, moaning softly as he gave in to the moment.

Judy looked up at him, licked him slowly, then without the slightest hesitation, pushed him as hard as she could. His head hit the side of the sink with a dull thud. Blood oozed from the back of his head as he slid down to the floor and was still.

Moments later, Judy walked out of the bathroom wearing his uniform. She ambled down the hallway and out the door with the red exit sign above it. Then she went down a flight of steps and out into the parking lot to find the car that matched the registration she'd found in the officer's wallet.

As she reached down to unlock his door, Judy looked behind her to see if anyone had followed her. When she saw that they hadn't, she got in.

Judy was going to find her man. After that, she was going to get her money. And then, one way or the other, Judy was going to get what she wanted.

She was finally going to get out of the Bridge.

Sonny was seeking a bridge of a different sort.

He found it just a few blocks from where he'd eluded the police and parked the green Mustang beneath the rusted structure that stretched across Thirteenth Street at Cumberland.

Snatching the backpack from the passenger seat, he looked around him before getting out of the car, then slid out into streets that knew him well.

It was a neighborhood where vast lots of packed earth filled spaces once occupied by row houses, a place where crack prostitutes lurched by like ghosts, and hundred-year-old buildings fell down, piece by tired piece.

As Sonny passed through, only one or two of the people on the nearly deserted morning streets noticed him. Not that it mattered. If anyone asked, no one with an ounce of sense would ever say they'd seen Sonny. The reward wasn't worth the punishment.

Still, something gnawed at him as he walked into the main entrance of his destination—the Fairview Apartments housing project. When he boarded the rickety elevator that would take him to Dot's eighth-floor apartment, the feeling grew-stronger.

It wasn't fear. Sonny rarely experienced that. It was desire—the same thing he always felt for the seventeen-year-old girl he kept for the nights when Judy wasn't enough.

When he'd met Dot, she was fifteen and living with her mother in a one-bedroom apartment in the Bridge. But even then, she was long black hair and firm, round flesh. Legs, thick and shapely. Eyes, wide and innocent. And a throaty laugh that revealed enough of her soft, pink tongue to make her delectable.

Sonny had quietly approached her, then paid a bribe to a Housing Authority supervisor to move her from one housing project to another. He assured her mother that Dot would be taken care of, and backed his promise with a two-thousand-dollar gift. She protested weakly, even tried to convince Dot not to go. But she was already overwhelmed with five other children—three of whom were under the age of five. So when Dot left, she really had no choice but to take the money and accept her daughter's decision.

Sonny wasted no time. Shortly after Dot moved to Fairview, he began to visit her there. Soon after that, she gave herself to him. Her passion was violent, clawing at his back, biting at his neck, squeezing him between her thighs until his breath rushed out of his wide-open mouth.

The sheer magnitude of it gave her power over him. Sonny couldn't resist her. And in truth, he didn't want to.

So he came back to her again and again. First with a car, then with a diamond, then with more money than she'd ever seen. Because when she wrapped his body in hers, pulling him down into a place so sweet he could never taste it completely, she always stopped just short of giving him her all. Sonny was always left waiting for more. He knew, just as she did, that it would never come. That she would still have power over him. But that was about to change.

As Sonny knocked on her door, he tried hard not to think of how her body felt against his. When she answered, though, he couldn't help remembering. Her face had the soft glow it always did right after she awakened. Her butter-colored legs extended from her short, silk robe like candy. He looked her up and down, taking it all in. And then he steeled himself, brushed past her, and hurried toward her bedroom.

"Well, damn," she said, closing the door behind him with an attitude. "Good mornin' to you, too."

Sonny grunted in response, then reached into her closet, took out an outfit, and threw it on the floor.

Dot walked into the bedroom behind him, nuzzling her face against his back as he reached down into the closet for a pair of shoes.

"What you come in here wakin' me up for?" she asked, her voice filled with a sensuous smile.

He took a deep breath before turning to face her. The first thing he saw was the mischief in her eyes. She looked like a child. He liked that. It would make it easier for him.

"Gimme your car keys," he said in a low, hard voice.

"I gotta go to the market today, Sonny," she said, clearly annoyed. "Why you can't just take your own damn car?"

There was a loud silence. And then the smack came from nowhere, his right hand sailing through the air and landing flush on her cheek. He smacked her again with his left hand, then punched her with his right. When he was through, she was on the floor, bleeding and startled.

"I bought you that car," he said calmly. "That mean it's mine. Now get up and get me the keys to my car."

Dot placed her palms flat on the floor and dragged herself to her feet. Her head was spinning as she walked across the room and retrieved the keys from her dresser drawer.

She watched Sonny warily as she brought them to him, moving slowly enough to duck another blow if it came.

"Hurry up, Dot," he said, never looking at her as he snatched off his pants and shirt and began to dress in the clothes he'd taken from her closet.

She scrambled over to him, pressed the keys into his hand, and moved backward until she was on the bed, cowering in the corner and wondering why Sonny had beaten her.

They were both silent while he dressed—Dot wondering what would come next, and Sonny reveling in the power he'd taken back from her. When he finished, he stalked over to her and took her chin in his hand.

"You ain't see me this mornin', Dot. Matter fact, anybody ask you anything about me, you don't know me, you understand?"

She shook her head yes.

"No. Answer me, Dot."

"I don't know you," she said, sniffing as she held back the tears welling up in her eyes. "I never did know you."

The weight of her words held him there for a moment. He looked around uncomfortably, not knowing quite what to say. Then he left.

Dot lay on the bed, knowing he was gone for good. She pulled her knees to her chest and wrapped her arms around them, holding herself because there was no one else to do so.

When the phone began to ring, she ignored it. By the tenth ring, when she reached across the bed and snatched the receiver from the cradle, she was angry. Before she could say anything, though, her mother was screaming in her ear.

"Dot, you heard about Sonny?"

She started to say something, but her mother cut her off.

"The nigga done did somethin' to Kenya, girl."

"Huh?"

"I tried to tell you about Sonny," she said, warming to the subject. "But you ain't wanna listen."

"Mom, what you talkin' about?"

"Kenya is missin', Dot," she said, placing emphasis on each word. "She been missin' since last night. The cops tried to stop Sonny 'cause they figured he knew where she was. He ran. Damn near killed a cop tryin' to get away. Then he musta stole a car and hit Judge Baylor. And from what they sayin' on the news, he hurt him pretty bad."

Dot held the phone and tried to digest what her mother was telling her.

"Dot?"

"Yes," she croaked, her voice barely a whisper.

"Dot, if Sonny come over there, don't let him in 'cause he might . . . just don't let him in."

When Dot didn't say anything, her mother's voice took on a nervous edge.

"He ain't there now, is he, Dot? Please tell me he ain't there now."

"He ain't here, Mom," she said, swallowing hard. "I ain't seen him."

"Dot, listen to me."

"Mom, I gotta go," she snapped, and slammed the phone into the cradle.

She sat for a moment, biting her lip as her eyes quickly shifted back and forth. It had all happened so fast, this falling-apart. But it was a moment that she'd known would come. And as she tasted the blood that oozed into her mouth from the places he had slapped her, she did what she'd always known she would.

Picking up the phone, she dialed the police, gave them Sonny's description, the location where he was last seen, and the description of her car.

A calm swept over her as she hung up. She wiped away tears with the back of her hand and sat for a full minute before a smile began to creep across her lips.

"You gon' be sorry you hurt me, Sonny," she said, her voice quivering. "I'm gon' make sure o' that."

The parking lot at Central Detectives was eerily still when Lynch arrived with Wilson and Daneen. But he didn't notice. His mind was filled with images of Sonny and the man who would surely die because of him.

As much as he tried, though, Lynch couldn't make himself care about Baylor. He was much too worried about himself.

"Come on, Daneen," Lynch said, roughly grabbing her arm and pulling her out of the backseat.

"Stop pullin' on me," she said, snatching her arm away and locking eyes with him.

Their stare was filled not with anger, but with longing. It was Lynch who looked away first.

Wilson watched as a slew of conflicting feelings hung like a thick fog between them. She turned and started to walk toward the building. There were more important things to worry about than that.

"Lynch!" a detective called out, running out of the back door with two officers following close behind. "She's gone!"

"What are you talking about?" he said, a lump swelling in his throat as he tore his eyes from Daneen's.

The detective stopped in front of Lynch. "Judy Brown," he said, panting. "Chalmers took her to the bathroom about twenty minutes ago. She must've hit him with something. Gashed the back of his head pretty good."

"So how did she get out?" Lynch asked, his face turning an ashen gray.

The detective looked down at the ground, clearly embarrassed. "We don't know. My guess is she put on his uniform and walked out through the parking lot. I mean, he didn't have it on when we found him on the bathroom floor."

Wilson's lip curled as disgust swept over her face.

"Why he was in the bathroom with her in the first place?" she asked, pausing for effect. "With his uniform off."

"I don't like your tone," the detective said, his eyes flashing anger.

"And I don't like your nasty-ass officers molesting our prisoners," Wilson said, moving toward the detective.

Lynch stepped between them and placed a hand on the detective's chest. "Where is Judy now?" he said.

The detective looked from Lynch to Wilson, then sighed in frustration before surveying the empty spaces in the parking lot.

"I don't know," he said quietly. "But it looks like Chalmers's car is gone."

"I don't believe this," Wilson said, throwing her hands in the air.

Lynch's reaction was cooler. "Let's put out a description of the car," he told the detective. "I'm sure she couldn't have gotten far."

But not even Lynch believed that. With the Ben Franklin Bridge and the state of New Jersey just minutes away, Judy could be anywhere. For that matter, Sonny could, too.

None of that mattered to Daneen. Sonny was just a means to an end. For her, it was about finding the one person who could help her to reclaim what had been lost in their months and years apart. It was about Kenya. And she wasn't about to let anyone forget that.

So she turned to Lynch with piercing eyes and spoke with the concern of a mother. "What about my baby?"

Lynch and Wilson looked at her, then at each other. But before they could answer, the handheld radio on Lynch's hip crackled to life.

"Dan 25?"

Lynch snatched the radio from his belt. "Dan 25."

"A complainant at the Fairview Apartments says your male just left her unit. He's wearing a brown shirt and black pants and driving a blue 1990 Ford Taurus with a Pennsylvania tag of B-Barney, W-William, D-David, five-six-four-three. Direction unknown."

"Dan 25, what's the complainant's apartment number?"

"Eight D. That's eight D-David."

He turned to Daneen. "That apartment number sound familiar to you?"

"No," she said. "But that's probably that young girl he mess with up there."

"And when were you going to tell us about that?" Wilson asked, clearly annoyed.

Daneen wasn't about to be bullied.

"I woulda told you when you asked me," she said. "Ya'll the cops, not me."

"Dan 25," Lynch said, ignoring Daneen and speaking into the

radio as he went back to his car. "I want that description broadcast over J band and East Division. Stand by for flash information on Judy Brown, wanted for investigation on narcotics violations, auto theft, and assault on a police officer."

Lynch jumped into his car with Wilson and Daneen while the detective who'd told him of Judy's escape rattled off her description to radio.

As Lynch drove the three of them toward the Fairview Apartments, verbal pictures of Sonny and Judy were painted over the airwaves of Philadelphia.

With Judge Baylor on his deathbed, and Lynch poised to take the blame, the search for them was about much more than Kenya now.

The knock at the door startled Dot. She thought it was Sonny, coming back to apologize, to take her with him, to do anything but what he'd done before he left.

She dragged herself from her bed, walked into her living room, and stared through the peephole at a police officer standing in the hallway with a notepad in hand.

She hadn't expected the police to arrive that quickly. But she opened the door, eagerly inviting the officer inside.

"You here about Sonny, right?"

"Yeah," the officer said, walking in while flipping through the notepad. "Where is he?"

Dot started to answer. Then the officer took off her hat and sat down on the couch. Dot's mouth dropped open.

"Why you so surprised?" Judy asked, smiling in spite of herself. "You thought I ain't know about you and Sonny?"

Dot stumbled to find the right words. "Know ... what?"

"Look," Judy said, her hard voice tinged with a quiet anger. "We ain't got time to play games, sweetie. I always knew. I saw the way he looked at you when you was livin' with your mama. Smelled you on his skin when he came back from seein' you. But I ain't care. Long as he brought home what was mine."

"So what you here for?" Dot asked.

" 'Cause Sonny got somethin' belong to me. And I got a feelin' you know where he went with it."

"Well, you wrong," Dot said with an attitude. "I don't know."

Judy got up from the couch, walked over to her and stood just a few inches away, staring at the cuts on her lips.

"You know somethin'," Judy said. "From the looks o' things, Sonny been here."

Dot self-consciously raised her hand to cover her mouth.

"Ain't no need to cover it up, honey," Judy said, her eyes boring into Dot's. " 'Cause if you don't tell me what I wanna know in the next five seconds, I'm gon' make sure everybody see it."

Dot knew she should be afraid, but she stood her ground with flat-footed defiance.

Judy took it in, and her eyes clouded over with a quiet rage. Her hand balled into a fist, her mouth turned down in a grimace, and as the seconds ticked by, Dot's resolve began to waver.

Judy made a sudden move. Dot fell to the ground in a shivering mess. Judy dropped to one knee and grabbed her by the neck. Dot reached up and tried to pry Judy's hands away. But as Judy's grip tightened around her throat, it was clear that Dot was too weak to fight her off.

"Niggas don't tell you 'bout this when they tryin' to get between your legs, do they?" Judy said through a maniacal grin. "They don't tell you they woman might walk up on you and choke the shit outta you."

The veins on Judy's forehead stood out as she squeezed harder, cutting off Dot's air. Dot's face turned red, then purple as she struggled to break free.

For a split second, Judy considered squeezing the life from the girl who had taken a piece of Sonny away from her.

But then good sense prevailed over anger. She let go, sitting back on her haunches as Dot coughed and tried to catch her breath.

"Where he at?" Judy asked.

Dot looked up at her, at once fearful and relieved.

"Gone," was all she could manage to say.

Judy got up from the floor and looked down at her menacingly. "Gone where?"

"To hell, I hope," Dot said with a gasp.

Judy continued to look down at her and wait. When Dot caught her breath, she repeated the description she'd given to 9-1-1.

Judy memorized it. Then she rushed from Dot's building and walked one block to the Salvation Army Corps on Huntingdon Street.

She told them that she needed clothing for a rape victim she was taking to police headquarters. When they gave her the clothes, Judy went outside, slipped into an alley, took off the police uniform she was wearing, and changed into the clothing herself. From there, she walked to Germantown and Rising Sun, where she took a room in a two-story hotel whose most loyal customers were crack prostitutes.

After checking into the room, she took to the street to find Sonny.

Chapter Seven

Lily looked from the cracked brown floor tiles in her hallway to the shadows that spilled across Darnell's ashen gray face. She thought that if she stared long enough, she would find answers. But the only things she found were questions. And all of them were about Kenya.

In the midst of her uncertainty, there were two things that Lily believed to be true. Sonny had molested Kenya. And somehow, he had arranged for her to disappear.

As far as Lily was concerned, Darnell's assertion that Judy was involved was wrong. No matter how much the drug game had hardened her, Judy wouldn't have harmed Kenya to hide the truth about Sonny and their drug enterprise. She just wasn't that ruthless.

So when Lily looked up through the shadows of her uncertainty and saw what she believed to be the truth, she spoke it without the slightest hesitation.

"It wasn't Judy," she told Darnell. "It mighta been some o' them people that hang around her place. But it wasn't her."

Darnell peered down the hallway at the living-room couch where Lily's daughter sat, watching television. Then he lowered his voice to a whisper.

"I wanna believe that, but I can't," he said. "Much as it hurt me to say it about my aunt, I can't stop thinkin' it was her."

"Much as it hurt you to say it?" Lily repeated sarcastically. "I don't think nothin' hurt you, Darnell. I don't even think you remember how it feel to hurt."

He didn't respond. Not outwardly. But inside, his mind was in another place—in a time when he and Lily couldn't stand this close to one another without touching.

"You'd be surprised what I remember, Lily."

"You said you came here about Kenya," she snapped. "Not about us."

"Us?" he said. "Ain't no such thing as us no more, is it?"

Lily stared at him for a moment. And then she looked away. The memories from their time together reminded her of what it was like to be happy. It was easier when she couldn't remember.

"You right, Darnell," she said finally. "It ain't no us. But it's a little girl that need to be found. And the cops damn sure ain't gon' do it."

"So you gon' find her?" Darnell asked skeptically.

"I don't even know where to start."

"Neither do I. Seem like I been walkin' in circles all mornin', hopin' I would run into her."

"You been out all mornin' and you ain't ran into nobody that seen her?" Lily said cynically. "Seem to me like you ain't really been lookin'."

"Well, I did hear somebody say she was with that girl from the tenth floor. What's her name?"

"Lakeesha or Shanequa or one o' them ghetto-ass names."

Darnell smiled. "Her name Tyreeka," he said.

Lily grunted, staring into the space between them as she conjured images of Tyreeka, the little girl who was too old for Kenya, but too young for the teenage boys she seemed to attract.

"I ain't never liked that li'l piss tail girl anyway," she said.

"Why not?"

"She one o' them sneaky heifers. Always up in some nigga face. And all the boys I ever seen her with was drug...

Lily's voice drifted off. Darnell stood quietly, waiting for her to return to the moment. When she did, it was as if something clicked.

"I wouldn't be surprised if Tyreeka know where Kenya at," she said.

"Why you say that?"

"Didn't you say Kenya was with her last night?"

"Yeah," Darnell said. "But when I knocked on her mother door this mornin', ain't nobody answer."

"Well, I'm goin' down there now," Lily said, hurrying toward the door and grabbing Janay's hand as Darnell followed close behind. "And I betcha a fat man that when I do, I'll find Kenya."

Sonny was on I-76, driving toward the airport in Dot's car. He was traveling at the posted speed limit of fifty, watching as other cars flew past him.

Sonny was in no hurry. He had already made contact with his Dominican connection—a man whose North Philadelphia drug corners paid for the private, guarded villas he'd built outside San Juan.

The Dominican had made arrangements for Sonny to stay at one of them once he reached Puerto Rico. It was a favor Sonny had earned through their decades-long business relationship.

But Sonny hated asking favors. And soon, he would no longer need to do so. With the money he'd taken from Judy, and the money he would have electronically transferred from his account, he could buy a private slice of the island. There would be women, young and nubile, who would bow to his every whim, and men whose daily chore would be to arrange his latest fantasy.

That's the way it would have worked if Sonny had planned to follow through. But he didn't, because he'd hurt cops while trying to escape, and they wouldn't rest until they found him. That reality changed everything.

Now, he only wanted to use the Dominican's influence to get him into San Juan. He would stay there for just a day, then decide upon a final destination and leave, telling no one.

Sonny knew that staying longer was not an option, because it would give the Dominican the opportunity to set him up. Sonny, after all, was in a position of weakness. The police were looking for him, his family was pointing fingers, and he had no backup to speak of. Regardless of their long-term business relationship, the Dominican, like any good hustler, would be loath not to take advantage of Sonny's vulnerability.

But Sonny wasn't going to give the Dominican or anyone else the chance to stick him. At least that's what he believed before he saw the flashing lights behind him.

Sonny looked in the rearview mirror and saw the patrol car moving closer. As he watched the car's dome lights swirl brightly against the pale expanse of morning sky, his mind began to race.

He had just passed the previous exit—Spring Garden—so he couldn't try to bolt from the expressway into the maze of West Philadelphia's streets. He couldn't turn around because a concrete barrier separated the northbound and southbound lanes. All Sonny could do was hope.

And at that moment, Sonny's hope was that the cop was trying to pass him. When Sonny switched from the middle to the far-right lane to give the cop the chance to do so, the cop switched lanes, too.

His palms began to sweat, causing his hands to slide against the steering wheel. He considered flooring it, but a chase on the expressway was not like a chase on the streets. There were only a few exits, and they could easily be blocked.

After a moment's pause, Sonny pulled onto the shoulder of the road. He did so in the hope that Dot hadn't given his description to police, and that this was just a routine stop. If it was, he knew that he could take care of the cop.

Sonny tapped the brakes and rolled to a halt. The police car pulled in behind him. When the cop got out, he unsnapped his holster and walked toward Sonny's car.

The gesture was ominous. Drivers who saw it slowed as they rode past, craning their necks to look inside the vehicle the cop was approaching.

Sonny ignored them. Instead, he watched the cop in the rearview mirror and removed his hands from the steering wheel. He knew that backup would arrive soon, which meant that he didn't have much time.

Grabbing the backpack, Sonny flung open the passenger door and plunged out of the car.

"Stop!" the officer shouted, drawing his gun and aiming at the spot where he believed Sonny to be.

Sonny rolled onto the ground and crawled on his belly, moving toward the back of the car. For a split second, everything around him was still. Then the officer opened fire, and the air was filled with the sound of flying bullets.

Suddenly, the cars that had slowed to watch the roadside drama were darting away as their drivers raced to avoid the onslaught.

Bullets punctured Dot's car, embedded themselves in the asphalt, whizzed past Sonny's ears. Sonny, still flat on his stomach, folded his arms in front of his head. Then he rolled beneath the car, pulling the backpack with him.

The officer stopped shooting and began to walk along the rear of the car. Sonny could hear the fall of his feet as he rounded the passenger side and stopped at the back door.

Sonny looked out from beneath the car at the cop's boots, which were just inches from his face. He could tell, even as the cop stood still, that his eyes were surveying the space around him, looking for Sonny.

Just as the cop started to bend to look under the car, Sonny reached out with one hand and pulled the cop's feet from under him. The cop fell hard, dropping his gun as his head bounced against the ground. Sonny rolled out from beneath the car. The cop tried to rise to his feet. Sonny jumped onto his chest, grabbed his head with both hands, and banged it against the ground. Blood spattered. The cop was still.

Sonny jumped in the car and peeled away, the spinning wheels spraying the cop's body with roadside gravel and dirt.

As he bore left at the fork in the highway, he looked in the mirror and saw the cop's backup arriving at the scene. Sonny pulled off at the next exit, Twenty-third Street, drove a half block to Twenty-second, turned right, and pulled into an open-air parking lot near a small street called Cherry.

Swinging the backpack onto his shoulder, Sonny walked out of the lot and cut down a side street toward the river. A few minutes later, when cop cars came flying into the area, Sonny disappeared into the high weeds along the bank of the Schuylkill River.

By the time they found Dot's car parked hard against the gate, with its lights on and its engine running, Sonny was gone.

Dot's door was ajar when Lynch arrived with Wilson and Daneen.

She was sitting in the middle of the floor, crying softly, chin on her chest, shoulders sagging under what appeared to be the weight of the world.

Her television was on, and the slapstick music of the Saturday morning cartoons sharply contrasted with the room's somber mood.

"Are you Dorothea Jones?" Lynch asked as he pushed open the door.

Dot looked up and saw Lynch—a man she vaguely remembered from the Bridge—walking into her apartment with a female detective and another woman.

Dot's expression was blank, just like her heart. She had poured out so much of it since Sonny's tumultuous departure that she wasn't sure there was anything left.

"They call me Dot," she said, wiping her tears with the back of her hand. "Not Dorothea."

"Okay, Dot," Lynch said, ignoring her apparent distress. "I'm going to keep this simple. We know you made the call about Sonny, but we need a little more. We need to know where he went."

Dot looked from Lynch to Wilson to Daneen. Their eyes were accusing.

"I don't know where he went," she said. "I told them everything I knew when I called 9-1-1."

Wilson, who had been standing by the door, closed it and walked to where Dot was sitting.

"Well, that's not enough," she said.

"Too bad," Dot said, rolling her eyes at the detective.

Wilson was inclined to snatch Dot to her feet and shake the answers loose. But then she saw something familiar in Dot's face. It was defeat, and heartbreak, and betrayal—the kind of all-consuming pain that a woman can only get from a man.

She tried to play on that.

"Sonny hurts people," Wilson said sympathetically. "But I don't have to tell you that, do I?"

She paused to give Dot a chance to respond. She didn't, so Wilson pressed on.

"He's still hurting people," she said. "On our way over here, there was a radio call for an assist. A highway patrolman who spotted Sonny driving your car on the expressway stopped him. Shots were fired. But before backup got there, Sonny bashed the man's head in and disappeared."

"So what you want me to do?" Dot asked, clearly agitated. "He took my car—punched me in my face and took it. I don't know where he goin', but wherever it is, I hope to God he stay there."

Wilson looked down at her and saw purple marks around her neck. She leaned in for a closer look.

"Did he do that to you, too?" she asked, pointing to the bruises.

"He might as well be the one who done it," Dot said. "It wouldn't have happened if it wasn't for him."

She turned away from Wilson, and the light from the television reflected against a shining welt near her right eye.

"Whole lot o' things would be different if it wasn't for him," she said, her eyes as far away as her voice.

"So why are you protecting him?" Lynch asked.

Dot laughed. It was a bitter sound. "Is that what you think?" she asked in disbelief. "Look at my face, man. Look at it and tell me why the hell I would be protectin' Sonny."

" 'Cause you fuckin' him, that's why!" Daneen shouted angrily.

"Wait a minute," Lynch said, jumping in.

"No, I'm not waitin'," Daneen snapped. "I been ridin' around with y'all all day tryin' to find my daughter. Sonny know where she at, Dot know where Sonny at. And she gon' tell me somethin', or I swear 'fo God, I'ma hurt her."

Dot smiled in spite of herself. She was past being afraid of pain.

"Oh, it's funny?" Daneen said, lunging at Dot as Lynch pulled her back.

"Yeah, it's funny. It's funny that you sound just like your aunt."

Lynch and Wilson exchanged puzzled looks.

"What aunt?" Lynch asked.

"Judy," she said. "Sonny woman."

"Are you saying you saw Judy this morning?" Lynch asked.

"She came right after I called 9-1-1," she said nervously. "I looked out and seen her, but I ain't recognize her, 'cause she had on this cop uniform. Then when I opened the door, she came in here trippin'. Said she knew all about me and Sonny and started askin' me all these questions. Then when I ain't tell her what she wanted to know, she started...Well, anyway, she said somethin' 'bout Sonny takin' somethin' that belonged to her."

"Did she say what it was?" Lynch asked.

"No," Dot said quietly.

"But you're sure she came here looking for Sonny and saying that he took something from her?" Lynch asked.

"Yeah."

"And do you know where she was going when she left?"

"No, but I—"

"Thanks Dot," he said. "You've been helpful."

As they walked out the door, Lynch relayed Judy's latest known location to radio.

After disappearing into the brush along the river, Sonny picked his way through the man-size weeds, hoping to go far enough downstream to avoid the K9 units that would soon join the hunt.

He made it as far as South Street, where he scrambled up the side of the muddy riverbank, dragging the money-filled backpack behind him.

Had he known that he was in the very spot where a priestess had only weeks before paid homage to the river goddess Oshun during the yearly Odunde festival, perhaps he would have prayed to her.

If not to Oshun, then to someone, because there was no way that Sonny would make it out of the city without divine intervention, especially after assaulting two police officers.

But Sonny wasn't one to pray. As far as he knew, the only god he needed was strapped to his hip, ready to rain fire and brimstone on anyone who got in his way. But if there was a bigger god than that, and he could help Sonny to San Juan, he would gladly accept the help.

But as far as he was concerned, he was more deadly than he'd ever seen God or anyone else be. And at that moment, as he jogged along the South Street Bridge, mud-covered and panting, Sonny looked every bit as dangerous as he thought he was.

His expression was fixed somewhere between madness and fear, his eyes darting nervously about him, searching for a car that would allow him to move faster. When he didn't find it, he began to run, taking to the street and threading in and out of traffic to the tune of blaring car horns and shouted profanities.

He ignored it all, running harder as he approached Graduate Hospital on the corner of Nineteenth and South.

When he reached the hospital's door, he abruptly stopped and limped into the lobby, with mud and sweat sticking to his clothes like dung. The guard—a young black man who looked uncomfortable in his blue security blazer and clip-on tie—looked up from the television behind the half-moon-shaped security desk.

"Can I help you?"

"I'm looking for the emergency room," Sonny said, wincing as if he was in pain. "I had a little accident down by the South Street Bridge."

"So I see," the guard said, staring at Sonny with increasing curiosity. "Go down the hall, make a left, and follow the signs. You can't miss it."

"Thanks."

Sonny walked away, his limp even more pronounced. The guard called after him. "Yo."

Sonny stopped and turned around slowly.

"You look real familiar, man," the guard said, dragging out his words as he tried to jog his memory. "Seem like I seen you somewhere before."

"Probably not," Sonny said, grabbing his knee. "Lotta people look like me, though. You probably got me confused with somebody else."

The guard stared at him a moment longer. "I guess you right," he said, his eyes dropping to Sonny's knee. "You better go 'head and get that leg looked at."

Sonny turned around and made the left toward the emergency room. A doctor walked past him, greeting him with an absentminded grin. A nurse hurried away from her station with a patient's chart on a clipboard. An orderly passed by the empty nurses' station pushing a wheeled cart filled with soiled linen.

When the orderly turned down a nearby hallway, Sonny followed him. The man opened a locked linen closet and pushed the cart inside. Sonny slipped behind him and grabbed the door before it could close.

The man turned around, irritated. Taking in Sonny's disheveled look, he dismissed him as a patient.

"The emergency room's that way," he said, then returned to what he was doing.

Sonny didn't respond. He shut the door behind him, reached into his waistband for the gun, and smacked the man on the side of his head with it.

The man went down, blood seeping from a widening gash near his temple. Sonny reached into the linen the man was sorting, tore a strip of cloth from a sheet, and tied it around his mouth. He tore another strip and tied his hands. Then he bent down until he was just inches from his face.

"Any clothes in here?"

The man nodded toward a cart on the other side of the closet. Sonny looked inside and saw what he needed. He stripped quickly, stepping out of his mud-stained clothes and into a clean set of surgical scrubs.

Sonny placed the gun in the backpack, then stood over the terrified man for half a second—long enough to frighten him into a silence they both understood he should maintain. Sonny left the room, locking the door behind him, leaving the man bleeding on the floor.

Walking quickly through the halls, he followed signs to the parking garage, took the elevator down to the lower level, walked to the darkest corner, and began trying car doors. Within moments, he was inside a black Maxima.

Breaking the steering column, he reached down and tried to hot-wire the car. There was a spark, and nothing else. Sonny looked at the display to see if the engine or battery indicators were lit. They weren't, so he felt along the bottom of the dashboard, looking for a kill switch. When he didn't find one, he tried the wires again. This time, the engine cranked.

Sonny shot out of the parking space and whipped the car through the underground lot, following signs to the exit. When he found it, the crossbar was down. Sonny considered ramming through, but decided against it, and stopped at the cashier's booth.

A bored-looking woman in her midthirties sat twisting a single braid of hair around her thick, brown finger. When she heard the car pull up, she held out her hand without looking at Sonny. He rolled down the window, reached into his bag and offered a twenty-dollar bill.

"I lost my ticket, so I'm not sure how long I been here," he said, thrusting the money into her hand. "But I guess this should cover it."

The woman started to respond, but fell silent when she glanced at him. From his face, her eyes made their way along the driver's side door, to the baby's car seat in the back, and then back to Sonny.

She had worked in the hospital parking lot for more than a year. She knew who owned the car, and it wasn't Sonny. When the reality of it struck her, she was suddenly afraid.

"I-I might be able to see what time you checked in if you give me your plate number," she said nervously. "Might save you a couple dollars."

"You don't have to do that."

"It's all right," she said quickly. "Just give me a second."

As she scrambled for a pencil with shaking hands, the phone in her booth rang. She answered, and as she listened to the guard at

the front desk tell her that a wanted man was loose in the building—
a man he'd seen on the news that very morning—the blood rushed
from her face.

When she looked at Sonny again, his gun was pointing out the
driver-side window.

"Hang up the phone, open the gate, and you'll live," he said
calmly.

Seconds later, the car sped out of the parking lot.

Lily banged on Tyreeka's mother's door with curses poised on her
lips. But when the door swung open, the self-righteous anger that
had sent her running down the stairs began to melt away.

Hattie Johnson stood in the doorway wearing a look that Lily
had seen in so many of her neighbors' faces. It was neither fatigue,
nor sadness, nor frustration, but a combination of all three. It was
the kind of look that came when tears no longer would, when the
reality of the projects sank down to the very marrow of the bone.

"Is Tyreeka here?" Lily asked, her voice more timid than she
meant for it to sound.

With three knee-high grandchildren grasping at her legs and the
television blaring in the background, Hattie fixed her glazed, tired
eyes on Lily.

"I ain't seen Tyreeka since ten o'clock last night," she said, her
eyes showing a spark of anger. "But when I do, she gon' wish she
ain't have to see me at all."

Lily stood in the hallway with Darnell and Janay, looking and
feeling uncomfortable. Hattie was about to step aside to let them
in, but then she glimpsed Darnell, and the look and smell of crack
gave her pause.

"If y'all don't want nothin' else..." she said, and started to close
the door.

Lily reached out and held it open.

Hattie looked at her expectantly. The spark of anger was gone, replaced by fatigue.

"We tryin' to find Judy's little niece, Kenya," Lily said. "Ain't nobody seen her since last night."

Hattie's dead eyes came alive again at the chance to gossip. "I heard about that," she said in an anxious, conspiratorial whisper. "Heard they took Judy outta here in handcuffs this mornin', and they lookin' for Sonny. They think they did somethin' to the child or somethin'?"

"I don't know," Lily said, looking up at Darnell, who stood quiet and still beside her.

"But from what we heard, Kenya was with Tyreeka last night," Lily continued. "I'm not tryin' to get in your business or nothin', but if you could tell us where Tyreeka went when she left here, it might help us find Kenya."

"Honey, if I knew where Tyreeka was at, I would be draggin' her home myself," she said, grabbing one of the children who had wandered too far into the hallway.

"'Cause if she think she gon' do what her sister did and stick me with her baby," she added, her lips twisting with attitude, "she got another thing comin'."

Just then, Tyreeka's twenty-week-old daughter screamed. She was sitting in the middle of the living-room floor, strapped in a tiny, padded rocking chair with curdled formula dribbling down her vomit-soaked sleeper.

The screaming continued for a minute straight. Then the baby settled into a low-pitched, constant whimper.

Lily looked at the child with concern.

"Don't worry 'bout her," Hattie said, reading her expression. "She all right. She just loud."

Lily didn't look convinced. But she continued anyway.

"So, you don't know if they was together at all?" she asked.

"I just know I told Tyreeka to go to the store and get some cereal so I could put it in this baby's bottle and put her to sleep. I mean, I knew she wouldn't come right back. But I ain't expect her to stay out all night."

"Okay," Lily said, sighing as she turned to leave. "I ain't mean to bother you."

"Wait a minute," Hattie said, calling Lily back. "There was one thing."

"What's that?"

"My cousin came up here last night. I guess she called herself tellin'. She told me Tyreeka was—"

Hattie turned around when she heard Sonny's name on television. They all stopped to listen.

"Police were in pursuit of a bright green Mustang driven by Williams," the reporter said. "He was wanted for investigation in connection with the disappearance of a little girl whose identity has not been released. Williams allegedly hit Baylor's car, causing the crash that killed the highly respected judge—a man widely expected to be the city's next D.A. Williams escaped, but the car he was driving has been found at Thirteenth and Cumberland, and right now, police are combing the vehicle for evidence.

"Channel 10 has also learned that Williams was stopped on the expressway by another officer about twenty minutes ago, but escaped after a struggle during which the officer fired his weapon. No word yet on the officer's condition. We'll have more details as they become available. But again, for those just tuning in, Common Pleas Judge John Baylor, community activist, respected jurist, prospective district attorney, has died of massive head injuries resulting from this morning's crash. He was fifty-two. Police are searching for Sonny Williams, the man believed responsible for the fatal crash. And highly placed sources say that an investigation into the department's role in the accident has already begun.

"This is Jim Wright, Channel 10 News, reporting live from Hahnemann Hospital in Center City."

They all stood silently for the next minute or so. Their faces were portraits of shock.

"Oh my God," Hattie finally said, her voice trembling with a mixture of rage and fear.

"What is it?" Lily asked.

"The car they said Sonny was in—that was the car my cousin told me the guy was drivin'."

"What guy?"

"The guy Tyreeka was talkin' to," she said, clenching her fist at her side. "The guy she got in the car with last night."

Chapter Eight

They looked like soldiers marching to Crispus Attucks—the housing project just a few blocks west of the Bridge.

Lily was first, walking so quickly that her feet flew over the cracked, uneven sidewalk in a blur. Janay was next, then Darnell. And bringing up the rear was Tyreeka's mother, Hattie, who had asked her cousin to watch her grandchildren while she went out to find her daughter.

Lily wasn't really concerned about Tyreeka. All she wanted was Kenya. And as they approached the corner of Twelfth and Parrish, where a half dozen boys stood huddled outside a graffiti-scarred Chinese take-out restaurant, Lily was almost running to find her.

Most of the boys saw her coming, and the group split to make room. But the one she wanted to talk to turned around too late. He wasn't prepared to meet her with the rugged disposition that the corner required. And before he knew it, Lily was in his face.

"Where Tyreeka at, boy?" she said menacingly.

"What you—"

"Look, nigga. I ain't got time to be out here playin' with you. Tyreeka cousin seen her get in the car with you last night. Now I wanna know where Tyreeka at, and I wanna know where Kenya went, too. And while you at it, I need you to tell me why you out here ridin' around with nine-year-old girls in your car."

At that, the other drug dealers backed away slowly, looking at the boy with a mixture of pity and disgust.

Soon after, the corner of Twelfth and Parrish fell silent. And that was no small feat.

The sounds of Twelfth Street had always come from the lives that passed through it. Even the bricks of the low-rise buildings had stories to tell. Like the timeworn trolley tracks that split the pothole-riddled street, the bricks had absorbed the spirit of those who'd lived there for the past fifty years.

And while the corner had transformed from a close-knit community to a disparate mix of fear and desperation, it had always been alive with children. But now, the sound of the corner was not the life that came from childhood games. It was the death that came from gunshots and drug deals gone bad.

But with Lily's arrival, even that changed. The ritual that the addicts and dealers had learned to perform came grinding to a halt. The banging pots and spatulas in the Chinese restaurant were still. The hum of traffic ceased.

The boy was silent, too, fingering the nine-millimeter that was tucked into his waistband as he nervously surveyed the faces of the other dealers. From the way they looked at him, he knew that the nine wasn't an option.

Though a dozen murders had been committed on that corner for less serious infractions than Lily's, she had asked him about the whereabouts of a little girl. And if the other boys on the corner could help it, Lily was going to get what she demanded. Because even the dealers knew that little girls were off-limits. Especially when there were grown women who were willing to perform any perversion they could imagine for as little as five dollars.

"Lemme talk to you for a minute, miss," the boy said, tugging Lily's arm to pull her away from the crowd.

Darnell stepped closer when the boy touched her. Two dealers moved to intercept him. Lily saw what was happening, pulled her arm away, and stood her ground.

"You can talk to me right here," she said defiantly.

Darnell and the dealers relaxed.

"All right," the boy said, looking increasingly uncomfortable. "But lemme straighten somethin' out for you. If Tyreeka younger than sixteen, she damn sure don't look like it. Plus she already got a baby by Bop, from down Twenty-second Street, so I know she ain't nine years old."

There were solemn nods of agreement from the other boys on the corner.

"That ain't the point," Tyreeka's mother said sharply. "I wanna know where she at, 'cause she damn sure ain't got no business with you."

The boy affected a cool bravado and tried to repair the damage the last few minutes had done to his reputation.

"She spent the night with me over my aunt spot up Yorktown," he said with a shrug. "We smoked a couple blunts, did what we had to do, and went to sleep in the basement. She got up and said she had to go home. So I threw her a couple dollars, and I ain't seen her since then."

Tyreeka's mother shrank back into the crowd, embarrassed by what she knew to be the truth about her promiscuous daughter.

"What about Kenya?" Lily asked insistently.

"If you talkin' 'bout that little girl Tyreeka was with last night, I saw her go back in the buildin' before me and Tyreeka started talkin'. She ain't never get in my car. Matter fact, *I* ain't been in my car since last night, 'cause..."

He hesitated. But with the entire corner awaiting his explanation, he knew he had no choice but to tell them why.

"I ain't been in my car since last night 'cause somebody stole it from in front o' my aunt house this mornin'."

"You sure about that?" Lily asked.

"Yeah," he said, feeling smaller than he'd felt just minutes before. "I'm sure."

"If it's the car I think it is," she said, "you might wanna look up Thirteenth and Cumberland for it. Sonny Williams stole a car like yours and crashed it up there this mornin'. They had somethin' on the news about it."

"Sonny, huh?" the boy said, his face filling up with anger as he turned to the other dealers. "I talk to y'all later. I got some business I gotta handle."

He left the corner with an exaggerated stroll, as if he was about to do something drastic. But while his furrowed brow and set jaw were theatrically perfect, the boy knew, like everyone else, that there was nothing he could do to Sonny. And as he walked away, that knowledge trailed behind him.

Moments after he'd left, Twelfth and Parrish came back to life. The boy became grist for the rumor mill. The man he was supposedly going to find became something else altogether.

Sonny left the hospital parking lot and gunned the stolen Maxima down South Street, hoping that the woman in the cashier's booth would be too afraid to call the police.

By the time he hit Sixteenth Street, he knew that she wasn't. Two blocks ahead of him, a police car rolled into the intersection of Broad and South, its dome lights flashing as two officers jumped from the vehicle with guns drawn.

Sonny, who had already passed Fifteenth by then, couldn't turn because there were no other cross streets. He couldn't take to the sidewalk because there were parked cars on either side. He had only one way out, and even as the officers aimed their guns at him, Sonny decided to take it.

Stomping on the accelerator, he steadied the steering wheel, lowered his head, and headed straight for the police car. The Maxima's engine went from a low-pitched hum to a rumbling scream. Glass broke over his head as bullets punched through the windshield. He raised his voice to a primal yell and lifted his head just before impact. Then he swerved to avoid a head-on collision.

The officers dived for cover as he smashed into the car's fender, causing it to spin into a nearby traffic light. The Maxima tilted on two wheels and the airbag deployed as the car crossed Broad Street, then came crashing down on all fours. Sonny braked, the car skidded, then he turned on tiny Clarion Street as the sound of police sirens filled the air.

He grabbed the backpack, jumped from the car, and bolted, heading toward the nearby Martin Luther King Housing Project. A police wagon pulled in behind him, and two officers jumped out and gave chase.

Sonny turned and fired. The bullets flew high, but the gunfire was enough to make the officers hit the ground. As they scrambled to their feet, Sonny rounded the corner, ducked through the broken basement window of a vacant house, and pulled the bag in behind him.

When the officers ran past with their static-filled radios blaring, Sonny stood atop the basement's three-foot-high pile of trash, trying not to breathe too heavily.

When they were far enough away, he quickly put his gun in his waistband, then turned around and surveyed the dark basement, looking for a way out. It took only seconds to find the daylight pouring in from a hole where a tree had grown through the back wall.

Sonny moved toward the light, stumbling over trash as rats scurried and squealed at his feet. When he reached the light, he realized that the opening was too narrow to accommodate him. He pulled at one of the bricks, and a row of them fell down, striking his head.

He ignored the pain as blood oozed into his eyes, pulling ever more desperately at the bricks until he'd opened a man-size space. Then he squeezed out of the house, crossed the overgrown weeds in the back alley, and climbed over the rickety wooden gate enclosing the house on the other side.

Sonny stood for a moment in the backyard, listening to the faint sound of a television. He didn't hear any other voices. But even if he had, it wouldn't have mattered. He didn't care if there were people inside.

Climbing the two crumbling concrete steps that led to the wooden kitchen door, he placed his shoulder against it, leaned in on an angle, and extended his leg for leverage. Then he pushed, splintering the doorjamb as he forced the door.

Seconds later, he was in the house, desperately hoping to find a way out.

When the call for an assist went out over the main band of police radio, Lynch and Wilson knew that Sonny had made his way to South Philadelphia.

They broke off the search for Judy, which had taken them through all of the tiny streets around Germantown and Lehigh, and raced to Broad and South with Daneen still in the backseat of their car.

Using the emergency lane that ran down the middle of Broad Street, it took them fifteen minutes to get to the scene. Once they arrived, they saw the devastation that Sonny had wrought.

The police car he'd struck sat against a leaning traffic light, its front grille twisted into a broken, toothless grin. One of the two officers who'd occupied the car was being carted to a nearby rescue vehicle with a back injury.

Just half a block away, the stolen Maxima sat in the middle of Clarion Street, its front end smashed and its driver-side door flung open.

Lynch, Wilson, and Daneen took it all in, saying nothing. But in their minds, they were all wondering if Sonny's elusiveness had cost them precious time in the search for Kenya.

It was Lynch who broke the silence.

"I'm gonna find out who's in charge," he said, after he'd parked among the dozen police vehicles that filled the intersection. "I'll be back."

As he jumped out of the car and approached a lieutenant who was directing officers to close off the corner's subway entrances, Wilson and Daneen sat quietly, each of them mulling her own thoughts.

Wilson watched as two district captains and the inspector in command of South Division arrived at the scene along with a dozen more patrol cars.

Daneen sat stoically in the backseat, consumed by the guilt she felt over her daughter's disappearance.

Wilson understood it, could feel it even without looking at Daneen. It was something that only a mother could comprehend.

She knew that there was no other woman for Daneen to turn to, so she broke an unwritten rule, throwing off her professional detachment and allowing herself—if only for a moment—to simply be Roxanne Wilson.

"Daneen," she said, turning to face her.

Stone-faced, Daneen stared out the window and ignored the detective.

"I know what it's like to want your child back," she said gently. "I'm not saying I know what you're going through, because that's the last thing you need to hear right now. But I will tell you this. I want you to find your daughter for more reasons than you know—personal reasons. And I'm going to make sure I do everything I can to help you. Okay?"

Daneen nodded silently. It was if she heard Wilson, but didn't hear her. Wilson understood that, too, and pressed on in spite of it.

"Now, you don't have to answer this if you don't want to," she said, "and I'm not asking you this to be nosy or anything like that. But I'm just wondering if Kevin is the best person to help you with this."

She stopped and looked at Daneen, trying to gauge her reaction. Daneen didn't turn to face her, so Wilson continued.

"I've been watching the two of you, and there's something going on there. It's like you're—I know this sounds silly, but I'm just going to say it. It's like you're in love with each other. Like I said, I know it sounds crazy, but I've been around for a long time, and I've learned that only love can make you despise somebody like that."

Daneen sat still for a few seconds, then looked at Wilson for the first time. When she spoke, it was with a quiet certainty.

"I can't tell you what Kevin feel," she said. "I can only tell you about me. I don't love Kevin. I never did. But I know him. Not the way a woman know a man. I know him the way you know somebody you watched grow up. Somebody you seen change in front o' your face. He seen me change, too.

"I guess he the only one left who can see me for who I used to be before . . ."

She paused, trying to remember the point when everything changed.

"He the only one who knew me, really knew me, before everything. So yeah, I think Kevin probably the only one who can help me with this.

"Far as everything else that's goin' on with us, that's somethin' we gon' have to work out down the line."

As she spoke, she watched Lynch speak to a gray-haired cop in a white shirt, then walk back toward the car. A news van pulled in behind the barricades that had been set up, and a reporter ran to the edge of one of them, calling Lynch and pointing to the car.

He waved the reporter away and got in.

"What did that guy from Channel 10 want?" Wilson asked, nodding toward the reporter.

"He wants to talk to Daneen," he said. "I told him no. Not yet, anyway."

Daneen didn't want Lynch speaking for her, but she knew that she wasn't ready to talk to the press yet. So she sat quietly in her seat and listened.

"I just talked to the inspector who's running the scene," Lynch said. "He told me he wants us to stay down here. But we're not going to be a part of the search. He wants South Division to handle it, along with whatever special units he might need to call in."

He turned to Daneen. "He wants you to be here in case they need someone to talk Sonny out of wherever he's hiding."

He paused for effect.

"You're the closest thing to family he has left."

Not that it mattered. Sonny wasn't looking to hear from family.

Judy descended the steps of the motel, then took to the sidewalk and lowered her head like she was struggling against the wind.

Her battle was not against the elements, however. It was against recognition. If she could hide her face long enough to make it to Germantown and Erie, she could pay a hack taxi driver to take her to the places where Sonny might hide.

She was going to carry out the plan she'd had in the back of her mind since escaping police custody and going to Dot's apartment.

She would confront Sonny for all he'd done to her. She knew how it would play out, because she'd seen it, time and again, in her mind: the slap she would deliver with the accusation, the startled expression that would fill his eyes, the feeling of triumph as she took back what was hers.

The moment would be sweet. In order to taste it, though, she would first have to find him. And she was determined to do that.

Judy made her way up Germantown Avenue, skirting the racks of detergent and baseball caps that littered the sidewalks outside the discount stores.

As she drew closer to Erie Avenue, the stores were replaced by greasy spoons, and then by bars. Shoppers no longer made up the crowds. Instead, there were commuters, anxious to make the connections that would take them to a safer part of town. Addicts and dealers stood along the periphery, mingling with the hustlers who took up their stations outside the infamous Eagle Bar.

Nearly everyone on the corner fit easily into a category. But Judy, walking up the avenue in jeans and sneakers, defied categorization. Even in her current state, she was too beautiful for Broad and Erie. And anyone who looked at her could see that.

"Hack cab," a man said as he spotted her approaching the corner.

She half looked at him, barely taking in the greasy jeans and filthy T-shirt that hung on him like an old man's skin.

"How much you charge me to go down Ninth and Indiana?" she asked quickly.

"Five dollars."

"I might wanna go a couple other places, too," she added.

"My car right over here," he said as he walked toward a green Chevy. "We can work all that out later."

He turned the key and the motor barely cranked. When it did, it lurched into gear and bounced down the avenue, its engine sputtering with the effort. Judy didn't notice. Her mind was filled with recollections of Sonny.

While most of them were of heartbreak and deceit, she held on to the ones that made the pain seem less real. She was caught in the throes of such memories when the car sputtered again, bucking and jumping before the engine stalled.

The driver cursed and turned off Germantown Avenue, using the car's momentum to ride down the slightly inclined street.

"I gotta run in this garage for a minute," he said, parking the car. "Guy got my jumper cables in there. I be right back."

He walked around the rear of the car and was gone.

Judy looked up and down the street, which was filled with closed factories, abandoned houses, and broken glass. The voices from the avenue that had been so close just moments before sounded like they were miles away.

Judy reached for the door handle just as the driver returned.

"What's wrong?" he said, smiling as he reached into his pocket for the car keys.

"I think I'm gon' walk," Judy said nervously.

"No," he said, pulling a knife from his pocket. "I think you gon' gimme my damn money."

Judy froze, looking down at the sharp blade and then at the driver's bloodshot eyes.

"Now!" he said, lunging toward her with the knife.

She hurriedly reached into her pocket and peeled off one of the bills she'd taken from the police officer's wallet.

"No," he said as he grabbed her hand. "I want all the money you got."

She threw the rest of the bills at him, then cringed against the car door, waiting for what she knew would come next.

He fingered the money and glanced at her, wild-eyed. "Get out," he said quickly. "Hurry up."

Judy didn't hesitate. She opened the door and ran up the hill, stumbling to get away from the car. She expected him to run, too. He didn't. And as she made her way to Germantown Avenue and looked back, she saw the reason why.

The flame from the lighter danced and flickered as he sat in the car and lit the pipe. Then his face disappeared behind white smoke as his eyes grew wide with the crack rush.

Judy watched him for a split second, then turned and ran back toward the motel. She had lost precious time. Now she needed to regroup.

Once he was inside the house, Sonny walked through the kitchen, with its dated fixtures and grease-stained pots, then the dining room, where dozens of ceramic and glass souvenirs teetered on rickety wooden tables.

When he passed through to the edge of the living room, he saw a couch along one wall, a television against another, and an old man sitting in a battered armchair across the room. He was wearing work pants and a flannel shirt buttoned to the neck. Surrounded by man-size stacks of dry, rotted newspapers, he was holding a pistol. And it was pointed at Sonny.

It took a second for everything to register. Sonny looked at the gun, then at the old man.

The man stared back, squinting as he took in the filthy green hospital scrubs and the bulging outline of the gun that was tucked into Sonny's waistband.

"Why don't you put that gun on that couch right next to you," he said, the words spilling over his bare gums as he pointed the gun.

Sonny hesitated. The man cocked the hammer of his revolver and placed his left hand under his right to support it.

Sonny knew the man was serious. He reached into his pants, pulled his gun out slowly, and placed it on the couch.

"Now before I bust a cap in yo' ass for breakin' in my house, I want you to tell me somethin'."

The man sat back in the chair, still pointing the gun.

"Did you do it?"

Sonny didn't quite know how to respond.

Seeing his confusion, the old man nodded toward the television. Sonny looked, and saw live pictures of the bedlam taking shape around them.

Police cars darted from South Street to City Hall. Police officers erected barricades. People gathered to gawk. And a television reporter tried to summarize it all.

"As you can see from these pictures from Chopper-6, police are moving to isolate Williams in the area of Broad and South," the reporter said, speaking as the pictures filled the screen.

"We've also heard from police sources that transportation hubs will see increased patrols in case Williams—now wanted on numerous charges including vehicular homicide in the death of Judge John Baylor—tries to leave the city.

"Williams first eluded police as they sought to question him in the disappearance of a girl who has now been identified as nine-year-old Kenya Brown. The girl's aunt, Judy Brown, is also being called a fugitive, and she, too, is being sought for questioning in the child's disappearance."

The old man hit the off button on his remote. He studied Sonny as the grief took hold, then sat back and watched him for a few minutes more.

When Sonny finally managed to croak a response, the only word his mouth would form was her name.

"Kenya," he said, choking on the sadness that enveloped him.

His eyes grew moist, and a chill ran through his body. He vacillated between anger and grief, and in that moment, came to know emotions that had always eluded him.

The old man watched the feelings take hold. He could remember a time when his own eyes had filled with those tears. But that didn't make Sonny right.

He reached for the telephone on his end table with one hand and held the pistol with the other. Both of his hands were trembling—with palsy, with fear, with weariness.

"I'm sorry 'bout the little girl," he said, squinting to read the numbers on the old black rotary phone. "But whether you did somethin' to that child or not, you still ain't got no business in my house."

Sonny watched as the man dialed the number 9. He squinted again to find the number 1, and Sonny pounced.

He dived forward and rolled on the floor, traversing the ten feet that separated them in two seconds as he bowled into the chair. The man squeezed the trigger. The ancient revolver jammed. Sonny knocked it from his hand and watched it spin across the hardwood floor.

The old man looked up into Sonny's eyes, terrified. Sonny stood up, grabbing the man's collar, and snatching him up from the floor. He stood him against the wall and spoke in a menacing whisper.

"Listen, man," he said, gulping air. "I ain't tryin' to hurt you. All I'm lookin' for is a way outta here. You gimme that, and you ain't never gotta see me another day in your life."

Sonny's grip on the man's collar was too tight, making his breath come in shallow gasps. He struggled to speak as he pointed to a hall closet.

"Coat," he said in a raspy voice.

Sonny eased his hold on the man's shirt. "Where? What coat?"

"Go in that closet over there and get my blue raincoat. I got a old raggedy Mercury station wagon out front. The keys should be in the coat."

The old man rattled on nervously as Sonny dragged him over to the hall closet.

"The car don't go past twenty-five, but it might get you 'cross town," he said quickly. "I guess it's enough gas in there to make it that far. I ain't drove it in a long time, but it's a good car. It still run."

"Shut up," Sonny said, taking the coat out of the closet and rifling the pockets.

He found the keys, a hat, and reading glasses.

"Anybody else in here?" he asked.

The man shook his head from side to side and watched Sonny nervously.

"Good," Sonny said, pushing the man into the closet and turning the lock.

"Hey," the old man said, his voice muffled by the closed door. "Don't leave me in here, man. I'll die in here."

Sonny ignored him, walked back over to the couch and picked up his gun and backpack. Then he donned the coat and hat and walked out of the house.

The news about Kenya was still there in his mind, bleeding like a fresh wound.

Fifteen minutes after Sonny ran from the corner of Clarion and South, the police set up checkpoints where the identifications of pedestrians and motorists were scrutinized and run through the national law-enforcement computer system.

They called in K-9 units to search through the dozens of vacant houses that dotted the area. They collaborated with housing police to search the high-rise apartments in the Martin Luther King Housing Project.

They even used four-man teams to conduct a door-to-door search of the twenty-block area they'd cordoned off.

With all of this in place, the inspector in charge was confident they would find Sonny. He put a SWAT unit on standby for what he expected to become a barricaded-man situation, with Sonny armed and holed up in a house, possibly holding hostages.

Lynch, Wilson, and Daneen were placed close to the staging area on the corner of Broad and Lombard, one block from South Street, in case Daneen was needed to help negotiate a surrender.

But after eight hours of searching, it was clear that Sonny had escaped again. And as they stood there watching it all unfold, Lynch, Wilson, and Daneen knew, like everyone else, that their chances of finding Kenya were growing slim.

"I think I'm going to take the complainant back to Central to file a missing person's report," Lynch told the Fourth District captain, who'd returned to the corner for the third time to check on his officers.

"Yeah, it doesn't look like anything's gonna come out of this," the captain said. "Damn shame I had to have my officers waste a whole day on this project bullshit."

"I don't know that anything's a waste when a kid's life is on the line," Lynch said, hesitating before adding the obligatory, "sir."

Before the captain could respond, Lynch walked away, waving for Wilson and Daneen to come with him. They all got in the car as Lynch angrily slammed the door.

"Wilson, I'm taking Daneen back to Central."

"What do you mean, taking me back?" Daneen said, her voice rising in a panic. "I ain't leavin' here 'til they find Sonny."

"Daneen," Wilson said firmly, "they're not going to find Sonny right now. He's gone. The best thing we can do now is have you file the report. In the meantime, we'll keep searching for Kenya."

"Yeah, but Sonny—"

"He's gone, Daneen," Wilson said again, louder this time.

The hopelessness of it took hold, and Daneen sat back in her seat, her eyes lost in the reality that came crashing down.

They rode back to Central Detectives in silence.

When they arrived, Wilson left them there, took her own car, and went home to rest and regroup before rejoining the search.

Daneen and Lynch took the long walk upstairs to document the hardest truth Daneen had ever faced.

It was five in the afternoon when Tyreeka got off the subway at Broad and Fairmount, carrying shopping bags filled with all the label-laden trinkets of ghetto fashion.

She'd spent the day downtown at the Gallery Mall, replenishing her wardrobe with the $300 the drug dealer had given her in exchange for her night with him. After the sneakers she bought, the money didn't pay for much—two pair of jeans and three shirts. But she'd tried to make it stretch, buying an outfit for the baby and saving $50 for her mother to make up for leaving her twenty-week-old with her.

She climbed the stairs to their apartment and opened the door.

"Bitch, where you been?" her mother said before she made it inside.

Tyreeka turned around. "I was—"

The first slap knocked her backward. She stumbled and hit her head against the door.

"I don't wanna hear no lies from you, Tyreeka," her mother said as she grabbed her daughter by the neck.

"Now, I'ma ask you one more time. Where you been?"

Tyreeka reached up and pried her mother's hand loose. "I ... can't ... breathe," she said, pushing her mother away from her.

Her mother's eyes widened, and she charged, hitting Tyreeka in the side of the head with a tightly balled fist.

The girl fell hard against the wall. Tyreeka's baby heard the ruckus and began to cry. The other children her mother was watching ran from the bedroom to see what was happening. They found Tyreeka cowering in the corner with her mother standing over her.

"Y'all get back in that room 'fore you get some o' this, too!" she yelled.

When they did, she turned on her daughter and snatched her up from the floor.

"Listen here, Tyreeka. You don't let these little boys buy you. That's why you got that baby in there now, 'cause you out here bein' a hoe."

"Mom, I wasn't with no boy!"

She smacked her hard across the jaw, knocking her down again. Tyreeka scurried backward like a crab.

"Don't lie to me. I just left the boy a hour ago. He stood right out there on Twelfth and Parrish, tellin' everybody how he gave you a couple dollars and sent your li'l dumb ass home."

"Mommy, I—"

"Shut up! I'm talkin'."

"Mommy, I just wanna give you—"

She picked her daughter up and threw her against the wall. "I said shut up!"

She started to speak in short bursts, punching Tyreeka each time she paused.

"I told you. About goin'. With these damn boys!" she yelled.

Tyreeka was curled up in a ball by then, trying in vain to block the blows.

"I ain't gon' tell you that shit no more!" her mother screamed, punching her one last time.

Tyreeka's neck snapped back with the blow. And as tears mixed with the blood that oozed from the cuts on her face, her mother stood over her, then crouched down and spoke softly in her ear.

"And if you think I'm playin' with you, I'ma show you what a real ass whuppin' look like you come in here with another baby. You understand me?"

Tyreeka nodded as she tried to choke back the tears.

"Now, where Kenya at?" her mother said.

Tyreeka looked up at her, confused. "I told her to come in here and ask you if she could spend the night. She ain't come?"

"No, she ain't come," her mother said sharply. "She ain't go with you?"

"No," Tyreeka said, sniffling as the pain of the beating began to set in. "She came back in the buildin' when I was talkin' with the boy. Did somethin' happen?"

"You don't know," her mother said, searching her daughter's eyes for her usual lies. "Do you?"

"Know what?"

"Kenya missin'," she said softly. "Ain't nobody seen her since she left you last night."

Tyreeka reached into her pocket, pulled out the crumpled fifty-dollar bill she'd brought back, and threw it on the floor.

Suddenly, the money was worthless. All that mattered was the dull ache that came with knowing her friend was missing.

She cried in silence, then folded her arms across her chest and tried to squeeze the grief away.

With each line of the missing person's report, the reality of Kenya's plight set in, and Daneen's grief grew that much deeper.

While going through Kenya's description yet again, she realized that her daughter was nine years old, and the years Daneen had lost to addiction had cost her the chance to be her mother. To tuck her in at night. To tell her right from wrong. To whisper the secrets that little girls keep. To know her.

Daneen didn't know her own child. And that, more than anything, caused her grief to explode in shoulder-shaking, snot-running, soul-stirring sobs. Tears that came not from her eyes, but from that place down deep, where lost years reside.

Kevin Lynch put down his hatred for Daneen when he saw her pain. He forgot about all of it, and he held her, right there in the squad room. Feeling her that close to him stirred something, though he didn't know what.

The other detectives turned away, embarrassed by his display of humanity. But Lynch was undaunted. He held on until the last tear had dropped. And then he let her go.

Daneen seemed to grow older after that. The energy that had filled her daylong search seemed to leave her. She looked worn, and Lynch could see it in her eyes.

When she finished filling out the report, he told her to go home and get some rest. She protested, arguing that she needed to stay until they found her baby.

Lynch told her that she could do more to help if she got some sleep. She argued for a few minutes more, but eventually relented, because she knew that he was right.

When he offered her a ride to her boyfriend's house, she refused it. She didn't want Lynch to meet the man whom she was seeing. And besides, she thought the forty-minute bus ride from Center City would give her a chance to think things through.

By the time the bus passed the transportation center at Broad and Olney, she was struggling to stay awake. The fatigue of the past day was set firmly in her bones, along with the deep, emotional toll of Kenya's disappearance.

She knew she couldn't go on without at least a few hours' sleep. She only hoped she would be able to get it.

When she got off the C bus at Nineteenth and Cheltenham, it was eight o'clock, and dusk swept across the border between Philadelphia and the suburbs of Montgomery County.

As she began the three-and-a-half-block walk to her boyfriend's house on Seventy-third Avenue, she tried to imagine what her life would have been had she been born on the other side of the county line.

Not that it mattered. Her life was what it was—a trash bin stuffed with people who were nothing more than empty husks. The ones who had used her, and the ones she had used. The only person who had ever really mattered to her was Kenya. And there were too many times when she hadn't mattered either.

Daneen tried to put that reality out of her mind as she turned the corner and walked up to the house. When she climbed the steps, fumbling in her pocket for her keys, the door swung open and her boyfriend Wayne was standing there, looking down at her with suspicion, his slight paunch pinched beneath the too-high waist of his pants.

"Thanks," she muttered, walking past him.

He closed the door and eyed her warily as she flopped onto the couch and flung her forearm over her bloodshot eyes.

"They find your daughter?" he asked in a clipped tone.

"No."

"And you here?" he said with raised eyebrows.

Daneen didn't respond right away. She didn't want it to escalate into something it didn't need to be.

She uncovered her eyes and regarded Wayne. He looked tired. His eyes, beneath his glasses, were ringed with circles. And his thinning, salt-and-pepper hair stood on end, like the stubble that sprouted from his face.

"Wasn't nothin' else I could do today," she said in measured tones. "Kevin told me I should come home and get a few hours' sleep, then maybe come back and help with the search tomorrow."

"Oh, Kevin told you that, huh?" he said sarcastically. "What else Kevin tell you?"

"Look, Wayne, I really ain't tryin' to go through this right now. My baby missin', and I'm tryin' to hold it together. I need you to help me do that."

"If you needed my help so bad, why you call Kevin and run down to the projects with him? Why you ain't ask me for my help if you needed it?"

"I'm askin' now, Wayne," she said calmly, refusing to be drawn into a fight. "Can you let me rest for a few minutes please? I just need to rest for a few minutes."

"Why?" he said, throwing out the word like an accusation. "You been up all night?"

She dragged herself to her feet and faced him with a hand on her hip.

"Yeah, I been up all night, Wayne, fightin' my aunt and the rest o' them no-good bitches down the projects, tryin' to find out the truth. I gotta come home and fight you, too?"

He didn't respond. Rather, he watched the way her lips moved when she spoke. The way words flowed from her mouth and cascaded down the curves of her body like water.

He watched her, and the blood rushed to his loins.

"No," he said, walking over to Daneen and folding her in his arms. "You ain't gotta fight me, too. I want you to find Kenya. And I wanna help you do that. But I just need to know where you are. When I ain't hear from you . . ."

He let the words trail off. He didn't want to give voice to his greatest fear—that the stress of it all would drive her to use crack again.

"I'm here, baby," she whispered. "Don't worry. I ain't goin' nowhere."

But even as she surrendered to his embrace, Daneen's mind was back at the Bridge. Minutes later, when she drifted off to sleep, she dreamed first of Kenya.

And then she dreamed of Kevin Lynch.

Chapter Nine

As Saturday spilled into Sunday, the voices recounting Kenya's disappearance grew louder. And as the whispers gave way to shouts, lies and truth locked horns in a pitched battle in which neither could prevail.

Before long, Kenya was more than a missing little girl. She was a cause—the kind that people grab hold of and refuse to let go.

Though the people of the Bridge had seen murders and beatings and lives torn apart by the heartless acts that were commonplace in the ghetto, Kenya's disappearance was different. Like everyone in the Bridge—from the smallest child to the oldest adult—she was small and frail in the scheme of things. And yet, she'd learned to make her way in a world where the odds were stacked against her. Kenya's disappearance made everyone realize that they, too, were vulnerable. That anything could happen to them, and no one would care. It made them afraid.

But the fear only lasted until the shock of Kenya's disappearance spun into grief, and then anger, and then something beyond emotion. Something dark, and primitive, and ugly.

Because, in truth, there was a part of it that was strangely delicious. The part that was so scandalous, so utterly barbaric, that it was like chocolate in people's mouths. And every time they spoke of it, they wanted to add another piece to what they'd said. To do anything to taste it again.

So after the preachers alluded to Kenya in their Sunday morning sermons, and parishioners retold the story in their homes and in their cars, their children rehashed it on the concrete where they played. Reporters reshaped it on the airwaves and in print.

By Sunday afternoon, everyone in Philadelphia had a take on Kenya's disappearance. The voices were everywhere.

In the beauty salon: "Child, you know that girl Tyreeka know more about this than what she sayin'."

"Girl, I heard she was messin' with Sonny, too."

"And Dot, with her li'l fast ass, she holdin' the money for him 'til he come back for it."

In the barbershop: "That boy Kevin Lynch, he in on it, too. That's why he was chasin' Sonny so hard. Didn't give a damn 'bout nobody, not even Judge Baylor."

This last was indicative of Baylor's stature within the Bridge. Because he had always been a man of action, even perceived indifference toward him was an offense approaching sacrilege.

Baylor's willingness to step beyond the bench, beyond the rhetoric, beyond his comfort zone, made him a hero. Not only in the projects, but throughout the city.

For that reason, the tears now being cried over Baylor came from black men he'd convinced to leave drug corners, from white widows whose husbands' murderers he had sentenced, from political strategists whose careers were linked to his impending run for district attorney.

In truth, it was only because of Baylor that Kenya's disappearance was important to anyone other than her neighbors and family. Her fate would not have mattered had it not spilled outside the confines of the projects and snatched a hero.

Though Sonny had injured two police officers and Judy had injured a third, though Kenya was an innocent child at the center of the storm, only the judge's death made her real to most people.

Were it not for that, the search for her would never have gotten as far as it did.

It was that thought that ran through Kevin Lynch's mind as he sat outside his captain's office at the Sixth District, waiting to be called inside.

They'd phoned him at home that morning, awakening him from his first bit of rest since early Friday morning, when he'd received the call from Daneen. When they ordered him to come into the district, he knew immediately that it was about Kenya.

In a little more than twenty-four hours, he'd watched her become a symbol for all that was wrong with the city, and with the department, and with the world. Now, there would be more symbolism. And Lynch would be at the core of it.

The captain stuck his head out of his office. "We're ready for you," he said, waving Lynch inside.

As Lynch entered, he saw inspectors on either side of the captain's desk. Behind them, there was a stenographer.

"Have a seat," the captain said, averting his eyes from Lynch's as he walked into his crowded office and sat down.

"I asked the inspectors to come down this morning so we could hold this here," the captain mumbled. "I know it's kind of awkward to have everybody down here on a Sunday. But I figured today would be good, because I didn't want to have to do it in a public way."

"How considerate," Lynch said sarcastically.

"Detective Lynch," one of the inspectors said as he pulled out a sheaf of papers, "I'll get right to it. We've reviewed the radio transcripts from the pursuit yesterday morning. We've also spoken with several of the officers and street supervisors who participated.

"What we've found is that you clearly violated procedure. You engaged in a high-speed chase while traveling in an unmarked vehicle, placed citizens in danger by refusing to break off the chase when it was clear that it had ventured into a residential area. And the speeds you reached, while traveling against the tide of traffic on one-way streets, were clearly dangerous, both to yourself and to the passengers in your vehicle.

"Further, you engaged in this chase while transporting a witness."

"The bottom line," the other inspector said, "is that we're giving you a thirty-day unpaid suspension with intent to dismiss."

Lynch's head began to swim. But even as his mind groped for words, his mouth began to speak.

"That's a little harsh for a procedural violation, isn't it, sir? I mean, I've spent the last twenty-four hours looking for this little girl. And there was no excessive force or anything with the chase. I just—"

The captain slid a copy of the Sunday *Inquirer* to the edge of his desk, and Lynch fell silent. The top half of the front page was filled with a picture of the fatal accident. Judge Baylor's bloody face was visible behind the car's shattered windshield. Lynch's police academy picture was in an inset photo. Next to it was a mug shot of Sonny Williams.

The headline read, "Dying to catch him: Baylor dead after deadly police chase."

The captain turned to the stenographer. "Don't type this," he said.

Then he turned to Lynch. "Son, if that judge had died in some other kind of accident, and you were at fault, that would have been one thing. But this..."

He paused, searching for the right words to describe what had happened.

"This was just plain bad judgment. This man is dead because you didn't think about what you were doing. You just reacted. And sometimes, not all the time, mind you, but sometimes, you have to do a little bit more than react."

Lynch stared hard at the captain, waiting for the other shoe to drop.

"I'm sorry, Kevin," the captain said. "But for what it's worth, I still think you would've made a hell of a lieutenant."

The captain turned to the stenographer and nodded.

"Detective Kevin Lynch, badge number 65943, it is the decision of this board that you are suspended for thirty days without pay. Further, you are—"

Lynch dropped his badge and gun on the captain's desk and stood up. "I'm what?" he said sharply. "You can't tell me what I am any more than you can tell me what Kenya was. But this isn't about her, is it? Not to you anyway."

"Look, Detective—"

"No, you look," he said, backing away from the captain's desk until his broad shoulders filled the doorway.

"You can sit here and act like this is all about procedure and right and wrong, but we all know that's bullshit. A little girl is missing, probably dead by now, and all you care about is covering your ass. Dragging me in here on a Sunday so you can hold a neat little press conference tomorrow morning and say you handled it.

"I guess the next thing you're gonna tell me is that Kenya Brown is a priority to you. Well, save your breath, because I grew up in the projects. I saw more niggers die than a little bit. Saw the cops come along and scrape up the bodies and never come back until the next one. So don't tell me this is about the rules, because I know better.

"You can make me the fall guy, blame me for the judge, do whatever you wanna do. I don't care.

"But if you plan on sending somebody down to the Bridge to look for Kenya Brown, you tell them I said to stay the hell outta my way. Because I'm gonna find that little girl, badge or no badge. And when I do, I want you to do me a favor."

He paused to look each of them in the eye.

"I want you to blame me for that, too."

Lynch stomped into the parking lot and stood next to his car, unsure of what to do. He was too angry to drive. So he opened the door, reached into the glove compartment, and took out a half-empty pack of Newports.

At that moment, he didn't care that he'd quit smoking months before. If the nicotine would calm the rage that rumbled in his gut, it was worth the risk of returning to his pack-a-day habit.

He lit one of the cigarettes and inhaled deeply, waiting for the rush. Instead, the stale smoke choked him. He began to cough violently. Moments later, when his coughing spell was complete, Lynch smiled in spite of himself.

He couldn't even smoke right. That's how bad his life had become. He wondered how it had come to this. How he had managed to jeopardize the career he loved for a child he had never really known and a woman he had grown to hate.

It was a question whose answer was rooted in a time when they were innocent. A time before children could go missing in the projects.

Lynch and Daneen had known each other even before they knew themselves. They'd played together as preschoolers, making mud pies from the packed dirt in the vacant lots near the projects. They'd gone on outings with the youth group from the church across the street. He'd chased her through the building's halls, playing catch-a-girl-get-a-girl.

But as he and Daneen grew older, they grew apart. He started to explore the world outside the Bridge. She confined herself to the world within it.

By the time they were thirteen, they'd become polar opposites.

Kevin Lynch went to private school on an academic scholarship, and Daneen played hooky, seeking education of a different sort.

He tried to remain close to her, but the things she began to do drove him away. He heard about her smoking marijuana, then snorting coke, then lying on her back in an empty project apartment as the boys from Poplar Street pulled a train—three of them having sex with her, one after the other.

By the time he got to high school, Kevin Lynch had abandoned Daneen. His only remaining friend was Tyrone Jackson, a boy from Eleventh Street who was a basketball star at nearby Ben Franklin High School.

Kevin and Tyrone did everything together. They tried beer for the first time, went to dollar house parties, talked to girls, tried manhood on for size to see what it felt like.

It felt good.

Daneen went on with her life, dropping out of school and leaning on her street savvy to survive while taking full advantage of her most stunning attribute—her looks.

By the time she turned sixteen, Daneen was exquisite. Her cocoa-colored face was set around thick, bow-shaped lips and large, mysterious eyes. Her jet-black hair fell to her shoulders in loose, bouncing curls. Her breasts were full and firm, and her wide hips curved into thighs that were at once muscular and soft, just like the rest of her.

Tyrone Jackson fell for her one summer afternoon when he saw her at the basketball courts at Sixteenth and Susquehanna, where he was playing in one of the outdoor leagues.

A good student and a handsome boy, Tyrone was well liked, but naive. He believed that his basketball talent, and the accompanying college scholarship, would carry him wherever he wanted to go.

He thought he could do anything, and that nothing could hurt him. So when he told his friend Kevin about Daneen, and Kevin warned him to stay away from her, Tyrone accused him of wanting her for himself. Kevin denied it. But the advice tore their friendship apart and pushed Tyrone even closer to Daneen.

In his senior year, when a severe knee injury cost him his college scholarship and virtually ended his basketball career, Tyrone wanted to turn to Lynch for help. But his pride wouldn't let him. Instead, he turned to the only other person he believed would understand—Daneen.

She convinced him that the only way to get the things he would have had as an athlete was to sell cocaine. He did, and shortly after he began selling, she became pregnant and told him the child was his. Nine months later, when Kenya was born, everyone in the Bridge knew that Tyrone wasn't the father. The child looked nothing like him.

In spite of the whispers, he accepted the child as his own. But the persistent rumors and the resultant humiliation became too much for him to bear. He wasn't used to adversity. As a top-flight athlete, he'd lived in a world in which everything had always been handed to him.

By the time Kenya turned one, the pressure had taken its toll. Tyrone was using the cocaine he was supposed to be selling. And as his casual drug use escalated to addiction, he fell hopelessly in debt to his suppliers.

In a desperate attempt to salvage something of his life, he set up a meeting with them, ostensibly to pay off his debt. In reality, he was planning to rob them, to take the money and fly Daneen and the baby somewhere, anywhere that would allow them to start anew.

It didn't work.

Five minutes into the robbery attempt, a hail of gunfire rained down on the corner of Ninth and Indiana, and Tyrone lay dead in the street. When the news made its way back to the Bridge, something inside Kevin Lynch died, too.

His friendship with Tyrone had been his link to a normal existence away from the regimented home life his grandmother demanded. When that link disappeared, Lynch was left to flail through the murky waters of his teenage years, trying desperately not to drown in them.

In the ensuing years, as he moved out of the projects and embarked on his police career, Lynch always told himself that he blamed Daneen for Tyrone's death.

But after watching his career go up in flames over his attempt to help Daneen find her daughter, Lynch had to admit the very truth that he'd been hiding for the past ten years.

He didn't blame Daneen for Tyrone's death. He blamed himself.

If he had admitted that Tyrone was right when he accused Lynch of wanting Daneen, his friend would never have gotten involved with her. He might have even lived.

But the past didn't matter anymore, Lynch thought as he got into his car. He was married now, with a child of his own, and a lifestyle far removed from his upbringing in the projects.

And though his love for Daneen had grown from mud pies and childhood games, it had all but died along with his friend, and then it had shriveled into hatred.

But none of that was important now. What mattered was the child.

As he started his car and rolled out of the parking lot in search of the man whom he believed to be Kenya's abductor, Lynch told himself that his feelings, whatever they were, didn't matter.

But not everyone was willing to live such lies.

Darnell knew what he felt for Lily. It had surged when the boy had touched her on the corner of Twelfth and Parrish, and he'd moved to protect her, forgetting the lost years and the abiding hurt that lingered from the time when she'd loved him last.

It was a time he remembered still. And a time he needed to forget.

So when he left her and came back to his aunt Judy's empty apartment, he searched for the crack Judy had managed to hide before she was arrested. When he found it, he tried to lose himself in a swirling cloud of smoke.

As always, the first hit brought a dizzying high that swept over him like a swarm of bees, at once stinging and pouring honey on him. But after that, there was nothing.

No matter how much crack he smoked, Darnell was left only with the realization that Kenya was gone, leaving Lily—the one woman he'd ever loved—with a grief that he could never understand.

The thought of Lily ate at him, even after his girlfriend, Renee, came to him with a bundle of crack she'd scammed from an old man for the unfulfilled promise of sex.

The thought of Lily consumed him, even as he and Renee engaged their every sexual whim in an effort to maintain the rush that came with each hit.

But in a matter of hours, when the drugs were gone, Darnell was left with the same thing that always waited for him at the end of the rainbow. He was left with reality.

And so it was that he and Renee ended up on Judy's living-room floor on Sunday afternoon, scraping the last of the brown residue from the car antennas they used for crack pipes. Scraping and hoping for one last hit.

Renee, as always, watched Darnell, taking her every cue from him. She was, after all, nothing without him. At least that's what she believed.

With chalk-white skin, and thick, yellow-white hair that came out in clumps beneath her ever-present scarf, Renee was an albino. And though she had always been an outcast in the Bridge, she'd spent her teenage years doing what all the other girls did—watching Darnell.

She'd fantasized about him, knowing that her dream would go

unfulfilled, like every other dream she'd ever had for herself. She'd watched him and wished for something better.

When crack came along, the choice for her had been easy. She'd never believed that she would be anything other than a failure. When Darnell succumbed to it, however, she didn't see the wasted life that everyone else saw. Instead, she saw an opportunity.

Renee became a slave to Darnell, sharing with him every bit of crack she could attain, giving herself to him in ways that were humiliating and painful. In exchange, he gave her one dream—tarnished though it was by addiction. He gave her himself. And she gladly took him. But the more she gave herself back to him, the more he despised her.

Renee couldn't see that. All she could see was Darnell. And as she sat on Judy's floor that afternoon, staring at the handsome teenage face she still saw beneath the ravages of crack, she was caught in the illusion of it all.

"What you lookin' at?" he asked when he noticed her eyes on him.

"I was just thinkin' they got some good treys down Crispus Attucks," she lied, referring to three-dollar caps that were sold in the nearby housing project. "You wanna get a couple?"

"My niece missin', and you talkin' 'bout some damn treys," he said, staring at her in disbelief.

"Your niece gon' show up," Renee muttered as she filled her makeshift pipe with residue and crumbs left over from her last cap.

"I don't know why you so worried about her now anyway," she added, raising the pipe to her lips with a self-satisfied smirk. "You wasn't thinkin' 'bout her last night."

Darnell watched with mounting anger as the crack in Renee's pipe sizzled beneath the first lick of flame. Then he suddenly swung his arm, knocking it from her hand.

The pipe skittered across the floor, and the crack spilled from the end of the tube. Renee scrambled after it, but Darnell grabbed her feet and dragged her back.

"That's all you worried about is smokin' some damn crumbs?" he yelled as he pulled her toward the door. "Get yo' li'l white ass outta here."

"No, Darnell, stop!" she screamed, reaching out in panic for the last of her crack.

He pulled her to the door, opened it, and pushed her into the hallway. Then he slammed the door in her face.

As she banged on the door and yelled his name repeatedly, Darnell surveyed the floor for every crumb she'd dropped, took the screens out of her pipe, and deposited them in his own.

When he lit the crack, the smoke rushed to his brain in a swirling play of light and sound. Judy's apartment became Lily's. Renee's screams became Lily's. She was there, in his mind, calling him. And Darnell had every intention of answering.

He knew that the only thing that could possibly bring her back to him was showing a commitment to finding Kenya. As he left the apartment and pushed past Renee, in the darkest recesses of his crack-addled mind, he believed that would be enough.

Judy spent the night in the motel room, staring at the ceiling and listening to the reality of her relationship with Sonny.

She heard it in the sounds of creaking mattresses and sizzling crack that filtered in from the rooms around her. The noises reminded her of his latest betrayal, and propelled her out of the room for one final search.

As she weaved between the prostitutes and customers who filled the dimly lit hall outside her room, something else pushed her. It was her love for Sonny. And try as she might, she couldn't deny that truth.

"I'm checkin' out," she said, dropping her room key in front of a dead-eyed desk clerk in the darkened, rust-colored lobby.

"You don't want another hour?" he asked, watching as her firm, round behind switched past him. "I'll pay for it."

But Judy was already outside, walking south on Germantown Avenue with her head down, hoping to avoid the man who had robbed her of her last few dollars.

She didn't look like one of the pencil-thin crack prostitutes whose gyrating movements separated them from the heroin-slowed whores with fuller forms and swollen hands. But men in cars still stopped, craning their necks and waving their arms in an effort to learn her price.

Judy ignored them, walking with purpose as she trekked down the twisting avenue, deeper into the heart of North Philadelphia.

She skirted the edge of the cemetery where abolitionists had been buried a hundred years before. Inside, she saw heroin addicts nodding against headstones, stuffing a new kind of slavery into their veins.

When she turned left from Germantown Avenue to Cambria Street, however, the vibes changed. The contented nod of those who'd gotten their morning wake-up disappeared. In its place, there was the violent desperation of those who hadn't.

Men and women ran up to cars, nearly plastering themselves to the windows to hawk their peculiar wares.

"Works, works!" shouted a man in a thick jacket, holding up packages of vacuum-packed needles.

"Glass, glass!" shouted a woman with hollow crack pipes hanging from her spindly, burnt fingertips.

These were the people on the fringe of the game—the bottom-feeders who sold paraphernalia to those who bought their drugs in the Badlands.

On the corners beyond them were the lookouts—the boys who

shouted *Agua* when police approached, warning the dealers to stash their bundles in hollowed brick walls and car shells.

And then there were the addicts whose lives played out like puffs of smoke in the dangerous space in between. They were everywhere, skittering about like roaches, slowly dying from the poison that was dropped between the crumbs.

The effect of it all was like that of a large bazaar, with deals, seen and unseen, taking place under its open-air tents. It was exciting in its way. But only to the untrained eye.

For those who knew what lay beneath it, Cambria Street was the gateway to its own special hell.

Judy had traveled down that street only once, when she'd accompanied Sonny to buy weight two years before. Since then, she had allowed him to handle that part of it. And watching the dangerous dance that passed for life there, she remembered why.

On the night when she'd come there with him, there was a drought—cocaine was in short supply because of a large seizure or some other unseen calamity.

During such times, hustlers sell fake coke, addicts cross invisible boundaries, and dealers die at each other's hands in greater numbers than usual.

Judy knew that. But when she watched Sonny get out of the car on the corner of Darien and Cambria, and the buzz of activity grew still, she was nearly oblivious.

She told herself that Sonny was at home in this place—that the danger she felt was nothing.

Ten minutes later, when Sonny came back from the house on the corner with half a kilo stuffed into each sleeve of his jacket, she watched him open the car door. And then she looked up as the barrel of a rifle eased out the shattered window of a vacant house just two doors away.

A man behind Sonny jumped toward him and reached for his

pockets. The rifle in the window belched fire. Blood and bone exploded from the robber's head. He grabbed at the wound as the life rushed out of him. Then he fell against Sonny's back, wrapped his arms around him, and slid to the ground in a puddle of blood.

For the next few seconds, nothing moved. Then Sonny smiled toward the window where the rifle had been, kicked his feet out of the dead man's grasp, got in the car, and drove away.

It was the first time that Judy saw someone die. When she finally mustered the courage to speak of it to Sonny, he just smiled and said a single word: "Pablo."

She never spoke of it again. But she always remembered that name.

And so it was that when she rounded the corner from Cambria to Darien Street, stopping at the house where she'd seen Sonny go on that fateful night, she knocked and waited for the metal cover to slide back from the rectangular cutout in the door.

When eyes appeared in the opening, she said the only thing she could: "Pablo."

The eyes watched her silently.

"I'm Judy," she said, trying not to look as nervous as she felt. "I'm here for Sonny."

The eyes watched her for a second longer. The metal cover slid back into place. And then the Dominican's door swung open.

When she went inside, Judy walked into something she had never expected.

Lily sat on her living-room couch while her daughter, Janay, sat on the floor between her legs. They were all alone now, in the bright-afternoon light that poured in through the window of their apartment.

Lily brushed her daughter's thick hair with one hand and smoothed it with the other. The repetitive motion was relaxing. It should have pulled Janay down into sleep. But after a day in which her best friend had disappeared, sleep came in bits and pieces. And when it did, it was filled with nightmares.

Kenya struggling to catch her breath as Janay tried in vain to help her. Kenya falling down one of the building's elevator shafts as Janay stood by, unable to move. Kenya smiling and waving good-bye as she floated skyward, with Janay grabbing desperately at her feet.

Janay was afraid to fall asleep again, so she sat with her mother in their apartment and tried not to think of Kenya. But everything—from the drip of the leaky faucet to the sound of children playing outside—reminded them of her.

Janay hadn't spoken of her all day. In fact, she hadn't spoken of anything. When she finally did open her mouth, her eyes opened, too, releasing the tears she'd been holding back for so long.

"Mom, why they had to do that to Kenya?" she asked, sniffing as she struggled to say the words.

"We don't know what happened to Kenya, yet," Lily said, brushing her daughter's hair gently.

"She woulda came home if ain't nothin' happen to her. She woulda least came back here. Right, Mom? She woulda least came back."

Lily stroked her daughter's hair, knowing she was right. She contemplated her answer for a few strokes more, then spoke what she hoped was the truth.

"Sometimes people do things, and they don't even know why they doin' it," she said. "Sometimes they hurt people just to be hurtin' 'em. And sometimes they hurt people 'cause they really wanna hurt theyself, and they just ain't got the guts to do it.

"I don't know why nobody would wanna do somethin' to Kenya, baby. But everything ain't meant for us to know."

"She ain't never do nothin' to nobody, Mom," Janay said.

She paused as the tears streamed down and dangled from her chin before falling to her lap.

"All she ever wanted to do was be friends. Even when people was mean to her, she tried to be they friend."

"I know, baby," she said, brushing gently. "I know."

"Why they couldn't hurt somebody else, then? Why they had to pick her?"

Lily couldn't lie to her. She couldn't pretend to know the reason why. "I guess only God know that."

"God supposed to know everything, right, Mom?"

"Yes, baby. God know everything."

"Well, how come God ain't do nothin' to stop somethin' from happenin' to Kenya?"

Lily brushed her daughter's hair for a little while longer. They sat in silence until, eventually, Janay fell asleep.

Lily never answered her last question. She didn't know the answer. The only one who could know that answer was God.

And He wasn't ready to reveal it yet.

Lynch sat in his car outside the projects, trying to convince himself that what he was doing was right.

He'd driven there after the impromptu hearing in his captain's office, and had spent the better part of the afternoon in his car, watching the projects breathe.

From what he could see, much had changed since he'd left there a decade before. But much had remained the same.

Drug dealers still shuttled back and forth from the corner to the entrance of the projects, while teenage boys walked shirtless to basketball courts and girls pretended not to notice. Young mothers still carried heavy bags and pushed strollers to the 23 bus stop. Children still looked happy, oblivious to the true burden of their poverty.

Perhaps most telling, streams of old folks still left the afternoon service at the church on the corner outside the projects, dragging children behind them as they returned to homes far from the projects.

He watched them as they walked down the church's concrete steps. A father holding hands with a girl in a yellow dress. A boy with a crooked clip-on tie, following his mother. A lone girl from the projects holding her grandmother's hand as she returned to a reality far different than that of the other parishioners.

Lynch took it all in, then got out of his black Monte Carlo SS, locked the door, and looked up at the high-rise. Against the bright, blue, afternoon sky, the place that had seemed so tall and imposing when he was a boy was now simply ugly.

He wondered if the ugliness had taken hold since Kenya's disappearance. But as he walked inside and began to climb the steps, he knew that it had been there for quite some time.

He could feel it in the frightening stillness that rose up through the pissy stairway fumes. It was more than the normal quiet of a Sunday afternoon. It was an entity—one that assaulted everyone who dared to come back to it.

Those who had sense would listen to the stillness, knowing that what they felt wafting through the air of the East Bridge Housing Project was death—plain and simple.

But Lynch wasn't one to listen to such things. He believed only in fact, and hoped to find it in the apartments and hallways of the Bridge. But before he could find it, he had to be found.

"Kevin!" Darnell said, calling after him as he reached the third-floor landing. "Wait a minute!"

When Darnell caught up to him, panting and doubled over, he smiled and spoke as if they'd never lost touch.

"I was comin' from 'round back, lookin' for my niece, and I saw you get out your car. I thought maybe I could help."

Lynch regarded Darnell's withered appearance with a mixture of sadness and anger. He could smell it on him—the days-old stench of crack. Yet Darnell stood before him like nothing was wrong.

"You've been doing more than looking for your niece," he said as he worked his eyes down Darnell's filthy clothing. "What the hell happened to you, man?"

Darnell's smile faded. It was replaced by a hardness that Lynch didn't remember seeing in his eyes before. "Life happened to me, man. Simple as that."

Lynch turned and resumed walking up the steps. "Yeah, well, I'm sorry to hear that. But I've got a little girl to find."

Darnell followed him, refusing to be dismissed that easily.

"So do I," he said firmly. "That's still my niece, Kevin. My sister baby. And if you really wanna find her, it shouldn't be about me. It should be about Kenya."

Lynch looked at Darnell again, closer this time, and decided that he was right.

"Did you see your niece before she left the house Friday night?" he asked, stopping on the steps.

"Yeah, I saw her," Darnell said, looking around uncomfortably. "But this ain't the place to be talkin'. I think we need to go to Judy place or somethin'."

Darnell walked past Lynch, then turned around, waiting for him to follow. After a moment's hesitation, he did. By the time they sat down in Judy's apartment, and Darnell began painting the sordid details of Kenya's life, Lynch could see it all playing out before his eyes.

Chapter Ten

On Friday, Kenya had begun her day by rolling off her bare twin mattress on the bedroom floor. She pulled her rumpled nightshirt down past her knees and stepped over Darnell and his girlfriend, Renee.

They had spent the last few days smoking, and they were clothed in the week-old funk of the streets.

As Darnell stirred and turned over to watch her, Kenya tiptoed to the window. She pulled back the tattered shade and the sun beamed in through the window, along with the sound of children's voices coming from the Twelfth Street playground. Their laughter moved in time with the rumbling bass of a passing car, and Kenya smiled.

"Kenya, what you lookin' at?"

Judy was standing in the doorway wearing her favorite robe. Her hands were in her pockets, holding on to the treasures Darnell and Renee and every other addict so desperately sought.

"I was trying to see if Janay and them was outside."

"You know you ain't goin' outside like *that*," Judy said, fixing her eyes on Kenya's nightshirt.

"I know," Kenya said with an attitude.

"Who you talkin' to?"

Kenya checked her tone.

"I was gon' ask you if I could go outside, Aunt Judy," she said sweetly.

"Yeah, that's what I thought you said," Judy mumbled.

"Well, can I?" Kenya asked. "Please?"

Judy glared at her great-niece.

"You got five minutes to get in that bathroom and wash up, girl," she snapped. "It's some cereal in the kitchen. Make sure you eat before you go out."

Kenya grabbed some clothes from the dresser drawer, bounded over Darnell and Renee, and ran quickly down the cramped hallway to the bathroom.

Darnell peered down the hallway and saw her emerge from the bathroom in a striped beige T-shirt, cutoff denim shorts, and sneakers. He listened as she went into the kitchen and ate something.

He saw Judy walk into the kitchen as Kenya finished. Then Kenya was out the door.

According to Darnell, that was the last her family saw of her before nightfall.

Lynch sat looking at the floor, trying to understand what it was to live in a place where life was worth less than a hit of crack.

"Do you always listen to Judy's conversations with Kenya?" he asked, still looking at the floor.

"They was standin' in the bedroom doorway, and me and Renee was layin' on the floor. I couldn't help hearin' it."

"How does Kenya feel about you lying around listening to everything she says?"

"Kenya hate me," Darnell said simply. "But it ain't got nothin' to do with me listenin' to her or watchin' her. I think I remind her of her mother. We look a lot alike, we sound a lot alike, we both smokin'.

"I mean, Daneen doin' better now, but she was bad as me 'bout a year ago. That's why Kenya had to move here in the first place. Human Services took her from her mother."

"But is there more to it than that?" Lynch asked. "Is there something that might have made her want to get away from here—to get away from you or somebody else?"

"Look around," Darnell said. "Who wouldn't want to get outta here? You left, didn't you? You was smart, right? Well, Kenya smart, too. She know the streets better than most people twice her age. She have to. 'Cause Daneen used to make her fend for herself when she was smokin'. I guess that's why, when Kenya moved down here, she learned what it was about pretty quick. She looked at me, and she seen the truth. Seen it real clear. On some days, I was her uncle. But mostly, I was just some nigga helpin' her aunt make money on the same shit that kept her from makin' it to school most days.

"Tell you the truth," Darnell said, looking Lynch in the eye, "I think Kenya looked at me and seen what she could turn out to be. And I think that scared her to death. I know it did. 'Cause it scared me, too."

"And what about Sonny?" Lynch asked.

"What about him?"

"You said Kenya knows the streets. Did she see what Sonny was about, too?"

"You gotta understand somethin' 'bout Sonny. He ain't the same with kids as he is with everybody else.

"Now, I heard about that little girl they say he raped and killed back in the day. And I still don't know if that's true. But I do know this. He treated Kenya like she was his granddaughter. Always buyin' her this, buyin' her that, takin' her places, playin' with her. And like I said, Kenya ain't slow. She saw what Sonny was about, and she knew to leave him alone when he was doin' business. But when he had time away from the hustle, time away from Judy, him and Kenya was tight. Sometime I think they was too tight."

"But was he molesting her?" Lynch asked pointedly.

"I don't know," Darnell said. "Kenya told some people Sonny was touchin' her—told some other people he was havin' sex with her. But I'm not sure about that now. The more I think about it, the more I think that mighta been a lie to get attention—to make people feel sorry for her. Kenya's a sweet girl. She just lies sometimes to get attention.

"But then again, watchin' the two of 'em together, I could see how people could think somethin' was goin' on. It was times when Sonny acted like he would rather spend time with Kenya than Judy. And Judy ain't like that. She ain't like that at all."

"Did they ever argue about that?"

"I don't know about all that. But I do know that Judy just up and kicked Kenya ass for nothin' the other day. Not bad enough to leave no scars. Just enough to get a message across."

"And what message was that?"

"She wanted Kenya to stay away from Sonny. That's what it was really about. 'Cause Sonny had took Kenya downtown to get her some clothes Thursday. When they came back, Kenya put on one o' the new shirts Sonny bought her. I think that got to Judy. It was like Judy was waitin' for a reason. And when Kenya ain't give her one, Judy just made somethin' up. Said Kenya had stole one o' her shirts and wore it."

"So do you think it's possible that Kenya got angry with Judy and ran away?"

"Anything possible," Darnell said. "But I still think the person y'all need to look at is Judy. Whatever Sonny did to Kenya, he wasn't tryin' to kill her. He wasn't tryin' to get rid of her either. But Judy was. She just ain't want her around no more. And she was willing to do whatever she had to do to get her outta here."

Lynch sat back and wondered if Judy was capable of such a thing.

———

The battered wooden door Judy had walked through was six-inch-thick reinforced steel on the other side. And unlike the world she'd left outside on Darien Street—with desperate addicts and ruthless dealers vying for their very lives—the place where Judy now stood was contrary to anything she could have imagined.

A black marble coffee table sat atop an intricately designed Oriental rug. The walls were mirrored, and the ceilings were dropped, with recessed lights shining from the stonelike tiles.

Burly men stood at either end of the living room, holding Uzis. The woman who had answered the door was similarly armed, and was joined by another woman as she lifted Judy's hands to search her.

Unbeknownst to Judy, this house was headquarters for an operation that controlled four nearby corners and the dealers who worked each one. Manned by a security crew and the manager who gave orders at the behest of the Dominican, the house handled only large quantities of cocaine. And only for a select few clients.

As Judy tried to take it all in, an older man sat silently on a crushed-suede couch, regarding her with a hint of a smile. When Judy had been searched, he patted the seat beside him, directing her to sit down. Looking around with an air of nervous uncertainty, she complied.

"You Pablo?" she asked in a self-conscious whisper.

"No I'm not," he said, smiling. "But it's a pleasure to meet you, Judy. Pablo wanted you to know that he's sorry about your missing niece. But our business relationship with Sonny, and of course, with you, has been very fruitful. We want to help you however we can. So tell me what you want, and we'll see what we can do."

She looked around at the people in the room, unsure of what to say.

"Tell me what you want," the man repeated slowly. He was no longer smiling.

"I want Sonny," she said nervously. "He got somethin' belong to me, and I thought y'all might know where I could find him."

"I see," the man said, placing a finger on his chin as he leaned back to contemplate her request. "Well, I'm afraid I can't help you there. Sonny's been one of our best clients over the years, and even if we did know where he was—and we don't—we couldn't tell you. We just don't do business that way."

Judy fixed her eyes on the man and tried to gauge his interest in her. She didn't see any. In fact, she thought she saw mild contempt. But she made her plea in spite of it.

"I just want to talk to him," she said, trying not to sound as desperate as she felt. "I don't know what Sonny told you about me, but I'm not here to hurt him. And even if I was, how could I? Like you said, the business relationship been good over the years. Y'all made a lotta money, just off what we moved down the Bridge. That couldn'ta happened without me.

"Now, I just wanna talk to Sonny. I want him to look me in my face and tell me why he did what he did. I just need you to point me in the right direction."

"I'm afraid that's not possible," the man said sternly. "But I'll tell you what. If you leave now, we'll forget you ever came here with the police looking for you. We'll forget the risk you posed to our business, and we'll let you walk out alive. If not..."

The guards on either side of the room leveled their weapons at Judy.

She wanted to get up, but she was frozen. She tried to move, but was too afraid of what might happen if she did.

One of the men raised his gun and took aim. Tears streamed down Judy's face, and her breath came in quick, shallow gasps. The guard's finger tightened on the trigger.

"Wait a minute," a voice said from the dining room. "Lemme talk to her."

When he walked in and Judy looked up into his face for the first time in days, she realized that her desperate search wasn't about the money at all. It was about the man standing before her.

Sonny. It had always been about him.

Daneen had to force herself to stay at Wayne's house for as long as she did. She spent half of Saturday night tolerating his clumsy touch, and the other half slipping in and out of a restless sleep.

By Sunday morning, when the first gray light crept through the bedroom window, she was ready to leave. But she didn't. Wayne made love to her and fell asleep, dozing well into the afternoon. Daneen was wide awake. Each time she tried to get up, guilt pushed her back down. It told her that she had never been a mother to Kenya, that no matter what she did from that point on, her daughter's disappearance would be on her head.

It told her, in short, that she was nothing. She tossed and turned for a long time, believing that.

Eventually, she turned to Wayne. But Wayne wasn't much of a communicator. The only thing he knew of her was how her skin felt against his. To him, that was all that mattered.

Since they'd met at a Narcotics Anonymous meeting two months before, he'd lavished her with attention. But not the kind that she wanted. He didn't talk to her. Rather, he talked at her, like a father to a child. He thought that because he had been clean for ten years, he could make every decision for her. He treated her as if she needed to be protected and was incapable of thinking for herself.

At first, that made her feel secure. She needed more than that now. She needed love. But she had no idea of how to give or receive it. Because in all her life, she'd never really known love. Not even for Kenya.

Knowing that left her more alone than she'd felt in a long time. It was that loneliness that caused her to slip out of bed and into the shower. When she finished, she padded back into the bedroom, dressed in jeans and a T-shirt, then tiptoed over to the bed and took a few dollars from Wayne's pants pocket.

Looking down at him as he slept, she saw a vulnerability that made him seem almost handsome. She smiled when she saw it, and hoped that her departure wouldn't change that part of him.

Reaching into the pocket of the jeans she'd worn the day before, she took out the house key and placed it on his nightstand. Then she walked down the stairs and out of the house, intent on doing the one thing she thought would give her peace.

Kevin Lynch sat on Judy's dingy couch, looking for the underlying truth in what Darnell had told him. But Lynch didn't see it. Not in what Darnell said about Sonny, or about Judy, or even about himself.

Lynch knew even before Darnell had begun to speak that Judy's home was no place for a child. After listening to Darnell, he didn't know any more than that. But if he was to have any chance of finding Kenya, he needed to go deeper, because Darnell's revelations had only scratched the surface.

"Do you know where Kenya went when she left here Friday morning?" Lynch asked.

"Same place she always go," Darnell said. "She went to Lily's."

"Well, I need to talk to her. She still on the fifth floor?"

"Yeah, she on the fifth floor. Her and her daughter, Janay. You want me to go down there with you?"

"You got something else to do?"

"No," Darnell said, getting up from the tattered armchair where Judy normally sat. "But lemme take a quick shower first."

"Why, you trying to impress somebody?"

"Nah," he said, avoiding Lynch's eyes as he walked toward the bathroom. "It's gon' take more than a shower to do that."

Lynch grunted in response. Then he got up and walked slowly through the apartment, trying to get a feel for what life was like there.

A pot of grease languished on the stovetop, next to a half-filled can of recycled Crisco. Above it was a grease-spattered clock. A counter ran alongside it, and a kitchen table with four scratched metal chairs stood against the back wall.

Dozens of burnt matches littered the living-room floor, along with empty caps, broken coat hangers, and metal pipes. Between the couch and chair that sat on opposite sides of the room, there was nothing. But along the wall, there were milk crates for Judy's nightly guests.

In the bedroom where Kenya normally slept, there was the stench of unwashed women, sweaty men, and dirty sex. Smells that a nine-year-old should never know.

There was a chest of drawers against one wall. The closet, or what was left of it, had no door. Clothes were piled inside in cardboard boxes.

The single twin mattress in the room had no box spring, and was covered with a single, dirty sheet. On the wall above it, across from the window, an old faded picture of Daneen hung from a cracked frame on the wall.

Lynch took the picture down and fingered its edges as Darnell, dressed in a towel, walked in behind him.

"That's Kenya picture," he said as he reached into one of the boxes for a change of clothes. "Funny thing about kids. No matter what they mother do to 'em, they still love 'em. Still wanna be with 'em, no matter what."

Lynch put the picture on the chest of drawers and walked back into the living room as Darnell got dressed.

Two minutes later, they were on their way downstairs to talk to Lily.

The old man never apologized, never acknowledged his threat to kill Judy. He simply directed two of the guards to take Sonny and Judy from the living room to the basement, where Sonny retrieved the backpack he'd taken from the Bridge.

It was a fluke that Sonny had come to the house at all. He'd wanted to leave Philadelphia. But when he tried to drive the old man's station wagon to the Ben Franklin Bridge, and into New Jersey, he could tell that the car was on the verge of breaking down.

With Port Authority police posted on the bridge, he couldn't take that risk. And because there was nowhere else for him to hide, he turned north on Fifth Street, drove as far as Germantown and Allegheny, then walked the back alleys to Darien Street.

He still cared about Judy, in his way. And he didn't want to think of what could have happened had he not been there. So as he and Judy were led through the basement to a set of rickety wooden steps, he tried not to.

The guards stood by as Sonny climbed the steps and pushed against one of two heavy metal doors. When he opened it, Sonny stepped up through an old loading bay. Judy followed him, and they heard a metal bar slide into place behind them, locking the doors shut.

Sonny grabbed Judy's hand and took her through the alley that ran behind the houses. At the end of it, he entered the backyard of the corner house. When Sonny knocked on the door, it was opened by a man with hooded eyes.

"Five dollars," he said in a gravelly voice.

Sonny gave him fifty.

"I'm goin' upstairs," he said. "I don't want nobody comin' up there, understand?"

The man looked at the fifty, stepped aside, and reached into his pocket for a key.

"Third room to the left. Works on the windowsill..."

Sonny and Judy were past him before he finished, climbing the stairs of the shooting gallery as nodding heroin addicts ignored them in favor of their hazy realities.

When they reached the room, Sonny pushed Judy inside and locked the door. Then he wheeled on her with an open hand, ready to unleash his wrath.

But when he looked at her, he froze, because the Judy who stood before him was someone he didn't know. She was a woman torn between heartbreak and anger. A woman unable to speak, because words had failed her.

His hand dropped to his side as she stood there, looking at him with eyes that said everything her mouth couldn't. It was a look of unyielding heartbreak. A look that went well beyond tears, because tears could never capture the depths of it.

He lowered his eyes and looked away, then sat down on the bed and placed his head in his hands.

She sat down next to him and asked the question she'd wanted answered for the past two days.

"Why, Sonny? Why you have to do it like this? I woulda gave you everything I had. You ain't have to do it like this."

He stood up and pulled back the sheet that covered the window in lieu of a curtain.

"I ain't mean for all this to happen," he said, looking across the rock-strewn backyard to make sure no one was approaching.

"Look at you, Sonny. You can't even sit down 'cause you scared somebody gon' run up on you. Is that what you wanted? Well, here it is. Life on the run."

He turned with fire in his eyes.

"You wanna know what I wanted, Judy? It's real simple. I wanted the money. I wanted to get out the Bridge for good and never look back."

"You was already out the Bridge, Sonny. You had another place somewhere in town, plus you had your li'l hoe up in Fairview. I'm the one needed to get out. You think I wanted be up in that li'l stinkin'-ass apartment sellin' five-dollar caps?"

"So why didn't you get out, Judy? I damn sure ain't stop you."

"I was waitin' on you," she said, raising her voice.

"Well, you shouldn'ta waited on me."

"Yeah, I see that. I saw it when the cops came, and you left me to clean up the mess."

They both fell silent as the truth filled the space between them.

"So tell me, Sonny," she said sarcastically. "What exactly was it that you ain't mean to happen?"

Sonny was almost ready to spring. But when he looked at Judy, the hurt in her eyes calmed him.

"Look, Judy. You keep tryin' to make me into somethin' I ain't. Tryin' to make me somebody that's gon' love you. I ain't that guy. I'm a hustler, and love just ain't in me."

"No, I think it's in you," Judy said with an acid voice. "It just ain't in you to love no full-grown woman. You can only love little girls."

"So what that's supposed to mean?" Sonny snapped angrily.

"I think you know what it mean," Judy said firmly. "I just ain't know what it meant. Not at first, anyway. I ain't wanna believe it when I heard about the little girl in the trash bin, 'cause I couldn't imagine that you would do some shit like that. But then I saw you with Kenya. Saw the way you was always tryin' to have her all up under you. The way you was always givin' her things.

"After while, it seemed like you was more interested in her than me. I ain't want to believe it, but I knew, Sonny. I knew, and I ain't do nothin', 'cause I thought the money was gon' keep it from mat- terin'. But I shoulda knew better than that, too. I shoulda knew you couldn't lemme have a little somethin', 'cause all you ever did in your life was take. You took me, and you took Kenya. And then you took the one thing that was supposed to make the hurt go away. You took the money."

She started to cry then, the tears rolling silently down her face as she glared at him. As she did so, her love for Sonny began to transform into hate.

Sonny saw it as her jet-black eyes—eyes like Kenya's—turned from shining black pearls to hard, flat coal. It was as if the light in Judy's eyes had finally disappeared. And it had taken Sonny to make it happen.

"You think you know a whole lot more than you do," Sonny said, looking down at his hands. "But the only thing you know 'bout me is what I let you see. You never got that, Judy. All I let you see was the hustler, 'cause that was enough for you. All you needed to know was I was gon' make some money—that I was gon' let you hope for somethin' different.

"You talkin' 'bout you ain't leave the Bridge 'cause you was waitin' on me. That's bullshit. You was scared to leave. Scared to just pack up and get yo' ass out the projects, 'cause you ain't never seen nothin' else but that. You was scared to go someplace where you woulda been just what you is—a little black nobody from North Philly.

"You ain't stay there waitin' for me, Judy. You stayed 'cause you could walk around there and pretend you was somebody. 'Cause people would look at you, and say, 'That's Sonny woman. Don't mess with her.' You stayed there 'cause you ain't know no better. Even worse, you ain't want no better. Not for real."

"That's a lie, Sonny, and you know it. All them times we talked about what we was gon' do with that money—how we was gon' just leave and not look back—you know I wanted to leave, but you ain't care, 'cause you ain't know how bad it was for me there. You could never know how bad it was."

"You right. I could never know 'cause I ain't come up in the projects, Judy. I come up off the street. I come up in a time and a place where you was either gon' learn to be a man real quick or you was gon' get took. So I decided I was gon' be the one doin' the takin'.

"They ain't have all this stuff like they have now—social workers and whatnot. So when they caught me robbin' old men out West Philly, they sent me to one o' them schools. One o' them places where the bad boys go to get worse.

"I come up in places where we had to fight just to eat, where you wore the same clothes 'til they fell off you, where the big boys took the little ones and made 'em they bitches at night."

Judy looked at Sonny, and he stopped for a moment, sitting silently as if he was reliving what his childhood had been.

"I ain't never had a chance to be a child, Judy. I ain't never eat no ice cream or buy no penny candy. Ain't never had no new clothes or funny toys. Ain't never had no friends. All I had was me and my fists. But you ain't know that, 'cause all you ever wanted to know about me was how much money I was gon' bring in so you could keep pretendin' you was gon' leave out the Bridge one day."

Sonny's words struck a chord in Judy. She almost wanted to comfort him. But she didn't quite know what to say.

"Maybe you right, Judy. Maybe I don't know how to love no woman. Maybe all I know how to do is love little girls. But whatever you seen me doin' with Kenya, whatever you heard about me doin' with any child, it was always about givin' them what I never had."

He reached out and took Judy's chin in his hand, then stared intensely at her eyes.

"I ain't never touched Kenya," he said. "Ain't never do nothin' to her but love her. I guess I could do that 'cause I saw a whole lotta me in her. I saw what she been through, and I saw how it turned her into a hustler. I guess I was tryin' to show her that she ain't have to be that. She could just be a little girl, and somebody would love her anyway.

"I thought you could see that, Judy. But I guess I was wrong. All you could see was how you wasn't gettin' all the attention you thought you should. And you took it out on Kenya. Now she gone, and you ain't even bother to look for her."

"Neither did you," she said. "You the one claim you love her so much. But I ain't see you breakin' down no doors tryin' to find her. You was too busy takin' my money."

"No, you was too busy worryin' 'bout the money," Sonny said. "Kenya your flesh and blood, not mine. And while everybody runnin' around talkin' 'bout I had somethin' to do with whatever happened to her, you come runnin' to find me.

"Well, you found me, Judy. And you ain't even ask me 'bout Kenya, even though you claim I was molestin' her. First thing out yo' mouth is 'bout some money. So who really the selfish one, Judy? Who really the one don't care 'bout nobody but theyself?"

"I ain't gon' let you turn this around and make it about me," Judy snapped. "I ain't the one took the money and tried—"

"You can have half the money," Sonny said. "But Kenya still missin'. And unless you know where she at, I don't see how you can sit here and not even say nothin' about tryin' to find her.

"So I want you to look me in my face and tell me, right now. Do you know what happened to Kenya?"

Judy looked down at her feet as the tears began anew.

But before she could answer Sonny's question, there was a knock at the door of their room.

Sonny pulled his gun. Then the doorknob began to turn.

Chapter Eleven

Lily had spent the better part of the past two days wondering why the police hadn't questioned her. After all, she was more of a mother to Kenya than Daneen, Judy, or anyone else had ever been.

But the police weren't doing all they could, in her opinion, to find Kenya. They hadn't gone door-to-door in the building where she lived. And they hadn't gone door-to-door in the rest of the neighborhood.

Worse, their investigation seemed to be more about finding Sonny than finding Kenya. But with Sonny still on the run, and Judy a fugitive as well, their options were running out.

So when the knock finally came on Sunday afternoon, she wasn't surprised. That is, until she opened the door and saw Kevin Lynch standing in the hallway with Darnell.

She paused for a moment, her eyes darting from one to the other before she opened the door wider.

"Come in," she said.

Lynch walked in. When Darnell tried to follow, Lily held out a hand to block him.

"Lily, I—"

"Look, I know Kenya your niece, Darnell. And I'm sorry she

missin'. But I can't keep bein' around you and havin' you all up in my house. If Kevin wanna talk to me 'bout what happened, that's fine. But we ain't got no more words, Darnell. I said what I had to say, and so did you. That's it."

He stood there, hoping that Lily would change her mind. When it became clear that she wouldn't, he turned to leave with a finality that hadn't been there before.

Lily closed the door, then leaned against the wall and let out a long sigh.

"What was that all about?" Lynch asked.

"It's personal," Lily said. "Have a seat and try to ignore the mess. It's been a long coupla days."

He walked around the coffee table and moved the hair grease and brush from the couch before he sat down.

"Can I get you somethin'?"

"No," Lynch said. "I really just came to talk with you, and hopefully your daughter, to get a little bit of detail on what happened Friday when Kenya came down here."

Lily looked at him and smiled in spite of herself. "I'm sorry, Kevin. It's still hard for me to believe you a cop," she said. "I still remember when you was livin' on the third floor—how your grandmother used to try and keep you outta all the mess that went on 'round here."

"Yeah," Lynch said softly. "That seems like another lifetime."

"But you look good, Kevin. I'm glad you could come back to help with this. I know that mean a lot to Daneen."

Lynch didn't respond. He didn't want to talk about Daneen.

"Far as what happened Friday," Lily said. "The only one who could tell you about that is my daughter. And I'ma be honest with you. I really don't want her doin' a whole lotta talkin'. You start talkin' 'bout people like Sonny—people that'll kill you soon as look at you—and I start gettin' real nervous 'bout havin' my daughter name comin' up as some kinda witness or somethin'."

"I understand. But I just want to ask her a couple of questions. It won't take long."

"No, you don't understand. If I let Janay talk to you, I don't want her name comin' up in no files, and I don't want nobody comin' 'round askin' her to testify."

"Lily, whatever she says won't go any further than this room."

"You a cop, Kevin," Lily said. "You can't keep what she tell you to yourself."

"Well, that's not exactly true," Lynch said with a sigh. "I was suspended this morning."

There was a moment of awkward silence, and then came the inevitable question.

"Why?" Lily asked.

"You heard about Judge Baylor, right?"

"They blamin' you for that?"

"Somebody had to take the fall. And since I was the one who started the chase, I got elected."

"So if you suspended, what you still here for?"

Lynch paused, then started to give her a simple explanation. But then he realized that there was no easy answer.

"I guess I'm here for a lot of reasons," he said haltingly. "But mostly, I'm here for Kenya. It seems like there was so much stacked up against her that there was nothing she could do to make it right. And she didn't have much help, either. Her mother could've been more than she was, but she didn't want to. Her father—or at least the man Daneen said was her father—died trying to be something he wasn't. And then when it all fell apart, Kenya had to come to live in a place that, for all intents and purposes, was a crack house."

He smiled uneasily, then fixed his eyes on Lily.

"I'm here because I can relate. If some things had happened just a little differently, my life could've been just like that."

Lily nodded, remembering the circumstances under which Lynch had come to the Bridge.

"But we're not here to talk about me," he said quickly. "We're here to find Kenya. And if Janay can shed some light on what she did Friday afternoon, maybe she can help us do that."

Lily was quiet as she made her way to a chair and sat back to consider what Lynch had just told her. She responded without looking at him, almost as if she was talking to herself.

"Janay all I got," she said. "And I can't see her gettin' mixed up in this. I done already lost Kenya to this place. I ain't gon' lose my baby, too."

"Lily, it won't leave the room," Lynch said. "Nobody ever has to know that Janay told me anything. I just need a starting point. Please. Let her give me at least that."

Janay came in from the bedroom and stood against the wall. She looked at her mother with a silent plea in her eyes. Underneath it was a hurt too big for a child to carry.

When Lily saw that, she knew there was no other choice.

"Come here, baby," she said, extending her hand as Janay came to her. "Tell Mr. Kevin what y'all did on Friday. Try not to leave nothin' out, 'cause he need to know everything he can if he gon' find Kenya."

Janay began to speak. Lynch listened intently. After a while, Lily joined in, adding the details that she could. As they spoke, they were all immersed in Kenya's reality.

It was as if Kenya was telling her story for herself.

When she left her aunt Judy's, Kenya ran down the hall, past the elevator and into the stairwell, with its piss-stained corners and stale smoke.

"Where you goin', Kenya?"

She turned around and saw Janay coming down the steps with jump ropes in her hands.

"I was lookin' for you," Kenya answered.

"You wanna play double Dutch?"

"Okay."

The two girls ran down the remaining steps together, hoping they would run into someone else who wanted to play.

They made their way out onto the sidewalk, anxiously looking up and down the street for some little girl who would be willing to turn the ropes. When she saw that there was no one else outside, Kenya sat down on the pole that ran along the length of the littered patches of grass outside the projects.

"Don't look like we gon' be playin' double Dutch no time soon," she said.

"What you doin' out so early, anyway?" Janay asked, sitting down next to her friend.

"I was tryin' to find you so we could play tag."

"Why you always wanna play them little corny games?" Janay snorted.

"Cause I got corny friends," Kenya said, smirking.

"Yeah, right," Janay said with a giggle. "I'm the one showed you how to be cool."

"No you didn't. It was them mice in your house—you know, the ones that be sittin' at the table at dinner, talkin' 'bout, 'pass the peas.' "

Both girls laughed. But beneath the laughter, they knew the truth. Kenya would much rather live at Janay's apartment than her own. In truth, anyone would.

For the next few minutes, they sat quietly, absorbed in their own thoughts.

"There go that bitch right there!" Rochelle yelled out from behind them.

Janay stood up and gripped the jump ropes in her hands as Rochelle and her cousins approached. Kenya stood up, too, because she knew what was coming.

Janay had been friends with the older girl until about a month before. That was when Rochelle found out that her boyfriend had tried to get Janay's number. Janay, who was developing more quickly than Rochelle and most other twelve-year-olds, didn't give it to him. In truth, she wasn't even allowed to accept phone calls from boys. But that didn't matter to Rochelle.

She had seen Kenya and Janay coming outside from the window of her first-floor apartment. And remembering the rage she'd felt after finding out about her boyfriend trying to talk to Janay, Rochelle gathered her two cousins and rushed outside to catch her.

Janay had managed to avoid Rochelle before. But from the look of the cornrows and the smear of Vaseline on Rochelle's face, there would be no avoiding her this time. But Kenya, ever the peacemaker, tried to reason with her anyway.

"Look, Rochelle," Kenya said, stepping in front of Janay, "why don't you go 'head with that? Janay ain't never say nothin' to that boy. You need to be steppin' to *him*, not her."

"Mind your business," Rochelle said, pushing her.

Kenya stumbled backward.

Janay dropped her jump ropes and punched Rochelle hard across the jaw, knocking her into her younger cousin, who fell down and clutched her ankle.

Rochelle swung a wild left hook at Janay, who ducked and hit Rochelle in the stomach with two sharp uppercuts.

Rochelle doubled over as Janay grabbed a cornrow that had shaken loose in the melee. Janay swung wildly with her left hand, hitting Rochelle repeatedly in the face.

Rochelle's older cousin, who until then had watched in stunned silence, grabbed Janay and wrestled her to the ground. But Janay still had a grip on Rochelle's hair, and Rochelle fell on top of both of them.

Rochelle's younger cousin, who was crying now, let go of her ankle, got up from the ground, and ran into the building.

Seeing her friend pinned under two girls, Kenya started swinging. The first punch landed squarely on the back of Rochelle's neck, and her forehead hit the sidewalk. She lay there writhing in pain as Janay got up and started punching Rochelle's cousin.

Kenya joined her, and by the time it was over, both Rochelle and her cousin were on the ground, curled up and trying to block the blows.

Janay and Kenya stopped, then stood there for a moment, surveying the damage they had done.

"Told you to stop messin' with me," Janay said.

Rochelle peeked out from behind her arms, got up, and stumbled back a little as she tried to regain her balance.

"This shit ain't over," she said as she helped her cousin get up from the ground. "Trust me, it ain't over."

Lily took it all in when her daughter Janay and Kenya walked into her apartment. Janay's clothes were filthy. There was a scrape on her knee. And the jump ropes she'd taken with her when she'd left the apartment were gone.

"What you done got into nine o'clock in the mornin'?" Lily asked from the kitchen as she wet a clean towel and rushed into the living room.

"It wasn't her fault, Miss Lily," Kenya said. "Rochelle and them started it."

"I told you 'bout hangin' around that girl," Lily said as she dabbed at Janay's scraped knee, "wit' her fast-ass self."

"I wasn't hangin' with her, Mom. She came outside and started messin' with me 'cause she thought I was tryin' to talk to her little dirty boyfriend."

Lily stopped dabbing at Janay's knee and looked up into her eyes, waiting for the rest of the explanation.

"She pushed Kenya," Janay said, looking down at her mother. "So I hit her."

Lily stood up, went into the bathroom, and came back to the living room with a Band-Aid.

"Lemme tell you somethin', Janay," Lily said as she bandaged her daughter's knee and sat down across from her. "Rochelle and the rest o' these little girls around here—they gon' grow up a lot faster than you. Some o' these same little hoodlums y'all call yourself fightin' over gon' be dead or in jail in two or three years. And Rochelle and the rest of 'em gon' still be here in these projects, carryin' they babies. And you know what's gon' happen to Rochelle and them after that? They gon' be stuck right here for the rest o' they life. And if you keep goin' out here runnin' behind 'em, yo' ass gon' be stuck here, too."

"But, Mom, I—"

"But nothin'. You nine years old, Janay. Ain't a boy on this earth worth fightin' over, especially these boys around here. You think I work two jobs every day so you can be out here fightin' over these nothin'-ass boys? I'm tryin' to get us the hell outta here."

"Mom," Janay said, explaining slowly as if she was speaking to a child, "I won the fight."

"That's even more reason for you to stay outta that foolishness. These people 'round here'll make a fight between little girls into somethin' it ain't even gotta be. Now I don't want you out there in that mess no more. You hear me?"

Kenya was sitting on a chair across from them, watching as Lily stared hard at her daughter and grabbed her arm.

"I said, 'Do you *hear* me?'"

"Yes," Janay said in a near whisper.

"All right then. Get in there and change your clothes. Kenya, you come here."

Kenya came and sat between Lily's legs as the woman reached over and grabbed a comb and hair grease from the end table.

"Look at you with your hair all over your head. I guess you jumped in it, too, huh?"

"They was gon' try to jump Janay," she said. "I ain't know what else to do."

Lily smiled. If her daughter was going to have a friend, she was glad that it was Kenya. At least the girl was loyal.

As Lily pulled the comb through a tangled patch of Kenya's hair, she thought of how the girl would stay at her home for hours— doing her homework during the school year, and then staying up with Janay, playing with dolls, and eventually, staying over.

"It ain't a lot of little girls 'round here I would let in my house," Lily said as she deftly twisted Kenya's hair into cornrows. "You know that, don't you?"

Kenya thought about that as she felt the comb working through her hair.

"I wouldn't wanna go to a lotta people house," Kenya said, looking down at her hands sadly. "Not even mine."

Lily started to respond, then thought better of it. She knew what the child meant.

"Sometime I wish I lived with you, Miss Lily," Kenya said softly. "I wish I could stay here so I wouldn't have to go back."

After Lily finished Kenya's hair, and Janay bathed and changed her clothes, the two of them went outside and played as if the fight with Rochelle had never happened.

Between trips to the store to get twenty-five-cent Hugs and bags of Andy Capp Hot Fries, they played until the sun sank down in the sky and rested against the rooftop of the high-rise.

By seven o'clock, they had switched games and were playing tag. That's when Lily came to her apartment window and called Janay in for dinner.

"Come on, Kenya," Janay said as she started toward home. "You know you want some o' that chicken my mom made. Don't even front."

Kenya hadn't planned on fronting. She was hungry, and she knew that Aunt Judy probably hadn't cooked. So Kenya followed Janay inside, and the two of them sat at the table as Lily zipped around the kitchen, placing chicken legs, corn on the cob, and mashed potatoes on plastic plates.

"Bless the food, Janay," Lily said as she wiped her hands on a towel and sat down at the table with the girls.

"God is great, God is good, and we thank Him for our food," Janay mumbled, pausing and lifting her eyes to glance across the table. "And thank you for sending my friend Kenya to eat it with us. Amen."

Kenya scooped up a forkful of mashed potatoes and slowly lifted them to her mouth.

"What's wrong with you, girl?" Lily said. "You don't like my cookin' no more?"

"I like it, Miss Lily. It's just that . . ."

She let the rest of the sentence trail off.

"It's just that what?"

"Nothin'," Kenya said, swallowing the potatoes.

She pushed the food back and forth on her plate. Kenya thought that if she stayed late enough, Miss Lily would call her Aunt Judy and ask if she could spend the night.

Lily nipped it in the bud with her usual forthrightness.

"You can't spend the night tonight, Kenya. Your Aunt Judy want you to come home."

"I wasn't tryin' to spend the night, Miss Lily," Kenya said in her best little-girl voice. "My mom supposed to be comin' over tonight, and I gotta be home when she get there. We goin' to the movies."

Lily started to call her on the lie. But she would see Kenya the next evening and talk with her about it then.

Lynch, Janay, and Lily sat for a long time after they finished talking. There seemed to be no sound in the room. But in reality, they were listening to the echoes of Kenya's story.

It was a story that was at once haunting and heart-rending, hopeful and sad. They all desperately wished for it to go on. They only hoped that there would somehow be more to tell. For now, though, there were only regrets.

"I wish I woulda just let her stay here with me," Lily said, shaking her head. "But Judy ain't want her stayin' here no more. She knew how Kenya felt about me, and she ain't like it. She ain't want us bein' that close."

"Had you and Judy had some kind of falling-out?" Lynch asked.

"Darnell and me was seein' each other for a while back before he started smokin'."

Lynch tried unsuccessfully to hide his surprise.

"What, I can't want a man, too?" Lily said with an embarrassed nile. "I was lonely, and he used to come here to get Kenya when she ·ould spend the night. I guess one thing just led to another. And Judy ain't like it when she found out. We stopped speakin', and after while, she stopped lettin' Kenya spend the night down here."

"So she could stay here during the day, but at night, she had to go home, even though Judy knew what was going on in her apartment?" Lynch asked.

"That ain't matter. Judy just wanted to be in control o' somethin'. She wasn't nobody otherwise—just Sonny woman. Some old has-been livin' in the projects. Kenya was the only thing in her life where she had some say, so she tried to control everything Kenya did. And even though she knew it woulda been better for Kenya to stay at my place—someplace safe and stable, without a whole buncha people runnin' in and out—-Judy wanted to call the shots.

"Sad part of it is, she ain't care about Kenya for real. 'Cause if she did, she wouldn'ta spent so much time tryin' to keep her from the people who loved her the most."

Lynch nodded and turned to Janay. "So what about the fight with Rochelle? Did you take her seriously when she said it wasn't the end of it?"

"Not really," Janay said. "I mean, Rochelle, she kinda crazy, and she like to fight. But usually, somethin' like that, we probably end up bein' friends again sooner or later."

"But when she said it wasn't over, did you think she would be coming back or trying to involve other people?" Lynch asked.

"It wasn't like we rolled on 'em or nothin' like that. Her cousin ran, and it was two-on-two. If they wanted to fight some more, they probably woulda came back outside when we did. But they didn't, so I thought it was over."

"Did you take it seriously, Lily?"

"If I woulda took that mess seriously, I wouldn'ta let Janay and Kenya go back outside. Far as Rochelle and them, I know her people, and I know they ain't even like that. Rochelle mom go to work every day just like I do, and she one o' the few people in this place I know I could go and talk to if I had to."

"So why'd you tell Janay that it could escalate into something bigger?"

"I told her for next time," Lily said. " 'Cause next time she get out there fightin', it might be some people that ain't tryin' to let it go at that."

"I'm still gonna have to talk to the girl and her mother," Lynch said. "Just to cover all the bases. What apartment are they in?"

"They in 1D," Lily said. "Rochelle mother name Florine. We call her Flo."

Lynch jotted down the information.

"But the person you really need to be lookin' at is that girl Tyreeka. She the last one seen Kenya. She was with her Friday night. But then she disappeared with some drug dealer from down Twelfth and Parrish."

"Where's the boy now?"

"I don't know. We went down there yesterday—"

"Who's we?"

"Me and Darnell and Tyreeka mother. We went down there to talk to him, and it turned out Sonny stole the boy car and used it to get away from y'all. So the boy act like he was gon' try to find Sonny. He left the corner, and ain't nobody seen him since. And

Tyreeka, she come traipsin' her li'l stank ass back here yesterday afternoon with a bunch o' shoppin' bags. She say she left Kenya at the front o' the buildin'. But I think she lyin'. 'Cause her and that boy claim he gave her some money, and that's how she bought all that mess down the Gallery. But I think somebody paid her to keep her mouth shut or somethin'."

"What apartment is she in?"

"Somewhere on the tenth floor. Ask somebody up there, they'll be able to tell you."

Lynch caught up on his notes and spoke without looking up. "Is there anything else I should know?"

Lily hesitated, then looked down at her daughter Janay.

"You ain't gon' say you talked to us. Right, Kevin? 'Cause I really don't want my name up in it."

"I already promised you I wouldn't mention you or Janay," Lynch said. "I'm going to stick to that."

"Well, I don't know if you know this or not," Lily said. "But Janay saw Sonny on the elevator Saturday mornin'. I started to call 9-1-1, but like I said, I ain't want Janay name in it. So I went up to the cop that was guardin' Judy door and told him I was the one who seen him. But really, it was Janay."

"How did you happen to see him?" Lynch asked Janay.

"I had came out to see if I could find Kenya after Miss Daneen came in here and said she was missin'. I thought maybe if I went outside, I might see her. But when I went to catch the elevator and the doors opened, Mr. Sonny was on there."

"What was he doing?" Lynch asked.

"Looked like he mighta been goin' up to the roof. He pushed the twelfth-floor button a couple times."

"Was anyone on the elevator with him?"

"No, but it was a piece o' Kenya shirt on the floor in the corner."

"Did he seem nervous?"

"He just seemed like he was in a rush. I don't think he seen that piece o' her shirt, and if he did, he ain't seem worried about it. I just remember him askin' me if I was gettin' on, and he kept lookin' at his watch. Then the doors closed, and I came back and told my mom I saw him."

"Do you remember what time it was?"

"I just know it was after seven o'clock, 'cause I remember the first cartoon was on Channel 29 'round that time. I tried to watch it, but I couldn't, 'cause I kept thinkin' 'bout Kenya."

"Thanks, Janay," Lynch said, turning to Lily.

"There's only one more thing I need to know from you," he said. "What's that?"

"In your gut, what do you really think happened to Kenya?"

Lily was quiet for a long time.

"I think she got mixed up in somethin' she ain't have nothin' to do with. And whatever it was, it had somethin' to do with that apartment up there. I don't know if it was Sonny and Judy, or if it was one o' them men that be up there smokin' and trickin'.

"But I tell you one thing. Kenya was loved. She still is. And the deeper you get into this, the more you gon' find out how much. People you thought ain't never give a damn 'bout that girl gon' come up out the woodwork."

"I hope you're right," Lynch said as he got up and walked to the door.

Someone knocked just as he started to twist the knob. When he opened it, he saw Daneen standing there, looking up into his eyes with a determination that hadn't been there before. He looked back at her, but only for a moment. He was learning that he couldn't look at her for long.

"Kevin," she said softly. "I ain't expect to see you here. But I guess it's a good thing I did. 'Cause I'm here to find my baby. And I ain't leavin' again 'til I do."

Chapter Twelve

Sonny wasn't about to be trapped in a run-down shooting gallery in the Badlands. Not after all he'd been through. So when the knock came, and the doorknob began to turn, he looked at Judy and held a finger to his lips. Then he moved his head to indicate that she should stand against the wall.

When she did so, Sonny flung open the door, leveled his gun at the man's chest, then reached out and snatched him inside, only to find that it was the owner of the house—the man who had let them in the back door a few minutes before.

The man threw up his hands to block his face, and his tired eyes widened in fear.

"I told you I ain't want nobody comin' up here," Sonny said in a low voice.

"I was just gon' tell you I had some ten-dollar bags out here in case you needed some more dope," the man said in his gravelly voice. "I try to take care o' my best guests—you know, the ones that pays real good. I ain't mean to—"

"Don't knock on the door again," Sonny said, leaning in close. "I don't need no dope, man. I just need to be left alone. Now don't let nobody else come to this door 'less they want some o' this lead in they ass, you understand?"

The man nodded nervously. "It won't happen again."

"It better not," Sonny said, pushing the man back out into the hallway and slamming the door.

Sonny and Judy listened as the sound of his footsteps faded down the hall. Then Judy let out a sigh of relief and sat down on the bed.

"You sure it's safe to be in here?" she said, looking at the dry wooden slats behind the plaster of the crumbling walls.

"It is for a little while," Sonny said, sitting down next to her. "Why, you scared?"

"I'm scared for you," she said, reaching out to stroke his face.

He grabbed her hand before she could touch him. "I wanna know about what I asked you," he said soberly. "I want the truth about Kenya."

She looked in his eyes and saw pain. She'd never seen that in all the years she'd known him. His eyes had always been guarded before. But now, he was allowing her a glimpse. It was a sight so rare that she found it difficult to look away.

When she did, it was to see inside herself.

"You told me it was a lot o' things I ain't know about you," she said hesitantly. "Things I ain't know 'cause I ain't wanna know.

"But it was a lot about me you ain't know either. And it wasn't 'cause I ain't tell you. You just wasn't listenin' when I did.

"You knew about my son dyin' in Vietnam, and my daughter bleedin' to death on the bedroom floor. You knew about they father gettin' killed in prison. You knew all that 'cause I told you. I guess I was hopin' it would make me real to you, and not just some old hoe for you to sleep with when you wanted to. But lookin' back, I guess all it did was give you what you needed to use me. To get my hopes up like you was gon' rescue me from losin' more o' the people I cared about.

"I guess that's what made me hold on to you so hard, Sonny. But the harder I tried to hold on, the more you backed away. And the more you backed away, the harder I tried to hold you.

"After while, I woulda did whatever you said just to be with you. That's why I started sellin' when you told me to. That's why I kept doin' it, even when I ain't see my life gettin' no better. That's why I saw things between you and Kenya that wasn't even there. And I guess the thought o' losin' you, and losin' that hope you gave me, I guess that made me think Kenya was in the way.

"I kept seein' you movin' away from me and closer to Kenya, and my mind started playin' tricks on me. I started tellin' myself you wanted her more than you wanted me. Then Thursday when you took her shoppin', I started thinkin' real crazy. Started thinkin' like I needed to get Kenya out the way. So I beat her. I guess I was hopin' she would just get tired o' me and run away. Then it could be me and you again, just like it used to be."

She stopped and looked up at Sonny, searching his eyes for sympathy. When she saw none, she turned from him and looked out the window.

Through the tattered curtain that covered it, she could see Cambria Street, where addicts scrambled and clawed for more.

She could see dealers, risking their lives on dangerous corners for the chance to peddle death—one hit, one pill, one injection at a time.

She looked at it all and saw herself. It was a sight she could barely stomach. She knew that Sonny had no such compunction. It was that heartlessness that had drawn her to him. She'd always believed that she could fix it.

When she turned from the window and looked back into his eyes, however, she realized for the first time that she'd never needed to fix his heart. It had been there all the time. It just wasn't with her.

"I knew what I was doin' was wrong, Sonny. I knew I shouldn'ta been sellin' that shit with that child livin' there. But after while, I just couldn't see makin' a choice between losin' you and doin' what was right for her. So I told myself I wouldn't be doin' it that long.

I told myself it was only 'til we took our money and got out. I lied to myself.

"I guess the craziest thing about it is, I was startin' to come around. I was gon' talk to Kenya before she left out on Friday. I was gon' tell her I was sorry for the way I was treatin' her and ask if we could start all over again. But I ain't get a chance to do that.

"By the time Kenya came back home that night, I had forgot all about it. I seen that first o' the month money rollin' in and I was back to that same old Judy. Kenya was in the way o' me gettin' my money, so I sent her to the store. By the time I looked up, she was gone. And so was you."

Judy reached out hesitantly and grabbed Sonny's hand, folding it gently in both of hers.

"But lemme tell you somethin', Sonny. And I want you to hear me real good. Much as Kenya was in the way, much as I thought she was comin' between us, much as I blamed her for everything that was goin' wrong, I would never do nothin' to hurt that child. I loved her, sure as I'm sittin' here. I guess, deep down, I had lost so much, I was scared I was gon' lose her, too. So I tried not to love too hard so it wouldn't hurt to lose her."

She let go of his hand, and her eyes took on a faraway look.

"But you know what, Sonny?" she said, her voice cracking. "It ain't work. It's still tearin' me up inside that Kenya gone. It's tearin' me up, Sonny, and I don't know how to make it stop hurtin'."

She leaned against him then, shivering with the pain of it all.

"Make it stop hurtin', Sonny," she said. "Please make it stop."

Sonny reached out and wrapped her in his arms, pulling her into his chest until her lips were against him. He held her there, the smell of her hair filling his nostrils until he pulled it back from her neck.

He kissed the soft skin there once, then twice, then licked it with his tongue. She reached down and squeezed until he stiffened beneath her touch.

He pulled her shirt down past her shoulders and let his tongue trail over her breasts, stopping and lingering at her nipples before gliding farther down.

She lay back, reveling in the feel of his lips skipping down the skin of her stomach, then brushing against her secret places until her moisture filled his mouth.

She worked her fingers into his thick hair and pushed until his face was buried there. Then she pulled his lips up to her mouth so she could taste it for herself.

Their tongues danced one around the other. Their bodies moved closer together. And when each part of them had touched, she lay back, opening herself even wider.

As he climbed inside her, the dance moved from their mouths, down their arms, into their hands and fingertips. They touched, gently at first, and then with a rhythm that grew faster with each stroke.

She wrapped her legs and arms around him. Sweat dripped from his chin into the hollow of her neck.

They gave themselves to one another, forever it seemed, in fear and in passion and in forgiveness. And as her moans turned to squeals, and then to screams, she buried her face in his chest as her passion poured out in liquid waves.

He met each wave with a stream of his own. And then they both lay spent, trying not to think of what the next moment would bring.

As he walked out of Lily's apartment, Lynch was angry. The sympathy he'd felt for Daneen had been swept away by Janay's sordid tales of Kenya's life.

The hard truths he'd heard spun through his mind like trash in a swirling city wind, giving new fuel to his hatred for Daneen.

Standing in the hall, watching his eyes move from sadness to disgust as he looked at her, Daneen tried to meet his gaze. But she couldn't, because somewhere inside, she knew that he was right to hate her.

Still, Daneen was well aware that it was no longer about her. It was about her daughter. And if the past was the barrier that stood between her and the man who could help to find Kenya, then the past had to be dealt with.

If it was up to Lynch, however, the past would stay firmly in its place.

"Excuse me," he said, and tried to walk past her.

She stood in his path. "We need to talk, Kevin."

"The only thing you can talk to me about is where this—"

He flipped through his notes until he'd found her name.

"Where this girl Tyreeka lives."

"She on the tenth floor. Apartment 10F. Why?"

"Look, you asked me to help you find your daughter, and I'm doing that. That's why I'm looking for Tyreeka. Seems she might be the last one who saw Kenya alive."

He stopped and looked her up and down. "But you wouldn't know that, would you? Because you're not around enough to know what Kenya does from day to day."

"You think I want it like that?" Daneen said sharply. "It ain't a day when I don't wonder where my baby at, what she doin', and who she with. It ain't a night that I don't pray and ask God to protect her."

"You should've been here to protect her yourself," Lynch snapped. "Maybe then she wouldn't have had to spend her nights wishing she lived with some other family."

Daneen fell silent. Lynch knew he'd hurt her, and he was anxious to do so again.

"You didn't know that, did you, Daneen? You didn't know your daughter was telling people that she wished for another family. I guess you were too busy smoking crack to pay attention."

Daneen could feel anger rising in her throat. But she knew this wasn't the time for that.

"We gotta talk, Kevin. Right now."

He stared at her and said nothing.

"Okay," she said. "If you won't talk, then I will. I know you hate me, Kevin. And I'm sorry you feel that way. But what happened between me and Tyrone was a long time ago. I was different then, whether you believe that or not. I was young and dumb, and I thought I had all the answers. Thought I could get whatever I wanted from any man I wanted to get it from. I guess I got that from Judy.

"I shoulda knew better than that, though. If I woulda really paid attention, I woulda seen that Judy wasn't gettin' much o' nothin', 'cause she was still right here in the Bridge with me."

"I don't have time for this, Daneen," Lynch said, pushing past her and making his way to the elevator.

She followed him, talking all the while.

"I thought I had me a basketball star," she said. "Thought Tyrone was gon' make some money, and I was goin' along for the ride."

Lynch jabbed the button for the elevator as Daneen spoke, trying his best to ignore her.

"I used him, Kevin. You knew it, and you tried to tell him, but he ain't wanna listen, so I used him some more. I gave him what he wanted, just how he wanted it, and he was happy with that. I was happy, too, I guess, 'cause I swore it was gon' pay off down the line. But then he got hurt, and all that was over.

"I saw all the things I wanted fallin' apart. Saw myself livin' in the Bridge and never findin' another way out."

Lynch jabbed the button again as his jaw set in a hard, angry line. When the elevator didn't come, he turned to her with years of built-up rage in his eyes.

"Is that all people are to you, Daneen? A way to get what you want? I always suspected you wasn't shit, but you just confirmed it for me. Now if you'll excuse me, I've got a little girl to find."

He walked quickly to the end of the hall.

"No, I won't excuse you," she said, following him up the steps. "You still holdin' on to somethin' that happened ten years ago, Kevin. It already done ate my life up. Don't let it eat yours up, too."

He walked faster. She was losing him, so she gave him the snippet of truth that he wanted.

"It's a lot to what happened with me and Tyrone."

Lynch stopped and turned around.

"No," he said. "I don't think there's a lot to it. You got him to deal drugs, then you got pregnant and told him Kenya was his. Everybody knew she wasn't. He couldn't handle it, and he died trying to."

"Okay, Kevin," she said as she caught up to him on the landing. "Kenya ain't Tyrone daughter. Is that what you wanna hear? You want me to say that out my mouth? Okay, she ain't his. I lied. But it wasn't like everybody thought it was. I lied 'cause I had to."

"Why, Daneen? What reason would you have to do that?"

She considered telling him the truth. But the truth, in all its ugliness, wasn't something she was ready to give up. It was something she'd promised herself she would take to her grave.

"I wanna tell you that, Kevin, but I can't," she said haltingly.

"You can't, huh? Well, tell me this, just to ease my mind because I've spent a lot of time wondering about it over the years."

Daneen looked at him expectantly.

"Is Sonny Kenya's father?"

Daneen stared at the steps as a range of emotions poured through her. She considered answering the question, but she couldn't. Not there. Not yet.

"I know who I wish her father was," she said, looking up at him.

Lynch shook his head with contempt. "You're the same as you've always been, Daneen. You say whatever you have to say to get what you want."

"I'm not tryin' to use you, Kevin. I was just sayin'——"

"Why don't you do yourself a favor, Daneen? Do us both a favor. Leave me alone. Go away and let me do what I have to do to find Kenya. You don't have to pretend you love her. And you definitely don't have to pretend you feel anything for me. I don't need that. And I don't need you."

As Lynch turned and continued up the steps, Daneen looked after him and decided that she could find Kenya on her own.

So as he went to Tyreeka's mother's apartment, she took to the streets. Because the streets were what Kenya knew best.

Tyreeka cradled her baby, looked into her eyes, and saw the love she'd never received elsewhere.

There was something pure in those eyes—a thirst that could only be quenched by Tyreeka.

As she watched her daughter explore every part of her mother's face, Tyreeka knew that this was what she had always longed for. Something of her own, something of substance that she had created.

Her daughter was the one genuine thing in a life covered over with masks and pretense. She made her feel like a child again. It was a feeling that she savored. Because even at thirteen, Tyreeka had seen more than most adults ever see in a lifetime.

The baby reached up and twisted her lip. Tyreeka winced and pulled the baby's hand away because her lip, like the rest of her face, was swollen. It hurt even to breathe.

When her mother called her from the living room, Tyreeka had to brace herself for the pain she felt when she spoke.

"Yeah, Mom," she answered, sounding like her mouth was filled with cotton.

"Come here, Tyreeka," her mother said. "Somebody here to talk to you about Kenya."

She carried the baby with her to the living room, where a dark-skinned bald man with tired eyes and hulking shoulders sat waiting on the couch.

"Is that your little sister?" Kevin Lynch said, leaning forward with a smile for the baby.

"This my daughter," Tyreeka said, sounding annoyed.

"Oh."

Lynch stopped smiling, embarrassed. "My name is Detective Kevin Lynch. I've been working on trying to find Kenya and I understand that—"

Tyreeka looked up, and Lynch noticed the bruises on her face for the first time.

"What happened to you?" he asked with concern.

"I fell," Tyreeka lied, looking sideways at her mother, who sat across the room in a folding chair.

"No, she ain't fall," her mother said matter-of-factly. "I beat her ass for stayin' out all night trickin' with some drug dealer while her baby was in here hungry. Now, if you gon' take me outta here for lovin' my daughter enough to discipline her, go 'head," she said, holding out her hands for the cuffs. "Jail probably better than sittin' up in here takin' care o' everybody else babies, anyway."

Tyreeka looked down at her baby and remained silent as Lynch looked from mother to daughter.

"I'm not here to judge you, Miss . . ."

"Johnson. Hattie Johnson."

"I'm not here to judge you, Miss Johnson. I just want to talk to your daughter about Kenya's disappearance, if that's okay with you."

"It's fine with me if it's okay with her."

Tyreeka nodded almost imperceptibly.

"I understand you saw Kenya on Friday night. Do you remember where you saw her and what time it was?"

"I guess it was a little after ten, 'cause the news had just came on Channel 29. I was goin' to the store to get some cereal for my baby, and I saw Kenya in front o' me. I called her and asked her where she was goin'.'"

"What did she say?"

"She never answered. She just said she was comin' with me. I told her she couldn't, and she asked if she could spend the night with us. Told me somethin' about some cousins comin' up from down South and Judy apartment bein' crowded.

"I knew she was lyin'. Kenya would lie sometime to keep from sayin' what was really goin' on down there. But somethin' about the way she said it made me take her serious."

"And what was that?"

"She started cryin'. I ain't know if she was fakin' or what, but I took her serious. I told her to go 'head up and ask my mom if she could spend the night."

"Why didn't you go with her?"

"I was talkin' to somebody."

"Who were you talking to?"

Tyreeka hesitated. Lynch sensed that she didn't want to give details.

"Look," he said, feigning exasperation, "we can do this down at Central Detectives if you prefer."

Tyreeka sighed and held her baby tighter, rocking her nervously as she answered the question. "This boy named Scott that hustle down Crispus Attucks."

"Scott what?"

"I don't know his last name. They call him Scott Playa. We was talkin' and then we went for a ride. One thing led to another and, you know, we ended up at his aunt house on Thompson Street."

"Do you remember the exact address?"

Tyreeka stopped to think. "It was 1185," she said. "I remember 'cause I was lookin' at it and thinkin' I ain't know the numbers went that high."

"Did you see Kenya go in the building before you left?"

"I saw her walk toward the buildin', but I ain't see her go in."

"Did you see her talking to anyone else after she left you?" Lynch asked as he jotted notes.

"No."

"Is there anything you remember about her state of mind when you talked to her?"

Tyreeka thought about it for a few minutes, then looked up at Lynch with a troubled expression.

"She seemed like she was nervous," she said. "She kept lookin' over her shoulder and actin' like she ain't wanna leave me."

"Tell you the truth, I think she was scared," Tyreeka said finally. "I think she was scared to go home."

Darnell sat with the shades drawn in the darkened living room, waiting for the hurt to subside. He'd been sitting there for hours, ever since Lily had dismissed him.

He was out of crack, and for the first time in months, he had no desire to scrounge for more. It was crack, after all, that had put him there, writhing in the pain that came with Lily's latest rejection.

It was the kind of hurt that twists in one's gut. The kind that comes after hope is built up, then crashes to the ground and shatters. It was an ache that Darnell had forgotten.

He had long ago stopped feeling. The crack had taken away his ability to do so. But in quiet moments like this, when the crack was gone and sleep refused to come, his emotions awakened and stabbed at him like needles.

Normally, he would turn to the drugs to make it stop. But all he wanted now was Lily. Nothing else would do.

He considered going out to join the search for his niece. But at that moment, he didn't care about the search, and he didn't want to act as if he did. The demand of doing so was too great. And Darnell was in no mood to meet demands.

He looked up as the doorknob turned, squinting at the dim hallway light that rushed into the darkness. He recognized the silhouette that filled the doorway. But not even the sight of his sister could pull him from his funk.

"Who that?" Daneen said, spotting him in the corner.

"It's Darnell," he said.

There was a moment of awkward silence.

"What you doin' here?"

"What you mean, 'What you doin' here?' I live here."

"Well, shouldn't you be somewhere lookin' for Kenya?" Daneen said, with a hand on her hip.

"Shouldn't you?"

"I just came in from lookin' for her," she said, walking to the window. "But it's only so many times you can keep goin' over the same streets."

She lifted the shade. Then she went about the task she'd come there to carry out. She went from room to room, rummaging though the drawers and closets, looking in vain for something that would give her a clue about Kenya.

She went into the kitchen, looked into a drawer, and saw the gun that Sonny kept behind the silverware tray. She quickly slipped it into her jeans, covered it with her shirt, and pushed the drawer shut.

"The cops already been through here lookin'," Darnell said, walking into the kitchen behind her.

Daneen jumped, but quickly regained her composure. She didn't want to have to explain taking the gun. She didn't even know why she'd done it. But somewhere deep down, she felt that she might need it.

"The cops couldn'ta searched the way they shoulda," she said haltingly. "Or else they woulda found my baby by now."

She looked at him nervously. When she realized he hadn't seen her take the gun, she leaned back against the counter and sighed. "I don't know what else to do."

"I don't think nobody do," Darnell said, going back to his spot on the floor.

Daneen walked over to the living-room couch and sat down across from Darnell. She took in the dark circles around his eyes, his pallid skin, his beaten expression.

"You look like you done lived a couple o' lives in the past few days," she said, almost sympathetically.

"So do you. But I expected that."

They sat quietly for a moment, lost in their own thoughts.

"You see Kevin?" he asked.

"Yeah, I saw him. He ain't wanna see me, though. Matter fact, he told me to stay away from him. Said he ain't need me to help him find Kenya."

Darnell laughed.

"What's funny?" she said.

"Seem like it's a whole lotta that goin' around. I went down Lily's like she was gon' fall for me if I washed my ass."

"So what happened?"

"You see where I'm at, don't you?"

"I don't know why you expected no different," Daneen mumbled.

"I don't know why you expected somethin' different from Kevin," he said in a tone that was almost angry.

Daneen was about to say something hurtful. But her brother was already in pain. His eyes held a sadness that had set in years before— the same sadness that had set into her own.

"I guess we always expectin' somethin' different, Darnell. I guess we think if we look past all the dirt we done did, everybody else gon' look past it, too. But it don't work that way.

"You live with the stuff you do," she said pointedly. "You live with it, and you can't kill it. 'Cause every time you think you done buried it, it get up out the grave. You can run from it, you can pretend it ain't there. But it's always standin' right next to you, remindin' you who you really are."

Darnell couldn't think of a response. There was no flip answer to the truth. There was no way to turn it around and point it at Daneen. It was what it was, and he knew it.

"Kenya more than a niece to me," he said, gazing at the floor as he changed the subject. "I wanna help you find her. It's just hard for me to keep lookin'."

Daneen stared at him. He looked tortured and pathetic.

"Help yourself, Darnell," she said as she got up to leave. "That's the best way you can help me."

"Oh, so you get a little two months clean and think you can tell me 'bout helpin' myself, huh?"

"Who said I was talkin' 'bout that? You got a whole lot more than that you need help with."

"First thing I need is somethin' to eat," he said, trying to lighten the mood. "You know the only thing Judy got in here is some damn grease on the stove. I can't eat that. Trust me, I tried."

Daneen dug into the pocket of her jeans, took out a crumpled bunch of bills, and handed him two dollars.

He looked at it. "What I'm supposed to do with this?"

"That'll get you three chicken wings and a rice and gravy from the Chinese store."

"Damn, sis, that's the best you can do?"

She looked at him, stretched out on the floor with his hand extended toward her like a beggar.

"That's what I should be askin' you, Darnell. I should be askin' if that's the best you can do."

With that, she turned and walked out the door.

———

The news van pulled onto the sidewalk in front of the projects and Channel 10's Jim Wright jumped out, holding a copy of the Sunday *Inquirer*, with Kevin Lynch's photo on the front page next to Judge Baylor's.

Within an hour of that morning's hearing, his department sources had told him that Kevin Lynch had been suspended for his role in the car chase that killed Judge Baylor. Wright had spent the rest of the day gathering other useful bits of information that no one else had thought to seek.

Now he was scrambling for footage so he could package the story in time for the five o'clock broadcast. Shots of the projects, perhaps even the apartment where Kenya had been staying, would do nicely for starters.

As he walked toward the building with his cameraman following close behind, he saw a group of boys sitting on the pole around the outside of the main building. They watched his cameraman to make sure he wasn't filming the project commerce they were posted there to protect.

He went inside, past the vacant guard booth. As he stood by the elevator, pushing the button and hoping that it would come quickly, residents shuttled in and out, looking at him with a curiosity that Wright misconstrued as aggressiveness.

When people started to gather and ask if they were going to be on television, Wright was anxious to move—to do something that would keep him from having to wait there for an elevator that obviously wasn't about to come.

"Let's get some shots on the first floor," he said, when he spotted the entrance to the stairway. "We can do a standup in the hallway and maybe just take the steps to the seventh floor."

They walked up the three steps that led to a door and the first floor, opened it, and walked into the dank hallway that ran between the apartments.

As the cameraman turned on the light and Wright began to speak, an apartment door opened and Kevin Lynch walked out. He was saying something to the woman who lived there when Wright spotted him and ran down the hallway, followed by the cameraman.

"Detective Lynch, Jim Wright, Channel 10! I saw you yesterday down at Broad and South when they were searching for Sonny Williams. I'd just like to ask you a couple questions."

Lynch was taken aback, but recovered quickly. "I'm busy right now. I don't have time to answer any questions."

Wright ignored that. "Regarding your suspension in connection with Judge Baylor's death, do you feel you've been unfairly made into a scapegoat?"

Lynch looked at the camera, then at the reporter, and wondered how they'd found out about his suspension so quickly.

"I don't have any comment on that," he said, pushing past them.

"Are you here working on the case in spite of your suspension?"

Lynch walked quickly down the hallway, with Wright and the cameraman close behind.

"Are you any closer to finding Kenya Brown? Is she even still alive?"

He stopped. "Look, man. This might just be a story to you, but these people have to live with it. It's not just some drama for you to put on television so people in the suburbs can shake their heads and talk about the poor little Negroes in the projects. It's people's lives."

"So does that mean you're still working on the case? And if so, under what authority, since you've been suspended from the force?"

"I'm just visiting," Lynch said. "I grew up here, and I'm just back visiting. Excuse me."

Lynch squeezed between Wright and the cameraman and was almost at the end of the hallway when Daneen came through the door.

she said, and stopped when she saw the reporter.

rown," Wright said when he spotted her. "You are Daneen

ght? Can I ask you a few questions?"

en looked from the reporter to Lynch as the cameraman approached and shone the bright light in her face.

Lynch was angry. He wanted to take the camera and smash it against the cinder-block walls. But he knew that the only way to keep the focus on Kenya, rather than Judge Baylor, was for Daneen to make some sort of public plea. Because no matter what they told themselves, there was still one cruel reality. The longer the search for Kenya went on, the more likely her disappearance would become a homicide. And Lynch knew that he could never live with that.

"Go ahead and talk to them," he said to Daneen. "It might help Kenya."

Daneen looked at Wright suspiciously. "Okay," she said. "Ask your questions."

"How does it feel knowing that the people who were supposed to be caring for your daughter allowed this to happen?"

Daneen hesitated, then looked into the camera. "I don't know what I feel about them yet. It's still sinkin' in that my daughter gone. I'm still tryin' to deal with that."

"What would you say to Judy Brown and Sonny Williams if you could talk to them?"

"I guess I would tell 'em we could deal with whatever they did later. Right now, I just want my baby back. So if they can help us find her, I would ask 'em, no, I would beg 'em to tell me where she at, so I could have her back with me where she belong."

"But isn't it true that the Department of Human Services took her from you and placed her here, with Judy Brown?"

Daneen hadn't expected that type of question. But Wright had done his homework, and what he'd learned was intriguing.

"I had some problems in the past," she said evenly. "But you tell me what's better for a child: a mother tryin' to get herself together or a house full o' drugs and God knows what else? I ain't gon' blame DHS for what's goin' on now. But I will tell you this. Kenya woulda been better off with me. Least then she wouldn't be missin'."

"Yes, but the fact is, your daughter was placed in this home and you could've—"

"Next question," Lynch said, his eyes flashing a warning.

Wright looked up at Lynch and decided not to press the issue.

"One last question, Ms. Brown. If Kenya was listening right now, what would you say to her?"

"I would tell her I love her. I would tell her to stay strong, 'cause Mommy doin' the best she can to find her. I would tell her that if she mad about somethin', she can talk to me about it. We can start over, baby. I wanna be your mother. I really do. But I need you to come home and gimme a chance to do that.

"Please, Kenya," she said, as the tears welled up in her eyes. "Come home."

She leaned against Lynch, who hesitantly put an arm around her. And then she allowed the tears to flow freely as the camera captured her pain in all its heartbreaking detail.

Chapter Thirteen

Three divisions of the police department, in various parts of the city, were swept up in the investigation. Officers in South Division, where Sonny had last been spotted, were still scouring the area for him. Detectives from East Division searched the area around Germantown Avenue, looking for Judy. Central Division detectives, along with Housing Authority officers, questioned neighbors in and around the Bridge and Crispus Attucks.

But in spite of the vast resources being committed to the investigation, it was painfully obvious that Kenya was not their concern. Though more than thirty officers were involved in the case, the police had questioned only a few neighbors, and none of them were the people who knew Kenya best. They hadn't extensively questioned the neighborhood children. They hadn't targeted any suspects other than Sonny and Judy.

In truth, most of the officers were only out to find Sonny, but not for what he might have done to Kenya. They wanted to even the score for the officers he'd injured, and to calm the public outrage surrounding Judge Baylor's death.

Roxanne Wilson knew that. And as she rose from the few restless hours of sleep she'd managed since going home on Saturday, she grabbed the Department of Human Services file that a friend in

DHS had managed to smuggle home after working some weekend overtime at the office.

As Wilson thumbed through it, she thought about the disappearances and murders she'd seen during her years in the police department's Juvenile Aid Division.

There was the case of the teen basketball star whose mother had murdered her in a fit of rage, then made a tearful plea for her daughter's safe return. There was the case of the foster mom who'd drowned her infant foster daughter, then had sex with her boyfriend as if nothing had happened. There was the case of the old woman who admitted that she'd smothered five of her infant children while claiming that they'd died from Sudden Infant Death Syndrome.

In all of the most heinous cases she'd seen while dealing with children, it was often the mother or caregiver who was to blame. It was that experience that told her the first finger should be pointed at Judy. But in her zeal to do what was right, she'd forgotten to look closely at Kenya's biological mother. And from what she saw in the file, she should have.

Wilson put the folder on her nightstand, got out of bed, and walked down the hall to her younger son's bedroom. Looking at its contents, which were arranged much the same as they'd been when her son was alive, she remembered why she was hesitant to blame Daneen. Because in some ways, Daneen's suffering had the same roots as hers.

Ten years before, Roxanne Wilson, just recently divorced, moved to her West Philadelphia home. She knew the neighborhood was bad. It had been that way for some time, because the cycles of change always seemed to make things worse.

The violence of the early seventies had died down, and street gangs had virtually disappeared. But as the culture of extended families and respect for elders eroded, so did the quality of life. The gang crimes that had once fulfilled a twisted sense of community were now committed for money.

Senior citizens foolish enough to believe that their struggles had earned them the respect of the younger generation became robbery victims. Women were no longer sisters, but bitches. Children, increasingly enamored of pop culture, grew up too fast. The church, which had been at the center of every significant community gain, turned inward. The result of it all was chaos. And it seemed that no one could do anything to change it.

Roxanne Wilson saw it all happening, and considered leaving the neighborhood. But she was convinced that as a homeowner who worked in law enforcement, she was a much-needed stabilizing force there. So she decided to stay.

On the balmy summer day that she allowed her twelve-year-old son Rafiq to go out to play video games at a nearby deli, the streets were alive. Playgrounds pulsated to the thump of bass-heavy music. Charcoal smoke from grills mixed easily with the pungent scent of marijuana. Girls wearing scarves over rollers and jeans over curves displayed their hardened femininity like only West Philly girls could. And in the midst of it all was Rafiq—a bookish boy who took his parents' divorce a bit too hard and his love of Pac Man a bit too seriously.

He'd taken his usual route to the deli, down Thirty-sixth to Brown Street, then over to the corner of Thirty-fifth. He walked past the drug dealers who gathered there and into the deli with his friend Brian.

Each boy had a pocketful of quarters, and set out to play until the machine's top ten spots bore their initials. They were on their third game when the black Oldsmobile swung around the corner.

Both passenger-side windows slid open, and two shooters sprayed the sidewalk with bullets from semiautomatic weapons. The dealers on the corner scattered. Two ran toward the projects, while a third ran into the deli and dived toward the floor near the video game.

A hail of bullets crashed through the window. Patrons fled. Women screamed. Men dived for cover. When it was over, the dealer who'd been targeted got up off the floor, brushing broken glass from his hair and clothing. Brian got up next. He was stunned, but unhurt.

Rafiq lay still, looking as if he was asleep. It was only when the storekeeper turned him over, and the blood poured out of the gaping chest wound, that they knew he was dead.

Roxanne Wilson remembered the date clearly. She'd had it inscribed on a bracelet that she still wore every day: May 27, 1981.

According to the case file, Kenya was born the very next day.

Wilson looked at the file and wondered if God had taken her son from the world and replaced him with Kenya. If so, perhaps it was Wilson's job to make sure that Kenya made it through.

The thought of it gave her a portion of the peace she'd lost when her son died. But as she looked through the file and saw the events that had led to Daneen losing Kenya, the peace turned to outright horror.

Human Services had first become involved in Daneen's case when a neighbor called anonymously, in 1987, and informed them that Daneen was living in an abandoned house with six-year-old Kenya. The child showed signs of abuse and neglect. She was taken and, in accordance with procedure, given to a relative who was willing to care for her. While Judy took temporary custody of Kenya, Daneen entered rehab, and sixty days later, was reunited with her daughter in a homeless shelter.

Later that year, Kenya complained of body aches at school. A teacher sent her to the nurse, and a short examination revealed bruises on the child's neck, arms, and chest. Human Services was called in again, along with the police, and it was determined that Kenya had been beaten. Daneen was charged, convicted of child abuse, and placed on probation.

Two years later, Daneen failed one of the mandatory drug tests that were required as part of her probation. Rather than turning herself in for what she thought would be a stint in prison, she went on the run, taking Kenya with her.

It took the police warrant unit six months to find them. When they did, Daneen and Kenya were living in another abandoned house.

Daneen was working part-time as a farm laborer, and hustling the remainder of the time to feed her raging crack addiction. Kenya, who was malnourished, filthy, and bruised, was taken again. Daneen pleaded guilty to a misdemeanor charge of child abuse, was sent to a county jail for six months, and did another six months in a rehabilitation center.

Meanwhile, Judy petitioned family court for full custody. Noting a clear pattern of abuse, the court turned Kenya over to her, and from what Wilson could tell, social workers' follow-up visits to Judy's home revealed nothing suspicious.

In one review, a social worker wrote that Kenya seemed to be adjusting well. In another, she noted that the relationship between Judy and the child appeared to be close.

As Wilson continued to flip through the file, however, she saw numerous handwritten notes warning of possible drug activity at Judy's apartment. There didn't appear to be any follow-up, though.

Roxanne picked up the phone and dialed a friend who worked as a supervisor in police radio.

"Get me John Sutton, please."

She waited as the call was transferred.

"John? Roxanne Wilson. Can you do me a favor and look up a location history for the East Bridge high-rise, Apartment 7D?"

She waited while he punched in the information. When he came back on the line, he told her of the flurry of police activity at the apartment over the past two days.

"Early Saturday morning, there was an unfounded missing person call," he said. "There was an unfounded person with a gun call, too."

"Do you know who made that call?"

"Came from a phone booth at Ninth and Indiana. Then there was a narcotics arrest and a crime scene detail assigned there on Saturday morning. The detail was resumed a few hours later."

"Was there anything prior to that? Any 'Meet Complainant' calls or anything?"

She waited while he double-checked. When he came back, he told her that there was nothing.

"Thanks," she said, and hung up.

From what Wilson saw, there was more than enough blame to go around. Between the police department, Human Services, and her own family, Kenya had been let down repeatedly. But it had all begun with Daneen.

And as Wilson dressed to go back to the projects, she did so with the intention of finding out if it ended with her, too.

When Jim Wright finished questioning Daneen, Lynch grabbed her by the arm and half dragged her outside to his car. After they'd both gotten in, she tried to cut off what she believed would be another argument.

"Did you find out anything new?" she said, fidgeting under his piercing gaze.

"I talked to Tyreeka," he said. "She told me she left Kenya in front of the building on Friday night and went to a house on Thompson Street with a boy named Scott.

"I checked it out. Scott Carruthers is the boy's name. He and Tyreeka spent the night at his aunt's house on Friday. The aunt saw the two of them come in. Of course she didn't say anything, because Scott's drug money pays her bills. But that's neither here nor there. The important thing is, she didn't see Kenya with them. And my gut says she's telling the truth.

"After I left there, I went to Rochelle's apartment. She lost a fight with Kenya and Janay and apparently said that she was going to get them. But she really had no intention of doing anything, and even if she did, she didn't have the means."

"Oh," Daneen said, withering under his stare.

After a full minute of silence, she turned to him.

"What you keep lookin' at me for?" she said.

"I'm looking at you because you're in my way, Daneen," Lynch said angrily. "You keep running me down like you need to talk to me so badly. Okay, I'm here. So talk."

Daneen opened her mouth, then closed it because she didn't know if there was much left to say. Not about the past, anyway.

"I just want to help," she said, finally. "I don't want to feel like I can't do nothin' to bring my baby back. I tried sittin' back already, and I couldn't do it, 'cause that ain't me.

"Matter fact, it's a lot o' things I'm findin' out ain't me. Like Wayne—that's the guy I was seein'. I mean, he was nice and he wanted to take care o' me and all that. But I was just usin' him."

Her lips turned up in a half smile. "I know you think that's all I do, Kevin, but I don't. Not no more. I just can't use people like I used to. I guess I know too much about what it feel like to be used."

Lynch laughed bitterly. "Nobody ever used you unless you wanted them to, Daneen," he said. "And they never used you unless you were getting something in return."

"I wish that was true, Kevin. I wish I could say I always got what I wanted out o' everybody that ever used me."

She sat for a moment, looking as if her mind was someplace else.

"But I guess that don't matter now," she said. "The only thing that matter is findin' Kenya. I can't sit here and wait for her to come home, Kevin. 'Cause when I sit back, my mind start tellin' me all kinda crazy shit.

"I start thinkin' I should be the one missin', 'cause Kenya ain't do nothin' to deserve this. All she was tryin' to be was a little girl—somethin' I probably ain't never give her the chance to do."

"Kenya's best chance is for you to leave me alone," he said harshly. "Just stay out of my way and let me work. I don't need any distractions."

"Is that what I am to you, Kevin," she said, looking up at him. "A distraction?"

He looked away and gazed out the driver-side window. "I don't know what you are, Daneen."

She looked down at his hand, which was resting on his knee. Then hesitantly, almost timidly, she reached out and held it in her own.

"I think you do know," she said softly. "I used to see the way you stared at me back in the day when you thought I wasn't lookin', Kevin. Even after we stopped bein' friends, and I would see you in the street. You would go your way, and I would go mine. But I could still feel your eyes all over me."

Lynch continued to gaze out the window. He didn't say anything, because he knew she was right.

"I used to wonder when you was gon' say somethin', Kevin. I used to wait for you to try to talk to me. In a way, I guess I wanted you to, 'cause you was different. You had went to that private school and talked all proper and shit."

They both smiled at that.

"But you wasn't no punk, either," Daneen said. "You knew how to hold yours. Lookin' back now, you was the kind o' boy we all shoulda wanted. But I guess we ain't know no better."

Lynch sat quietly, recalling his youth with Eunice Lynch, the woman he'd called Grandmother. He remembered the way she controlled him from the time she'd become his foster mother. He remembered the vicious beatings that she would administer for violations of her strict rules. He remembered that, as he got older, she warned him to stay away from Daneen. He remembered, most importantly, that he listened.

He sighed as the memories came back to him. And with the return of those memories, the hostility he'd been harboring for years seemed to lessen. It didn't disappear, however. It only changed shape.

"I guess it didn't matter what either of us wanted," he said wistfully. "Like my grandmom used to tell me: Everything that look good to you ain't good for you.

"That's what I used to think of when I would look at you. I would see the little girl who made me feel welcome when I came here. I would see the one person who played with me and didn't make me feel like an outcast. And when I saw you growing older, it hurt me to see what your life was turning into."

"So why didn't you ever say anything to me?"

"I did, Daneen. I said what I had to say, and you ignored me. I talked, and you kept right on doing what you were doing. I wanted to come to you. I wanted to grab you by the hand and take you with me, take you to something more than what you were heading to. But then after I heard you let the guys from Poplar Street pull a train—"

"That was a lie, Kevin. That never happened. Them niggas on Poplar Street couldn't get nowhere near me. And when I kept tellin' 'em no, they started goin' around makin' up these lies about me. I knew people was gon' believe what they wanted to believe, so I just ignored it. Wasn't nothin' I could do to change nobody mind, anyway."

"So why didn't you tell me that?"

"Would it have made a difference, Kevin? You already had your mind made up about me, and so did your grandmother. I guess, lookin' back, I can't blame her for tellin' you to stay away from me."

Lynch looked at her, then looked past her, back to the time when, as a teenage boy, he'd tried to stand up to Miss Eunice for the one person in the Bridge who mattered to him—Daneen.

It was a Saturday, around six o'clock, on one of the hot summer nights when the projects seemed poised to bubble over into something dangerous.

Kevin was fourteen and he wanted to go to a house party that night, in the first-floor apartment where redboned twin sisters lived with a young mother who was almost as fine as they were.

He'd already finished the list of chores he had to do every Saturday morning, and he had promised Daneen that he would meet her there. The only thing left to do was to get past Grandmom. And that wouldn't be easy to do.

He was in the bathroom peeling Ms. Eunice's old knee-high stocking off his head. And just as he was preparing to melt another layer of Royal Crown grease into his hair with a hot washcloth before brushing over his waves with a soft-bristled brush, she walked past and spotted him.

"Where are you going?" Ms. Eunice said, stopping at the bathroom door wearing the flower-print housecoat that hung like a tent over her considerable girth.

"Remember I asked you about that party downstairs? You said if I finished all my chores I could go."

"Yes, I remember saying that," Ms. Eunice said, watching him with shining eyes set in smooth, reddish brown skin.

He looked in the mirror, slowly brushing his hair, and studied her reflection as she stood in the doorway behind him. He could tell that she was turning the thought of the party over in her mind, because her eyeballs were pointed toward the silver-gray hair that extended back from her forehead in long, silky strands.

"Who's going to be at this party?" she asked.

"Heads, Eric, Shawn, Steve, and Tyrone, probably Benny and Robby."

"No," she said, folding her arms and exposing the jiggling fat underneath them. "Turn around, look at me and tell me who's going to be at this party."

He complied, trying not to show his exasperation. "Heads, Eric—"

"I heard that part already. Tell me what girls are going to be there."

"The twins, Freda, Gail, Crystal, Tonya, Roberta. You know, just some girls from the building."

"What about Daneen?" she asked, cutting straight to the point. "Is Daneen going to be there?"

Kevin considered lying. He knew he only had a second's hesitation before she would scrap the idea and tell him no.

"She might," he said, studying his freshly washed Jack Purcell sneakers in an effort to look nonchalant.

"Then you can't go," she said, turning and walking toward her bedroom.

Kevin felt his face grow hot with anger. He'd always listened to her before. But this time, after he'd worked so hard—after she'd already told him yes—he couldn't let it go.

"Why can't I go to the party?" he said, following her into her bedroom.

She was reaching down into the space next to her bed as he spoke.

"What did you say?" she asked with her back to him.

"I said, 'Why can't I go?'" he repeated, already regretting that he'd questioned her.

She turned around wielding a walking stick, pointing it at his head and walking toward him as he backed slowly out of the bedroom.

"Let me tell you something, boy," she said, reveling in the fear that swept over his face as she waved the stick.

"I didn't raise you all these years, make sure you did well in school, wash your clothes, take care of you, just to watch you throw it all away over some whore from these projects."

"Grandmom, I just wanted to go to the party," he said, his eyes filling with tears.

She ignored him. "I figured when you got big enough, you would try something like this. But boy, don't ever try to test me. Not for Daneen or for anybody else. Because I told you once, and I'll tell you again. That girl Daneen is trouble. She smokes marijuana, and I've smelled alcohol on her more than once. She's having sex, too. I can see it in the way she walks. And I'll be damned if you're going to go messing with that girl and come back here talking about she's having your baby."

"We're just friends, Grandmom. I wasn't trying to—"

"Shut up," she said, backing him against a wall in the hallway. "I see how you look at her, Kevin. Don't tell me what you're not trying to do.

All that playing together was fine when you were kids. But that's over now. So don't ever let me catch you with that girl again. Because if I do, I swear, as God is my witness, I'll kill you myself, just to save you the trouble of spending your life tied to somebody like that."

She held the stick aloft for a few minutes more, searching his eyes for any remaining signs of rebellion. Then, suddenly, she swung the stick with all her might, striking his skull and splitting open his skin. He screamed out in pain, and she sent him to his bedroom. He remained there for the rest of that weekend, licking his wounds and trying to purge himself of the girl who'd stolen his heart.

"Kevin," Daneen said, dragging him back to the present.

He looked at her, sitting just two feet away, and realized that he still hadn't managed to get her out of his system. Though their lives had gone in completely opposite directions, they had come together again for Kenya.

And as the two of them sat in his car, trying to work through the emotions that had always been there, Lynch fingered the scar that he still bore on top of his shaved head—a reminder of his grandmother's disapproval of Daneen. He knew that he might never truly purge himself of her. And that, more than anything else, frightened him.

"Kevin, I wanna ask you somethin'," she said in a whisper.

He looked at her and felt the lost years pulling at him, even as the thought of his wife and child lingered in the back of his mind. He looked at her, and they were both teenagers again, with a world of endless possibilities in front of them. He looked at her, and she spoke his very thoughts.

"I need to know what it coulda been like if things was a little bit different," she said, leaning toward him.

He looked down at her hand, which was still holding his, and then at her lips moving toward his. The answer to her question spun through his mind like a flash of light. It was a picture of them wrapped around one another in the steamy heat of a long-ago summer. He tried to see if there was anything after that.

Then his cell phone rang.

Daneen jumped back. Lynch reached into his pocket for the phone, knowing that he wanted her as much as she did him.

"Hello?" he said, answering the phone.

The blood rushed from his face as he listened to the voice on the other end of the line.

"I'll be right there," he said.

"What is it?" Daneen asked.

"It's my wife," he said, reaching over to open her door. "She's at the hospital. I have to go."

As Daneen stood at the curb and watched him drive away, she knew that there was something to what they'd felt a few seconds before. She wondered if they would ever feel it again.

The walls of the shooting gallery seemed to close in on them, even as Sonny lay next to Judy, watching the color of night play against her face.

She'd just fallen asleep, worn-out, no doubt from the stress of two days on the run. Sonny stayed awake on pure will, because he knew that he couldn't afford the luxury of rest.

He got up and looked out the window, watching the streets grow thick with the chaos of nightfall in the Badlands. The number of addicts—riding through in cars and walking up to dealers and hustling to get more—seemed to grow with each passing minute. And so did Sonny's need to get out of the house. He couldn't stay there any longer. It just wasn't safe.

He slipped on the shirt and pants he'd gotten from the Dominican's house and tucked the gun into his waistband. Then he reached down for Judy, who lay on the mattress, half dressed.

He caressed her face, and at his touch, she brought her knees up to her chest.

Sonny was about to shake her awake, but stopped when he heard the sound of a creaking step. He was still for the next minute. When he heard nothing else, the hairs on his neck stood up, because a heroin shooting gallery shouldn't have been that quiet.

He reached for Judy again. But this time, it wasn't the sound of a step that stopped him. It was greed.

Sonny looked at the backpack at the foot of the bed and thought of the thousands of dollars inside it. The moment he decided that he needed the money more than he needed Judy, all hell broke loose.

A man burst through the door feetfirst, tumbling into Sonny as Judy came awake with a start. The force of the collision knocked both men against the wall, but Sonny recovered quickly. He snatched the gun from his waistband and in one smooth motion, brought it crashing down on the back of the man's hooded head, knocking his hunting knife to the floor.

A second hooded assailant was through the door before the first one fell, squeezing off three rounds that punched holes in the already crumbling wall. Sonny ducked. Judy dived to the floor and landed next to the first man.

As Sonny prepared to squeeze off a round, Judy came up from the floor with the hunting knife, slicing into the flesh between the second man's legs. He dropped his gun with a scream and fell to one knee. Sonny stood over him, kicking the gun away.

The first one got up and tried to attack, but Sonny turned quickly and fired. Blood and bone exploded from his head as the man fell back against the wall, and was still.

As Judy fastened her clothes, Sonny snatched the bag from the foot of the bed and dragged the one with the knife wound over to the wall, sitting him next to his dead partner.

He aimed the gun at his head, then reached down and snatched off his hood.

When they saw his face, both Sonny and Judy knew they'd been betrayed.

"Who sent you?" Sonny said to one of the guards who'd escorted them from Pablo's house.

The man smiled through the pain of his shattered leg.

"Nobody sent us. Our shift was over at the house. We knew you had a bag full of money, and we came to get it."

"So Pablo ain't know about this?" Sonny said.

"Pablo would kill me if he did."

Sonny straightened his arm.

"I'ma save him the trouble," he said.

The man tried to go for a gun that was tucked in the small of his back, but he didn't have a chance. Sonny shot him dead with such an easy brutality that, for the first time, Judy was truly afraid.

She stood frozen until Sonny grabbed her hand, and they made their way down the steps to the front door. The heroin addicts had been evacuated prior to the robbery attempt. That's why the house was so quiet. The owner was sitting on a stool by the door with his throat slit—a victim of the would-be robbers.

Judy watched it all and was suddenly overcome with a fit of uncontrollable shaking. She'd seen two men die in front of her, and was standing next to a third dead man whose body was still warm.

Sonny ignored her and looked out the front window, examining the streets and the rooftops for signs of more men. He didn't see any, so he turned to Judy.

"Get up against the wall," he said as he held the gun at her temple.

"What you doin', Sonny? I thought——"

"I know what you thought, Judy," he said coldly. "But I told you I can't love you. I never could. Now get up against the wall."

She backed up, looking at him with slack-jawed disbelief.

He ripped her cotton shirt from her chest and used the cloth to tie her hands as she struggled in vain.

When he'd finished with her hands, he tied her feet. Then he stood up, panting from the struggle.

"Good-bye," he said simply.

And with that, he walked out of the house, leaving her there in the midst of death, with hurt and anger and fear and betrayal pouring out from her eyes in bitter tears.

Sonny had no time for such feelings. He walked quickly toward the bustling drug corner of Eighth and Cambria Street, looking for a way out. When he found it, he moved slowly, waiting for the car he'd targeted to stop in traffic. It did, and Sonny reached inside the open window and held the gun at the head of a blond-haired boy whose baseball cap bore the logo of a local university.

"Get out the car," he said quietly.

The boy's three young passengers looked from Sonny to the driver. Then they looked down at the crack they'd bought two minutes before, and suddenly, the drugs didn't seem so important.

"I said get out the car," Sonny said. "All o' y'all. Right now. And take them drugs and shit with you."

The four of them did as they were told.

Sonny got into their car and sped toward Germantown Avenue, leaving the students in the middle of Cambria Street, at the mercy of those who would abuse them.

Hopefully, it would take a while for them to get to the police, Sonny thought as he zoomed toward Center City. That would give him the time he needed to get out of Philadelphia.

But now that Pablo's men had tried to kill him, receiving help from the Dominican was no longer an option.

He would have to make his escape on his own.

Chapter Fourteen

A few minutes after Kevin drove away, Roxanne Wilson pulled up outside the Bridge, spotted Daneen walking toward the building, and called after her.

"Wait a minute," she said, getting out of the car and running toward her. "I need to talk to you."

Daneen folded her arms in quiet defiance. She had just talked through almost twenty years of bitterness and resentment. She didn't know if she could talk anymore.

"Do you have a minute?" Wilson asked as she caught up to her.

"It depends on what it's about," she said.

"It's about Kenya," Wilson said, walking back toward the car. "Take a ride with me."

"A ride where?"

"Nowhere in particular," Wilson said, stopping. "There's just a few things I need to go over with you."

Daneen hesitated.

"Come on," Wilson said, smiling. "It won't take long."

Daneen followed the detective to her car, and the two of them got in and rode slowly through the streets Daneen had walked a thousand times in the last two days.

"I was doing some reading a little earlier," Wilson said as she turned the corner at Fairmount Avenue. "Seems there's a lot to your relationship with your daughter. You want to tell me about it?"

"Ain't a whole lot to tell. I had a daughter. I got on drugs. They snatched her from me and gave her to Judy."

"That's a real simple explanation."

"Well, what is it you wanna know?" Daneen said, sounding more than a little irritated.

"Let's start with why you got on drugs in the first place," Wilson said, turning north on Sixteenth Street and riding through a pocket of poverty rivaled only by the projects.

Daneen tried to figure out where to start. Unable to think of a place that would allow her to sum it up easily, she chose to start at the beginning.

"My mom died when we was real little," she said softly. "I was, like, five, and Darnell was seven. We ended up movin' up here with my aunt, 'cause we ain't really have no place else to go. I guess that's why I made friends with Kevin, 'cause I knew what it was like for him to have to come here from someplace else.

"By the time I was maybe thirteen, I was smokin' weed and drinkin' beer like everybody else. I guess I was kinda young to be doin' all that, but it really wasn't no thing to me. I could take it or leave it.

"I ain't really start havin' a problem 'til I was in my late teens. My body had changed a lot, men started payin' attention, and my life started gettin' real complicated.

"Niggas was runnin' around sayin' I was a hoe, sayin' they slept with me, tryin' to say all kind o' shit that wasn't true. My girlfriends started shyin' away from me, guys was scared to talk to me, especially the ones I wanted.

"By the time I did have sex for the first time, it was with some guy from down Eighth Street. I was like, this is it? This what y'all been sweatin' me for? Shit hurt like hell, it lasted for, like, two minutes, plus the nigga was smellin' like forties and cigarettes. I'm like, 'Damn, least you coulda slapped on some cologne or somethin'.' "

Wilson cracked a smile at that. She could relate.

"By the time crack came out, I guess 'round '85, I had dropped out o' high school, and I already had Kenya. Then Tyrone died."

"Who was Tyrone?" Wilson asked.

"He was my boyfriend when I had Kenya."

"Was he her father?"

Daneen smiled ruefully. "No," she said, growing more comfortable with the truth. "No, he wasn't."

"So where's her father now?"

"I'm not sure who her father is," she said, looking out the window as they passed by the crowd of people who were gathered at Broad and Girard.

"Well, we don't have to talk about that now. You were telling me about the drugs."

Daneen skipped over all the things she'd told herself she'd forgotten. And she gave Wilson only what she could bear to say.

"I was just kinda driftin' after Tyrone died," she said. "I was workin' here and there, but mostly I wasn't doin' much o' nothin'.

"A lot o' stuff happened, things I still can't really talk about, but I guess the reality o' my life just came down on me all at once. But that wasn't why I started smokin'.

"At first, it was just, like, somethin' to do. Judy was sellin' it, so I tried it. Course I had to sneak and do it. But when I did, I ain't see what the big deal was. So I tried it again.

"I guess it was like the fourth time when I finally got this rush that made me feel like I was someplace else. I mean, it was like I was seein' and hearin' shit that wasn't even there. I was feelin' somethin' inside me that I had been lookin' for all the time. Somethin' that was too good to be true. Turned out that it was.

"I took Kenya with me all through my addiction, and she seen some things that she really shouldn'ta seen. I did some things I shouldn'ta done, too."

"Things like what?" Wilson said.

There was a long pause as Daneen ran through a litany of offenses in her mind.

"I don't want to talk about it," she said quietly, turning to look out the window again.

Wilson didn't press. She drove around the block, stopping in front of the family shelter on Broad Street off of Fairmount Avenue.

"Let me jog your memory," she said, pointing at the building. "You lived here for a while, but before that, you lived in an abandoned house. And when they found you there with Kenya, there were bruises all over her body. And that wasn't the last time. There were two more times after that. When they finally gave Kenya to Judy, you'd been labeled as an abusive mother, and there was no way you were going to get your daughter back."

Wilson turned to Daneen and looked her in the eye.

"I understand disciplining your children, Daneen. I spanked both my sons when they were coming up. But when you take a little child and beat them black-and-blue—when they've got bruises up and down their arms and around their neck—there's something wrong with that."

Daneen sat still and said nothing, afraid to look at the detective for fear the truth would show in her eyes.

"Tell me why you beat your daughter every time she lived with you, Daneen. What was it that made you treat her that way?"

Daneen's face filled with sorrow at the memory of what she'd done. She tried to think of an answer, but all the explanations sounded convoluted when she listened to them in her mind.

"I ain't sure," she said as she wrung her hands nervously. "I mean, I guess it was a lot o' things goin' on."

"You keep saying that. But that's not telling me anything. What kind of things were going on? Was it the addiction? The homelessness? Or was it something else—something deeper than that?"

"It was me!" Daneen said, screaming as she turned to Wilson with anger etched on her face. "I ain't want no baby tyin' me down, holdin' me back, and every time I looked at her I thought o' that. That's what you wanna hear?

"How about this? It was my childhood. It was my mother's fault. I ain't never know my father. My aunt was mean. Pick one.

"It was all that shit the therapists tell you it is when you go to rehab, and they sit there and try to pick your life apart when they don't know nothin' about you.

"It was all that, okay? That's why I beat my daughter."

Daneen rolled her eyes and turned slowly, retreating back into herself.

"I don't think it was any of that," Wilson said as she studied Daneen's face. "I think you regret every time you put your hands on that child. I think it still hurts you to think about it, especially now that she's missing."

She paused. "I came down here to see if we should be looking at you as the main suspect in your daughter's disappearance, what with your documented record of abuse. But I think now there's something else I need to ask you—something that's very important for us to know if we're ever going to find your daughter."

Daneen turned to her and waited.

"We need to know where her father is," Wilson said earnestly. "For all we know, her father might have abducted her. Parents do it all the time, Daneen. And if that's what Kenya's father did, we need to start looking for him."

"Her father ain't do that."

"How do you know?"

The question threw Daneen for a loop. She hadn't expected it.

"I know 'cause he with Kenya," she said haltingly. "He in everything she do and say. He in the way she talk. He in her smile. He in her eyes. Maybe that's why I would get high and beat her like that. Told you that shit made me see things that wasn't there, and when I smoked it and looked at my daughter, I would see him."

Daneen shivered at the pictures in her mind. And then she sighed and admitted the truth she'd always known.

"I guess when they took her it was the right thing to do," she said.

"You told me a few minutes ago that you didn't know who her father was," Wilson said firmly. "But if you saw him in your daughter, you obviously do. Now I'm gonna take you down to Central Detectives, and I'm gonna have you make a statement. And before we leave there, I need you to tell me who Kenya's father is. And I need you to tell me where I can find him."

Lynch sped north on Germantown Avenue, from the filthy ghettos of impoverished North Philadelphia to the quiet prosperity of Chestnut Hill.

He weaved in and out of traffic, expertly navigating the narrow, two-way street, with its slippery trolley tracks and slow buses. And he did it while dodging in and out of oncoming traffic as his heart pounded in his chest.

The Chestnut Hill Hospital nurse had told him that his wife, Jocelyn, was hemorrhaging and about to undergo surgery.

The fear was compounded by the guilt he felt over admitting his feelings for Daneen. While his marriage wasn't perfect, and had been in a steady decline since the loss of their baby six months before, he still belonged to Jocelyn. More important, he still wanted to.

It was Jocelyn, after all, who had dragged him, kicking and screaming, from his shell during his sophomore year at Penn. It was Jocelyn who had showed him who he was.

They'd met during an annual campus screening of black independent film. He'd come alone, and sat in the far corner of the lecture hall, hoping to avoid those conversations that invariably came down to background.

He often found himself deflecting questions, changing subjects, hoping to hide where he'd come from. He hadn't learned to celebrate who he was because he'd spent too much of his life trying to rise above it.

That night, as the lights went down in the lecture hall, the first film—an intense short that examined the lives of Africans on a slave ship—shocked most of the audience into silence.

Lynch was silent, too. Not because he was shocked, but because he'd learned that even among his own, it was frowned upon to be too black in the Ivy League. So he never laughed too loud, or smiled too broadly. And when everyone else was silent, he went along with the crowd, holding back who he was for the benefit of the whole.

Jocelyn had no such reservations. She was high-yellow with waist-length dreadlocked hair. She wore African garb that flowed with the perpetual breeze that cooled the tree-lined campus. She laughed loud, hard, and often. And silence just wasn't her style.

She came to the screening late, made an entrance that drew stares from the bourgeois students she loathed, and sat next to Lynch in the corner. When the first short was over, and she'd observed their staid reaction to the stark realities of slavery, she shook her head sadly.

"Most of these folks come from those same people on those ships," she said, loud enough for some of them to hear. "And yet they come to a little Ivy League university and they feel like they've arrived."

Lynch had remained silent. He hadn't even looked at her. But from the moment she spoke, he loved her. Not romantically. That would come later. He loved her for giving voice to what he'd always felt, but never had the courage to share. He loved her because she was the only genuine person he'd encountered since moving from the Bridge to the campus.

After the screening, he mustered the courage to ask her to a coffee shop. She accepted. They talked for hours. Or rather, he talked. She just listened.

He told her about his grandmother, and how she'd raised him with harsh words and heavy sticks that forced him into manhood. He told her about the public tongue-lashings and private beatings that took that manhood away.

He told her of the time she'd burned him with a hot iron because he hadn't finished pressing his clothes. He told her of the weekend he'd spent locked in a closet for refusing to finish a bowl of cereal, and the night he'd spent in the hallway for missing his nine o'clock curfew. He told her of the beatings with extension cords and walking sticks, and showed her the scars he'd hidden for years.

He told her about it all. And when he'd laughed and cried, remembering the woman who'd abused him into surviving the Bridge, he shared the biggest secret of them all.

He told her that his grandmother had been dead for three days. The funeral was the next day, and he was thinking of staying away.

Jocelyn looked at him with eyes the color of honey, and she wrapped both his hands in hers.

"You can't stay away from that funeral," she said. "So I'm going with you, Kevin Lynch. I'm going with you to celebrate the woman who loved you enough to protect you."

"I wouldn't call scarring me for life protection."

"Scarring?" she said incredulously. "She might've been rough on you, but you're nineteen years old, and you've got friends who are dead. You're alive. But not only that, you're at Penn, getting the kind of education most people just dream about. You're not scarred. You're blessed."

She shook her head. "I don't care if there's not another soul at that funeral. You're going, and I'm coming with you, because without Miss Eunice Lynch, you wouldn't even be here. And we would all be a little bit poorer."

They married a year before Lynch graduated with a degree in criminal justice. They had one daughter, Melanie, and were devastated by the loss of their second child, who was conceived six years after the first.

When Jocelyn lost the baby, everything, including their sexual intimacy, was nearly destroyed. It was like they were physically and emotionally absent from one another.

Lynch was at once angry and saddened, deprived and desperate because his marriage was falling apart. So he chased Sonny more relentlessly, remembered his childhood with more pain, hated Daneen more intensely, and wanted her a little more. But within the lies that his emotions told, there was this reality: He wanted his wife to love him the way she used to.

Somewhere beneath the pain of their lost child, she did. And as he barged into the hospital, past the uniformed guard who asked him to sign in, Kevin Lynch was propelled by that love.

"Where's my wife?" he said to a doctor standing next to a curtained-off cubicle.

"What's her name?" the doctor said.

"Excuse me, sir," the guard said, coming in behind him. "You have to wait outside. You can't come in here until you sign in."

"My wife is supposed to be in surgery right now," he said. "I want to know where she is."

"Sir—"

"It's all right," the doctor told the guard. "I can show the gentleman to his wife."

The guard left. Lynch gave the doctor her name, and a few minutes later, he was with her in a room in intensive care, holding her hand and fingering her dreadlocks as he gazed into her drowsy eyes.

"Are you all right?" he asked.

"I am now," she said, smiling as her sedative took effect.

"How did the surgery go?"

"I didn't need surgery," she said slowly. "I did have some bleeding, though. They think it's residual effects from the baby. They're going to keep me overnight for observation and run some tests. Mom's got Melanie at the house."

"So you're all right?"

"I'm fine, baby. I've just been lying here thinking about you. Seems like I haven't seen you in days."

"I didn't think you noticed," he said despondently.

She closed her eyes and licked her lips, then opened them and studied his face, trying to remember how his mouth looked when he laughed. She hadn't seen him laugh since they'd lost the baby. She missed that.

"You must have the patience of Job," she said. "I know it must be hard living with someone who blames everybody for something that nobody can control."

"I don't know that I'm all that patient," he said soberly. "I guess I'm just learning to wait. You do that when you don't have a choice.

"And the way I see it," he said, playfully pulling at her hair, "I don't have a choice, because I love you."

She closed her eyes and smiled as he reached down and kissed her forehead.

"I saw the news today, Kevin. They said you were suspended. When were you going to tell me?"

"I didn't want you to worry, Jocelyn. And I still don't. We've got some money saved up, and this thing'll go to an arbitrator in a few months. In the meantime, we'll survive."

"Are you sure? Because I can—"

"We'll survive," he said firmly. "I'm sure."

She was quiet because she knew that he would take care of things financially. It wasn't the suspension that worried her. But something did, and Kevin knew it.

He sat back and waited for her to tell him what it was. He didn't have to wait for long.

"I saw the interview with Jim Wright," she said, avoiding his eyes as she spoke. "That woman looks like she's heartbroken over her daughter."

"She reminds me of you," he said gently. "She wants to do something to bring her baby back. But sometimes there's nothing you can do."

"Kevin," she said, suddenly staring up at him, "why are you still working on this case when you've been suspended?"

He fingered her hair for a few minutes more.

"I'm working on it because Kenya was my friend Tyrone's daughter. At least he thought she was."

"Are you sure that's the only reason?" she asked worriedly.

"What's that supposed to mean?"

"I saw the end of the interview on Channel 10. I saw the way she leaned on you when she started crying. I saw the way you held her. That's not your job, Kevin. So I'm going to ask you, and I want you to tell me the truth. Do you feel something for her?"

Lynch touched his wife's face and kissed her hands.

"You're my wife, Jocelyn. I feel something for *you*. And even though we're going through a rough spot right now, I still only feel for you."

"But Kevin—"

He kissed her and she responded, placing her hand on his face. The kiss was tender, reassuring, gentle.

"Get some rest, Jocelyn. And trust me. I need you to trust me."

A few minutes later, when Lynch left the hospital to head back to North Philly, he knew that his wife would do that.

He just wondered if he trusted himself.

Sonny drove to Center City and jumped from the car with its engine running, smiling at the irony as he left it in front of the offices of the Philadelphia Parking Authority.

He knew he didn't have long to make his move, but with darkness descending over the city, he had more of a chance than he would have had in daylight.

So he walked up tiny Filbert Street to the Greyhound bus station, where taxis stood ready at the curb, then waved at the first one he saw. Before the cab could pull out, another cabbie shot in front of it from the other side of the street.

A man jumped out of the first cab, speaking in Swahili as he berated the Hindu cab driver who'd cut him off. Horns sounded as traffic backed up. The cab drivers continued to argue. It looked like they might come to blows.

A police officer came out of the bus station and walked up to the cab drivers.

"Both of you move your cars now."

"He tried to cut me off from my fare," the African said.

"I didn't," the Hindu driver said. "He's lying."

"Where's the fare?" the cop said. "Show him to me."

"He's right over ..."

The African looked around for Sonny, pointing to the spot where he'd stood just seconds before. But he was gone.

Walking around the corner to Center City's busiest thorough-fare—Market Street—Sonny hoped that the beat cop hadn't seen him and that the police car that was approaching him from behind would pass by.

When the car drew near to him, he put down the backpack and reached down as if he was tying his shoe. It passed, and he picked the bag up, walking as quickly as he could without running.

When he reached Market Street, there were cars everywhere. Too many cars for a Sunday, he thought. And in Sonny's paranoid mind, all of them were undercover police.

He sat down in a bus shelter and hunched over as he watched for cabs. He saw everything but. Buses passed by him. So did cars, bicycles, and pedestrians.

All of them seemed to look at him as if they knew who he was. He sank down even lower in his seat, telling himself that he was imagining things.

When he finally saw a cab, he stood to flag it down, and the cabbie pretended not to see him.

"Racist bastard," Sonny muttered, returning to his seat in the bus shelter.

Another cab approached from the opposite direction. Sonny took out a twenty-dollar bill and waved it. The cabbie made a U-turn and screeched to a halt in front of him.

Sonny opened the door, threw his backpack in the backseat and got in. Before the cab could pull off, however, a police car approached with dome lights flashing. Sonny reached into his waistband and put his hand on the butt of his gun as the police car pulled alongside the cab.

The cabbie rolled down his window. "Yes, Officer."

"There's no U-turns here," the cop said. "Next time, go around."

"Sorry, Officer," the driver said.

The cop nodded and drove away. Sonny released his grip on the gun. The driver looked in the rearview mirror.

"Where to, buddy?"

"How much would you charge me to drive me down to Bear, Delaware?"

"That's an hour drive," the cabbie said. "I'd have to get the money up front. And it'd have to cover my cost there and back."

"I'll give you $400," Sonny said, peeling off four crisp hundred-dollar bills.

"You sure about that, buddy?" the driver said, taking the money and placing it in his shirt pocket. "I was only gonna charge you $350."

"You drive the speed limit and let me get a nap on the way down, I'll pay you another hundred when we get there."

"You got it," the driver said, pulling off and heading in the direction of I-95.

As he did so, Sonny sat back and thought of the whirlwind of the past few days. He thought of Judy and Daneen, Lily and Darnell. And even as the motion of the car lulled him to sleep, his last waking moments were filled with the little girl he'd loved as his own.

Darnell's head was swimming with memories of his childhood, visions of his future, shadows of his past, all mingled together like a vivid, unending nightmare.

It was a nightmare he could no longer endure. So he sat on the floor, wondering how he would get his next high. Wondering how he would forget everything that had happened in the past two days. He sat there, wanting crack so badly that his empty stomach flipped at the thought.

One way or another, he was going to feed that hunger. And then, somehow, he was going to forget what had happened to Kenya.

He fingered the two dollars that Daneen had given him. He thought of the things Daneen had said to him, and the things she'd done over the years, and he realized, at that moment, that he resented her.

He disliked the way she spoke down to him, as if her newfound sobriety made her better. He hated the way she insulted him when he asked her for money. But more than that, he hated himself for having to do so.

He sat there, remembering the way Daneen had always treated Kenya, and he was saddened. He remembered how Daneen had cast her daughter aside when she was clean, and the way she had beaten her when she was high. He remembered how Daneen would always act as if she was sorry about it all.

But none of that mattered now. Kenya was gone. And in Darnell's mind, it was Daneen's fault. He didn't want to have to deal with that reality. The less he had to think about it, the better off he would be. So he hoisted himself off Judy's floor, intent on hustling up enough money to get high.

Before he could make it out the door, however, someone knocked.

Darnell looked up and thanked God for the visitor he believed to be his girlfriend, Renee. She must have come to her senses and returned to apologize, he reasoned. Maybe she even had some crack.

He snatched the door open with a grin that quickly faded when he realized that it wasn't her.

"Judy got somethin'?" the visitor asked in a slow Southern drawl.

Darnell looked at the old man they called Monk, with his gray hair and hunched back, standing at the door looking desperate.

He wondered why Monk kept coming back to Judy's apartment. Each time he came there, he was victimized. And the last time Darnell had seen him was no different.

Monk had paid Judy five dollars to go into the bedroom with a woman on Friday night, shortly before Kenya had left the apartment to go to the store. As always, the woman emerged from the room first. Monk came out a few minutes later, his face etched in crack-induced confusion. It was a look that soon disintegrated into anger, because Monk knew that the woman had picked most of his Social Security money from his pockets. She hadn't even given him the sex she had promised in return.

But in spite of what had happened to him on Friday, here was Monk again, standing at Judy's door, waiting for more of the same. As bad as Darnell knew his own addiction to be, he believed that Monk's was worse. Because a man so old shouldn't want to be abused that way.

"You ain't hear Judy got popped?" Darnell asked.

"I been sleep," Monk said. "I can't stay up two and three days like y'all. I needs my rest."

"You could get your rest if you stop comin' in here smokin' that shit and take your crusty ass down the Senior Center somewhere."

"Ain't enough goin' on down there for me," Monk said with a mischievous grin.

"Well, Judy ain't here," Darnell said as he started out the door. "Ain't nothin' happenin'."

"Why don't you stay here and smoke this reefer with me then?" Monk said, pulling out a Phillie Blunt filled with marijuana. "I be done keeled over tryin' to smoke this by myself."

Darnell smiled. There was something about Monk that always made him smile.

"Come on in here, Old Head."

Darnell closed the door and sat on the floor as the old man sat in Judy's chair, watching him.

"Can't sit on that floor," he said, grinning as he took a toke. "Time I bend down that far, I won't be able to get back up again."

He coughed, then sat back in the chair and handed the blunt to Darnell, who took a puff and handed it back.

"You heard Kenya missin', right?" Darnell asked.

Monk, who was preparing to take another toke, stopped with the blunt halfway to his mouth. His eyes filled with a momentary grief, then he held it to his lips and inhaled.

"I seen Kenya Friday night after I left outta here," he said.

"Where you see her at?" Darnell asked quickly.

"I was walkin' down the street out front, lookin' for that girl who got me for my money," he said, passing the joint back to Darnell before continuing.

"Don't ask me what I was gon' do to her, 'cause I don't know my damn self. But by the time I figured I needed to come on back inside and go to bed, it was after ten. I came on up to the fifth floor and tried to go to sleep. But with them knuckleheads down the hall playin' that music all loud, I couldn't, so I came out. I was gon' try to go on back downstairs and look for the girl again."

"That was kinda late for you to be out, wasn't it, Monk?" Darnell asked, passing the blunt back to him.

Monk took a long drag of the marijuana, watching the smoke swirl from the tip and float toward the ceiling.

"Ain't matter to me," he said, smiling contentedly as his eyes closed to slits. "Wasn't like I had nothin' for nobody to take. So I went on down the hall and pressed the button for the elevator. Course it took all long—longer than usual—so I turned around to go 'head back in my apartment."

He passed the blunt back to Darnell, who greedily sucked in the smoke.

"I heard the doors open, though, and when I turned around I seen Kenya."

"What was she doin'?" Darnell asked, taking another toke and passing the blunt back to Monk.

"She was standing there lookin' cute," the old man said, smiling again as the marijuana brought on a slight dizziness. "Almost looked like a little woman. Like a real pretty little woman."

"So what you sayin', Monk?" Darnell asked, growing tense.

"I'm just sayin' I seen her, and she was pretty."

"What you doin' lookin' at a little girl like that?" he said.

"Come on, Darnell," Monk said nervously. "You know I ain't mean it like that. I just seen her on the elevator, and I thought she was pretty, that's all. I ain't mean nothin' by it."

"Well, where she go when you seen her?" Darnell asked, standing up. "Was she with somebody? Did you see who she was with?"

"Course I seen who she was with," Monk said as Darnell towered over him.

Darnell reached down and lifted the confused-looking Monk from Judy's chair.

"I want you to show me who she was with."

Chapter Fifteen

Wilson and Daneen walked into the cigarette smoke that shrouded Central Detectives and emerged from it like ghosts, standing in the middle of the room and looking for Lynch.

A few detectives looked up from their battered steel desks as the clatter of ancient typewriters and the hum of inane conversation filled the room.

Wilson walked up to a detective who was busy typing up a report. "Where's Kevin?"

He stopped and looked up at her like she was stupid to ask such a question. But then he saw the earnestness in her face.

"You didn't hear about it?" he said.

"I heard he got suspended over the Baylor thing, but I didn't know whether it was true because I haven't talked to him."

"You heard right," he said offhandedly. "Thirty days with intent to dismiss."

Wilson stood there for a minute, unsure of what to do.

"So who's the lead detective now?" she asked.

"You might want to talk to the captain about that."

Wilson looked around for someone she knew. When she didn't see anyone, she turned back to the detective in front of her.

"This is the missing girl's mother—Daneen Brown. Is it okay if she sits with you for a few minutes until I come back?"

"Sure," the detective said, pointing behind him. "Captain's office is that way."

"Thanks," Wilson said, walking over to the office and tapping on the door.

The captain opened it. "Come in and have a seat, Detective Wilson. I've been expecting you."

She did as she was told, watching him with a cynicism that came through in her silence.

"I just got off the phone with your captain over at Juvenile Aid," he said, sitting down and leaning back in his chair. "We've decided that since you've already been sort of working the case unofficially, we're going to give JAD the lead on this. You'll be assigned to it, which should give us a head start."

"Sir, if you don't mind me asking—"

"That's just the point, Detective. I do mind. The only thing you need to know is that Kevin Lynch has been suspended for his role in that chase yesterday, and we don't want anybody else's career to suffer because of that unfortunate incident. Do I make myself clear?"

"Crystal," she said sarcastically.

"I'd check that attitude if I were you," the captain said as he picked up a file from his desk.

Wilson pursed her lips as he put on a pair of reading glasses and began flipping through the file.

"Central will provide whatever support you need—manpower, equipment, whatever," he said. "And of course we've still got people assigned to the search for Sonny Williams and Judy Brown. South and East Divisions do, too.

"But you won't be involved in that. You'll focus on the girl," he said, handing her the file.

She opened it as he spoke.

"We're still treating this as a missing person, as you know, and we believe that there's still a good chance of finding her. It's only been two days. Of course, the longer it goes, the more likely it is that we'll have to start treating it differently."

Wilson didn't respond. She didn't have to. They both knew what that meant.

"That file's got everything we have so far," the captain said. "It's based on the few interviews we've been able to conduct with neighbors and the missing person report that was filed by the child's mother. You'll also find a copy of the DHS file there. You might want to take a look at that."

"I already have a copy of the DHS file," Wilson said.

"How'd you get that?"

"I called in a favor," she said. "But what I saw there was a little troubling. That's why I brought the mother down here to question her. She's sitting outside with one of your detectives."

"Good," the captain said. "I just perused the file myself, and from what I see, we might need to take a closer look at her. I'm sure you can handle that."

"I'm sure I can, sir," she said, looking more confused with each page she turned. "But these interviews—I mean, is this all we've got?"

"We really haven't been able to get much from the people up at East Bridge," the captain said. "Maybe that's my fault for sending a bunch of white cops to the projects with notepads and pencils and expecting them to come back with answers."

"Can I be frank, sir?"

"I wouldn't expect anything less."

"I think Kevin Lynch probably needs to be involved in this investigation. He grew up there, he knows the people, and he knows the rules. But with him being suspended..."

"I see where you're going," the captain said. "Now I'm going to be frank. The decision to give Lynch the suspension didn't come from me. It came from the top. The media had the story, and we couldn't just sweep it under the rug. Baylor was a hero to just about everyone in this city. He was getting ready to run for D.A., and if he'd lived, he would've won. If we sat back and did nothing, people would've been on that black talk-radio station tomorrow saying it was some kind of setup. That woman on that morning show would've dragged the commissioner in there and grilled him on the air. Then the mainstream papers would've gotten a hold of it, and before long, it would've looked a lot worse than it is."

Wilson didn't argue. She knew the truth when she heard it.

"But I know Kevin Lynch," the captain continued. "I've worked with him for three years, and I've never seen a guy as committed to finding the truth. The suspension's gonna be overturned—hopefully sooner than later. I mean, none of us are stupid here. I've literally seen cops kill people, get fired, and reinstated within a year by an arbitrator.

"But the suspension's not the issue here. Because suspended or not, nobody's going to stop Kevin Lynch from going up there and finding out what happened to that little girl. He said as much when he left here this morning, and I believe him."

"But can I work with him on this?" Wilson said.

The captain looked down at the floor as he spoke.

"Officially, I don't know if Lynch is still working on this case or not. Unofficially, I'm getting word back that he's already got a lot more than we do."

The captain paused before he continued.

"What I'm saying to you is, if the two of you share information on an informal basis, I don't see any harm in that. My concern—whether you believe it or not—is finding the girl. Not the politics of it, not making the department look good, not covering my ass. I want that little girl found, and I don't care how that happens. I just want to make sure that it does."

Wilson closed the file and sat in her seat, reflecting on what the captain had just said.

"Thank you, sir," she said, her mind already back to the case. "Is that it?"

"No," he said. "There's one more thing. When you go back up to the Bridge, I want you to deliver a message for me."

"What's that, sir?"

"Tell Kevin Lynch I said hello."

"I'll do that," she said, standing up.

But as Wilson left the captain's office and grabbed Daneen for the return trip to the projects, she wasn't the only one carrying a message.

Judy looked across the dark hallway at the dead man. He was leaning back against the wall, his bloodless face frozen in surprise.

His throat was slit in a straight line, and blood dried in ragged clumps against his shirt. But even in death, his upturned hand was extended, as if he was waiting for payment from one of the many addicts who patronized his house.

The hallway, which would have normally been filled with people shooting heroin, was silent. With two dead men upstairs and another just a few feet away, that silence frightened Judy. And as she tried to free her hands from the bonds Sonny had fashioned from her shirt, the sounds of the street scared her even more.

She heard breaking glass and imagined more robbers coming for her. She heard laughter and imagined the dead men coming back to life. She heard running water and imagined blood, pouring down the steps. She heard gunshots and imagined that she would soon be dead, too.

She worked feverishly to untie the bonds that held her hands behind her back, twisting and rubbing and pulling at them until the skin broke and the warm blood ran against her wrists.

Several times during her struggle, people knocked at the door.

They were stuffers—heroin addicts—looking to come in and get high. She considered calling out to them, but never did. She was, after all, bound and helpless. And if someone were to find her that way, there was a chance she might never make it out alive.

After a half hour of pulling at the strips of fabric, she realized that her struggle had tightened the bonds. She was starting to lose feeling in her hands, and as the desperation set in, the fear increased. She started to cry. Not because of the fear, but because of the pain Sonny had inflicted on her.

She looked around, trying to find something she could use to cut the ties. She didn't see anything sharp enough, so she leaned back against the wall and tried to push herself up with her feet. She fell the first few times. But after fifteen minutes of trying, she managed to stand up.

She hopped down the hall, then up the stairs and into the back bedroom. Though the two men had been dead for less than an hour, the smell of congealing blood, torn flesh, and gunpowder combined to form an almost unbearable stench.

Judy tried not to look at them as she scanned the room for the hunting knife she'd used earlier. She spotted it on the floor, near their feet, and bent down to get it. She fell, bumping into one of them, and let out a startled yelp as the dead man's hand brushed against her back.

Trembling, Judy scooted along the floor until her hands were next to the knife. Then she reached down and grabbed it, feeling the man's dried blood on the handle as she worked the knife against the cloth.

After a full minute, she felt the fabric give way, and when her hands were completely free, she reached down and untied her feet. When she was finished, she stood up, zombielike, and walked down the hall to the bathroom. She ignored the black mildew that seemed to grow in every corner, and turned on the faucet, rinsing the blood from her hands.

She didn't bother to dry them. She didn't see the need. She simply walked down the stairs, past the dead homeowner, and out the door.

With her tattered, bloodstained shirt hanging from her shoulder in strips, she walked down Cambria Street, nearly naked from the waist up.

Dealers and addicts alike watched her as she passed them, her glassy eyes and slow gait convincing them that she was high.

"She musta smoked some wet," someone said, garnering nods of agreement.

But Judy hadn't smoked the embalming-fluid mixture that made its users think they could fly or walk naked in the street. She'd succumbed to a high of a different sort.

Hers was the kind of high that made her believe there was love in the drug game. The kind that convinced her that she could change a hustler into something more. The kind that told her she could dream of a new life.

Her high was lies. And she'd believed every one she'd ever told herself.

So as she made her way to Germantown Avenue, walking past the cemetery she'd passed on her way into the Badlands, Judy no longer believed anything. The only thing she knew to be real was death, because she'd seen it up close and lived to tell about it.

She walked up the hill and into the busy street, ignoring the sounds of blaring horns as cars swerved to avoid her. Her eyes were focused on everything and nothing as she moved toward her new reality—the one in which Sonny no longer existed.

She knew what she was looking for. It was only a matter of finding it. And as a police van rolled toward her with flashing lights, she stopped in the middle of an intersection and waited for it to come to her.

When the officers got out of the van and turned her around to cuff her for what they believed was public drunkenness and nudity, she smiled and spoke in a clear voice that froze them in their tracks.

"I'm Judy Brown," she said. "Y'all been lookin' for me since early yesterday. I wanna talk to Detective Kevin Lynch. I got somethin' to say about Sonny Williams and my niece, Kenya."

The officers looked at each other, unsure of what to make of it. Then one of them pulled off his hat and looked inside at the pictures of Sonny and Judy that had been distributed at roll call.

"That's her," he said to his partner, who got on the radio and called for a supervisor.

Within minutes, they were transporting Judy to the Twenty-fifth District, where she was placed in a locked cell before being transferred to police headquarters in Center City.

She was put under guard and taken into an interrogation room. And then they lit into her, one after the other, wielding their questions like bludgeons.

But after hours of questioning by a team of four detectives, Judy sat at the table with a half smile, feeding them the same response she'd given from the beginning.

"I ain't talkin' to nobody but Kevin Lynch," she said, staring straight ahead with eyes that had forever been changed by Sonny's betrayal.

"Y'all can either get him in here, or I'll take it to my grave. I done already died anyway, so it don't make no difference to me."

As he returned to the Bridge from the hospital, Kevin Lynch felt like he was walking out of his new life and back into his old one.

Since Friday, transitioning between the two had become increasingly difficult, especially with thoughts of his wife and career piled atop childhood memories of beatings and unrequited love, dead children and friends killed for drugs.

He forced himself to ignore those things, however. Because he was determined to face his ghosts.

As he got out of his car and walked toward the building, he marveled at the darkness that enshrouded the Bridge. He knew that it came from the grief over Kenya's disappearance. But he also knew that in spite of the pall that hung over the building, it still held light.

There were childhood games and innocence, mother love and healing, selflessness and dreams. All these things existed within the walls of the Bridge. Lynch knew that, because those things had allowed him to escape.

He only hoped those things could emerge once more. He hoped that they could save Kenya.

And so, Lynch walked into the building and did what he'd intended to do before he'd received the call about his wife. He stood in the middle of the foyer and tried to imagine that he was Kenya, preparing to go up to the tenth floor and ask for permission to stay the night at Tyreeka's.

He immediately noticed that the guard booth was occupied for the first time since he'd come there on Friday.

"How you doin', man?" he said, walking over to the gray-haired, bespectacled man sitting behind the inch-thick glass.

The security guard nodded warily. Lynch figured he had seen more than his share of everything while working there, and found silence to be the best response to most of it.

"My name is Kevin Lynch," he said, smiling. "I'm working on the Kenya Brown disappearance, and I was wondering if I could ask you a few questions."

"Cops already been through here," the man said as he smoothed down his light-blue uniform shirt. "But I'll tell you like I told the other ones. The guy that was supposed to be here Friday night probably wasn't on his post when all that happened."

"Well, if he wasn't here, where was he?"

"I don't know. But I'll tell you this. He miss a lotta nights. I ain't tell them other cops this, but I think he on that stuff. Course it ain't my job to supervise him, so . . ."

The old man let the sentence trail off.

"Was he supposed to be here last night, too?" Lynch asked. "Because I was here yesterday, and I didn't see a guard in the booth."

"Listen, man. The company don't really pay us nothin', so it's a lotta nights when guys don't show up."

"What about you? Do you miss nights, too?"

"I been workin' all my life," the old man said. "I don't know how to do nothin' else but show up. They pay me, and I do my job the best way I can."

"So what exactly is the job?" Lynch asked.

"Well, we supposed to make people that don't live here sign in when they come to see somebody in the buildin'. A lot o' times that don't happen, 'cause people just walk on by. But that's what we supposed to do."

"Did you ever notice the people who visited Judy Brown's place?"

"Judy Brown on the seventh floor? Shit, you can't help seein' the people that go in and outta there. It's like the Hit Parade up there. And I ain't talkin' about no music."

"What do you mean?"

"The hit parade, man. That's what I call it, anyway. 'Cause every time I come in here, I see people paradin' up to Judy place to get a hit."

Lynch couldn't help smiling as the old man pressed on.

"You could look at most of 'em and see they was on that stuff. Most of 'em ain't sign in, but the people that did, they usually put phony names on the sheet. Matter fact, here go a old sign-in sheet right here. Take a look. You'll see what I'm talkin' about."

The man reached underneath the desk in the guard booth, pulled out a few curled sheets of paper on a clipboard, and handed them to Lynch.

Lynch looked at the names with Judy's unit number next to them and copied them down in a notebook.

"Did you or any of the other guards ever call the police and tell them what you thought was going on up there?"

"You learn to mind your business," the man said. "You gotta get off work at night, and you don't want nobody knowin' you tried to cause problems in here, 'cause it's a long four blocks to the subway."

"I understand," Lynch said. "You see and you don't see."

"That's right," the old man said, bobbing his head vigorously.

"What about Kenya Brown, the little girl I'm looking for," Lynch said, pulling out her picture. "Have you ever seen her before?"

The man looked at the picture. "Yeah, I seen her. It's hard not to see her. She different from a lot o' these other little girls you see runnin' in and outta here. She still got a little bit o' innocence about her."

"Ever talk to her?"

"She would wave, and I would wave back. But no, I never talked to her. People get funny when you talk to they kids."

Lynch thought for a moment, looking around the foyer and trying to imagine where Kenya would have gone first when she came back in on Friday night.

"I guess, if you saw her coming in and out a lot," Lynch said as he looked around, "you would have noticed if she liked the elevator more than the stairs."

The man nodded. "I did. She took the stairs most o' the time. Course she knew, just like everybody else, that the elevator was real slow. But there was one other thing I noticed about her."

"What's that?"

"At night, especially if it was a lot goin' on in the buildin', she would wait for the elevator. I think she mighta been scared to take the stairs by herself. Tell you the truth, I can't blame her."

"Why do you say that?"

"A lotta shady folk be hangin' in that stairway at night, especially on the weekend. One boy like to hang in the stairway and act like he crazy—talkin' to hisself and what not. I think he on that stuff, too."

"Do you know his name?"

The old man was about to say it, but a group of residents came into the building, watching as he talked to Lynch.

Figuring it would be better if they didn't hear him give the name, he wrote it out on a piece of paper, folded it, and handed it to Lynch, who opened it and read it.

"He usually be up there at Judy apartment," the guard said. "That's where he like to hang at when he ain't in the stairway. But I guess with Judy gone and everything shut down up there, you might find him in that apartment up there on six."

"Thanks," Lynch said, folding the paper and putting it in his pocket. "I appreciate your help."

"Don't thank me," the old man said. "Just find that girl. She a good little girl. She ain't never bother nobody."

Lynch nodded and walked over to the elevators a few feet away. He pushed the button, then looked at his watch to time its arrival. It took a little over a minute and a half for the doors to open.

And when he got on, he could feel the very thing he'd been hoping to find. He could feel Kenya's spirit.

Wilson heard the news of Judy's arrest as she left Central Detectives. But instead of going to police headquarters by herself, she dialed Lynch's cell phone.

When she got an automated message saying the phone was inactive, she loaded Daneen into the car, and the two of them tore out of the parking lot with a portable siren blaring in the unmarked car.

"Did I hear them say somethin' about Judy?" Daneen said, as they raced through Chinatown on the way back to North Philadelphia.

"They said Judy's at the Roundhouse," Wilson said, referring to Philadelphia police headquarters. "She's asking for Lynch. I'm going to go get him."

"How you gon' do that when he suspended?" Daneen said impatiently. "Why don't you just ask her whatever you gotta ask her yourself?"

"Why should I start questioning Judy again when I still haven't gotten a straight answer from you, Daneen?" Wilson replied, as the car sped past the male prostitutes who frequented the dark corners of Thirteenth Street near Callowhill.

"I don't know what you talkin' about," Daneen said.

"Sure you do. I'm talking about Kenya's parents. You and her father."

"I can't get into that," Daneen said through clenched teeth. "Why can't you just respect that? Why you tryin' to make me tell you somethin' that ain't got nothin' to do with findin' my daughter?"

"Can I tell you something, Daneen? I just left Captain Silas Johnson, commander of Central Detectives, who placed me in the lead of this investigation and told me to do whatever I have to do to find your daughter.

"He thinks like anyone else would think after taking a look at the file from DHS. He thinks you look like a pretty good suspect, based on the way you used to bounce your daughter around when she was with you."

"He can think what he wanna think," Daneen said flippantly. "I know I ain't have nothin' to do with it."

"I know that, too," Wilson said. "But you're hiding something from me—something that might help me find your daughter. That's obstruction of justice, and I can lock your ass up for that, Daneen. So you can either tell me what I want to know, or we can hold you in the Roundhouse and feed you cheese sandwiches for a week because somebody accidentally lost your paperwork."

They pulled up in front of the Bridge and parked behind Lynch's car.

Wilson got out first. "Don't answer me yet, Daneen. Right now, we've gotta find Kevin. Because if Judy says she'll only talk to him, he needs to be there. But I'll tell you this much. You will answer me. One way or the other, you're going to tell me who Kenya's father is."

Renee had spent most of the afternoon trying to figure out what she'd done to anger Darnell. She knew that his temper was volatile— especially when he wanted to get high. But the way he'd blown up when she'd mentioned Kenya wasn't about a high. It was about grief. And Renee was determined to make that grief go away.

As she made her way back to the Bridge with the crack she'd hustled turning tricks for the past few hours, she hoped that the peace offering she'd brought with her would be enough to earn his forgiveness.

When she walked in through the back entrance of the building and saw Darnell coming toward her in the foyer, she had reason to believe that it was.

"What's goin' on, baby?" Darnell said, smiling as if nothing had happened.

"That's what I should be askin' you," Renee said cautiously.

He sighed and threw an arm over her shoulder.

"I'm sorry about earlier," he said. "I guess this thing with Kenya just startin' to get to me."

"I know it is. But I got somethin' to make you feel better."

She opened her hand and showed him ten capsules of crack. He reached out for them, and she pulled them back, stroking his crotch with her free hand.

"You gotta earn these," she said with a grin.

"Don't play with me, Renee. I ain't in the mood for that shit right now."

Her grin faded, and her pale skin grew red. And in a rare moment of defiance, she told him what she thought.

"I know you don't really want me, Darnell. But you ain't gotta act like it. I mean, I ain't Lily, but at least I'm here with you. That's more than I can say for her."

"Lily ain't got nothin' to do with this," Darnell said.

"No, she got everything to do with it. I think that's why you treat me the way you do—'cause I ain't her. That's why one minute you sayin' you sorry and the next minute you tryin' to take it out on me again. Maybe I should just take my little shit someplace else and smoke it. Maybe then you'll be happy."

She fell silent and waited for a slap, or one of the other abuses she'd come to expect from him.

Darnell just stared at her. He wasn't used to her standing up for herself, and he didn't know quite how to respond.

When finally he spoke to her, it was with a vulnerability she didn't know he possessed.

"It ain't you," he said. "It ain't Lily, either. It's Kenya. I guess I ain't know I cared about her that much, 'til it hit me a little while ago. I was smokin' a blunt with Monk, and he started talkin' about how Kenya look like a pretty little woman. I'm listenin' to him, and I'm thinkin' this the man that did somethin' to my niece.

"I started to kick his ass right then. But somethin' told me not to. I guess it was a good thing, 'cause a few minutes after that, he said he saw Kenya on the elevator with this dude Friday night. I made him take me out to try to find him. We walked around the block a few times, even looked around the buildin', but we ain't see nobody."

"Who was the guy Monk seen her with?" Renee asked.

"He said he ain't know who it was. But I think Monk just old. He probably thought he seen Kenya and ain't seen nothin'."

"So where Monk at now?" Renee said.

"I guess he went back upstairs to his apartment. I don't know. All I know is I can't look no more. Seem like that's all I been doin' these past couple days is lookin'."

Renee looked at him with something approaching sympathy. Then she reached up and rested her pale hand against his dark brown skin. "Let's get outta here for a minute. It's a house down Poplar Street we can go to. You ain't gotta think about Kenya for a little while."

Darnell stared down at Renee, almost gratefully. But when she took his hand and led him out the back entrance of the building, Darnell knew, for the first time in years, that crack wasn't going to solve anything.

Chapter Sixteen

Lynch got off the elevator and walked down the deserted hallway to 6D—the apartment number the guard had written down for him. When he knocked, the unlocked door creaked open.

A cold puff of air whisked out of the apartment and clung to him as the pungent scent of smoke filled his nostrils.

He walked in coughing, noting that the plastic floor tiles were burned black. Some of the walls were charred, revealing gray cinder blocks behind the damaged Sheetrock. Water damage had left plaster and paint peeling from the others.

Lynch was so caught up in the sight of it all that the slamming sound startled him.

Reaching for the gun that he kept under his jacket, Lynch wheeled on the man who'd shut the door.

Bayot didn't move. He simply stood against the wall, staring at Lynch with more curiosity than fear.

"Who are you?" Lynch said.

A wide smile creased Bayot's face.

"Had a fire in here a while back," he said, ignoring Lynch's question. "Floor a little burnt up."

Lynch chambered a round in the gun. The sound of the metallic click filled the space between them.

"I said, who are you?" Lynch repeated forcefully.

Bayot's smile disappeared quickly and he stared down at the floor.

"Who are you, who are you?" he chanted, as his face transformed into that of an angry little boy.

Lynch started to respond. But then the man looked up, and Lynch caught a glimpse of his eyes.

The person trapped behind them was not the burly, forty-year-old man whose gray-flecked, unkempt beard grew out from leathery, almond-colored skin. The person behind those eyes was a child.

"Bayot," Lynch said, easing the gun back into its holster as he spoke in soothing tones. "That is your name, isn't it—Bayot?"

His eyes grew wide and his head moved in circles as he tried to form a word.

"My name is Bay-ard Jack-son," he said with much effort. "They call me Bayot."

"Okay, Mr. Jackson—"

"Bayot."

"Okay, Bayot. I'm sorry I had to come in without your permission. But I needed to ask you about something. Is that okay?"

The soft words seemed to relax Bayot.

Lynch reached into his jacket pocket and pulled out the picture of Kenya. "Do you know her?"

Bayot looked timid, almost afraid.

"It's okay," Lynch said. "You can tell me. I'm looking for her, and I thought you might have seen her, that's all."

Bayot stuck a finger in his mouth and smiled. "That's Kenya," he said.

"That's right," Lynch said. "Kenya Brown. Can you help me find her?"

Bayot covered his face with both hands and smiled mischievously. "She pretty," he said, giggling. "Pretty little girl."

Lynch felt a knot forming in his gut.

"Are you friends with her?" he asked cautiously.

Bayot's smile faded as sadness turned down the corners of his mouth.

"She don't wanna be my friend," he said. "She scared o' me."

The sadness turned to dejection.

"She too little to play with me anyway. Plus Mommy said don't play with little girls, so I don't."

"Who's your mommy?" Lynch asked.

"Mommy don't live here no more," he said matter-of-factly. "She died."

"So you've been living here by yourself since then?"

"I don't live here. I live in a group home on Eighth Street. They keep takin' my SSI check, talkin' 'bout it's for my rent and for my food. So I be leavin' sometime, and when I do, I get my check and I go upstairs with Judy and them, or I come down here so nobody won't bother me."

"Were you there on Friday? At Judy's, I mean."

Guilt swept over Bayot's face, and he was silent.

"What's wrong?" Lynch asked.

"You gon' tell on me."

Lynch watched him for a moment, trying to figure out what he meant. He decided to gamble.

"I already know you smoke the crack Judy sells," Lynch said. "You know you could get locked up for that, right?"

Bayot averted his eyes and nodded slowly.

"I don't want to see that happen," Lynch said. "And if you help me find Kenya, it won't. But if you don't help me, I'm going to have to tell. And then they're going to put you in jail for smoking crack. You don't want that, do you?"

Bayot's eyes filled with tears as he shook his head vigorously from side to side.

"Good. Now I'm going to ask you again. Did you see Kenya on Friday?"

Bayot shrank back against the wall and began to cry. Then he sat down on the smoke-damaged tiles, trembling.

"Did you see her on the staircase?" Lynch prodded. "Somebody told me that you like to play on the staircase."

"You gon' tell," Bayot said, rocking back and forth with his arms around his knees.

Lynch hesitated, then came over and sat down next to him. "I promise I won't tell," he said, looking the man in the eye.

Bayot studied Lynch's face. Then he let out a long sigh and stared straight ahead as the memories poured out.

"I just wanted her to play with me," he said nervously. "I ain't want to do nothin' to her. I just wanted somebody to play with. But Mommy said I'm too old to play with little girls. So I just followed her."

Bayot looked down at the floor, then over at Lynch, who sat silently waiting for the rest.

"I ain't want her to be scared o' me," Bayot said. "I ain't want her to think I was crazy, neither. 'Cause I ain't crazy. I just don't learn like other people do. Sometime it take me a while to figure stuff out, know what I mean?"

Lynch nodded.

"I figured Kenya out a long time ago, though. I knew she was nice, 'cause everybody wanted to be her friend. I guess that's why I wanted to be her friend, too. That's why, when I seen her comin' out Lily place the first time on Friday, I was gon' ask her to play with me."

"Do you remember what time it was when you saw her?" Lynch asked.

"It was nine o'clock, 'cause when I seen her, somebody had a radio playin' real loud, and they had said the time on the radio."

Bayot stopped and looked at Lynch for approval. He nodded. That pleased Bayot, so he continued.

"When I saw Kenya come out and start walkin' upstairs, I started comin' up the steps behind her. She looked back and I ducked down, 'cause I thought she wanted to play hide-and-go-seek. But then she started walkin' up the steps again. So I followed her again. She stopped and looked back like she was tryin' to find me. When she ain't see me, she started lookin' kinda scared, and she ran up to Judy apartment and went in."

"When I asked you if you were in Judy's apartment, you said I was going to tell. Did that mean you were in there?"

Bayot nodded bashfully.

"So if you were in there, how could you have been outside the apartment, watching Kenya go in?"

"I was in there early. But then I had spent all my money, and Judy told me I had to go."

He furrowed his brow and stuck out his bottom lip. "She always tell me I gotta go when I ain't got no more money."

"So why were you on the steps?" Lynch asked.

"I told you, that's where I be at," Bayot said. "Don't nobody mess with me there. They don't be callin' me crazy and stupid and all that other stuff."

Lynch felt sorry for him. But he didn't have time for compassion, so he pressed on.

"You said you saw her the first time around nine o'clock," he said. "So I guess that means you saw her again after that."

"Yeah, she came back out after while. I seen her comin' down the steps, and I thought if I let her see me, she might want to play. So I waited 'til she got down to, like, the third floor, and then I stood in front of her."

"Did she say or do anything at that point?"

"She told me to move. First I thought she was playin'. But then she pushed me and ran outside."

"Was that the last time you saw her that night?"

"I thought I saw her one more time. But I ain't sure, 'cause she was in the elevator."

"What did you think you saw?"

Bayot's eyes darted about like he was unsure of what to say.

"What is it, Bayot? What did you see?"

"I don't want to get nobody in trouble," he said.

"Just tell me what you saw."

"You gon' tell him I told," Bayot said, as more tears formed in his eyes.

"Tell me!" Lynch shouted.

Bayot jumped, covered his ears and began to babble. "I came up the steps, and I was just gon' go to sleep in here, but it was a lotta noise 'cause they was havin' a party, and I stopped on the steps and looked. Then I seen the elevator doors open and then Kenya was on there, and I ain't want her to see me 'cause I knew she was mad at me, so I backed up and peeped around the doorway. This man got on the elevator with her and it looked like she hugged him. And he hugged her back. And then the doors closed, and then I ain't see her no more after that."

He sat breathing heavily when he was finished. Lynch watched him, waiting for more. When nothing more came, he asked another question.

"Do you know who the man was who got on the elevator with her?"

Bayot nodded quickly.

"Who was it?"

"I don't know his name," he said. "He be up in Judy apartment, though. He be up in Judy apartment all the time."

Wilson and Daneen rushed into the building and up to Judy's, rightly assuming that they would find Lynch there.

When they walked inside and found Bayot standing next to him, Daneen was confused.

"What you doin' with him?" she asked, her eyes shifting from one to the other.

"The same thing I've been doing since Friday," Lynch said, avoiding her eyes for fear of rekindling their last conversation. "I'm trying to find Kenya."

"With him?" Daneen asked incredulously.

"He says he saw Kenya on the elevator on Friday night," Lynch said. "A man who hangs around Judy's got on with her when it stopped on the sixth floor. Kenya apparently knew the man pretty well, because she hugged him right before the doors closed."

Wilson glanced at Bayot. "Do you know who the man was?"

He looked down at the floor and shook his head no.

"Did you see what he was wearing?" Wilson asked.

Bayot looked away, afraid to speak to her.

"It's okay," Lynch said patiently. "She's a friend of mine. Her name is Roxanne. You can trust her just like you trusted me."

"Why are you talking to him like that?" Wilson said. "Is something wrong with him?"

"Bayot slow," Daneen said with a hint of annoyance. "People usually don't pay him no mind."

Wilson looked at Lynch. "Don't you think you're reaching here, Kevin?"

"I've talked to everybody else, and I've pieced together everything Kenya did on Friday, except what happened when she left Tyreeka. Bayot's the only one who saw her after that. Are you saying I should ignore that just because he's slow?"

"No, Kevin. I'm just saying he might not be all that reliable as a witness."

"Well, I don't care what you think," he said sharply.

Wilson took a step back, stretched her eyes wide, and met his attitude with one of her own.

"Look, Kevin. I know things have been a little rough for you with the suspension, and your wife getting sick, and whatever this thing is between you and Daneen. But don't try to take it out on me. In case you forgot, we're both on the same side, here. So you'd better start caring what I think, because when it all comes down to it, I'm your only link to the department—the same department that turned its back on you as soon as it needed a fall guy."

"That doesn't give you the right to question my judgment."

"If I question what you're doing, it's only because I'm trying to help you," Wilson said. "That is what you asked me to do when you called me in on this, isn't it? Or did you forget that, too?"

There was a moment of awkward silence. Then Lynch sighed.

"I'm sorry," he said. "This whole thing is just getting a little frustrating. When I came up here with Bayot, I was hoping he would see something that would jog his memory. But Darnell wasn't here— I guess he's somewhere smoking again—and Bayot says he doesn't remember the man's name that got on the elevator with Kenya."

Wilson reached into her pocket and pulled out a picture of Sonny. "Was this the man you saw?"

Bayot looked at the photo, squinting and turning his head sideways in an attempt to focus in. "I ain't sure."

"You ain't never sure," Daneen snapped. "Every time you open your damn mouth, you talkin' about you ain't sure, with your dumb-ass self."

Wilson turned to her. "Daneen, I think you need to calm down."

"No. I think y'all need to find my daughter."

"Tell you what," Wilson said, her eyes flashing anger. "You tell me what I asked you about, and we can start trying to find your daughter."

"I told you I can't do that, because I don't know who her father is."

"You're lying," Wilson snapped.

"You don't know that," Daneen said coolly.

"Look, we don't have time to waste," Lynch said. "So this is what we're going to do. I talked to the guard downstairs and got a list of people who come up here on a regular basis. Daneen's going to look it over and see who's legitimate. Then we can cross-check the list against police records and get Bayot to look through some pictures down at Central.

"Of course, I can't be the one to go with him. So maybe you can do that, Roxanne."

"Actually, that's what I came here to talk to you about," Wilson said. "The answer to this whole thing might already be down at the Roundhouse."

"What do you mean?" Lynch asked.

"They found Judy. They're holding her at homicide."

"So why aren't you down there questioning her?" Lynch asked.

"Because she says she has some information about Kenya and Sonny that she only wants to talk to you about."

"Well, that can't happen right now."

"Kevin, you don't understand," Wilson said. "It has to happen. I know you're angry that this thing came down to a suspension. But I talked to Captain Johnson today, and I don't think he'd object to you getting in there and doing what you have to do. That's just the feeling I get."

"Well, they're shit out of luck if they think I'm going down there to bail them out after what they did to me."

"Kevin," Wilson began.

Then Bayot chimed in.

"You told me you was tryin' to find Kenya," he said, looking at the floor and swaying back and forth. "You lied to me."

"No, Bayot, you don't understand. I was—"

"If you cared about her, you wouldn't care who made you mad. If you really wanted to find her, you would talk to Judy."

They were all silent as the truth of Bayot's words split the differences between them.

"You tricked me, just like everybody else be tryin' to trick me," Bayot said. "You don't care about Kenya. You only lookin' for her 'cause you wanna make yourself feel better."

Lynch looked at the faces around the room, and he knew that they'd all been wrong about Bayot.

And as they all left Judy's apartment to head down to the Round-house, Lynch was certain of only one thing.

Bayot was right about him.

Sonny struggled mightily, fighting against the hands that clutched at his throat, squeezing his windpipe shut and crushing the life from his body.

No matter how hard he fought, he couldn't break free. The fingers of the hands were too thick, the arms they extended from too heavy, the will of the attacker too strong.

"How it feel to die?" someone asked him through the darkness.

The words grated against Sonny's ears. Each one of them was a knife, cutting him as the question repeated, louder each time.

"How it feel to die?"

The voice was deep, frightening, ominous. And it carried the unmistakable stench of death.

"How it feel to die?"

Sonny tried to answer, but there was no wind to carry his words. He tried to fight, but there was no strength to wage his battle. He tried to pray, but there was no god he'd ever known.

And so he drifted, falling back into a place where his only link to life was the voice. He fell as his vision faded to black. He fell until the smell of death was gone. He fell until the voice called out to him again.

"How it feel to die?"

Sonny snapped awake, looking around in a panic as the cab driver tapped against the taxi's glass partition. Sonny blinked to clear his eyes, and when the fog began to lift, he looked around the cab to get his bearings.

He saw the backpack on the seat next to him, then looked out the window at the bright lights that illuminated the bus station. He looked at the man who was tapping on the partition, and all of it came roaring back to him.

"What you say?" Sonny asked in a drowsy voice as he rubbed the sleep from his eyes.

"I said, 'How do you feel?' You were moving around back there like you were having some kind of attack or something."

"I'm fine, man," Sonny said as he sat up. "What I owe you?"

"That depends. Bear doesn't have a bus station. We're in Wilmington. It was the closest one. That okay?"

"Yeah, that's okay," Sonny said, suddenly in a rush to get out. "What I owe you."

"Another hundred."

Sonny peeled it off, handed it to him, and got out of the cab.

As the taxi drove away, Sonny hoisted the backpack onto his shoulder and walked across Martin Luther King Boulevard to the bus station. His mind replayed everything that had happened since Kenya's disappearance—from his initial escape, to the daylong chase, to the murders in the shooting gallery. And finally, his mind went back to Judy.

He absently wondered if she was still there against the wall, her hands tied and her mind consumed with money. He smiled at the image, because in his mind, it confirmed what he'd always believed.

Sonny was better than Judy. He was better because he knew that in the dope game, money was all that mattered. He didn't confuse sex with love, or power with loyalty. Judy, on the other hand, had twisted it all into what she hoped it could be. That had weakened her. And that weakness had allowed Sonny to take everything.

As he walked into the bus station to purchase his one-way ticket to Miami, he was filled with the satisfaction of knowing he'd gotten over yet again. His only regret was that he didn't know what had happened to Kenya.

That, more than anything, wore on him. It made his sweet escape into a hollow victory.

After all, he'd never known love until Kenya. He'd never known that he could hope for someone else, hurt for someone else, want for someone else. But in her innocence, she'd shown him how to do all of those things. And he loved her for it—loved her like the granddaughter he'd never had.

That love had been tested daily as he watched Judy take away everything he'd ever given to Kenya. And while he'd pretended not to care, it had pained him to see Judy hurt her.

That's why it was so easy for him to betray Judy. In truth, it had given him pleasure to do so.

But now, as he stood in a near-deserted bus station in Delaware, he realized that the pleasure had faded. The one person he'd ever really cared about was gone. Nothing could bring her back. That saddened him. But not enough to deter him from what he had to do.

"What time that bus to Miami comin'?" he asked the clerk behind the sales counter.

She looked up at him with tired eyes. "Should be here in a half hour. About ten or so."

"Can you tell me where the bathroom at?"

The woman pointed to an arrow on the wall. Sonny followed it to the men's room, where he went into a stall, sat down on the toilet, and opened the backpack.

It was the first time he'd really looked at the money since he'd taken it from the roof of the Bridge. The sight of it was breathtaking—an endless sea of green.

He parted the stacks and reached down to the bottom. There were dozens of loose bills there—money that had worked its way out of the rubber bands that held the stacks together.

Sonny decided to take them out and arrange them into a separate stack. But as he gathered up the last few bills, he realized that there was something else.

When he pulled it out, he saw that it was an old diary of Judy's. He opened it and found that the white paper was turning yellow, and the blue ink was faded in some places. But the words were unmistakable.

Sonny began to read them, and he learned something about Judy that he hadn't known before. He learned that she had a conscience that wouldn't allow her to turn a blind eye to everything she saw.

As he read on, he discovered something about himself, too. He had a gift for peering through the details, sorting through the secrets, sifting out the lies, and seeing truth.

If the ten-year-old secret that the diary exposed was real, then he knew that the truth had come to him in his dream. He had seen it through Kenya's eyes.

He walked out of the bathroom and past the desk, headed for the door.

"Excuse me!" the desk clerk called after him.

Sonny turned around.

"There's been a change. The bus that was supposed to make the trip to Miami broke down. They had to get a replacement out of New York, but it won't be here 'til morning."

Sonny considered going someplace else—anywhere that would get him far away from Philadelphia. But going just anywhere wasn't an option. He had a plan, and he was going to stick to it.

"You're welcome to go to sleep in one of the chairs," the clerk said. "The bus should be here by six o'clock in the morning. That'll be here before you know it."

Sonny stood in the middle of the near-empty bus station for a moment, then shook his head slowly and sat down in one of the plastic chairs that were bolted to the floor.

The contents of the diary were still swirling in his mind. So he took it out of his pocket and stared at it for a moment. Then he walked over to a trash can and threw it away.

A few moments later, he leaned back in the chair and closed his eyes, hoping he could forget what he had read.

Chapter Seventeen

When they left the Bridge, Lynch took Bayot, while Wilson transported Daneen. They drove to the prisoner's entrance on the Seventh Street side of police headquarters in order to avoid the reporters who were camped out front.

Lynch could see them milling about as he got out of his car with Bayot and walked down the ramp that led to the basement holding area. He wondered how much of the real story the reporters actually knew. More important, he wondered how much of it he would learn by speaking with Judy.

Lynch walked through the door, and the police officers who worked as guards stopped to watch him as the prisoners raised their usual raucous cry from the large holding area known as the bubble.

Lynch stood still for a moment, unsure of why the officers had stopped working. Then one of them began to clap. Two more joined in, and then three. After that, the room exploded in applause.

Embarrassed, Lynch worked his way through the crowd to backslaps and words of encouragement.

"We're with you, Kevin," a gray-haired white officer told Lynch.

"Don't let 'em hold you down," said a female officer seated by a typewriter.

"You'll be back," said an officer who was standing next to the fingerprint station.

What they didn't know was that Lynch was already back. And he was going to make the most of his return.

He nodded his appreciation for the support of his fellow officers, and with Bayot, Wilson, and Daneen close behind, took the elevator up to the second floor.

When the four of them walked into homicide, a lieutenant scrambled to the door to meet them.

"Detective Lynch," he said, extending his hand. "I guess you've already heard that Judy Brown is asking for you."

Lynch took his hand hesitantly. He didn't know the man, and didn't care to. The only thing he was concerned about was finding Kenya.

"This is Bayard Jackson," Lynch said. "He says he saw Kenya on Friday night, and he may have seen a man who was with her on an elevator around ten o'clock. This is Kenya's mother, Daneen Brown, and this is Roxanne Wilson. She's the lead detective on the investigation into Kenya's disappearance."

"Good," the lieutenant said. "I can get some of my guys out here to take a statement from Mr. Jackson. Then we can interview Ms. Brown."

"No," Lynch said. "That's not the way we're going to do it. Your guys can interview Mr. Jackson. But Detective Wilson is going to question Ms. Brown while one of your detectives sits in."

"I don't know if you heard this, Lynch, since you're suspended and all," the lieutenant said sarcastically, "but Judy Brown did make one statement to us before she asked for you. She said Sonny Williams murdered two people in a heroin shooting gallery down in the Badlands. We found two bodies in the bedroom and another one downstairs. We're charging Williams with all three, which makes this a homicide investigation."

"Homicide or not, you've got one witness who says she knows

what happened to Sonny and Kenya. She only wants to talk to me. So we're going to do it my way. And it really doesn't matter to me whether you like it."

"I don't think you know who you're talking to, Lynch."

"I don't think I care," Lynch said. "I'm in charge here, or I walk."

Captain Silas Johnson, who'd sat in the back of the office watching them, got up from his perch on the side of a desk.

"So is that what we're doing now, Kevin?" the captain said as he approached the front of the office. "Giving everybody hell because poor Detective Lynch wasn't treated fairly?"

"No," Lynch said. "We're letting me do what I do better than anybody else you've got. But hey, we don't have to do that. I can turn around and go back out that door. Then you can explain to those reporters out there why a man who killed three people and injured three police officers is still on the loose, and the only one who's been punished for it is me."

"Come here," the captain said as he walked to a small office in the back of the room. "I need to talk to you for a minute."

"Last time you told me that I lost my job."

"Well, I guess that means you don't have anything to lose this time. Besides, it'll only take a minute."

He stopped next to a door, holding it open for Lynch, who eventually relented and walked back to meet him.

When they were both inside, the captain closed the door.

"Have a seat, Kevin."

"I prefer to stand."

"Suit yourself," the captain said, sighing as he sat down. "I didn't come down here to argue with you. I came because I wanted to be here when you arrived. I wanted to make sure you understood that I've already talked to the commissioner, and there's a good chance we can make all this go away."

Lynch looked at him with a cynicism that bordered on contempt.

"Okay, there's more than a good chance," the captain said, reading his expression. "We will make it go away. But we need you to do this thing with Judy. We need you to talk to her."

"I'm not here to get my job back," Lynch said. "I'm here to get the truth. And I guess I've already gotten part of it."

"Which part might that be?"

"The part about the department not giving a damn about me. Anytime you can make a suspension with intent to dismiss go away just like that, then there really was no need for the suspension in the first place, was there?"

"Look, Kevin—"

"Where's Judy?" Lynch asked. "You want me to talk to her, and that's what I'm here to do. You don't need to explain the politics of it, Captain Johnson. I get the politics."

The captain stared at him. "She's in the back."

Lynch walked out the door without another word, slamming it behind him and storming into the interrogation room, where Judy sat quietly between two detectives.

"Well, lookee here, it's the man of the hour," one of the detectives said bitterly.

Lynch ignored him. He'd seen his kind before. Young, white, and angry that a black cop was better at the job than he.

"How are you, Judy?" Lynch asked.

She looked at him with a quiet madness playing in her eyes. "I been better."

"I won't be needing either of you," Lynch said to the detectives. "You can both leave."

"We usually don't do one-on-one interviews in homicide," one of them said. "Especially with a male detective and a female prisoner."

"Well, homicide isn't handling this interview," Lynch said. "I am. And the video camera's on, isn't it? It'll all be documented. So if you'll excuse me, I need some time alone with Ms. Brown."

They walked out reluctantly, watching him over their shoulders as they left the room.

"They don't like you," Judy said, after the door closed.

"Fuck them."

"You shouldn't talk like that, Kevin. You know Ms. Eunice wouldn'ta liked you talkin' like the rest o' the folk from the projects."

Lynch picked up a chair from the far side of the room, put it down in front of Judy, and sat down.

"No," he said wearily. "She wouldn't like it. But then, there's a whole lot of things going on in the Bridge that she wouldn't have liked."

"I guess you right," she said, stopping to reflect on the truth in Lynch's words.

"You know, Kevin, I used to watch your grandmother and wonder why she was so rough on you. I thought maybe she ain't like you 'cause you wasn't her blood. But lookin' at you now, I guess she knew somethin' the rest of us ain't know."

"Yeah, she knew how to kick my ass when I didn't do what she told me to do," Lynch said.

"I think it was more to it than that. I think she knew somethin' I'm just now findin' out."

Judy smiled, but just barely.

"She knew the key to life is the company you keep," she said. "That's why she told you to stay away from Daneen."

"Judy, she didn't—"

"Yes, she did, Kevin. She told you to stay away from Daneen 'cause she saw where things was headed with her. She saw it even before I did.

"And when she saw that, she saw what this thing with Kenya is really about. I know you think it's the drugs and the hustlin' and all that. But that ain't what made this happen. The trouble with Kenya started before she was born. It started with everybody in my house, from me on down, lookin' for a way to feel better. Lookin' for somethin' to make the truth go away. See, you was there, but you ain't live the Bridge like we did, Kevin. Your grandmother made sure you hoped for somethin' different. We ain't have that. All we had was what we saw. And to us, the only way out was to hustle.

"We all thought Eunice was crazy for watchin' everything you did and everyplace you went. But I guess she wasn't. 'Cause while she was makin' sure you was comin' up right, everybody else in the Bridge was fallin' apart. Especially us."

"What do you mean by falling apart?" Lynch asked.

"That ain't important right now," Judy said earnestly. "What you need to know is what I called you down here to tell you. Sonny ain't do nothin' to Kenya. I thought he did in the beginnin', but that was just me bein' crazy. The truth is, I knew he had my money, and I was gon' try to get it back."

"What money?" Lynch asked.

"The money we had stashed in a backpack on the roof. The money we was gon' use to start over. Least that's what I thought. But Sonny had other ideas." She shook her head. "That's why he ran, Kevin. Not 'cause he did nothin' to Kenya."

"So where do you think he is now?"

"My guess would be he headed down Miami. I know he had some people down there he did business with sometime. He ain't never give me no names or nothin'. I guess he figured the less I knew, the better. And he was right, 'cause if I knew where Sonny was right now, you best believe I would tell you."

Lynch looked at her for a long time before he spoke.

"I don't believe that, Judy. I think you're just trying to buy time for him. Deep down, I think Sonny could do anything to you, and you would still love him. I think you need him to treat you the way he does."

"You mighta been right about that a couple days ago," Judy said. "But you ain't right no more. Sonny took everything I had and left me for dead up in a damn drug house. You think I'm still tryin' to protect him after he did some shit like that? You can believe what you want. But the truth is the truth."

"You've gotta give me more reason to believe you than that."

"It's like I told you," Judy said. "It all go back to Kenya and the fact that she ain't really have no business here in the first place."

"What's that supposed to mean?"

"It mean Daneen ain't have no choice but to lie about that baby and who her father is," Judy said.

"So you know who he is?" Lynch asked.

"I was never really sure. Daneen told me somethin' about it, but I ain't never believe her. I thought she was just makin' it up to get my attention. I ain't know 'til she had Kenya that it was true."

"Well, who is it?" Lynch said anxiously. "Who's Kenya's father?"

"You mean Daneen ain't tell you yet? All this time y'all done spent together these past couple days, and she still ain't tell you the truth?"

"Why should I have to hear it from Daneen?" Lynch asked "Why don't you tell me?"

" 'Cause she the only one who really know," Judy said. "I just think I do. She swore she wasn't never gon' tell nobody. And in all these years, she never did."

Staring across a scarred wooden table in another interrogation room as a homicide detective looked on, Daneen was getting annoyed with Wilson.

"Why you keep askin' me the same shit over and over again?" she said.

"Because you keep telling me everything but the truth," Wilson said. "But I'm going to do you a favor and share a little truth with you. Sonny's wanted for four murders, if you include the vehicular homicide that killed Judge Baylor. If you're holding something back from me to protect him, some smart prosecutor is going to want to try you as an accessory to those murders. So before we go any further, you might want to get a lawyer in here, Daneen, because this is serious."

Daneen stared at Wilson, trying with all her might to maintain her tough exterior. But she couldn't, and as her face crumpled, and the tears began to flow, the pain Daneen felt was not about Wilson and her questions. It was about herself.

She was tired of the secrets and lies that, for years, had helped her to maintain her sanity. She was tired of pretending that the truth didn't exist.

"Are you all right?" Wilson asked.

Daneen nodded.

"Do you want a lawyer?"

"I ain't do nothin', so what I need a lawyer for?"

"I don't know," Wilson said. "But I do need to know why you won't tell me the truth."

Daneen breathed in deep, steeling herself for what she was about to do.

"I guess it been so long since I took the truth out and looked at it, I don't even know what it look like no more. I just know it hurt."

"What's so painful about the truth, Daneen?"

"Same thing that's painful about it for everybody else," she said. "Truth don't dress up. It just stand there smilin' through them raggedy-ass teeth, lookin' at you like you crazy for callin' it ugly."

Daneen began to play with her hands, nervously pulling her fingers out of the sockets and causing her knuckles to crack.

"Truth was when my mom died and we had to come up in Judy house with nobody to look out for us. I guess that's what made me and Darnell so close. It's what made us look out for each other. See, if I was around, couldn't nobody mess with my big brother. Not even Judy. I remember the first time she tried to give him a spankin' for stickin' his hand in a socket. I stepped in the middle, little as I was, like I was gon' do somethin' about it."

Daneen smiled. "She whupped us both that day."

"But it wasn't all pain. It was plenty o' days when me and Darnell had all the fun in the world. We would push each other on the one Big Wheel we had between us. We would race up and down the sidewalks with our shoes off. We would hide in the closet and act like we was campin' out in the woods somewhere. When I got my first little boyfriend—I guess I musta been about nine—I kissed Darnell to see if I knew how to do it right.

"I guess it was around that time shit started gettin' ugly. Sonny was around—had been around for a while, to tell you the truth. And so was a lot o' his boys. Uncle this and Mister that. I don't remember half they names. I just remember a lot of 'em used to be drunk all the time. They would come in and sit around, lookin' at me, and lookin' at Judy. I think I even caught a couple of 'em lookin' at Darnell. Course none o' that mattered to Judy. She just wanted Sonny to keep bringin' home money. And that's what he did. He brought home money. But it's always a cost to that, ain't it? Like Judy used to tell me, ain't nothin' in this world free.

"Sonny cost us. Not that he was all that bad. He wasn't. It's just that it felt like, once he came around, we was left to raise ourselves. After while, I started runnin' away to get Judy attention. But all that did was make it worse.

"I still remember the last time I ran away," Daneen said, breathing heavily. "I ended up down the basement, hidin' and tryin' to figure out where I was gon' go next. It was dark down there, and hot. Plus I thought I heard rats scurryin'. I started cryin' cause I was scared, and then I started runnin' toward the door.

"Somebody grabbed me. I tried to scream, but he put his hand over my mouth. Then he tripped me and threw me down on the floor. He pulled my shorts and my panties down, and then..."

The tears began to run down Daneen's face.

"I was nine years old," she said. "Same as Kenya is now. I came home all bloody, with my elbows all scraped from tryin' to fight my way off that cement floor. I told Judy what happened."

Daneen's voice caught in her throat. Wilson reached out and held her hand. When Daneen finally gathered herself, she continued.

"She ain't take me to the hospital or to the cops or nothin' like that. She just said, 'That's what your dumb ass get. I bet you won't run away no more.'

"That's when I knew I hated Judy," Daneen said. "But she ain't the only one I hated. I hated that guy who raped me, too. And even if I couldn't see his face in the dark, I knew one thing. I was gon' find out who he was, and his ass was gon' pay for what he did to me."

"Did you ever find out?" Wilson asked.

"Yeah, I found out," Daneen said. "But it wasn't 'til eight years later."

Daneen paused.

"That's when he raped me again," she said in a voice barely above a whisper. "Nine months after that, I had Kenya."

Bayot was afraid. Being in a police station for the first time in his life made him feel like he'd done something wrong.

The two white detectives stood over him, staring down as he thumbed through the book of mug shots they'd had shipped down from Central detectives.

"You see him yet?" the blond-haired detective asked.

"I ain't sure," Bayot said.

"Not sure, huh?" the detective said, jabbing his partner with his elbow. "I'm starting to think it was you in that elevator with her."

"What you mean?" Bayot said, looking up at him with a terrified expression.

His brown-haired partner, smelling blood in the water, chimed in.

"What were you doing on the stairway looking at a little girl on the elevator? What are you, some kind o' child molester or something?"

"What's mo-les-ter?" Bayot asked, struggling to pronounce the word.

"Oh, we got us a slow one here," the blond detective said to his partner.

Both detectives laughed. It was a harsh, humorless sound. It was meant to intimidate. And it accomplished its purpose.

"Tell you what, Mister Learning Disabled," the blond said. "Why don't you do us a favor and take another look at the book."

"I don't wanna look at it no more," Bayot said, folding his arms and pouting like a little boy. "I wanna go home."

"Well, that's just too bad. You're not leaving here until you tell us who you saw with that girl. That's if you saw anybody at all, because I think you're lying."

"No I'm not," Bayot said. "I ain't lyin'. I seen him. He be up in Judy house. I know him, too, 'cause he always be tryin' to act like my friend when I see him up there."

"Well, if you're not lying," the brown-haired detective said, "then why don't you show him to us in the book?"

Bayot looked from one detective to the other, then reached for the book and flipped quickly through the pages. He was sure that he would spot the man he'd seen. But then he flipped the last page, and there was nothing.

"Lemme look at it again," Bayot said.

"Go ahead, we've got all night."

Bayot went back through the book again, more slowly this time, and when he got to the page where Sonny was pictured, the blond-haired detective placed his hand on the book.

"I want you to look at this page very closely," he said. "There's two pictures there, and I think one of them might be the man you saw."

Bayot stared up at the detective, searching his eyes for approval, then looked at his partner, who nodded to indicate that he wanted Bayot to take another look.

He buried his nose in the page for a moment, then sat up and pointed to the man on the left.

"Are you sure that's him?" the brown-haired detective asked. "Because it would be okay if you weren't sure."

Bayot looked up at him, confused.

"You're not sure, are you?" his partner asked. "What about the other one? Do you think it could be the other one?"

Bayot looked at the opposite page, and moved his finger until it was pointing to the man pictured there. He looked up at the detectives again.

"Do you know who that is?" the blond one asked.

Bayot wasn't sure of anything anymore. He just knew that he wanted to leave.

"I seen him before," he said.

"Where did you see him?"

"I think he be at Judy's."

"You said the man who got in the elevator with Kenya is always at Judy's, right?" the brown-haired detective asked. "So it's possible this is the man you saw?"

"I guess so," Bayot said.

"What the hell do you mean, you guess so? Either you saw him or you didn't."

"I don't know," Bayot said, covering his ears as he always did when he was frustrated and afraid. "Leave me alone."

The blond-haired detective had seen enough. He snatched Bayot out of his seat and held him at arm's length.

"He's the one you saw," he said, tightening his grip on Bayot's collar. "Do you understand? He's the one you saw."

"Get off me," Bayot said quietly.

"Tell me that the man in the book is the one you saw, and I'll let you go. After that you can go home."

"Get off me now," Bayot said.

The detective looked at his partner, who leaned back against the table, laughing at the two of them.

Bayot's face began to tense. His muscles rippled beneath his shirt as he took on the look of a two-year-old poised to throw a tantrum.

"Get off me!" he yelled.

Bayot lifted up one arm and brought it crashing down on the detective's wrist. The detective drew back, cradling the wrist in his hand as his partner stopped laughing and sprang toward Bayot. As he was about to swing, the door flew open.

"Stop it!" Wilson yelled, running into the room. "What are you doing to him?"

"He just identified Sonny Williams as the man he saw with the girl," the brown-haired detective lied.

"No he didn't," Wilson said. "Because Daneen Brown just identified someone else as Kenya's abductor."

"Who?" the detectives asked, almost in unison.

Wilson paused to look from one to the other.

"Herself."

Lynch rushed to join Wilson in the interrogation room. Judy could wait. So could everything else. If what Daneen was saying was true, Lynch wanted to hear it for himself. And he wanted to hear it from Daneen.

Sensing his need, Daneen stared past Wilson and the homicide detectives who sat in the room with them. She took a deep breath and focused her eyes on Lynch, staring as if her words were for him alone.

"The last thing I wanted was for my baby to end up livin' down the Bridge with Judy," she said. "She had already messed my life up—or at least let it get messed up—and I wasn't about to let her do the same thing to Kenya. They took that outta my hands, though. Not that I'm blamin' nobody for what happened. I shoulda treated Kenya right when I had her. But that was hard to do, 'cause she was a trigger for me. She reminded me o' that basement floor."

Lynch looked down as he realized that he didn't want to hear it after all. It was too late, though. Daneen wasn't about to spare him anything.

"I was raped, Kevin. Once when I was nine, and again when I was seventeen."

"Why didn't you say anything at the time?" Lynch said. "Why didn't you tell me?"

"What you was gon' do, Kevin? What was anybody gon' do? When I said somethin' the first time, Judy blamed me. So when it happened again, I thought everybody would think I was lyin'. And I couldn't take that. So I kept my mouth shut, wore my clothes loose, and hid my belly 'til I couldn't hide it no more.

"Then I told Tyrone the baby was his, 'cause I just couldn't see bringin' that child in the world with a rapist for a daddy.

"But I couldn't even do that right, could I? Tyrone died, and everybody blamed me for that, too. And all Tyrone left behind was the truth. So every time I seen Kenya, I would see the truth about her real daddy. I would feel his hands on my ass, his breath on my neck, his tongue on my skin. I would feel him poundin' into me while I scraped my elbows tryin' to fight my way up off that floor.

"I could ignore what I saw in her when I was clean. But when I smoked that shit, I couldn't, 'cause the high always turned from magic to poison. I would smoke, and then I would feel him inside me again—hurtin' me, rapin' me.

"And when I looked at Kenya, it was like she was him. When I would hit her, it was like I was hittin' him—gettin' him back for what he done to me."

She stopped and stared at Lynch for a long time.

"That's why I killed her, Kevin. I couldn't take seein' her daddy no more. So Friday night, I waited 'til Wayne went to sleep, took some money out his wallet, caught a cab down the Bridge, and I took me a blast. And right after I did that, I saw Kenya comin' out the projects."

"What time was that?" Lynch said.

"I guess it was around ten o'clock. Coulda been later, I don't know. All I know is I seen her comin' out. I called her over to me. Then I told her I was gon' take her to the store."

"When you say you called her over, where were you?" Lynch asked.

"I was across the street from the building, near the corner, right in front o' that lot with them real high weeds. When I called her, she came runnin' up to me."

"Was there any conversation?"

"She told me my eyes looked funny. Then somethin' musta clicked. She started lookin' scared, 'cause she know how I get when I get high. She started sayin', 'No, Mommy, no.' Then she tried to run.

"I grabbed her and pulled her in the lot. I pinned her arms down with my knees and put my hands around her neck. Then I just squeezed 'til she wasn't breathin' no more."

"And she didn't manage to bite you or scratch you or anything like that?" Lynch asked. "I mean, it would seem to me there would have been some kind of struggle."

"I had her arms pinned down," Daneen said. "She kept bringin' up her legs and kneein' me in my back. She tried to bite me, too, but she couldn't move her head. After while, I guess she knew it wasn't nothin' she could do, so she just stopped fightin'."

"So where did you put the body?" Lynch asked.

"I left out the lot and went under that bridge down Ninth Street. I found me a stick and pried off a manhole cover. Then I went back and got her and threw her down in the hole."

"Where exactly?" Lynch said.

"Somewhere on Ninth Street. I don't know exactly where. I was high. I was scared. But if y'all go out there and look, you'll find her."

"You're sure about—"

"Look, I killed her, Kevin! I killed her, and then I went back to Wayne house and acted like I ain't know nothin' about it. Now stop pressin' me, 'cause I ain't answerin' no more questions. If you wanna know somethin' else, get out there and find Kenya. I'm finished talkin'."

Daneen sat back, arms folded, chest heaving as her admission sank into the very walls of the room.

"We need to know one more thing," Wilson said gently. "We need to know who the man is who raped you."

Daneen turned to her with cold, dead eyes.

"It was Sonny," she said, shivering with a lifetime of rage. "He Kenya father."

Chapter Eighteen

By Monday morning, Philadelphia was in an uproar. The police department was issuing hourly statements to keep pace with media demands. When that proved too slow, the press turned to the neighbors to fill in the blanks with rumor and innuendo.

What had started out as a missing child had ballooned into a scandal. Even Judge Baylor's death was now background noise, submerged beneath the story's discordant harmonies.

With the murders in the drug house, and Judy's tale of bondage and escape, Sonny's crimes had reached far beyond the scope of anything in the city's recent history. The fact that he was still at large was at once chilling, and in a twisted sense, exhilarating.

But even Sonny's ruthlessness paled in comparison to Daneen's stunning admission that she had murdered her own daughter. That macabre detail had taken the story national. Television news magazines scrambled to get crews to Philadelphia from New York and Los Angeles. And while Daneen and Judy remained in custody on murder and drug charges respectively, new developments continued to take shape.

Daneen's former lover Wayne bolstered her account when he told detectives that, unbeknownst to him, she'd stolen money from him on Friday. Dot—Sonny's mistress at the Fairview Apartments—lent credence to Daneen's stories of rape by telling detectives of Sonny's penchant for young girls and violence.

The man who owned Sonny's Old City loft told police of his double life, describing a quiet man that paid his rent on time and kept to himself. And in the biggest break in days, the cabbie who'd driven Sonny to Delaware came in and told detectives about the trip.

The media's rush to plumb the depths of the story made Lynch's reinstatement almost a nonissue. That enabled him to work unmolested as he scrambled to find the truth beneath the madness.

While Wilson teamed with homicide detectives and Water Department employees to search the sewer system around the projects for Kenya's body, Lynch headed back to the Bridge to talk to the woman whom he believed could tell him what he needed to know.

When he arrived at her apartment, Lily was waiting.

"I was wonderin' when you was comin' back," she said, opening the door. "I only got a few minutes to talk, Kevin. I gotta be at work down the bar in a half hour."

"It won't take long," Lynch said, walking in as a picture of Sonny flashed on her television screen. "Especially since you're already watching what's going on."

"Whoever don't know what's goin' on by now must not have no TV, 'cause it's on every channel."

"From what I can see, it's more drama than anything else," Lynch said as he sat down. "The reality is, everybody's just waiting for the body to be pulled out of the sewer."

"Well, they'll be waitin' for a mighty long time," Lily said sarcastically.

"I take it you don't believe Daneen's story."

"Do you?"

Lynch smiled ruefully. "I don't think it would have been possible for Daneen to come across town on a busy Friday night, take Kenya into a lot and kill her, then dump the body in a hole without anyone seeing her."

Lynch paused, rubbing his chin as he thought about the case.

"The only thing I can't figure out is why she would lie about it."

Lily looked at him expectantly.

"That's why I came here, Lily. I figured you might know."

"Only Daneen can tell you that, Kevin. I just know it's a lot more to her than what you see. The girl been hurtin' since y'all was runnin' around tryin' to figure out if y'all was gon' be boyfriend and girlfriend."

Lynch looked up, embarrassed that Lily knew.

"You wanna know what I think about Daneen?" Lily said, ignoring his embarrassment. "I'll tell you. I think she seen too much when she was little. That's what turned her into the type o' person she is now.

"She can't sit back and watch other people get hurt, even after they hurt her. She just can't stand to watch pain, 'cause she know what it feel like."

"She hurt Kenya, though," Lynch said. "There's no denying that."

"Yeah, she did. And that's why she ain't try to get her back after they took her the last time," Lily said. "She thought she was doin' the child a favor by lettin' her go."

Lynch sat quietly and considered what Lily had told him.

"I think you've got Daneen all wrong," he said. "She's a user and a liar who'll say anything to get her way."

"You right, Kevin. But even when she usin' people, she don't do it to hurt 'em. She just do it to get what she want. And when she start feelin' like she hurtin' 'em, she start backin' up."

"So what does that have to do with her lying about this?" Lynch asked.

"Don't you see, Kevin? She lyin' to keep somebody else from hurtin'. I don't know who it is no more than you do. But I'll tell you this much. Daneen blamin' herself for whatever happened to that baby. I know if it was me, I probably be askin' God why He ain't take me instead o' my child.

"What I'm sayin' is, Daneen ain't lyin' just to be lyin', Kevin. She punishin' herself. And I bet she probably doin' it to keep somebody else from gettin' the pain she think she deserve."

Lynch looked Lily in the eye.

"She told us Sonny raped her," he said. "She said he's Kenya's father."

Lily was stunned.

"I don't know what to say about that," she said. "But you know I always thought he had somethin' to do with this. I said it from the beginnin', and I'll say it now. Sonny the only person I know mean enough to hurt a child.

"But mean as Sonny is, it's one thing I ain't never see him do," Lily said. "I ain't never see him mistreat that baby. He always treated Kenya like one o' his own. So if Daneen say he Kenya father, you might wanna take her serious. You know it's always a little bit o' truth up in a lie."

Lynch sat for a moment before getting up to leave.

"Where you goin'?" Lily asked.

He stopped and looked back at her. "I'm going to see if I can find that little bit of truth," he said.

And then he was gone.

Homicide detectives believed they had just enough truth to find Sonny. They combined the information the cabbie had given them about Sonny's trip to Delaware with Judy's tip concerning his Miami business connections. Then they pinpointed the bus Sonny had boarded in Wilmington, and communicated the bus number and license plate to every state police force from Delaware to Florida.

The bus pulled into a Maryland rest stop a half hour after the communiqué. A few minutes later, it was surrounded by police.

Most of the passengers were still on board, staring out the windows with mild curiosity as plainclothes and uniformed officers jumped from their cruisers and fanned out across the tarmac.

Two of the officers boarded the bus, quietly instructing the driver to evacuate the passengers because of a possible leak at the gas station.

As the passengers walked calmly to the restaurant at the far end of the rest stop, three officers discreetly checked their faces against a picture of Sonny.

While they did that, three officers entered the rest stop's gas station, fast-food restaurant, and convenience store.

Sonny was in the fast-food restaurant's men's room, splashing water on his face in an effort to shake the remnants of the dream he'd had as the bus barreled southward on I-95.

Staring at his red-eyed reflection in the bathroom mirror, Sonny could still picture Kenya's mouth opened wide in the same silent scream that had haunted his sleep. He could still see her assailant standing before her. He could still see that it was someone they both knew.

As he left the bathroom and walked out the side door of the restaurant, the dream still haunted him. But when he heard the distinctive crackle and hiss of a police radio, it was forgotten.

Sonny's heart beat faster as he lowered his head and glanced sideways at the officers milling about.

As he made his way between the cars that were parked throughout the lot, the sounds of the crackling radios faded. So did the voices of the increasingly restless bus passengers. Then someone yelled out.

"Hey, wait a minute!"

Sonny slowed and reached for the gun in his waistband as a white man approached him from behind.

"You forgot this inside," he said to a woman walking in front of Sonny.

"Thanks," she said, taking her purse from him.

Sonny relaxed and walked toward two minivans parked next to one another at the far end of the lot.

When he reached the vehicles, he crouched between them, tried the sliding door on the first van and found that it was locked. He tried the other. It was open. As he slid the backpack inside the van, his gun dropped to the ground.

He was about to crawl out to pick it up when two men approached. One of them was talking on a cell phone.

"We'll be home soon, honey," he said. "We're only three hours away."

Sonny left the gun, scrambled back into the van, and shut the sliding door as quietly as he could. He crawled around the seats and curled into a fetal position, covering himself with a blanket that lay crumpled in the back of the van.

Seconds later, the man on the cell phone disconnected his call and climbed into the driver's seat.

"How many times are you gonna call your wife?" the passenger asked as he got in.

"She gets all crazy if I don't call her every couple hours when I'm on these business trips."

"I think you're just whipped," the passenger said.

The two of them laughed as the van made its way back to the highway. But Sonny wasn't listening to them. All he heard was the fading chatter of the police radio as they drove away from the rest stop.

The only other sounds that mattered were the engine's hum and the whisper of tires against asphalt.

He didn't care where he was going anymore. But wherever it was, he was sure of one thing. He would have to take his memories of

Kenya with him. Because try as he might, he just couldn't make them go away.

Darnell was hoping to erase some memories of his own as he sat alone in Judy's living room, waiting for Renee to return with more crack.

But when the knock came and he opened the door, the reminders came flooding back again.

"I wasn't expecting you to be here," Lynch said as he walked inside.

"I don't see why," Darnell said. "I ain't got no place else to go."

"You weren't here yesterday when I came by with Bayot," Lynch said.

"That's 'cause I was with my girl Renee. She bought me a little somethin' to take my mind off Kenya. But I'm here now, so wussup?"

"I'm sure you heard about Daneen's confession," Lynch said, sitting down in Judy's chair.

"Why you think I'm in here instead o' lookin' for my niece?" he said. "Everywhere I go, I hear it. I just can't keep listenin' to people sayin' that shit."

"Then you don't believe what Daneen said about killing Kenya?"

Darnell contemplated his answer.

"My sister real messed up in the head right now. She want it to end so bad she tellin' y'all she did it 'cause she think that's gon' make it go away."

"There must be more to it than that," Lynch said.

"Only if what she said about Sonny bein' Kenya father is true."

"Do you think that's a lie, too?" Lynch asked.

"I don't know. I remember her sayin' somebody did somethin' to her when she was around Kenya age. Judy ain't believe it, so nobody else ain't believe it, either."

"Did you?" Lynch asked.

"Not at first. I thought she was lyin'. See, after we lost our mom, Daneen spent a lot o' years tryin' to get that mother love from Judy. When she came home and told Judy somebody had raped her, I ain't wanna believe it. But when we got older, and I started seein' what Sonny was into, I started thinkin' it was true.

"You saw what he did with that little girl back in the day, Kevin. The way he stuck her in that trash bin. You saw that young girl over Fairview he been messin' with since she was fifteen. So don't ask me if I think he Kenya father. Look at all the shit he did over the years, and you tell me what *you* think."

"Doesn't matter what I think," Lynch said. "But I'm curious about you. If you thought that Sonny had done something to your sister, why didn't you do anything?"

"I was a boy, Kevin. I was eleven the first time, and I was nineteen the second time. Sonny was takin' care o' the whole family. What was we gon' eat if he was out the picture?

"So when I got the feelin' he was messin' with Daneen, I just told myself I ain't see nothin'. I ignored it just like everybody else. Not sayin' it's right, but that's what I did."

"Did you get the same feeling later on with Kenya?"

Darnell lowered his head.

"I did, but I ain't face it 'til it was too late. I know that was wrong, Kevin, but that don't change the truth. Judy did somethin' to Kenya to protect Sonny, 'cause Kenya was gettin' ready to tell what he was doin' to her."

"How could Judy have done something to her if she was here the whole time on Friday?" Lynch asked.

"Maybe she got somebody to do it for her."

"Maybe," Lynch said. "That would explain what Bayot told us."

"What's that?"

"He said he saw a man get on the elevator with Kenya on Friday night—a man who hangs out at Judy's."

Darnell looked surprised. And then he looked disturbed.

"What's wrong?" Lynch asked.

"I was with Monk the other day, and he said the same thing," Darnell said.

"Who's Monk?"

"This old head that be in here sometime. He live up on the sixth floor, in 6G. He said he saw some dude get on the elevator with Kenya after he left here Friday night."

"When did Monk tell you this?"

"Yesterday. Matter fact, I told him to show me where the dude was at, and he couldn't. I asked him his name, and he said he ain't know."

"Why didn't you say anything to us?" Lynch said.

"Monk old and crazy. Plus he be smokin' more than I do. He liable to see anything."

"If two people say they saw Kenya getting on the elevator with a man, it probably happened," Lynch said. "Now I want you to think about this, Darnell. And I want you to answer me honestly. What man was here on Friday who spends a lot of time in this apartment and left shortly after Kenya did?"

Darnell didn't have to think about it for long.

"Sonny," he said. "He left to pick up another package of coke right after Kenya went to the store."

By the time Wilson and other detectives conducted a third search of the area where Daneen claimed to have dumped Kenya, it was apparent that they weren't going to find the body there.

Leaving a skeleton crew behind to continue the search, Wilson did the only thing that was left to do. Accompanied by a homicide detective, she returned to the Roundhouse to talk with Daneen.

When they arrived, Daneen had already been taken from homicide to be processed in the basement holding area, in the very place where she had entered police headquarters as a complainant just one day before.

There, she was placed in a one-person cell to wait for her video hearing before the bail commissioner. Shortly after the hearing, when her paperwork was processed, she would be transported to a municipal prison called the Detention Center.

But Wilson didn't care about the hearings. She didn't care about procedure. All she cared about was finding Kenya.

So when she walked in through the prisoner's entrance, she didn't stop for idle chat. She simply grabbed one of the turnkey officers and barged down the dim hallway to Daneen's cell.

When Wilson and the homicide detective walked in, there was only one question on Wilson's lips.

"Why did you lie to us?"

Daneen looked up from the cold bench that served as a cot.

"I ain't lie," Daneen said calmly. "Y'all just ain't listen."

"I don't understand you, Daneen," Wilson said. "Don't you want Kenya found? Don't you want whoever did this to be caught?"

"You got me. I'm caught. What more you want?"

"I want the truth," Wilson said. "But obviously, I'm not going to get that from you."

Daneen took a long, hard look at Wilson.

"This whole thing is like shit," she said calmly. "You leave it alone long enough, it'll get hard and dusty and blow away, just like it wasn't never there. But if you take a stick and stir it up, it start stinkin'. So save yourself some trouble and stop stirrin' it up. I killed my daughter. So just go ahead and take me up State Road now."

"If you'd killed her," the homicide detective said, "there would be a body."

"It is a body," Daneen said. "I already told you that."

"Then show it to us," Wilson said.

It took a while for Daneen to respond.

"What you mean, show it to you?" she asked.

"I can call up an inspector right now and get permission to take you to find the body," the homicide detective said. "If you can show us the body, then you can keep whatever secrets you want to keep. Nobody'll stir up anything else."

Daneen looked from one detective to the other, and for the first time, she looked afraid.

"Where's the body, Daneen?" Wilson said.

She paused before uttering the answer they knew she would.

"The Bridge," she said, hoping to buy time with the lie.

A few minutes later, they had the paperwork they needed. They took Daneen out in shackles and whisked her into an unmarked vehicle.

And then they did the one thing that the police hadn't done to that point. They set out to conduct a real search of the projects.

But someone had already beaten them to it.

Lynch headed for Monk's apartment with pieces of Daneen's and Darnell's stories intermingled with his own.

He thought of the abuse he'd suffered at the hands of his grandmother. And then he thought of Daneen's stories of the basement, with its dank air and scurrying rats.

He thought of the way his grandmother had staved off his manhood with heaping portions of pain and humiliation. And then he thought of the way Daneen's womanhood had been forced upon her in the dark maw of the Bridge.

He thought of it all, and after he'd knocked on Monk's apartment door and gotten no answer, he started down the steps to see the basement for himself.

In all the years he'd lived there, he'd never ventured down that far. He'd never had the nerve. And as he walked in through the broken gate that was supposed to keep the basement secure, he saw why.

He opened the unlocked door and saw that the room was dark, but vast. He could tell that it was massive by the hollow echo that came from the dripping water in the back.

As he ventured farther inside, he could feel dampness resting on his shoulders like a cloak. Thick, round columns with twenty feet of space between them extended from floor to ceiling. He bumped into two of them before his eyes adjusted to the gray light.

When they did, he sat down on his haunches and rubbed his hands against the rough cement.

He imagined Daneen on that floor, writhing beneath a grown man, fighting to preserve what little innocence a child of the Bridge had left by the age of nine. The thought of it was almost too much to bear, so he got up and started toward the door.

Just as he did so, there was a squeaking sound, followed by a tiny scraping noise that came from the back of the room. Lynch wasn't sure what to make of it, so he turned around and walked into the darkness.

The closer he got, the more scraping he heard. It was followed by a rapid, repetitive tapping. When he was almost there, he thought he heard a hiss.

Lynch took his gun from his holster. Then he fished his lighter from his pocket. He flicked it, but it failed to light. He flicked it again, and the yellow flame cast an otherworldly glow against the darkness.

It took a moment for Lynch to make out the large, square shape before him. It was one of the old trash bins, much like the one where the little girl's body had been found years before. The scraping he heard was coming from behind it.

Lynch took a deep breath and tried to prepare himself for whatever he was going to see. Then he aimed his weapon in the direction of the noise, stood slightly aside, and kicked the trash bin away from the wall.

A swarm of flies flew toward him, their wings beating the suddenly putrid air. A half dozen rats scurried away, revealing spindle-thin legs extending out from the wall. Lynch squinted to get a better look, covering his nose with one arm as a foul odor filled the air.

He bent toward the body and it all came into focus. Teeth protruding from an open mouth. Bushy hair in disarray. Shining eyes wide open in death.

It was a dog. And it had been dead for a while. Lynch breathed a sigh of relief as he turned to walk toward the door. When he reached it, something suddenly drew him back to the dead animal.

It wasn't the shedding fur that looked like hair. It wasn't the shining eyes that grew dimmer by the moment. It wasn't the vermin that the animal's corpse attracted.

Lynch was drawn by the childhood memories that had haunted him for a lifetime. He was drawn because he wanted to face the fear he'd had since seeing that first dead body as a child. He was drawn by his desire to defeat his demons.

Lynch approached the dog again, looked down at its body, then did what he'd come back to do. He flung open the trash bin.

And in a moment that was frighteningly reminiscent of the one he'd experienced as a child, he saw the body of a little girl inside.

It was Kenya.

Wilson and the homicide detective pulled up outside the Bridge, dragging Daneen from the car in shackles. As a uniformed escort pulled in behind them, they walked her quickly inside the foyer and instructed her to show them where she'd hidden her daughter's body.

"Somewhere upstairs," Daneen said vaguely. "Like I said, I was high. But I know I took her to one o' them empty apartments on the twelfth floor."

"You're sure it's the twelfth floor?" Wilson said.

Daneen nodded, casting her eyes downward as the residents of the building gathered around and stared at her with damning silence.

"Okay, we'll check the twelfth floor then."

Wilson pushed the elevator button as two uniformed officers came in and held back the growing crowd.

Just as the elevator arrived, Kevin Lynch walked into the foyer with tear-stained cheeks.

"Wait a minute, Roxanne," he said, calling out from behind them. "I don't think you need to go up there."

"Why not?"

He turned to one of the uniformed officers.

"Get on the radio and get a detail together," Lynch said, wiping his eyes. "Hold them out here on a crime scene."

"Where's the scene?" Wilson asked.

Lynch pushed through the crowd and met them at the elevator. Then he spoke so that only the four of them could hear.

"It's in the basement," Lynch said. "In one of the old trash bins, same as the last little girl Sonny raped and murdered."

They all looked at Daneen, who turned away to avoid their accusing eyes.

"Sometime a lie a whole lot better than the truth," Daneen said.

"No," Wilson said. "It's not. Because no matter how many times you tell a lie, the truth eventually comes out. Maybe one day you'll understand that."

Daneen didn't respond. She didn't have to. Because they all knew that the focus was now back on finding the truth.

And as they piled into Wilson's car for the trip back to police headquarters, the truth was looking more like Sonny Williams.

Now all they had to do was find him.

From what he could tell, they'd been riding for almost three hours when the minivan rolled into the darkness and came to a stop.

And as the men closed the doors and walked away, Sonny lay

still beneath the blanket, listening as the sound of their footsteps moved across a concrete floor and faded to nothing.

He could hear other vehicles moving in and out of what sounded like an enclosed space. And a few minutes later, when he raised his head and looked out the back window at the other cars lined up in neat rows, his feeling was confirmed. It was a parking garage.

Sonny got out of the van, slung the backpack over his shoulder, and began trying doors on the cars.

When he tried the handle on a Lexus, the door opened, the car alarm filled the garage, and several security cameras trained their lenses on the area, pinpointing the vehicle—and Sonny—within seconds.

He desperately fingered the steering column, ripping at the plastic casing with his bare hands in an attempt to expose the wires. When finally he got the vehicle to start, he bolted out of the space just as a security guard in a Jeep pulled in behind him.

Gunning the engine, Sonny drove toward the open garage door and flew out from underneath it, making a hard left and speeding away from the building.

Looking up at lights and street signs, he tried to get his bearings as he darted in and out of thick traffic on a tree-lined boulevard. He wound his way around a traffic circle, then hit a straightaway that ran toward an oddly shaped building.

Sonny still didn't know where he was. That is, until he glanced up, spotted the nearly forty-foot-high bronze statue of William Penn atop the building, and nearly drove into oncoming traffic as reality came crashing down.

The men in the minivan had indeed driven for three hours. But instead of going south from Maryland, they'd gone north. And the trip that he'd believed would get him farther away from his troubles had brought him right back to them.

His getaway had returned him to Philadelphia.

As he struggled to digest that fact, a police car with sirens blaring fell in behind him.

Sonny turned onto Fifteenth Street and sped around the circle leading past City Hall, weaving through the tangled traffic surrounding the building.

When he'd gone almost all the way around, he skidded and made a sharp right, heading north on Broad Street, with the police car gaining steadily.

As he passed Race Street, where the traffic to New Jersey slowed the flow of the southbound lanes, he knew that there were few options for escape. He would have to make his move within the next few seconds, before backup arrived.

Making a hard left, he jumped the median and plunged into oncoming traffic. The car screamed toward a truck that was preparing to enter the turning lane. Just before impact, Sonny jumped from the car, rolled toward the curb, and ran away from the explosion as the Lexus barreled into the truck.

In the ensuing confusion, he took to the streets of Center City with the cop hard on his heels.

The call went out over police radio's central band as Lynch and Wilson were dropping off Daneen and the detective at homicide.

"Cars stand by," the dispatcher said. "Assist the officer, civilian by phone, at Broad and Vine Streets. An officer there is in foot pursuit of a black male, west on Vine from Broad."

The officer came on the air almost immediately.

"Six-eleven, resume that assist," he said, breathing heavily into the radio. "I lost the male around Sixteenth and Callowhill."

He released his talk button and came back on the air, still breathing hard.

"I've got flash information when you're ready."

"Go ahead, 611."

"Suspect is wanted for investigation for auto theft, and leaving the scene of an accident at Broad and Vine. He's a black male, forty-five to fifty-five years old, six-foot-two, dark-complexioned, with brown eyes, black hair and a mustache. He's wearing black jeans, white sneakers, and he's carrying a backpack. He made his escape on foot from Sixteenth and Callowhill within the last five minutes."

Wilson turned to Lynch as she pulled out of the Roundhouse parking lot.

"Didn't Judy say the money Sonny took from the roof was in a backpack?"

Lynch snatched the radio handset from the dashboard.

"Dan 25, I'm en route," he said, as Wilson turned on the car's lights and raced toward Broad and Vine. "Tell all responding units to use caution. That male fits the description of Sonny Williams. He's wanted for several murders and assaults against police in Central and East Divisions, and should be considered armed and extremely dangerous."

A gaggle of voices exploded over the radio as every officer within two miles of Broad and Vine joined the chase.

But as Wilson drove the relatively short distance from police headquarters to the accident scene, it was apparent that their cars would soon be useless in the search.

The truck Sonny rammed had burst into flames, blocking the Broad Street entrance to I-95 and limiting access to the Ben Franklin Bridge, City Hall, and the Vine Street Expressway.

The Fire Department was on the scene, and traffic was already backed up for miles in all directions. Callowhill Street, where Sonny was last seen, was being used as an alternate route. So even the officers who managed to make it there on foot were hampered by the sheer volume of traffic.

Lynch jumped out of the car looking for the officer who'd initiated the chase. When he saw him, still bent over and sucking air, Lynch reached into Wilson's glove compartment and took out a picture of Sonny. Then he ran over to the officer and stuck the picture in his face.

"Is this the guy you were chasing?" he asked.

The officer looked up from his crouch and nodded vigorously.

"I guess you didn't see which way he went on Callowhill."

The cop shook his head no.

Lynch got on his cell phone and called Captain Silas Johnson at Central Detectives. When he answered, Lynch tried not to let his still-simmering anger with the captain show through.

"It's Kevin Lynch," he said. "I'm down at Broad and Vine. I've got an officer who's positively identified Sonny Williams. He was last seen at Sixteenth and Callowhill five minutes ago."

"I'm on the other line with the commissioner now," the captain said. "We're shutting everything down. Nothing leaves that area, nothing leaves this city until we find Sonny Williams."

"I understand."

"And Lynch?"

"Yes, sir."

"I heard about you finding the girl. Good work."

There was a long pause as Lynch held the line.

"It would've been good work if I'd found her alive."

Chapter Nineteen

By nightfall, it was clear to everyone that Sonny had eluded the police yet again. But after the commissioner approved the captain's plan, the city was tightly sealed in the hope that he would eventually resurface.

Both airports were placed under surveillance, as were the bus and train stations. Photographs of Sonny were issued to cabbies and store owners. Even day-care centers were warned that Sonny was in the area. He was, after all, suspected of murdering a child.

That reality was now the driving force behind the search. And even as authorities sought Sonny in connection with the other murders and assaults he'd been involved in, the investigation of Kenya's murder began to take precedence over everything, even the death of Judge John Baylor.

The police department's crime lab spent a full day gathering evidence from the basement where the little girl's body had been discovered. But they didn't find much of anything.

The fingerprints they collected were virtually unusable. They found no physical evidence to link Kenya to a killer. The autopsy, which was performed just hours after she was found, revealed the official cause of death as cardiac arrest, no doubt brought on by the struggle with her killer. But the autopsy yielded no evidence of sexual activity. On the contrary, it showed that she was a virgin.

By Tuesday morning, the D.A. had disregarded Daneen's trumped-up confession, and sought instead to charge Sonny, because the circumstantial evidence against him was so compelling.

He was known to have a penchant for young girls. He had a long history of violence. He remained a suspect in the similar murder of the child who'd been found in a trash bin twenty years before.

And though the story of Kenya being sexually active had proven to be false, detectives still believed that Sonny had made some improper contact with the girl and that he'd murdered her when the child threatened to tell.

In addition to motive, Sonny had opportunity, having left Judy's apartment shortly after Kenya to replenish Judy's drug supply.

There was only one problem. Bayot—the man who could place Sonny with Kenya on the night of her death—was unsure of what he'd seen. And the only other person who could corroborate his story was Monk.

That's why Lynch rode back to the projects with Wilson on Tuesday afternoon. He was determined to convince the old man to come forward. Moreover, he was determined to figure out how everyone else fit into the equation.

"What do you think about Judy?" he asked Wilson, as they drove toward the Bridge.

"I think Judy's greedy," Wilson said. "Greedy and insecure about a man who never gave a damn about her in the first place."

"Her nephew seems to think Judy wanted Kenya out of the way so Sonny wouldn't have to deal with molestation charges."

"He's doing an awful lot of thinking for a piper," Wilson said derisively.

"Think about it," Lynch said. "Judy broke her neck to tell us that Sonny hadn't done anything to Kenya. Then she gave us some bullshit about him being on his way to Miami. Maybe the hunch I had back at homicide was right. Maybe she was doing whatever she had to do to make sure he got away."

"I think that's a stretch," Wilson said, as they pulled up in front of the building. "What does his getaway do for her now? She still can't run a crack business without him."

"Doesn't make a difference," Lynch said. "She doesn't want to see her man in jail."

"I still think it's a stretch," Wilson said.

They got out of the car and went into the building, walking past the elevator and taking the steps to Monk's sixth-floor apartment. When they reached it, they knocked on the door for five minutes before they realized that he wasn't going to answer.

Wilson tried the doorknob. It opened.

As the two of them walked inside, they were greeted by a rush of air that smelled of marijuana and ointments, cleaning solutions and sweat. And just beneath those odors, there was sickness—the smell of an old man.

The television in the bedroom was on. There were matchsticks and beer cans scattered about the floor. The remnants of marijuana cigarettes were everywhere. And so was the feeling that the old man had nothing left to live for.

When they walked back into his bedroom, they saw why. Monk was sitting in a chair, his face fixed in a look of permanent surprise, his hand reaching for a glass crack pipe on the floor.

Lynch walked over to him and checked for a pulse. But even before he touched him, he knew that there hadn't been a pulse for days.

Monk was dead. And as Wilson radioed in the news, and Lynch called the Medical Examiner's Office to have the body removed and autopsied, they knew that their chances of finding an eyewitness to place Kenya with Sonny had died with the old man.

———

The heat in the storage closet was stifling. With no windows and little space, Sonny was beginning to wonder how much longer he could survive there.

He'd considered himself lucky when he eluded the cop before walking into the library at Nineteenth and Vine. He'd thought himself brilliant when he waited until closing and slipped into the little-used basement closet.

But after a day of breathing his own recycled air in the cramped and pitch-black space, Sonny knew that it was just a matter of time before he would have to move.

He was contemplating a way to do that when someone opened an office door and the faint sound of a radio made its way across the hall.

When he heard his name, the broadcast seemed to grow louder. And the announcer's words lent urgency to his plight.

"The D.A.'s Office is going forward with plans to charge Sonny Williams—the man wanted in connection with the murder of nine-year-old Kenya Brown—after witnesses identified him as the perpetrator in Sunday's triple murder in a North Philadelphia drug house. Meanwhile, funeral services for Kenya Brown have been scheduled for one P.M., tomorrow, at the Calvary Baptist Church of Philadelphia. KYW Newstime at the tone is five o'clock."

Sonny didn't hear what came over the radio after that. He only heard the reality that rang in his ears as he stood there, realizing that his life was now in jeopardy.

If the drug-house murder charges stuck, he would surely get the death penalty—especially if the D.A. had her way.

And even if he was somehow able to get out of Philadelphia at some point—which he now doubted more than ever—he would still be in real danger of being brought back to the city to face lethal injection.

He couldn't allow that to happen. So Sonny waited. And when

he was sure that the building was empty of most of its workers, he ventured out of the closet and found a maintenance man who was almost his size.

With the last few ounces of strength he had left after so many days on the run, he pummeled the man, then dragged him into a bathroom, changed into his uniform, and transferred the money from the backpack to a trash bag.

As he slipped out of a side entrance of the library, Sonny knew he had to do one thing before making a final push to flee the city. And he knew that he'd have only one chance to do it.

Judy sat in the dank basement cell she'd occupied since Sunday, contemplating all that had happened to her family over the years and wondering if they could ever truly heal.

Kenya's death, which she'd learned about just an hour after the body was found, had left her shocked, then angry, and, finally, guilty.

She cried, but her grief wasn't just for Kenya. It was for Daneen: the child whose tear-filled eyes told tales of rape in the basement; the frightened teenager who'd been forced to make a choice between a moment of truth and a lifetime of lies.

Each time Judy thought of Kenya, she grieved for Daneen. The last time she'd done that—on the night when she'd learned of Daneen's secret—she'd scrawled the words in a diary because she just couldn't keep it inside. Then she hid the book in her son's old backpack—the same bag Sonny had stolen from the roof.

As she sat in her cell watching a detective and a uniformed officer walking toward her, she wondered if Sonny had bothered to look at anything other than the money. More than that, she wondered if the words in the diary meant anything to him.

"Ms. Brown," the detective said, as the uniformed officer opened Judy's cell door. "Come with us."

She got up and walked with them down a dimly lit hallway. At the end, a heavy steel door slid open. She blinked to adjust to the fluorescent light that washed over her.

The detective walked her over to an area with mounds of paperwork in metal racks on a Formica desk. One of the papers had her name on it. He thrust it in front of her and waited.

"What you want me to do?" Judy asked, looking up at the detective.

"The drug charges have been reduced to what amounts to disorderly conduct, and the district attorney has decided against filing assault charges in connection with the officer you injured at Central Detectives, since there were, um, mitigating circumstances. The bottom line is, we want Sonny, not you. Your testimony will help us get him. So if you sign this paper, you're free to go."

Judy looked at the letters scrawled across the top of the page.

"What does S.O.B. mean?" she asked.

"It means sign your own bail. It's basically a promise that you'll show up at your preliminary hearing."

"How y'all gon' send me outta here after I told you Sonny killed them men on Cambria Street? He know I'm the only one who seen him do it, so if I go home now, and he somewhere in Philadelphia, what you think gon' happen?"

"Ms. Brown, we're going to have a detail posted outside your door for the next few days. If you need anything, those officers will get it for you. If you have to go anywhere, they'll take you. We're going to make every effort to protect you until Sonny Williams is caught."

"Can't y'all put me in some kinda witness protection program and send me outta Philadelphia or somethin'?"

"You're going to be protected, Ms. Brown."

"If you wanna protect me, keep me in jail. I'm safer here than I am on the street."

"We can't do that."

"Why not?"

"There's a federal consent decree that sets a limit on the number of prisoners we can hold. Under the guidelines, we've gotta let you go. Now please, sign here. There's a car waiting to take you home."

"I ain't got nothin' to go home for," Judy said, taking the form.

"Sure you do," the detective said. "Your great-niece's funeral is tomorrow."

As she signed the form and turned to leave the Roundhouse, Judy put aside her fears in order to deal with that very present reality.

Kenya was dead. She would have to be buried. And so would all the secrets of the past.

As the last few residents left the building for Kenya's funeral, Kevin Lynch got out of his car and strolled down the street outside the front entrance of the Bridge.

He walked in through the building's foyer and out toward the back entrance. Then he stood in the rear of the building, looking at the space where he'd seen the little girl's dead body all those years ago.

As he stood there, the memories of his childhood came flooding back. He remembered his grandmother, and the stern manner in which she'd raised him. He remembered Daneen, and the heartbreak she'd caused him. He remembered Tyrone, and the death that embittered him.

And in the midst of those memories, Lynch lowered his head and began to do something he hadn't done in years. He began to pray—for strength, for healing, for closure.

He stood there for what seemed to him an eternity—head bowed, eyes closed—and soon felt a soothing calm wash over him. It told him that his wife and daughter were still the most important people in his world. It said that his childhood and everyone from it were firmly in his past. It assured him that his attraction to Daneen was little more than a fantasy from long ago. It wrapped him in its arms and gave him peace.

A few minutes later, as he walked back through the building, that peace was interrupted by a faint rustling from the bottom of the ramp that led down to the basement.

He stopped to look into the shadows. At first, he didn't see anything. But as his eyes adjusted to the dim light, he saw a man standing in the darkness.

Lynch drew his gun and aimed at the figure.

"Come up here right now, with your hands where I can see them!" he shouted.

Nothing moved, so Lynch took a few steps down the ramp, trying to make out a face.

Suddenly, the man rushed at him, bowling him over and knocking the gun from his hand.

As Lynch got to his feet, the man lost his footing and fell facefirst on the ramp. Lynch dived on his back and the man reached back with both hands, grabbed Lynch by his jacket, and threw him over his head.

Lynch landed on his back, but scrambled quickly to his feet. When he turned to face the man again, he found himself staring into the eyes of his attacker. It was Sonny.

Lynch swung wildly, missed with a left hook, then connected with an uppercut. Sonny fell backward, but managed to hit Lynch, who landed three blows of his own, knocking a weakened Sonny flat on his back.

Sonny looked to his right and saw his last chance lying next to him, shining in the darkness. Lynch caught sight of the gun at the same time.

Sonny crawled toward it, but Lynch reached it first, then wheeled around and struck Sonny with the butt of the gun.

Falling against the wall with blood oozing from his wounds, an exhausted Sonny raised his hands in surrender.

Lynch took out a pair of handcuffs and chained Sonny to a pipe, that ran along the wall. Then he lifted the gun and jammed it into Sonny's mouth.

"Tell me about Kenya," he said, panting through clenched teeth. "Tell me how she died, or I'll kill you."

Sonny slid down the wall and sat on the cold concrete floor, mumbling something about dying and words on a page.

"It's in the diary," he said wearily. "Judy wrote it all down in the diary."

The church across the street from the projects wasn't big enough to accommodate the throng. So the funeral was held on Sixteenth and Fairmount, at a Baptist church called Calvary.

But even that church, which was considerably larger, had never seen so much activity.

Unmarked police cars with detectives slouched low in their seats, traffic units whose dome lights swirled against the bright summer sky, uniformed officers with radios hooked to their ears. And standing on a flatbed truck, a single homicide detective, videotaping the mourners in hopes of capturing some clue about the killer.

There were television crews and paparazzi, snatching bits and pieces of mourning, photographing the people of the Bridge and converting Kenya's death into a Hollywood production.

When the hearse arrived and her casket was carried into the church, its diminutive size spoke volumes. Most people who saw it cried bitter tears as they grieved over the dark realities of life and death in the projects.

There was no such display from the family.

Daneen stood outside and hugged Darnell's girlfriend, Renee, who whispered condolences in her ear. Daneen seemed taken aback by that. But she thanked her anyway, then went inside, looking as if she was determined not to cry. Darnell followed

Daneen, wearing quiet grief with a dignity that didn't exist in any other aspect of his life. Judy was last, looking more fearful than anything else.

As they passed by, the whispers followed them. Daneen, for one, pretended not to hear them. There was nothing anyone could say that she hadn't already told herself a thousand times.

When they'd finished the long walk down the center aisle, they sat quietly on the front pew. Those who loved Kenya—Lily and Janay among them—sat close behind. Kenya's classmates and friends were there, too, sprinkled in among the people who'd come to bask in the twisted air of celebrity surrounding the whole affair.

Daneen spent most of the funeral looking rather than listening.

During the final viewing, she watched as Judy looked down at the body and collapsed with screams and flailing arms, nearly knocking over the casket before a group of men came forward and carried her out.

A group of children from Kenya's school read a poem. The preacher quoted I Peter, 3:16—something about keeping your conscience clear, so that when you're abused, people who hate your good behavior in Christ can be ashamed.

Daneen felt a terrible sadness upon hearing that passage. More sadness than she'd felt at any time since Kenya disappeared. More pain than she'd felt after piecing together the truth about Kenya's murder and taking the blame rather than revealing it. More grief than she'd felt when, shortly before the funeral, she'd gone to retrieve the one thing that would make it right.

As the church rose and fell with emotion during the spirited eulogy that followed the reading of the passage, Daneen only heard the words *abuse* and *shame*. She had, after all, abused Kenya when she was alive. And now, she was ashamed.

She was mired in that shame, even as the church exploded in applause when the preacher wiped his brow and sat down.

There wasn't anything else to be said, she thought. And there was only one thing to be done. But apparently, not everyone shared that sentiment.

As the sanctuary continued to rock with a soulful chorus of amens and hallelujahs, Darnell jumped up from his seat, stomped to the front of the church, and grabbed a microphone.

When he began to speak, the spirit of the service changed from uplifting to ominous.

"I wanna say somethin' to whoever did this!" he shouted angrily.

Feedback from the microphone rose in an earsplitting hum, and everyone in the church fell silent.

"Whoever did this to my niece might be in here right now," he said. "But I wanna tell you somethin'. God don't let you get away with killin' babies. And the people who loved this little girl—the ones who watched her grow into the sweet child she was—we ain't gon' let you get away with it either."

Darnell dropped the microphone, and with tears streaming down his face, he stormed down the aisle and out the back door of the church.

Everyone watched as the door slammed shut behind him. No one knew what to do. And then Daneen got up and ran out, too.

Lynch stood in the dim light of the ramp in back of the building, his face etched in shock as a handcuffed and beaten Sonny recited what he'd read in Judy's diary.

When Lynch thought about it, he didn't believe him, because the words in the diary—even if they were true—didn't fully explain what had happened to Kenya.

So Lynch asked Sonny about his relationship with the girl. And Sonny recalled the truth with quiet sadness.

"I was like her grandfather," he said softly. "Kenya reminded me what it was like to be young and scared, like I was when they used to send me to them homes."

Sonny looked at Lynch, who still held the gun at his side.

"I guess bein' good to Kenya was my way o' fixin' some o' the wrong I did over the years."

Lynch's eyes bored through him. "Nothing could fix all the wrongs you did, Sonny."

"Maybe you right. But I ain't do nothin' to Kenya. You gotta believe that."

"Why should I?" Lynch said angrily. "You're a murderer. You killed those people in that drug house, and you came back here to kill Judy. And you can deny it 'til the day you die, but I know you killed Kenya, too."

"No, I didn't," Sonny said earnestly.

Lynch was silent for a moment. "I'm giving you one more chance to tell me the truth."

"I am telling the truth!"

"Okay," Lynch said, lifting the gun and tightening his grip on the trigger. "I warned you."

When he saw the maniacal look on Lynch's face, Sonny believed he was going to die. He closed his eyes to welcome his fate. A second later, there was a gunshot.

Lynch left him there, cuffed to the pole, and ran out the front of the building. He stopped when he saw Daneen, who calmly handed her gun to Lynch, then fell to her knees and cradled her victim while he died.

Darnell looked up at Daneen with a whispered, "I'm sorry."

Then he exhaled for the last time as Daneen pressed his head to her bosom before laying him gently on the sidewalk.

Daneen stood up slowly. Lynch watched her with a measure of disbelief before fishing out another pair of handcuffs, getting on his radio, and calling for a wagon.

"I blamed Sonny for raping me," Daneen said stoically, " 'cause it was the easy way out."

The wagon arrived, and a slack-jawed Lynch pointed to the foyer, where Sonny was handcuffed to the pole, next to the money-filled trash bag.

When the officers emerged with him, Daneen turned to Lynch. Somehow, she needed to make him understand.

"I ain't lie about everything, Kevin. I told you I was raped. And I told you I couldn't stand to look at Kenya father no more."

"So the diary thing is true," Lynch said matter-of-factly. "Judy knew Darnell raped you."

"Yeah, she knew," Daneen said calmly. "My brother liked to hurt women, Kevin. And it all started here in the Bridge with me. I held on to that secret for years, 'cause I ain't want Kenya to have to live with it. Secrets catch up with you, though. That's what cost my baby her life."

"Are you saying Darnell killed Kenya?" Lynch asked quietly.

Daneen stared at him with tear-filled eyes. "When I came back to search Judy's apartment, he was just sittin' there in the dark. He knew she was dead. I guess I did, too. Maybe that's why I took Sonny gun out the kitchen drawer and hid it in that lot across the street. Deep down I knew I'd need it, 'cause when we was at Judy's, Darnell said, 'Kenya more than a niece to me.'

"When he said that, it was like he was finally admittin' he was Kenya father. And right then, things I had been holdin' on to for years started comin' up. The rapes, the lies, the secrets."

Daneen clenched her jaw. "Then y'all brought Bayot up to Judy's, and he said he saw a man who hung at Judy's huggin' Kenya on the elevator."

Lynch looked confused. "But Darnell said Kenya hated him. Why would she hug him?"

" 'Cause she didn't hate him, Kevin. She loved him. She just didn't trust no pipers. Not after the way I treated her when I smoked. And anyway, Bayot wasn't the only one who saw Darnell with Kenya on that elevator. Monk saw him, too."

"How do you know that?"

"Right before the funeral, Renee gave me her condolences. And she gave me somethin' else. She told me Darnell went with Monk to find the man Monk saw with Kenya. Right after that, Monk turned up dead. That wasn't no accident, Kevin. Darnell killed Monk to keep him from tellin' what he saw. Renee knew that, and she couldn't live with it."

Daneen looked down at her brother for the last time as Lynch tugged gently at her arm, leading her toward the waiting police wagon.

"But we ain't gotta keep secrets no more," she said, turning to stare at mourners trickling back from her daughter's funeral.

"We can all rest now, especially Kenya. 'Cause like Darnell said at the funeral, God don't let you get away with killin' babies."

As she spoke, neighbors and television cameras assembled in shocked silence, recording the look of peace that had set her face aglow, recounting the final justice that had set her free from secrets, repeating the haunting mantra that had given her back her life.

"No," Daneen said as she took her final look at the Bridge. "God don't let you get away with killin' babies. And the people who loved my little Kenya—the ones who watched her grow into the sweet child she was—we don't let you get away with it either."